EX
LIBRIS

Romance Treasury

THE ROMANCE TREASURY ASSOCIATION

TORONTO · NEW YORK · LOS ANGELES · LONDON
AMSTERDAM · PARIS · SYDNEY · HAMBURG
STOCKHOLM · ATHENS · TOKYO · MILAN

These stories were originally published as follows:

ROMANCE TREASURY is published by
The Romance Treasury Association, Stratford, Ontario, Canada.

Dust Jacket Art by Wes Lowe
Story Illustrations by Wes Lowe
Book Design by Charles Kadin
Printed and bound by R. R. Donnelley & Sons Co.

ISBN 0-373-04091-1

Printed in U.S.A. AO91

CONTENTS

A HANDFUL OF STARS

A Handful of Stars

Lucy Gillen

Charlotte regretted not knowing the uncle who had left her Blanestock. She was thrilled, however, to know that the beautiful old estate was now hers and settled down to enjoy it.

Then the intriguing Scott Lingrove came into her life. Charlotte found him charming, yet couldn't help wondering if she was really as interesting to him as he claimed. After all, it was said that he'd set his sights on owning Blanestock, that he'd go to any lengths to get his way.

Surely that wouldn't include a cold-blooded marriage! Her heart drowned out the rumor, but her head told her not to trust him—or herself.

CHAPTER ONE

CHARLOTTE OPENED her handbag yet again and once more read that very important letter through to its very end. It was still so hard for her to believe that by simply answering a small advertisement she had seen by chance in a newspaper, her whole life was probably about to be changed completely.

No more office routine, no more frequent changes of employer or the need to save for every little luxury. It was just possible, of course, that she was counting her chickens rather too soon, but she thought not, for everything pointed to big changes. The prospect before her had the excitement of novelty whether it proved lucrative or not.

For seven years now, ever since she had left secretarial school at eighteen, Charlotte had been gainfully employed as a secretary, and if the number of posts she had held was in excess of the number of years it was only because she had been unfortunate in her choice of employers. A succession of them had been far more keen to appreciate her physical attributes rather than her professional ones.

She was efficient at her job, she knew that, for she had been well trained, but it seemed to matter more that she was a petite and shapely five feet two, with rich brown hair and huge violet-coloured eyes. It was a situation she found frustrating to her professional talents, however flattering it may have been in a personal sense and, since her latest employer was proving no different from the one before, the advertisement in the newspaper had come as a welcome opportunity to make yet another move, although she had not anticipated quite how long it would take.

The brief, but specific, notice had been inserted by a firm of solicitors, and asked that any existing relatives of the late Ezra Albert Blackwell, Blanestock in the county of Derbyshire, should communicate with Messrs. Clee, Banbury and Chartres of Chedwell in that county.

When Charlotte had first seen it she had been immediately reminded of the many stories her paternal grandmother had told her as a child. She had spoken often and longingly of her own childhood in the beautiful, but sometimes bleak, Derbyshire hill country. Her grandmother's maiden name had been Blackwell, and she had had a brother, although Charlotte did not immediately remember his christian name.

Those intriguing little notices in newspapers had always drawn her eye, but she had never for a moment expected to see one that in any way concerned her. Not that she had been very sure that this one did at first and she had done a great deal of heart-searching and undergone many changes of mind before she had at last written to Messrs. Clee, Banbury and Chartres.

Now at last she was about to experience the culmination of that correspondence. Over what seemed like an interminable time, letters had been exchanged and proof of her identity despatched, and then, after months of waiting and having almost forgotten the matter, she had received a letter informing her that, no other claimants having been forthcoming, she was the sole beneficiary under the will of her great-uncle, Ezra Albert Blackwell.

She had never met her great-uncle, never even consciously realised that he existed, and that seemed now to be a cause for regret. For surely she should have had some communication with an old man who had left her all he possessed, and who must have been a very lonely old man if it was necessary to advertise for members of his family.

She had no idea if he had ever been married or not, but even if he had it was obvious that he had left no family, and she pitied him in his solitude. Charlotte herself had been orphaned for the past five years, and she knew something of the feeling of loneliness.

What her inheritance would amount to, she had no idea, except that it involved property, and she had perhaps been a little too rash in giving up her latest job to travel northwards. But the solicitors' letter had mentioned a substantial estate, and that in itself was encouraging.

In these days the house alone must be worth quite a considerable amount, if her grandmother's stories about it were true, and in any case just owning a house of her own was worth the journey. At any time now she would know just how worthwhile it had been.

The last letter from Messrs. Clee, Banbury and Chartres had informed her that she would be met at Chedwell station by a member of their firm, and that knowledge too gave her hope that possibly her inheritance would be quite considerable. For surely such honour would not be afforded anyone less than a wealthy heiress.

Charlotte had never been this far north before, and the journey had been something of a revelation to her. There had been cities and towns certainly, along the way, but quite a deal of the latter part of it had been through unexpectedly wonderful scenery and she had been impressed with the quite overwhelming grandeur of the green-grey crags and sweeping hills.

Now and then the hills cradled a small town or village in their midst, but it in no way detracted from their stark beauty. It was magnificent, awe-inspiring scenery and she felt herself almost anxious to live here, among these great sweeping hills. It was almost as if she was returning rather than coming to it for the first time.

From what she could see of it from the train as they drew into the station, Chedwell appeared to be a small, quiet town, mellow and attractive in the late summer sun.

Charlotte stepped down from the train with a light skip of excitement in her heart, prepared to enjoy this change to the full. There were several others alighting at the same time as herself, and quite a few people about on the platform, so that she stood down her suitcases for a moment and looked around her, trying to guess which of them looked most like a representative of Messrs. Clee, Banbury and Chartres.

She could see no one that looked in the least like her own idea of a man from a solicitor's office, but a good-looking young man in a light grey suit did appear to be looking at her curiously.

Not that she would have given his interested scrutiny a second thought in normal circumstances, but at the moment he seemed to be the only person taking any particular interest in her, so she smiled at him, a little hesitantly, and waited while he came across to her.

He was of medium height, dark-haired and blue-eyed and *very* good-looking, and he proferred a hand as he came nearer, evidently convinced of her identity. "Miss Brown?" Charlotte nodded, pleasantly relieved, she had to admit. "I'm Noel Chartres."

So—they had sent one of the partners to meet her! Charlotte was very impressed and put on her nicest smile in gratitude for the honour. "Thank you for meeting me, Mr. Chartres," she told him.

"We felt it would be more fitting for someone to meet you," he told her, making signs with his hands to someone out of her sight. He turned a slight but quite charming smile on her. "It's a great pleasure, Miss Brown."

"Thank you." She responded to the quiet compliment with unusual feeling. "I'm not very happy about wandering around a strange town in search of someone I've never met. It was very good of you to come."

There was an earnestness in the blue eyes that impressed her as genuine. He was obviously a young man who took everything he did very seriously and, as an efficient secretary, Charlotte approved of that.

"Did you have a pleasant journey, Miss Brown?"

He had seen her through the ticket barrier with the minimum of fuss, and commandeered the services of the one and only porter wih no trouble at all. For all his seemingly quiet manner and the appearance of reticence, Noel Chartres was obviously a man used to having his wishes attended to without argument.

Charlotte smiled thanks as he saw her into his car and dismissed the porter with a discreetly palmed coin.

"It wasn't a bad journey at all," she said in answer to his question. "And the latter part of it, coming through the Peak District, has been wonderful."

He smiled quiet approval at her over his shoulder and purred the car engine into life. "You've never been to this part of the world before?"

"Never," Charlotte agreed. "I'd no idea how beautiful it is."

"You expected factory chimneys?"

She nodded, a wry face admitting it. "Although my grandmother used to tell me about it, but somehow one expects everything to have changed completely in all that time."

Noel Chartres shook his head. "This kind of country changes little and very slowly, Miss Brown." They drove in silence for several minutes, then, "I'm sure you'll enjoy living here," he said.

"I'm sure I shall," Charlotte agreed wholeheartedly.

Noel Chartres cast a brief, enquiring glance at her as he guided the car through quite busy traffic. "You *will* be keeping on Blanestock?"

"Oh—oh yes, I think so," Charlotte said, brought face to face with her first decision. "I'll have to decide when I've seen it, of course."

"Yes, of course." He smiled again. "You mustn't allow yourself to be rushed into anything."

Something in his voice and his manner, as well as his choice of words, made Charlotte suspicious that there might be something more than mere polite curiosity in the question, and she watched the good-looking profile curiously as she spoke.

"Is there anything I'm likely to be rushed into, Mr. Chartres?"

It was a second or two before he replied, and she knew she had guessed correctly when she saw his expression, but he was possibly having second thoughts about mentioning it. "You know from your correspondence with us," he said at last, "that Mr. Scott Lingrove is Mr. Blackwell's designated executor. He's also a neighbour, if one can call it that."

"Yes, I remember his being mentioned," Charlotte said, eyeing him warily.

"Since Mr. Blackwell's decease," Noel Chartres told her, "Mr. Lingrove has more than once expressed a desire to purchase both the house of Blanestock and the adjoining land."

"Oh, I see."

It came as something of a shock to Charlotte to hear that someone was apparently already seeking to relieve her of her inheritance, no matter how legally, and she decided impulsively that she would give short shrift to Mr. Scott Lingrove when she met him, whoever he was.

"But naturally you must see the property first before you make any decisions about disposing of it," Noel Chartres told her. "As I say, you mustn't allow yourself to be rushed into anything."

Charlotte smiled confidently, in no doubt what her decision would be. "You'll find that I'm not easily rushed into *any*thing, Mr. Chartres," she told him.

This time she thought his smile definitely approved of her answer, and he nodded. "Good," he said firmly.

The offices of Clee, Banbury and Chartres were well in the tradition of family solicitors, and Charlotte was not disappointed or surprised here at least. There were well worn, dark leather chairs and shelves of impressive-looking books, and to complete the picture, behind a huge desk sat an elderly man with glasses perched somewhat precariously on his nose. So much the personification of the traditional family solicitor that Charlotte instinctively smiled when she saw him.

He looked up when she came into the room with Noel Chartres, and hastily got to his feet, a ready smile disturbing the spectacles even further so that he jabbed a hasty finger at them to prevent their sliding off altogether. "Aah!" He came across the room, one hand already outstretched, while Noel Chartres introduced them.

"Miss Brown, this is my father, Philip Chartres: Father, Miss Charlotte Brown."

It was only as she shook the proffered hand that Charlotte remembered the name on the firm's notepaper was Philip Chartres and not Noel. Evidently the son had not yet acquired the status of full partner. "Good day, Miss Brown." A firm plump hand enfolded hers enthusiastically, and he beamed his pleasure. "Delighted to meet you at last. Please do come and sit down."

He ushered her into a chair and reseated himself, glancing at his son who had seated himself at a discreet distance, on a chair over by the window, half hidden by his father's bulk. "It was good of you to have someone meet me," Charlotte told him, seeing now that her escort, however willing, had more likely been a delegate than a volunteer.

"Not at all, not at all," she was assured. "Your late great-uncle was a valued client—least we could do for his heir."

"I never knew him, of course," Charlotte said. "I

wish I had. He must have been a very lonely man, having no family. We—we might have been friends."

"It's a pity," the lawyer agreed, returning his errant spectacles again, with another sharp jab of a finger. "But alas, he was a difficult man in the latter years, Miss Brown. No disrespect, you will understand, but he became something of a recluse in his last years, and no one really got close to him. He wouldn't even make out a proper will, hence our need to advertise for kith and kin."

"And there's no one?" Charlotte asked, still not quite daring to believe it. "No one else beside me?"

"No one at all," Philip Chartres said. "No one else has come forward, which was only as we expected, of course, but one must do these things properly. We know that Mr. Blackwell had only the one sister, your grandmother, and no brothers. He never married, so there are no direct heirs, and I understand that your father is deceased, Miss Brown?"

Charlotte nodded, her eyes clouded for a moment. It still hurt to talk about it even after all this time. "Both my parents were killed five years ago, Mr. Chartres, and my father was an only child."

"Sad, sad." The greying head shook sympathetically. "And your grandmother too is no longer alive?"

"She died last year."

'So—" Plump hands spread expressively. "There remains only yourself, my dear Miss Brown, and, if you will allow me to say so, you are a very fortunate young woman."

Charlotte gazed at him with her deep, violet-coloured eyes and hardly dared ask, "There's—there's a big estate?"

"A very handsome one," Philip Chartres agreed, almost smugly. "Mr. Blackwell invested very heavily and very wisely both overseas and in this country, and the income from these investments is in the region of twenty thousand pounds per annum."

Charlotte could say nothing for several seconds, too stunned to find words, her brain whirling chaotically with the very idea of it. Working as a secretary it would take her more than a lifetime to accumulate even one fortune of twenty thousand pounds—the idea of it as an annual income was just inconceivable.

"I—I can hardly believe it," she said dazedly.

"There is, of course," he warned her cautiously, "a good deal of paper work and a number of formalities to go through before you can expect to take possession of your entire estate, but as you are the sole beneficiary, there should be less delay with probate than there would have been had others made claims as well." He looked at her with a broad, satisfied smile. "You may safely leave all that sort of thing to us, of course, Miss Brown."

"Oh yes, of course," Charlotte agreed readily. "But there is one thing that's rather puzzling me, Mr. Chartres. About the executor of the will. I thought, I mean I understood that a—Mr. Lingrove was my great-uncle's executor. Surely he—"

"Mr. Lingrove very wisely put the whole matter into our more experienced hands," Philip Chartres told her smoothly. "Such vast sums of money and complicated investment interests need expert handling, Miss Brown. I can assure you that we will do our very best on your behalf."

"Oh yes, I'm sure you will!" Charlotte glanced over at Noel Chartres, sitting quietly and half hidden, over by the window, and she smiled. "I'm quite happy to leave it all to you, Mr. Chartres."

NOEL CHARTRES had offered to drive her out to see the house, but Charlotte had declined the offer with thanks. Much as she would have enjoyed his company, she felt that she would like to see Blanestock for the first time on her own. It was probably naïve of her, but she felt there would be something so very special about the moment that she was unwilling to share it.

She was already feeling quite light-headed with the excitement of the prospect and when she at last saw solid proof of her new-found wealth she would much rather be alone, with no one to witness her feelings.

She took a taxi, revelling in the sheer extravagance of not having to count the pennies, and told the driver to take her out to Blanestock. It pleased her enormously too, when he did not ask her where it was. He obviously knew it, and looked at her speculatively via the driving mirror as they drove off.

It was a mile or two outside Chedwell and among those sweeping grey hills, but when they eventually arrived she was forced to admit that the approach to the house was something of a disappointment to her.

What must once have been a neat and tidy driveway was now deeply rutted and badly overgrown with weeds, and the trees and shrubs that lined it were in need of trimming, so that she was conscious of an air of neglect even before she saw the house. By the time they had driven the length of the drive she was already wishing she had left her first visit until later, when she was less tired from travelling and therefore less easily dismayed by what she saw.

The taxi driver, she thought, was puzzled about her, and he looked at her even more doubtfully when she paid him with the obvious intention of dismissing him. His weather-beaten face smiled at her anxiously.

"'Ow you going to get back, miss?" he asked.

Charlotte looked round at the big, shabby old house and could see the logic of the question herself, although she was not prepared to admit as much at the moment. "Oh, I'll be all right," she assured him.

"You wouldn't like me to come back for you? Say in about an hour or so?" he offered, and Charlotte hesitated, then finally shook her head.

"No. No, thank you," she told him, determined not to be put off so early on. "I'll be quite all right, thank you very much."

He touched his cap, still eyeing her doubtfully. "O.K., miss, you knows best, I 'spect."

Charlotte, watching him drive back along the weed-grown drive, wondered if she really did know best, but it was too late now to call him back. She had more or less committed herself to spending her first night at Blanestock.

She had booked herself a room at a hotel in Chedwell, but had decided that if it was at all possible she would sleep at the house and she had accordingly notified the hotel of her intention and brought an overnight bag with her.

She was, she supposed, being rather optimistic, but Noel Chartres had told her that Blanestock was still fully furnished, although he could not guarantee what state the furnishings would be in after so long. She consoled herself, however, with the thought that the weather had been so warm lately that there was little likelihood of it being too damp.

Nevertheless, as she inserted the key in the lock and pushed open the door, she experienced a sudden cold feeling of doubt at the sheet-covered mustiness of it. Perhaps after all she had been too rash in parting with that friendly taxi driver.

It must once have been a very beautiful home, she realised with a thrill of pleasure as she walked into the nearest room. Its ceilings were high and beautifully carved, and the fireplace, she felt sure, must have been the work of Robert Adam.

It was not an enormous house, as country houses go, but it had a promise of grace and elegance even in its neglect, and Charlotte took to it on sight. She would restore it, she decided without hesitation, standing there in the centre of the hall a few moments later. It deserved to be looked after when it had been so long neglected, and her mind was off on daydreams about how it would look with its former grandeur restored.

There was a wide, shallow staircase that swept up gracefully to the upper floor, the paintings on either side of it glowing with rich colours where the sun shone in through a long window about halfway up. To let such a place fall into neglect was disgraceful and she would remedy the matter as soon as she had funds enough to do so.

In the meantime she would have to see if it was possible for her to sleep there that night. What she had so far seen had not encouraged her, but she was not prepared to be too easily *dis*couraged. Only those shapeless, sheet-shrouded ghosts of chairs and settees made her uneasy, and the utter and complete silence of it, like an air of expectancy.

She had her back to the door, very conscious suddenly of the silence and the stillness so that when she heard the sound of a key in the lock she spun round swiftly, wide-eyed and with her heart thudding wildly in her breast, almost as if she had been caught trespassing.

The newcomer came straight in without hesitation, and was too busy for the moment looking at the key he held in his hand to notice her. He was obviously puzzled to find the door already open. Then he caught sight of Charlotte and stopped in his tracks, seemingly stunned at the sight of her, for he stared at her as if he could not quite believe what he saw.

His sudden appearance had startled Charlotte so much that she held her hands clenched tightly in front of her, her bag on the floor at her feet where she had dropped it. He was the first to recover, however, and he smiled suddenly and came across to her, still looking as if he did not quite believe her.

"Hello," he said. "Who are you?"

It was not at all the kind of question one should be asked in one's own home and by a complete stranger, Charlotte decided, and stuck out her chin. "I might ask *you* that," she told him, recovering her nerve.

His smile was wide and completely self-confident, and he looked down at her from a vastly superior height. His face was considerably less good-looking than Noel Chartres's, but somehow much more attractive and, at such close quarters, very disturbing.

"You must be Miss Brown," he said, and practically

commandeered one of her hands, holding it firmly and for longer than was strictly necessary, and all the while studying her with a pair of hazel eyes that did nothing to conceal the interest that gleamed in their depths.

"I'm Charlotte Brown," she admitted, involuntarily wary of him.

The strong fingers still retained their hold and the interest was undiminished, undeterred by her slightly cool manner. "I didn't even realise you'd arrived," he told her. "I'm Scott Lingrove."

Yes, of course, Charlotte thought as she attempted to ease her cramped fingers, he would be Scott Lingrove. She had somehow visualised him as a man who saw what he wanted and made no bones about getting it as best he could. He was the man who wanted Blanestock, and now that she had seen both the house and him she was more than ever determined that he should not have it.

The fact that he could let himself into the house with a key surprised her until she remembered that as the executor of old Ezra Blackwell's estate he would be entitled to have a key. At the same time it passed through her mind, quite unreasonably, of course, that he could have better carried out his duties by having the place cleaned up a bit.

He was an overpowering man, definitely so in appearance, and his initial introduction would seem to prove that his character might very well match his looks.

He was very tall and broad-shouldered, with a lean muscular look that suggested strength, and features that betrayed a strong will and possibly stubbornness. He would not, she decided, be an easy man to move.

He had thick fair hair that curled just slightly above his ears and in his neck, and it was obvious that he spent a good deal of his time out of doors, for there was no other way he could have acquired such a deep tan.

The rugged, almost stern features were a deep golden brown, and a light-coloured shirt with short sleeves revealed arms and a strong brown throat as tanned as his face. Altogether he looked a formidable antagonist should she ever have cause to cross him. Not a comforting thought in the circumstances.

"I—I arrived today," Charlotte told him, hating to admit, even to herself, that he made her feel nervous. "I didn't expect to find anyone else here," she added with deliberate bravado.

He smiled. "Oh, I come in several times a week to keep an eye on things," he told her. "The place is more or less in my charge until it's taken over by its new owner."

"Then I'll be able to relieve you of the responsibility," Charlotte said, and wondered why that idea should amuse him so much.

The hazel eyes took in the overnight bag she had dropped when his coming in had so surprised her, and he raised a brow in query. "You're not thinking of staying here tonight, are you?" he asked.

Charlotte frowned at the proprietorial tone, and nodded firmly. "Yes, I am staying, Mr. Lingrove," she said, now certain of her decision. "The house is fully furnished and it can't be damp at this time of the year."

"Of course it can," he argued. "It's stood empty all last winter, it *must* be damp. And anyway, it's never been cleaned since the old man died." One brow dared her to argue and his eyes challenged her to stay after his next argument. "Apart from that, heaven knows what you'd find in the beds after all this time."

Charlotte's involuntary shudder brought a smile to his face, and she decided there and then that she did not like Scott Lingrove very much, so far. He was, of course, very obviously trying to put her against Blanestock from the outset, so that she would be more than willing to sell it to him. But if that was his intention he had chosen the wrong tactics as far as Charlotte was concerned.

"Oh, I think I can deal with a few creepy-crawlies," she told him airily, and with far more confidence than she was feeling. "Don't worry about me, Mr. Lingrove."

For a moment he said nothing, but there was a small, speculative smile at the corners of his wide mouth and she disliked it intensely, for it made her feel as if he was prepared to indulge a rather wilful child, but would attempt to change her mind, for her own good, if he could.

"I'm not exactly worrying about you," he told her. "But I don't like to see anyone walk into something without realising all the drawbacks."

"I'm fully aware of them, thank you."

He was nodding his head, that smile still in place and rapidly getting on her nerves. "I doubt if you do, but it's your funeral, and I suppose you're old enough to know your own mind."

"*Quite* old enough," Charlotte agreed firmly.

"O.K." He shrugged, as if he at last realised that argument was useless. "Have it your way, Miss Brown. But eleven months is a long time for a house to be empty."

"I'm surprised there hasn't been a—a cleaner or something in to look after it," Charlotte told him, and he smiled, following her meaning well enough, she thought, and probably resenting it, although he showed no outward sign of doing so.

"As I told you," he said quietly, "I've been keeping an eye on it myself, but I didn't see myself in the role of charlady, and it hardly seemed worthwhile getting a woman in to keep it spick and span when it could easily have been donkey's years before the next owner moved in."

He was right, of course, Charlotte was forced to allow, but she still did not like the idea of this lovely old place being allowed to accumulate dust all that time. "I wish I'd known," she told him. "I could have done something about it."

This time he laughed quite openly, so that she felt her hands curl into her palms. "Could you now? I doubt it, not until you were officially the new owner, and that mantle's sitting importantly on you at the moment, isn't it, Miss Brown?"

Charlotte's dark-fringed eyes blazed at him indignantly. "How dare you speak to me like that?" she demanded, and had the satisfaction of seeing him sober again, although the laughter still lingered in his eyes.

"I apologise." He bobbed his fair head, and the rugged features crinkled into a smile again, while he studied her with a lack of inhibition that stirred some emotion in her that she could neither recognise nor control. The sensation was new to her, for never before had any man ever made her feel so infuriatingly unsure of herself, and she wished he would go and leave her alone.

"I—I appreciate your concern about my staying here tonight, Mr. Lingrove," she told him as coolly as she could manage. "But I'll be quite all right, I assure you, and I have quite a few things I want to do before it begins to get dark."

"Can I help?"

She shook her head—his help was the last thing she wanted. "No, thank you."

He studied her for a moment longer, then shrugged airily. "Right, then I'll leave you to it." He strode back across the hall to the door. "I'll see you in the morning."

Charlotte followed his progress with startled eyes. "I—I don't think so," she said, and he turned and smiled at her.

"You will," he insisted. "You're cut off completely here. You can't even make yourself a cup of tea because there's no water or electricity or gas, but if you prefer roughing it for the night, who am I to argue? Goodnight, Miss Brown."

CHAPTER TWO

IT WAS NOT really surprising that Charlotte did not sleep very well in her very makeshift accommodation that night. It was true she had found all the bedrooms furnished, as Noel Chartres had promised, and having chosen one to use, she had stripped the bed to make sure there were no unwelcome visitors.

Relieved on that point at least, she had sought out bed linen from a well stocked but chillingly damp cupboard, and hopefully spread out sheets and blankets in the sun to air. A couple of hours in that warm sun, she thought, would take care of any lingering dampness. But the bed itself was another matter and she had settled finally and very reluctantly for the much harder surface of the floor.

She had slept only fitfully, for there were any number of strange creaks and scratches that disturbed the dark silence, and she dared not even try to identify them, much less unroll herself from the enshrouding blankets to seek them out.

It was early morning before she really fell asleep, from sheer exhaustion, and the first thing she was aware of when she woke again was the sun streaming in through uncurtained windows and across her face. She hid her head, lingering for as long as possible in the comforting limbo between sleeping and waking, then reluctantly she sat up and yawned. So much for her first night at Blanestock, she thought, ruefully.

Getting out of her blanket roll, she walked across to the windows and stood gazing out at the view. It surpassed anything she had expected to see before she came and she gazed at it for several minutes, feeling some of her first enthusiasm returning as she looked at it.

The green and grey ruggedness of the Peaks with the thin, spiralling ribbon of an occasional road winding, apparently aimlessly, like a lone touch of civilisation in a vast expanse of wildness.

it was beautiful, and at the same time a little awe-inspiring, and she knew that in winter many of those roads could become impassable for days on end. It was a sobering thought for a girl born and raised in the comparative security of a big town, but it offered a challenge and a sense of freedom and adventure that Charlotte was more than willing to accept.

A glint of something shining in the distance caught her attention for a moment, and she narrowed her eyes, trying to decide what it was. Possibly a stream or a small roadside waterfall, for such things abounded among the rocks, so her grandmother had told her.

It was a wonderful place to have spent a childhood, and Charlotte, reassured by another day, was ready to enjoy it all. It was all so vastly different from the town garden and paved streets she was used to, and much more exciting.

She was already decided, when she turned away from the window, that she would go into Chedwell this morning and see about getting a woman in to clean up the house before she did anything else. A gardener could come later, when the estate was more settled and she felt more sure of herself. But in the meantime she would move into Blanestock as soon as water and electricity could be restored.

It was only when she faced the prospect of doing without a bath because there was neither water nor the means to heat it that she realised just how right Scott Lingrove had been about her roughing it.

She could neither cook herself a breakfast, nor, as he had pointed out, make herself a cup of tea, but the worst dilemma of all, she realised as she came downstairs, was that she could not even call a taxi to take her back to Chedwell, and for a moment the runaway excitement of it all cooled in the need to be practical.

Isolation, she realised ruefully, was only enjoyable when it was well organised, and she had cut herself off from everything and everybody without giving even the most basic essentials a second thought. It was a situation that made rather a joke of her much prized efficiency.

Perched on a sheet-shrouded ghost of an armchair a little while later, she was faced with the fact not only that she was very hungry, but that her best and probably only way of getting help and the use of a telephone was to seek out Scott Lingrove. Much as she disliked the idea of it, he was her nearest neighbour.

Probably he would not be too surprised to see her, for he had promised that he would see her this morning, and it looked as if he was going to be right. It also occurred to her a few minutes later as she walked down the weed-grown driveway to the road, that in this sort of country one's neighbour was as likely to be five miles away as just over the fence.

Thanks to a good memory she remembered his address from her correspondence with the solicitors, but she had no idea how near it was, and she prepared herself for a long walk. She had gone less than half a mile, however, when she spotted the name "Wainscote" carved deeply in one of a pair of stout stone pillars at the bottom of a curving drive, and smiled her relief.

The outlook here was very different from that at Blanestock and she eyed it with envy. The name was clear and plain for all to see, and the drive was neat and elegant, but one thing that caused her to raise a scornful brow was a notice board attached to a post just inside the black iron gates.

WAINSCOTE, it announced in large black letters. HOUSE AND GARDENS OPEN TO THE PUBLIC. Daily 11 A.M.—6 P.M. Admission 40p.

So, Charlotte thought, her lip curling in superior disdain, for all his autocratic manner Scott Lingrove was not above opening his home to the public. She could see now why he was so keen to buy Blanestock, he either wanted it as an added attraction or as somewhere he could sneak away to when he got tired of being part of the show.

One thing puzzled her about it, however, and she frowned over it as she started along the drive. Why should *his* house be of any special interest to visitors? Usually, or so she had always understood, a house opened to the public belonged to some ancient family of honourable lineage, and surely Scott Lingrove did not come into that category.

The fact that he possibly could made her feel less sure of herself, but she nevertheless continued on up the beautifully kept driveway, through an avenue of tall, elegant oaks and beeches, with neatly laid out flower borders visible on smooth green lawns. She was daydreaming about how Blanestock would look when it was similarly cared for when she stopped short suddenly as another bend in the drive confronted her with the house itself.

It was much bigger than Blanestock, as was to be expected, and much better cared for, but otherwise contemporary, and the graceful elegance that could have been Blanestock's too seemed almost to taunt her as she gazed at it in envy.

Now that she had arrived she was uncertain just what she ought to do. Whether she should ring the bell and ask for assistance as a neighbour in need, or whether to be quite casual and merely ask to use the telephone as if she was simply a passing stranger.

A great deal would depend on who answered her summons. If she was seen by Scott Lingrove himself then she would be bound to eat humble pie, and that she was very reluctant to do. The decision was made for her a moment later, however, when she heard the crunch of footsteps on the gravel and turned to see who it was.

Scott Lingrove came round from the back of the house, and was evidently returning from a morning ride, for he wore slim-fitting cream trousers with short, soft leather boots, and a white shirt open at the neck, a riding crop tapping lightly against one leg as he walked.

So far he had not seen her, half hidden by the trees bordering the drive, and his mouth was pursed in a soft whistle. Some slight movement on her part must have caught his eye then, for he looked across to where she stood and a moment later smiled recognition. "Good morning," he called to her. "Come on over, you don't have to hide in the trees."

Since she had had no intention of hiding, Charlotte resented the implication, but she was undecided just how to approach him without demolishing too much of her dignity. She went across the intervening yards of drive still wondering how much appeal she should put into her greeting.

"Good morning," she said, and almost involuntarily responded to his smile. "I'm afraid I'm rather an early caller."

A wide and completely friendly grin reassured her, and one large hand waved in the direction of the house. "I told you I'd see you this morning," he reminded her. "Come in."

Charlotte eyed him doubtfully, wishing he had not been so obviously ready to prove himself right about his forecast of last night. "I only wanted to use your telephone," she explained, and he nodded.

"Why not? It's just inside the hall."

She followed him up the steps to the half open doors, and blinked when she saw the splendour of the hall he had so casually referred to. No wonder that Wainscote was open to public viewing if this small section was any guide to the rest of it; it must be quite beautiful.

The telephone stood on a small table against one wall and he indicated it with a casual hand. "Help yourself," he told her.

"Thank you." She felt suddenly and dismayingly overawed by her surroundings, but she would hate him to know it.

"Would you rather make your call first, or wash and

breakfast first?'' he asked, and grinned amiably. ''If you've got your priorities right, you'll settle for a wash and brush up and breakfast.''

Charlotte blinked at him for a moment, startled by such unexpected hospitality. ''Oh, but I—I didn't—'' she began, and he eyed her almost as if he was daring her to deny the increasing pangs of hunger that gnawed at her empty stomach.

''Now don't try and tell me you're not hungry,'' he interrupted with another grin. ''You must be.''

A small, rueful smile admitted it at last. While she was not altogether sure that she liked his rather officious manner that took her acquiescence for granted, she felt sure he meant well in this instance, and she was unwilling to jeopardise her chances of a breakfast.

''I'm starving,'' she confessed, ''and I *would* enjoy a breakfast, thank you.''

''Good!'' The hazel eyes swept over her briefly and expressively. ''I hoped you wouldn't be too suspicious to behave sensibly. Now—which are you going to do first? Wash and eat or phone?''

''I—I'd like to wash, if I may,'' Charlotte said. ''I feel awful, if you're sure it's—''

''I'm quite sure,'' he said, interrupting again. ''There are twelve bathrooms here, so I'm sure we can fit you in somewhere.'' This time the waving hand indicated a magnificent curved staircase. ''You start on your way up and I'll send Mrs. Crayle to give you a hand with whatever you need.''

''I can manage,'' Charlotte said, automatically, and he smiled, ignoring her protest and giving his attention to an elderly woman who came out from the nether regions of the house, almost as if on cue.

"Ah, Mrs. Crayle," he said, "show Miss Brown the bathroom, will you? And give her anything she needs, then you can see about some breakfast for us, we're both on the point of starvation."

The woman smiled and nodded. "Yes, of course, Mr. Lingrove. Will you come this way, madam?"

Charlotte followed her up the beautiful staircase, walking a little self-consciously stiff-backed because she knew instinctively that Scott Lingrove was watching her from the bottom of the stairs.

She wished, too late now, that she could have sought the help of some other neighbour, if indeed there was one within walking distance, but then she would probably not have been given the facilities she was offered here. Scott Lingrove was proving much too disconcerting for her peace of mind, but at least he provided breakfast and she was prepared to take a great deal at the moment to feed the inner man.

Whether any more than one of the twelve boasted bathrooms was in use, Charlotte had no way of knowing, perhaps they were merely for show in these days of economy, but the one she was shown into had certainly been in use quite recently and, she guessed, by her host.

There was still a warm steamy atmosphere left from a bath, and an electric razor shared the glass shelf over the wash basin with a brand of after-shave that she recognised as having been used by the man downstairs.

She was provided with a towel and soap and told how to find her way down to the breakfast room when she was ready, then left to her own devices. The bathroom was sheer luxury, Charlotte decided, as she washed and cleaned her teeth. Its fittings were the last word in elegance and its size made her smile ruefully as she worked out that her entire bed-sit in London would have fitted comfortably into it.

She had not dared to bath because she was not too sure how much time she was expected to take, but a wash refreshed her, and she prepared to go downstairs again feeling a little better able to face Scott Lingrove's rather disturbing brand of hospitality.

Her host, she discovered, having located the breakfast room, was already drinking coffee from a large and surprisingly inelegant pot mug. Not at all the sort of thing she would have envisaged on the table of a stately home. However, pottery aside, he rose politely when she came in and smiled a greeting.

"Feeling better?" he asked, and Charlotte nodded.

"Very much better, thank you, Mr. Lingrove."

"Breakfast is on the way." He saw her seated and poured her coffee, then went back to his own brew. "Did you sleep well at Blanestock?"

She sought an answer that would not give him the satisfaction of knowing he had been right about the state of the bedding, but it was not too easy. "Not too badly, thank you," she said cautiously.

"No creepy-crawlies?" She shook her head. "Or spooks?"

Charlotte kept her peace while the woman was in the room with them, but her mouth tightened when she thought she saw his reason at last for giving her breakfast and being so solicitous about her welfare. By fair means or foul he meant to have Blanestock, and he was trying a little of both at the moment.

The unexpected hospitality, the warnings about the place being too damp and the insinuations that she might be made uncomfortable at Blanestock by either marauding insects or by something more sinister were all too clearly done with the intention of making her as uneasy as possible.

"I'm not afraid of creepy-crawlies, Mr. Lingrove," she told him as the woman closed the door. "And I don't believe in spooks."

"No?" One brow questioned the truth of that, and the hazel eyes gleamed with either laughter or malice, she was very unsure which at the moment. "You wait until you've spent a few *winter* nights there, with a howling north-easter screeching round the chimneys."

Charlotte looked at him steadily, her small and slightly tip-tilted nose in the air. "I don't mind the wind either," she informed him. "I expect it can be pretty noisy in the winter, but as long as I know what it is, I shan't mind."

He was smiling again and he eyed her for a moment before answering. "You're a stubborn little creature, aren't you?" he said then, and Charlotte flushed bright pink. It was very tempting to be rude to him, but she did not really want to descend to that.

"I just have no intention of being driven off my property by *any*thing, that's all," she told him. "I like Blanestock and I mean to stay there."

"Come what may, eh?" he laughed, and shook his head. "Well, I just hope you won't let your determination to stay there at all costs lead you into doing anything foolhardy, that's all."

"I'm not a complete idiot, Mr. Lingrove," she declared haughtily.

"Oh, I had no intention of suggesting that you were," he said mildly, a tone denied by the malicious gleam of laughter in his eyes. "But the place *must* be damp after all this time and you'll be getting pneumonia if you spend any more nights in those beds until they've been thoroughly aired."

Charlotte looked down at her plate and hesitated about being too forthcoming about her sleeping arrangements. "I—I managed," she said.

"On the floor?" The accuracy of the guess startled her for a moment, and she looked up swiftly, wide-eyed, so that he knew he was right and smiled.

"I—I was quite comfortable," she told him.

"You'd have been more comfortable in a hotel in Chedwell," he retorted.

"Maybe, but I wanted to stay in Blanestock!"

He was nodding and his smile made her want to hit out, it was so all-knowing. "So that you could establish your claim," he guessed.

"If you like!"

"Any special reason?"

She blinked for a moment uncertainly. "I—I don't know," she admitted at last. "I just like the idea of owning a house like Blanestock, that's all."

"I see."

Charlotte looked at him from the shadow of a dark sweep of lashes. "Why do you want it, Mr. Lingrove?" she asked softly, and for a moment Scott Lingrove looked at her steadily, then the brown face crinkled into a smile.

"So Noel Chartres has told you, has he?"

"I have been told that you want Blanestock, yes," she agreed cautiously, wondering, now that the step was taken, if she had been very wise to let him know she was aware of his plans.

He was smiling as he helped himself from the dish of bacon and eggs. "It must have been Noel," he told her with annoying certainty. "Old Philip would never have been so indiscreet, especially on a first meeting. Also," he added with a smile that suggested all manner of things, "he wouldn't have been so influenced by a beautiful face."

All of which was probably true, Charlotte realised ruefully. Noel Chartres had obviously been impressed, for all his reticence, and he should probably not have mentioned the matter of Blanestock changing hands. Whatever his reasons had been she doubted if the elder Chartres would view his son's indiscretion with much pleasure, and she made a vow that Philip Chartres would not learn of it from her. Whether Scott Lingrove could be relied upon to be quiet about it was another matter.

"Whoever told me about it," she said, "the fact remains that you do *want* Blanestock, don't you?"

"I want to buy it," Scott Lingrove agreed with a smile. "You sound rather as if you think I'm out to commandeer it by fair means or foul." The hazel eyes held hers for a moment steadily. "My intentions are strictly honourable, I assure you, Miss Brown."

His choice of phrase, she felt, was probably used with the intention of embarrassing her, but she had no intention of allowing herself to be swayed, no matter how it was done. "Whatever your intentions are," she informed him, politely but coolly, "I'm not parting with Blanestock—I like it."

"I can see your point," he said quietly. "It's a lovely old place, or it would be if it was restored."

"Which is precisely what I intend to do," Charlotte said.

"You've really made up your mind to live there, then?"

She nodded firmly. "I have. But first I have to see about making it habitable by having the water and electricity, etc., turned on again."

"Is that what you wanted to use the phone for?" he asked, and she shook her head.

"Not exactly," she said. "I can see about all that once I get back to Chedwell. I presume that's where the powers-that-be reside?"

"It is."

"No, I wanted to use your phone to ring for a taxi to come and fetch me, actually. I—I never gave a thought to how difficult it would be to get away from here again," she confessed unwillingly, especially when she saw his smile.

"Can you drive?"

The question was unexpected, and she shook her head. "No. I've never had reason to learn."

"Well, if you're going to live out here," he told her, "you'd better learn. I'll teach you if you like."

Again she blinked at the unexpectedness of it, and shook her head somewhat vaguely. "I—I don't know," she said. "I'll have to see whether I like the idea or not. Of learning to drive," she added hastily when she saw his raised brows.

"It's up to you, of course," he told her. "Now you're such a wealthy woman, you could have a Rolls and a handsome chauffeur. But in the meantime you needn't bother getting a taxi to fetch you—I'm going into Chedwell myself after breakfast. I'll run you in."

Charlotte was unsure if she wanted to be any further

indebted to him, but she could see no reasonable way of refusing his offer, so she nodded.

He smiled. "My pleasure. Incidentally, you don't have to bother about seeing the powers-that-be about getting the services restored."

"But I—"

"Philip Chartres mentioned that the new owner would be here some time yesterday," he told her. "So I rang them all and organised it. They'll be along any day now, to fix you up."

Charlotte's small frown was instinctive, although she knew she should have been very grateful to him for taking the trouble. It was simply that she had always been a very independent type of girl, especially in the last five years, and she was not at all sure that she liked being looked after quite so completely and efficiently as Scott Lingrove was doing.

"Thank you."

One brow recognised her reticence and he smiled at her across the table. "You don't really mean that, do you?" he asked, and Charlotte hastily lowered her gaze.

"Yes, of course I do," she told him quietly. "But—well, I *am* a trained secretary, Mr. Lingrove, and I'm used to doing things for myself."

"I do beg your pardon!" The hazel eyes gleamed wickedly, although his features were suitably composed into an expression of apology. "I forgot for the moment that you're one those super-efficient business women. One expects a woman, especially such a beautiful woman, to be just a little dependent. You must forgive my anxiety to help, but I hadn't met you then, of course."

It was difficult to know whether he resented her independence or if he found it amusing, but she had no hesitation in deciding that he was quite the most disconcerting man she had ever met, and she found herself wishing she had known him long enough to be downright rude to him. He had that sort of effect on her.

'I'm a secretary," she said, stiffly polite. "And I pride myself on being reasonably efficient, Mr. Lingrove. I hope I am."

"Not to the extent of making sure you weren't stranded miles from the nearest transport, or that the house was fit to sleep in," he reminded her quietly. "But I suppose that scarcely comes under the heading of duties for an efficient secretary, does it?"

"It doesn't," she agreed shortly.

"Ah well," he smiled, and shook his head slowly, his gaze wandering slowly over her face in obvious appreciation of what he saw. "You won't need to be anything but beautiful now that you're going to be a lady of leisure, will you?" he said softly, and she hastily hid her eyes with a sweep of dark lashes.

His expression was one she had seen many times before and always been able to cope with, but somehow with this man she felt so much more vulnerable. "I—I haven't quite got used to the idea of being a lady of leisure yet," she confessed.

"You've hardly had time," he agreed. "And you won't be taking up residence right away, will you?"

Charlotte nodded. "As soon as the place is habitable," she said. "Then I'll see about getting it restored and the gardens cleaned up. It could be such a beautiful place, it's such a shame it's been allowed to fall into neglect."

"It could be lovely," he agreed. "And it's so much less cumbersome than Wainscote."

"Oh, but this is beautiful!" Charlotte exclaimed without hesitation. She looked at him curiously for a second through her lashes. "In fact I can't quite see why you want Blanestock when you have this."

His eyes glowed with laughter again, and he shook his head as he disposed of the last of his breakfast. "I doubt if I should want it if Wainscote *was* mine," he told her, and Charlotte stared at him for a moment, uncomprehendingly.

"I—I don't understand," she said at last. "*Is*n't it yours? I thought—"

He was shaking his head. "It isn't mine," he told her. "I only manage it for Simon—Lord Everslade."

"Oh! Oh, I see." She thought she could see at last, why he was so anxious to buy Blanestock for himself. If he was merely managing this huge house, then it was more feasible that he would want somewhere of his own, and being so close to Wainscote it would kill two birds with one stone as it were. One thing occurred to her, however, and that was that he must be drawing an enormous salary as manager if he could even consider buying Blanestock.

"It'd be perfect for me, as you can imagine," he told her, "to be right next door. I'd be on the spot without, as it were, living on the job."

'Yes, yes, of course I can see that."

The hazel eyes quizzed her speculatively for a moment, and he smiled. "But you won't let me have it?"

Charlotte shook her head. "No," she said firmly, "I won't let you have it."

"Ah well!" He shrugged, still smiling. "*Audaces fortuna juvat*. We'll see."

"I don't—" Charlotte began, and he laughed softly as he got to his feet.

"The Everslade family motto," he told her. "Fortune favours the bold—and it's amazing how often it does, Miss Brown."

CHAPTER THREE

IT CAME as something of a surprise, albeit a pleasant one, to discover how swiftly the various authorities acted in response to Scott Lingrove's request for action in restoring the services to Blanestock. By the end of the week they already had the water and electricity working again, and Charlotte was so encouraged by their promptness that she had left the hotel after having spent only five nights there, and moved out to Blanestock, despite the doubts of both the Chartreses and Scott Lingrove.

Electric fires had aired one of the beds sufficiently for her to sleep on it without risk of pneumonia, and she was less troubled about being cut off from transport when the telephone engineers came and reconnected the telephone service. Altogether she was quite enjoying herself, even if her mode of living could perhaps be considered a little primitive at the moment.

Her first night at Blanestock, sleeping in a proper bed, she did not even notice the sounds that had disturbed her before, and slept well, waking again to find the sun streaming into her room. She bathed and took her time over breakfast, then decided to ring for a taxi to take her in to Chedwell to do some shopping.

She was putting away her breakfast things when someone rapped on the back door. For some inexplicable reason she was quite sure it would be Scott Lingrove and she instinctively put a hand to her hair before she called out to him to come in.

Her suspicion was confirmed when he stepped through the doorway and smiled at her. "Good morning," he said. "I see you're independent now, able to cook yourself breakfast."

"Yes, thank you." She remembered in time that he had been responsible for the electricity being on. "They were very quick."

He cocked a brow at her and smiled. "I thought they might be," he said. "How are you getting on?"

"Fine," she told him, wondering why he had come and wishing she did not feel quite so uneasy whenever she was alone with him.

"No problems?"

"No."

"How are you managing about cooking?" He smiled then and dismissed his own question with a shrug of his shoulders. "Of course, you *can* manage, can't you?"

"Can't you?" she retorted swiftly, and he laughed.

"Not a chance," he said. "I'm as helpless as a baby without somebody to cook for me." He perched himself on the edge of the kitchen table and she realised suddenly how remiss as a hostess she was being.

"Oh, please sit down," she told him. "We can go through into the sitting-room if you like, although it isn't very spick and span yet, I'm afraid."

"I'm quite happy here," he replied, swinging one foot back and forth, and studying her in that way that she found so disconcerting. "You're a great improvement on the last owner," he said then. "Although old Ezra wasn't a bad fellow when you knew him. I must admit I didn't expect anyone quite like you—I was thinking more along the lines of a middle-aged spinster with tweeds and a tight mouth."

"Really?" Charlotte decided to ignore the very obvious appreciation of her looks and concentrate on finding out as much as she could about her great-uncle. This man professed to have known him quite well and it seemed so important to her somehow to learn as much as she could about the old man who had, however unconsciously, made her an heiress.

She had considered asking the Chartreses about him, what he had been like as a person, but somehow their position as lawyers deterred her. Lawyers always seemed such distant people. Not that she felt at ease with this man, but at least he would not be tied by professional etiquette to telling her only polite generalities about a client.

"Did you know my—my great-uncle very well?" she asked, and he nodded.

"As well as anyone did, I suppose, especially in the last five years. He saw almost no one after he lost Mary."

"Mary?"

He nodded, looking up with a wry grin for her obvious curiosity. "You wouldn't know anything about that, of course, would you?"

"I know absolutely nothing about him," she admitted, "and I wish I did. I'm curious about him, I confess."

"So I gather."

His smile did nothing to further peace between them and she wished he need not always make her feel so angry and resentful. "I suppose you think I'm just a—a nosey-parker, trying to find out all I can about him," she said defensively. "But I would *like* to have known him when he was alive. As it was I didn't even really know he existed until I saw that advert in the newspaper, and that was purely by chance.

"Purely by chance?" he echoed, and laughed shortly, so that Charlotte flushed.

"You probably think all sorts of uncomplimentary things about me, Mr. Lingrove," she said, still defensive. "But I *am* his only surviving relative and if I'd known of his existence before I'd have been happy to have visited him. Perhaps made him a little less lonely."

"He *was* lonely," Scott Lingrove said quietly. "He was a *very* lonely man, especially when—" Large hands dismissed a moment of pity almost impatiently, but Charlotte was unwilling to let it rest there.

"You—you imply that there was a special reason for his being so lonely," she said. "And you mentioned someone called Mary." He said nothing, and she almost resigned herself to the fact that he would enlighten her no further. "Please tell me about him," she begged, unconsciously appealing. "He was all the family *I* had left too, and I'd like to know something about him."

For a moment the hazel eyes studied her with disconcerting steadiness, then he smiled and their corners crinkled into a myriad of fine lines. "It's the old story," he said. "A woman."

"Oh!" That much was unexpected and she looked at him uncertainly, wondering if it was something best left unsaid. "I—I didn't realise there was anything like that."

"There wasn't anything like that, as you call it," he

told her with a smile twitching the corners of his mouth. "He was an old man and it was only six years ago, but I imagine it comes harder at that age."

Charlotte stared at him, uncertain just how much of it was truth and how much speculation. "You—you mean that he wanted to—to marry her?"

He shrugged. "I gathered that was the idea," he told her.

"Oh—oh, what a shame. Was she nice, this—Mary?"

He nodded, smiling. "Very nice," he said. "Mary Bishop she was then."

Charlotte was silent for a moment, genuinely sorry for the lonely old man. "Poor man," she said softly. "To love someone and they marry someone else."

"It was only to be expected," he said quietly. "After all, she was forty years his junior."

"Oh!" Charlotte's eyes widened with surprise. "Oh, I see."

It was easy enough to see, she thought, a lonely old bachelor suddenly finding himself wildly infatuated with a woman young enough to be his granddaughter, and being rejected for someone else. No wonder he had become what Mr. Philip Chartres referred to as "a difficult man" in his last years.

Scott Lingrove's eyes regarded her speculatively, as if he followed her train of thought all too easily. "I suppose the Chartreses told you the old man was crazy in his last years?" he suggested, and her expression was confirmation enough. "Well—" he shrugged, "he wasn't, not by a long way. He was lonely and miserable and he always hoped that one day—" He shrugged again and left the rest unsaid.

"It's—it's so sad," Charlotte said, feeling quite misty-eyed. "And such a waste of a life."

"It's always a waste of a life to moon too long over a woman, whoever she is," Scott Lingrove declared brusquely. "But there you are, he didn't marry Mary, so you get the estate. It's an ill wind." And that, Charlotte felt, was an adage she could not very well disagree with.

IT WAS quite a pleasant surprise the following day when Noel Chartres telephoned and asked her to have lunch with him, and Charlotte accepted without hesitation. He would fetch her, he said, and they could have lunch and talk about Blanestock at the same time.

He was not happy, he said, about her staying there on her own, and Charlotte was quite touched by his concern, although she assured him that she was perfectly all right until she could get someone to come in either full or part-time.

He was really very nice, she decided, and also a very attractive man, and she was glad he had been impressed enough with her to ask her to lunch. At least, she thought, between them her new acquaintances were making sure she did not go hungry.

"It's fortunate you found Scott Lingrove," he said as they sat over lunch, his blue eyes looking earnest. "If you hadn't noted the name of the house and gone to find him, it could have been very uncomfortable for you. I didn't realise you intended staying the night at Blanestock or I'd have tried to discourage you, so would Father."

Charlotte smiled. "It wouldn't have done any good,

I'm afraid," she told him. "I'd made up my mind to stay, and I really wasn't too uncomfortable, even though I did sleep on the floor."

"Did Lingrove know you were staying there?" he asked.

"Yes, and as you would have done, he tried to discourage me. I was very pleasantly surprised to find he was prepared to give me breakfast and the use of his bathroom, though."

"Oh yes, he'd do that," Noel said, a little sourly, she guessed.

"He'd also arranged for the services to be reconnected too, which was useful, although I *am* used to doing things for myself."

He smiled, though much less sarcastically than Scott Lingrove had done in the same circumstances. "You're very independent," he said. "But now that you don't have to do things for yourself, you must learn to let others do the worrying for you."

Charlotte laughed, wondering if he had himself in mind in particular. "I'm not sure I'll be able to, Mr. Chartres," she told him. "It's not an easy habit to break, being independent."

"Well, please believe me, we'll be only too glad to take care of everything for you," he assured her. "And, for myself, I'll be glad to help in any way I can, even if it isn't strictly on a professional basis."

Charlotte did nothing about the brief, reticent brushing of his fingers against her hand as it lay on the table, but she smiled. "Thank you," she said softly. "I'll remember that."

He said nothing for a while, then he looked up at her

suddenly, eyeing her curiously for a moment before he spoke. "How did you get on with Scott Lingrove?" he asked.

Uncertain just what kind of answer she was expected to give, Charlotte hesitated. "I—I got on quite well with him," she admitted at last. "He's rather a—forceful character, but he seems quite thoughtful, and I appreciated his help."

He looked down at his plate for a moment or two, as if he sought inspiration for what he had to say next. "I—I don't quite know how to put this," he said then, still not looking at her. "But the truth is, Miss Brown, I'm afraid I was rather indiscreet the other day—Saturday, when you arrived. I mean," he added hastily, "I shouldn't have mentioned anything about Mr. Lingrove wanting to buy Blanestock from you. I'm afraid I rather jumped the gun by telling you about it before you were made a proper formal offer, and if my father knew I'd said anything—"

Charlotte smiled understanding, wondering how on earth she was going to explain that she had mentioned it to Scott Lingrove too, and wishing she had not. "I promise I won't say a word to your father," she promised.

He looked so unbelievably grateful that she hated to have to confess the rest and tell him that she *had* mentioned it to the man most concerned. "I'm very much obliged to you, Miss Brown," he said. "I can't for the life of me think what made me say anything about it without first consulting my father. However" he shrugged and smiled "—there's no harm done.'

Charlotte pulled a wry face, and shook her head. "I'm afraid it might not be as simple as that," she told him. "You see, I spoke to Mr. Lingrove about it on the Sunday."

"Oh, lord!" His look of dismay might have struck her as comical at any other time, now she was only sorry she had been unable to resist raising the subject with Scott Lingrove.

"I really am *very* sorry," she said. "But you see I didn't realise that I wasn't supposed to know about it."

"No, no, of course you didn't," he hastened to reassure her. "It was entirely my fault, Miss Brown, please don't apologise for anything."

"Will—will your father be very angry about it?" she asked, and he shrugged.

"I suppose it all depends on whether Scott Lingrove sees fit to say anything about it," he told her, already almost resigned, she thought. "If he complains about you being forewarned, as it were, then it might be awkward for me."

"Yes, of course, he would want to spring it on me, I suppose, wouldn't he?" she guessed. "Then if I was feeling disillusioned enough I'd probably have sold it and been only too glad to let him have it."

"Something like that. It's difficult, you see, because he's a client as well. Not one of ours, actually, but of Basil Clee's, the senior partner."

"Oh dear!"

He looked suitably gloomy, and Charlotte wondered what on earth she could do to help. "The Everslades are valued clients," he told her, "and the old man would never forgive me if, through me, they lost the Everslade business."

"The Everslades?" Charlotte frowned curiously. "But I thought—I mean surely the Everslade family wouldn't take away their business because of some minor complaint of their—their manager, would they? I understood from Mr. Lingrove that he only managed Wainscote for Lord Everslade."

"So he does," Noel agreed. "The Everslades are abroad for a couple of years, and Scott Lingrove's keeping an eye on Wainscote while they're away, but it's all in the family. Simon Everslade and Scott Lingrove are cousins."

"They're cousins?"

"That's right. Their mothers are sisters and the two of them have always been as thick as thieves." He hastily glanced at her face to see if he had been too frank, but was evidently reassured by her expression. "I mean, they've always been very close. The two boys, of course, are much too young to take on the duties of heir, so rather than bring in an outsider, they left Scott Lingrove in charge."

"Oh, I see."

It seemed, Charlotte thought ruefully, that there was a great deal she had to learn about her new neighbour. She had had no idea that she was moving into quite such a high stratum of society when she took up her new residence, and the thought of it momentarily dismayed her.

"Anyway, don't let it bother you," Noel told her, after a moment or two. "He probably won't say anything about it, and it's unlikely they *would* take their business elsewhere because Clees have handled the Everslade *and* Bishop family affairs for donkey's years."

Something, somewhere, struck a chord in Charlotte's memory, and she looked at him curiously for a moment before realising what it was. "Bishop?" she said. "You said the Bishop family?"

"That's right," Noel agreed, apparently unaware of any reason for comment. "Lady Everslade was Miss Mary Bishop before her marriage."

AFTER A WHOLE WEEK at Blanestock, Charlotte was still discovering things about the old house. It had numerous cupboards and alcoves and, behind a locked door, she found some dark and worn wooden steps leading down to a cellar, although she had not ventured further than the door to investigate it too thoroughly.

She could make herself much more comfortable now that everything was working again, and she already felt quite at home there. The house was much too big for her to live there alone, of course, and especially without help, and she had no illusions about how bleak and lonely it would seem in the winter months.

Trying to find the services of a full-time housekeeper, however, was not only difficult but well-nigh impossible. She had managed to obtain the services of a daily woman, but even she could not start for another week yet, and Charlotte was impatient to see some improvement before then.

Noel Chartres seemed to think that she should have stayed in the hotel until the place was made ready for her, but she would not hear of it. Blanestock was hers and she wanted to live there, no matter if it was less than perfect at the moment.

Never a girl to sit around and wait for things to happen, she was prepared to start on the cleaning up process herself, although the thought of tackling the whole house was rather too daunting.

Setting to one morning, she spent some time cleaning out a large cupboard, and the success of that so inspired her that she decided to extend her ministrations to one of the bedrooms. Whether her aristocratic neighbours would approve of the new mistress of Blanestock scrubbing her own floors or not, she was uncaring.

She had looked out an old frock and covered it with a large print apron, then tied back her hair with a scarf tied peasant fashion. She was bound to get filthy, for the place was inches thick in dust.

There were any number of brooms and brushes and mops in a cupboard in the kitchen, and she armed herself ready for work. Carrying a big bucket full of water and disinfectant for laying the dust, she went upstairs somewhat precariously, depositing the bucket at the top of the stairs, on the landing. Then, working on an Eeny, Meeny, Miny, Mo system, she selected a bedroom for attention.

It was a warm sunny day and she flung wide all the windows before starting, wondering as she stood there for a minute taking in the view of the wide, sweeping countryside, whether she would not have been as well going for a walk instead.

Dismissing such temptations, she shrugged and turned back into the room. The first thing to be done was to take off those shrouding sheets from the furniture. Seeing it draped like that always made her feel horribly creepy, and she thought of Scott Lingrove's remarks about spooks.

The bedroom was at the back of the house, so that she had only brief second thoughts about gathering up the dust-laden rugs from the board floor and hurling them out of the window to be brushed later. Then she picked up a broom and a big feather duster and faced her task with a gleam in her eye.

She had registered the expected thud below when the rugs landed, but that was not all she heard. There was also a loud and indignant yell at almost the same moment and she put her hands to her mouth when she realised what had happened. There was no possible doubt in her mind what she had done and she closed her eyes in silent prayer that it was not too important a caller that she had submerged under a pile of very dusty rugs.

It was a moment or two before she could bring herself to look out of the window and then she saw only the rugs themselves lying on the stone-paved terrace that spanned the back of the house. She thought she caught a glimpse, however, of a pair of heels just disappearing in through the kitchen door, and groaned inwardly.

Whoever it was must surely be furiously angry at receiving such cavalier treatment, and she stood there for a moment with her heart beating an anxious tattoo at her ribs, wondering what on earth she could say to excuse herself.

It was only a few seconds later that she heard the sound of a heavy tread on the stairs and stared at the closed door in dismay. Whoever it was was obviously bent on making an issue of it, and there was no doubt it was a man from the heaviness of the tread. He must be really angry too, she thought wildly, to have come straight in to the house like that in search of his attacker.

Before she could summon enough courage to cross

the room and open the door to identify her visitor, however, another and much more ominous sound shattered the quietness of the house, and once more a hand flew to her mouth.

"Oh no!"

There was no disguising the obvious. Her caller had not only been smothered with dusty rugs, he had now fallen foul of the bucket she had left at the top of the stairs, and the rattle and clatter of the metal bucket against the balustrade was followed by a masculine voice passing an opinion in no uncertain language.

Opening the door, Charlotte almost fell over Scott Lingrove bent double as he tried to brush some of the water from the bottoms of his trouser legs. Finding him so close at hand and doubled up like that, she let out a squeak of surprise and dropped the broom and the feather duster she carried. The broom, fortunately, fell with a clatter against the wall, but the duster found its mark on the back of the caller's neck before floating to the floor.

"Damn you!" Scott Lingrove complained loudly. "Not content with half drowning me, you have to smother me with your blasted mop as well!"

"I'm—I'm sorry." It appalled her to realise it, but her first instinct was to laugh, and she hastily smothered it for fear he was really as angry as he looked.

"So you should be!" he retorted.

Not prepared to take the entire blame for his falling over the bucket, Charlotte frowned. "Well, you should have seen the bucket standing there," she told him unsympathetically. "It's big enough."

"You don't have to tell me that!" He shook each leg in turn, spattering the wallpaper with little showers of water. "But in case you hadn't realised it, I was already half blinded with dust from a load of rugs or something. And that blessed mop's moulting—look at my head!"

It was true, Charlotte realised, the feather duster was old and it was very definitely moulting. She stood there for a moment, looking at the spectacle he made, and most of it her doing, she was bound to admit, if only to herself.

His once white shirt showed more than a trace of dust from the rugs—evidently they had landed right on top of him, and the bottoms of his trousers were soaking wet almost to the knees. To crown it all there were several brown and white feathers from the mop adhering to the thick fair hair, where it curled just above his ears.

Try as she would to control it, she could do nothing more about the laughter that bubbled up inside her. It showed first in her eyes and made them sparkle darkly, then it touched the corners of her mouth as she made one last desperate attempt to stifle it, and finally burst out in a peal of merriment that echoed round the sun-streaked walls of the long landing.

For a moment she thought he was actually going to hit out at her, for there was an unmistakable gleam of anger in the hazel eyes that boded ill for her sense of humour. "Why, you little—" He actually had a hand raised, she would have sworn it, but then, suddenly he shook his head and his own wide mouth twitched with laughter. "All right," he told her quietly. "Have your fun, Miss Brown, but don't think you'll get away with these sort of tactics."

"Tactics?" Charlotte queried, her voice still unsteady with laughter. "What tactics?"

He pulled the last feather from his hair, and looked at her steadily. "It used to be a drawbridge and boiling oil to keep out the invader," he told her. "Now it seems it's a pile of rugs on the head, buckets of water and a feather mop thrown in for good measure. You intend making a firm stand for your castle, don't you?"

Serious now, Charlotte stared at him. "You—you surely don't think I did all that on purpose, do you?" she asked.

"Didn't you?" The hazel eyes held hers steadily, and she felt a strange, erratic fluttering in her pulse as she hastily looked away again. "I thought it was your way of repelling boarders."

"Oh, but that's—that's utterly ridiculous," she protested, retrieving her duster and shaking loose another shower of brown speckled feathers. "I didn't even know you were down there when I threw the rugs out, and I certainly didn't expect you to come galloping up the stairs and fall over the bucket. That was entirely your own doing."

"I came upstairs to protest about having a pile of filthy rugs thrown at me from a great height," he informed her, obviously bent on arguing. "And if ever there was a well laid booby trap, that bucket was it. It was perfectly placed for anyone coming up the stairs to fall over."

"But I told you, I didn't expect anyone to *come* upstairs," Charlotte insisted, and stifled another giggle when he shook a wet leg. "But I'm sorry about you getting wet for all that."

"Sorry?" He raised a doubtful brow. "Forgive me if I doubt that, won't you?"

"You can please yourself whether you believe it or

not," she retorted. "If you *will* come barging into people's houses, uninvited, you have to take your chance on the sort of reception you get."

"I see." He spoke quietly, so quietly that it made Charlotte suddenly wary of him, and she watched him uneasily from beneath lowered lids.

"I'm sorry about the rugs *and* the bucket," she told him hastily. "But there was nothing intentional about any of it, honestly."

"Not even the way you laughed?" he asked, his own eyes showing signs of amusement again, much to her relief.

"Oh, that!" A small, soft giggle escaped her. "I'm sorry if it offended you, but you *did* look funny with wet feet and feathers in your hair."

"Oh, I'm quite sure I did," he said softly. "And you've got a wicked little sense of humour, Charlie Brown."

Charlotte looked at him indignantly. Not only was he being much too familiar on such short acquaintance, but she had never allowed anyone at all to abbreviate her rather quaint old-fashioned name. "I beg your pardon," she said coolly, and looked at him meaningly.

The meaning was lost, however, because he refused to interpret her words in the way she intended. "Oh, think no more of it," he told her airily.

"I was referring to your distortion of my name," Charlotte told him, firmly refusing to let the matter drop.

His eyes crinkled into a smile and he surveyed her steadily for a moment, daring her to argue. "Oh, but surely you've been called Charlie Brown before," he said. "It's just too much to resist."

"No doubt," Charlotte said. "But I don't allow anyone to call me anything else but Charlotte—or Miss Brown," she added meaningly, and he grinned.

"Sorry," he said blandly, "but I shall always think of you as Charlie Brown. I have done ever since I first heard your name from Philip Chartres, and old habits die hard."

"Well, this one had better die right now," Charlotte declared firmly.

For several breathless seconds she held his gaze steadily, then very unwillingly she lowered her eyes, biting her lip on the sensation that had made her do it. It was virtually impossible to outface him, and she had never before been made so uneasy by any man.

"Charlotte?" he asked softly, and she nodded, almost without realising it.

"I'm—I'm sorry about you getting wet, and—and about the rugs," she said, talking about anything to break that long, discomfiting silence. "Why—why did you come over? Was it anything special?"

He smiled wryly. "By a strange coincidence," he said, "I came to ask you if you still want a housekeeper."

Charlotte looked up swiftly, nodding her head in case there was any chance of his misinterpreting her answer. "Oh yes, I do!" she told him. "Don't tell me you've actually managed to hear of one."

"I've more or less engaged one for you," he said, and smiled over her swift and instinctive frown. "Oh, I know you like being independent about things, but Mrs. Borden came to my notice and one has to be quick to take advantage of opportunities like that these days, so I took the liberty of asking her to come and see you tomorrow."

"Tomorrow?" There should have been some reason, she thought, why tomorrow should have meant something to her, but she was so anxious to be fixed up with a housekeeper that she did not dwell too long on possible snags. There could not be anything very important that could not be put off.

"It's convenient?" he asked, noting her brief frown.

"Oh yes, of course." She smiled, prepared to forgive a lot, if he had really found her a full-time housekeeper. "I can't really believe it," she told him. "I was given to understand that there was no such thing to be had in the whole of England. I'm very, very grateful to you, Mr. Lingrove."

"My pleasure," he said, and smiled, one brow cocked in query. "But I'd be even more pleased if you'd return the compliment and call me Scott—after all, we're old friends, aren't we?"

Charlotte blinked, her heart racing wildly for some inexplicable reason. "After one week?" she asked and he shook his head.

"It's nearly ten months since I first heard about you," he told her. "I feel as if I know you by now."

It was indeed a long time since she had first learned that Scott Lingrove was the executor of her great-uncle's estate, and she supposed that his name had become familiar even though its owner had been known to her for only a few days.

"I—I suppose it could seem as if we'd known one another for a long time," she allowed.

"Long enough to call me Scott?"

She nodded. "And in view of the way I've treated you this morning and the fact that you've found me a housekeeper, will you let me make you coffee as a sort of peace-offering and thank-you combined?"

He looked down at his wet clothes and the dust still on his shoulders, and smiled. "I don't usually dress like this in the company of a beautiful woman," he said, "but since most of it is your doing, you'll have to take me as I come." He bowed from the waist, one arm extended as she walked past him to the stairs. "After you, fair Charlotte."

CHAPTER FOUR

THE VERY IMPRESSIVE Mrs. Borden had come and gone, leaving Charlotte feeling very uncertain just who had been interviewing whom. She was, Mrs. Borden insisted firmly, accustomed to working in only the best houses and she did not usually consider herself a cook-housekeeper, but in the circumstances she was prepared to adjust her standards to suit.

The circumstances, Charlotte suspected, had something to do with the fact that Mrs. Borden was the wrong side of sixty, there would only be one in family and, not least, she thought, the fact that Mr. Lingrove had personally asked her to consider it. Mr. Lingrove was first cousin to Lord Everslade and therefore definitely Mrs. Borden's idea of "the best people".

She would be unable to start for another two weeks yet, but if that suited Miss Brown—Charlotte said it did, and saw her rather intimidating prospective employee to the door with a sigh of relief. Scarcely had she sat down, however, to give herself time to recover her self-confidence, when the door bell rang and she got to her feet again with a sigh.

"It's me," Scott Lingrove informed her when she opened the door. "I just saw the Grand Duchess Borden leaving—did she suit?"

A smile acknowledged the aptness of the description,

and Charlotte invited him in, wondering what today's reason was for his calling. "She's starting in another couple of weeks," she told him. "I only hope I can come up to her standards."

His grin recognised, and sympathised, with her feelings as he followed her across the hall and into the sitting-room. "She's a bit much, isn't she?" he said. "But I'm sure you'll cope."

"I hope so," Charlotte said with feeling, and he laughed, perching himself on the arm of a chair.

"Well, don't let her get you down, for heaven's sake, I'm sure you've come across a few dragons before, in the world of big business."

"But it's not quite the same," Charlotte told him. "I have the feeling that Mrs. Borden looks on me as not quite up to her standards—not what she's used to. I shall probably do all the wrong things and she'll leave again in high dudgeon because I'm not good enough for her."

Scott looked at her steadily for a moment, his eyes half teasing. "Oh, come on now, Charlie Brown," he said with a laugh. "That's a dangerous state of mind to let yourself get into. Don't let yourself be brow-beaten by the likes of Mrs. Borden. Stand up to her, let her know who's boss."

"At the moment," Charlotte retorted, "I'm not at all sure who *is* boss." She looked at him through heavy lashes, a small frown on her brows. "And *don't* call me Charlie Brown."

He laughed again, undeterred by her disapproval, one hand thrust carelessly into a pocket, the other hugging his bent knee across the other. "You'll be a real Charlie if you let your housekeeper bully you," he told her, and she pursed her lips.

"I suppose I will," she admitted. "But I've never crossed swords with anybody like Mrs. Borden before, and she petrifies me."

He left his perch on the chair arm and shook his head as he came across to her, so that intinctively Charlotte's fingers curled into her palms. One hand slid beneath her chin and gently raised her face while he studied her for a moment without speaking.

"I'm afraid I'm going to be disappointed in you," he told her softly. "I thought you had spirit."

For a long moment Charlotte said nothing, then she raised her eyes and looked at him. "It's all right for you," she told him, "you're the *best* people, so Mrs. Borden said, and she should know after all her years' experience. Me, I'm just a—"

His mouth very effectively stopped whatever derogatory name she had been going to call herself, and his breath was warm on her lips when he spoke, softly, and with a half smile touching his wide mouth. "You're an independent, self-reliant, very beautiful girl," he said. "And you'll wave the big stick over *la* Borden or I'll know the reason why. O.K.?"

Charlotte could only nod for the moment. Her heart was hammering so hard at her ribs she felt breathless and a little dizzy. "O.K.," she agreed in a strangely husky voice, and wondered how on earth she had allowed herself to get into *this* situation.

"Good!" He smiled approval at her apparent compliance. "Then get your bonnet and shawl and I'll take you for a drink and a bun at the local hostelry."

Charlotte looked at him curiously, still not quite understanding her own reactions. "Can you spare the time?" she asked. "Haven't you got a stately home to run, or something?"

Scott shrugged. "The stately home season is dying off now," he told her solemnly. "What few that may turn up, Crayley can deal with quite efficiently. Now—are you game for that bun and beer or not?"

It was only a very brief hesitation she made, but in that time she felt his eyes on her, challenging her to refuse. "Why not?" she said at last. "I'd like a sandwich and a drink at the local. Just give me a minute."

"I'll give you no minute," he argued firmly, taking her arm. "For one thing I'm on the point of starvation and for another I don't want you dolling yourself up and putting the Everslade Arms in the cocktail class. It's beer and doorstep sandwiches—and there's absolutely nothing wrong with the way you look now."

"But I—"

She stopped in mid-sentence, turning startled eyes when the door bell rang yet again, and as she gazed out into the hall the realisation dawned at last. Yesterday when Scott had asked if today was a convenient time for her to see Mrs. Borden she had thought it struck a chord in her memory briefly. Now she knew why—she had promised to have lunch with Noel Chartres and he was here to fetch her, completely unaware that she had just this minute committed herself to another lunch with Scott Lingrove.

"Trouble?" Scott asked curiously, seeing her expression, and she nodded vaguely, wondering how on earth she was going to get out of it.

"Very much so," she told him. "That's Noel at the door, and he's expecting me to have lunch with him."

"Aah, I see."

He evidently had no intention of being helpful, and she was uncertain whether the gleam in his eyes was anger or amusement as he stood watching her, waiting to see how she would cope with the situation.

"Scott, I'm sorry—I quite forgot about Noel."

"Very flattering for poor old Noel," he said, quite calmly and quite unhelpfully.

"I—I promised him yesterday."

He nodded. "I see, so I'm to be discarded as an embarrassing mistake while Noel takes you to the fleshpots of Chedwell."

"I've said I'm sorry, Scott," she protested. "I—I know it's my fault, but I—well, I just forgot."

He grinned then, as if something had just occurred to him. "I suppose I could take *that* as a compliment in a way, couldn't I?" he asked. "You were so carried away in my company that you forgot you'd already promised to see Noel Chartres." He shook his head, going on before she could speak in her own defence. "Oh well, I'll let you get away with it this time, Charlie Brown, but if you ever do it again I shall be much less cooperative next time."

"Will there *be* a next time?" Charlotte asked, meekly, while Noel rang the bell again. It would not do, she decided, in the circumstances, to object to the Charlie Brown.

The hazel eyes held her gaze steadily for a moment. "Oh yes," he said softly, "there'll be a next time."

He strode across the room and out into the hall, with Charlotte following a little dazedly, and he opened the door to Noel Chartres with a small, slightly malicious smile touching the corner of his mouth for the other man's surprise.

"Oh! Oh, good morning, Mr. Lingrove." He was a valued client, Charlotte remembered. "I—is Miss

Brown—" He saw her then just behind Scott, and smiled his relief. "Oh, there you are."

She smiled a greeting at him while Scott turned in the doorway, in no hurry to depart, apparently. "Hello, Noel," she said. "Do come in."

"If you're—" Noel began, but she shook her head hastily, and distinctly heard a faint chuckle from her first visitor.

"I'll see you tomorrow, Charlotte," Scott said, fixing her with a challenging gaze that defied argument.

"Yes. Yes, of course," she agreed vaguely, and he smiled as he turned to go. "Scott!" He turned back, his eyes glinting as he cocked a brow in query. "I'm—I'm sorry about today."

Noel was trying to follow the rather confusing exchange with a curious frown, and Charlotte wondered if he had some inkling of what had happened. "If you've something else to do instead," he began, but Charlotte shook her head. "I haven't," she told him. "Come in, Noel."

She turned again, feeling rather like a mechanical doll with her head going from side to side as she gave each of them in turn her attention. "Goodbye, Charlotte."

"Goodbye," she echoed. "And—and thank you."

He laughed softly as he went down the steps to the drive. "'Bye, Noel," he called back over his shoulder. "Look after her for me."

Noel looked quite startled for a moment, then he looked at Charlotte, seeking an explanation, but she was already closing the door on that disconcerting laugh and fighting to keep the embarrassment she felt from showing on her face.

"What on earth does he mean?" Noel asked, as he followed her across the hall, and she shook her head impatiently.

"Oh, it's his idea of a joke, I suppose," she told him, turning to face him when they stood in the sitting-room. "It's—well, it's a bit embarrassing really, Noel. You see, I—I'm afraid it completely slipped my mind that I was having lunch with you today. I've been seeing someone about the housekeeper's job, and she turned out to be a very formidable female."

"Oh, you've managed to get somebody, have you?" he asked, knowing how anxious she had been about it.

"She starts in a couple of weeks' time," Charlotte said. "It's someone Scott found for me, actually, that's why he came over. To see how I'd fared with Mrs. Borden."

"I see. I wondered why he was here."

It was obvious from his expression that the idea of Scott Lingrove visiting her was something he did not view with much favour, and she guessed he did not like the other man very much. Undoubtedly he was obliged to be polite to him because he was a client of his firm, but his manner left no doubt as to what his private feelings were.

"He drops in occasionally to see how I'm getting on," Charlotte explained.

"And you don't mind him sounding as if—as if he has some sort of proprietorial claim to you?" he asked, remembering Scott's parting words.

"Oh, that!" Her laugh dismissed it as unimportant. "I suspect Mr. Scott Lingrove enjoys stirring up as much mischief as he can."

"And I endorse your view," Noel assured her shortly.

"You don't like him?"

It seemed he was unwilling to go so far as to actually admit it, his professional caution probably curbed his tongue. "I wouldn't go that far," he said warily. "But he can be rather annoying at times."

"He can be maddening!" Charlotte declared, not bound by professional etiquette. She smiled up at him. "But we're not bothered about Scott Lingrove," she told him. "I really am sorry that I forgot our lunch date, Noel. I can't think how I could have been so woolly-headed."

From his expression it was difficult to decide whether he was most offended or hurt, but the latter showed most plainly on his face, and he thrust his hands into his pockets and looked down at the highly polished toes of his shoes.

"It doesn't matter if you have something else to do," he told her, making it obvious that it *would* matter.

"I haven't," Charlotte denied. "If you don't mind waiting just a little while, while I make myself presentable. I won't be very long."

"I don't mind waiting in the least," he assured her, but still looked uncertain. "I thought I heard you say—I mean I wondered if you had arranged something with Lingrove."

"I did," she admitted, making a face over the admission. "I said I'd have a drink and a sandwich with him at the local, but that was before I remembered I was seeing you. And I'm quite sure he couldn't have cared less either way."

"I'm sure he could," Noel told her morosely. "Believe me, Charlotte, I know him, and one thing Scott Lingrove doesn't like is losing something he's set his heart on."

Such as Blanestock, Charlotte thought ruefully, and wondered just how far he would go to gain his own ends. So far he had done nothing to exert pressure on her to sell him the house, but there *were* more subtle ways of achieving the same end, and Scott Lingrove, she guessed, would not be above using them.

It was only three days later that Charlotte received a letter from Mr. Philip Chartres containing the information that Mr. Lingrove had made an offer to buy Blanestock, just as it stood, and for a very generous amount considering the state of the house itself.

She felt annoyed because he had made no mention of an official offer either during their public house lunch two days ago, or during a couple of subsequent short visits to the house. Feeling that he was, in a way, applying legal pressure she was prepared to do battle with him when she saw him again, and in the meantime she prepared a formal letter of refusal for the solicitor.

She was angry that he had even made another offer when he knew quite well she had no intention of selling, and she made up her mind to go along to Wainscote and tell him so. Some days before, when she was taking an exploratory walk, she had discovered that it was possible to gain access to Wainscote property without the need to walk along the road and in through the main gates.

It was possible because there was a narrow spinney

bordering a field belonging to Blanestock which acted as a boundary between the two properties. It dispensed with the need to walk along the road and then along that all too impressive drive which rather overawed her. She had no intention of being overawed by anything or anybody at the moment, so she left the house by the back door and made her way via the neglected gardens to the field beyond, bordered by the communal strip of woodland.

It was quiet and still and utterly peaceful out here, and it was not long before it began to have an effect on Charlotte as she made her way through the trees in the spinney. The rich brown loam underfoot smelled warm and spicy, and the autumn sun was persuading the birds to sing as gaily as if it was summer, so that by the time she had worked her way through the trees to the far edge of the spinney she was feeling a little more kindly disposed towards Scott, and almost prepared to see his point of view.

At the Wainscote side of the trees she struck something of a snag, for there were tall, thick rhododendron bushes growing all along the edge and their thick, solid growth made getting through them something of a hazard. Thick, strong branches wove a barrier between her and the smooth green parkland she had seen on the other side, and she was forced to turn and extricate herself at almost every step.

Almost through, she was imprisoned by a particularly strong branch that required brute force to move it, and she had her back to the open space behind her, deaf and blind to anything at the rear as she concentrated on freeing herself from the tangle.

She managed, at last, to free herself and jerked backwards suddenly on to the smooth green sward behind her, half stumbling as she came. "Look out!" The cry came too late, for she had turned at the sound of it, so quickly that she stumbled again and fell.

She had a brief and quite terrifying glimpse of some huge creature with flaring nostrils and staring eyes just before she fell and rolled right in front of it. For a moment it towered over her, its legs and feet waving above her, and she closed her eyes tight, resigned to being pounded to a pulp where she lay.

It seemed like an eternity that she lay there, hearing a strange kind of snorting sound and the heavy thud of hooves, mixed and muddled in with a familiar voice sharp with command. Then the thudding stopped and the voice spoke again, followed by a sharp slap and the hooves racing away over the soft ground.

"Charlotte!" She still lay there curled up tight and not daring to move, and she still had her eyes closed when hands lifted her gently and arms cradled her against a heart that thudded unnaturally loud under her right ear. "Charlotte?"

She had no difficulty in identifying the voice and she played possum for a moment or two because she knew that the gentle cradling would come to an immediate end when he realised she was unhurt. And she opened her eyes only reluctantly.

"What—what happened?" she asked meekly.

"What happened?" As she expected he pushed her upright, none too gently, and got to his feet, looking down at her like some huge figure of vengeance. "Suppose *you* tell *me*?"

Charlotte made sure she was in good repair, then scrambled to her feet, brushing down her coat more as a reason for not looking at him, than because it was dirty. "I—I fell," she admitted, and the sound he made was more snort than laugh.

"You burst out of the shrubbery like a rabbit out of a hole," he told her. "You're damned lucky Satan didn't pound you to a pulp."

Satan, Charlotte assumed, was the fiery creature who had towered over her with flailing hooves, and she looked across to where he galloped across the parkland for home—riderless. "I'm sorry if I startled him," she said, looking up at last, "but I got caught in the branches and—I don't know, I suddenly got free and shot out."

"You're telling me!" He stood regarding her, feet apart, hands at his sides, one hand tapping a riding crop against one leg with ominous impatience. "You damned near unseated me!"

"I'm sorry."

"Let alone risking getting your own neck broken, you could have broken mine too," he went on relentlessly, and Charlotte sighed.

"I'm sorry, Scott."

"So you said," he retorted. "What are you doing sneaking in through the shrubbery, anyway?"

Remembering her original errand, Charlotte dismissed her momentary meekness and her mouth tightened as she stuck her chin in the air and looked at him down the length of her nose. "I was on my way to see you," she told him.

"Oh? I'm flattered." He was less tense now, and the first glimmer of laughter showed in his eyes as he put a hand under her elbow and turned her towards the house. "You'd better come and tell me why." He raised a brow that challenged her to argue. "I know it isn't simply for the pleasure of my company," he added.

"It isn't!" She walked along beside him, wondering if here and now was a good time to discuss it. The circumstances and the surroundings were scarcely businesslike, but she was unwilling to wait any longer before having her say. "I've had a letter from Mr. Chartres."

"Oh? Which one?"

"Mr. Philip Chartres, of course, as you know quite well."

She waited for him take the matter from there, but apparently he had no such intention. "Well, go on," was all he said, and Charlotte frowned at him.

"You're just being difficult, Scott," she accused. "You know perfectly well that he's made me an offer for Blanestock, on your behalf."

"Not quite," he argued. "Basil Clee's made an offer on my behalf. Philip Chartres has conveyed the offer to you."

"Oh, whatever the legal niceties are," she said impatiently. "You've made an offer for Blanestock."

"That's right."

She looked up at him, at the rugged, almost stern features in profile to her. He was determined not to be co-operative, she thought, and wished she had never come, for he had long since sabotaged any hope of her original plan of telling him exactly what she thought of him, even if it meant quarrelling with him. She had certainly intended to arouse something more than the cool and annoyingly matter-of-fact response she *was* getting.

She drew in a deep breath that sounded almost like a sigh. "You know quite well I have no intention of selling Blanestock," she said. "So why make the offer?"

"Actually that offer was put in hand before you came here," he told her. "It was intended to be all very legal and proper, and if Noel Chartres hadn't jumped the gun, the letter would have been your first intimation that I wanted to buy it."

"In other words you'd have sprung it on me and hoped I wouldn't have time to think about it first."

"Something like that," he admitted with a grin. "As it was Noel successfully scuttled my surprise."

She looked at him, momentarily anxious for Noel. "You—you didn't let them know I'd been told about it, did you?" she asked, and knew he followed her thoughts from the way he smiled.

"No, I didn't," he said. "I wasn't particularly anxious to land Noel in the mire with his firm. He's not the first man to have been led into indiscretion by a pretty face."

"I didn't—" she began, and he laughed.

"I know you didn't intentionally," he told her, "but you *were* the reason he forgot his professional ethics, I've no doubt, so I didn't let on."

"Well, I'm grateful to you for that, anyway," she told him. "But I still don't see why, when you know I have no intention of selling Blanestock, you let the offer be made."

"Because I intend having it."

Charlotte stopped in her tracks, and glared up at him, ignoring the fact that he was very obviously amused by her annoyance. "Over my dead body!" she declared fiercely, and he laughed again, urging her on towards the house.

"Battling Charlie Brown," he taunted. "Fighting to the last ditch for her inheritance."

"That's the whole point," Charlotte told him firmly. "It *is* my inheritance, and I've no intention of relinquishing it to anyone."

"Not even if you get married?" he asked with a smile. "Does your spouse automatically get barred from your fortress too? Or will he be the one exception?"

The choice of subject made her uneasy for some inexplicable reason and she looked at him warily. "There's no question of it arising at the moment," she said. "When it does—*if* it does—"

"Oh, it will," he assured her softly.

"Then it'll be a different matter altogether, of course. What's mine will automatically be his—whoever he is."

They were walking through the beautifully kept gardens at the back of Wainscote, and he still kept a hand under her arm as they approached the house itself. "Then the obvious solution to the problem is for you to marry me," he told her blandly, and Charlotte stared at him unbelievingly for a moment.

When the full meaning of it dawned on her at last, she snatched her arm away from his hold and her eyes blazed furiously, looking almost black in her anger. "You *would* too," she declared. "You *would* stoop as low as that to get what you want. Noel said you didn't like losing anything you'd set your heart on and now I believe him—wholeheartedly!"

"Did he now?"

He spoke quietly, and Charlotte's brain rang a warning bell. She was pretty certain that the Everslade family would not lightly change their allegiance from Clee, Banbury and Chartres, but another indiscretion by Noel might well be food for thought and she must guard her tongue. Scott Lingrove had already proved that he would go to any lengths to get what he wanted.

"I—I shouldn't have said that," she confessed, looking at him anxiously through her lashes. "Please—don't blame Noel."

"For what?" he asked, taking her round the side of the house. "He's quite right, I don't like losing a thing I've set my heart on, but neither, I imagine, does anyone else, do they?"

"I—I suppose not."

"Of course they don't," he retorted. "Noel Chartres has his sights set on you, it'll be interesting to see if he likes it when he doesn't get you."

The conversation, Charlotte felt, was becoming much too embarrassingly personal and she wished she could find some way of changing it. "I—I don't think you have any right or any reason to talk like that," she told him. "And I wish you wouldn't."

The hazel eyes gleamed wickedly and the fingers encircling her arm tightened fractionally when he spoke. "All right, Charlotte," he said softly. "But if you really do imagine Noel Chartres is seeing you simply with the idea of drumming up business, you're in for a big shock one of these days."

"I don't," she denied. "But I just don't think it concerns you, that's all."

He shrugged, smiling as he led the way into the

house. "And I happen to differ on that point, that's all."

It was useless, she thought, staying longer with him for she had little hope of making him see that she firmly and finally meant it when she said she had no intention of selling Blanestock. She might just as well go home, and let her continued residence there show him how much she meant it.

"I won't come in," she told him, withdrawing her arm from his grasp. "There's really no need, I might as well get back."

"I thought you'd come to see me." He smiled. "It's been a very brief visit—eventful, but brief."

"I came to see you about the letter and the offer you made," she told him. "And—"

"You mean," he interrupted with a grin, "you came to put me firmly in my place."

"All right, I did," Charlotte retorted swiftly, chin in the air. "Well, I've made it quite clear now. I have no intention of parting with Blanestock, now or ever, and since that subject's settled, there's nothing else to discuss."

"All right, all right!" He laughed softly, taking her arm again, drawing her into the hall. "Round one to you," he allowed. "So there's nothing more to discuss, but you don't have to go storming back to your fortress yet. Nobody's going to lay siege to it while you're gone, so come and have some lunch with me, hmm?"

"I—I don't think I should." She was not at all happy about his apparently easy capitulation, it was too out of character, as she felt sure Noel would agree, and she regarded the invitation to lunch with open suspicion.

"But why on earth not?" he demanded. "*I'm* the loser in this battle, remember? If I'm not bearing a grudge, I don't see why you should."

"I—I don't exactly bear any grudge," she began, and he hugged her arm against his side as he persuaded her further into the house, his face crinkling into another smile that was irresistibly persuasive.

"Then come and have lunch with me," he coaxed, and eventually she heaved a great sigh of resignation and allowed herself to smile. As well as being infuriating, he was also disarmingly attractive, and she spared a moment to wonder at his still being unattached.

"Very well," she agreed at last. "Thank you."

"I should make one stipulation, I think," he told her solemnly, and turned her to face him, both hands now on her arms.

"I don't know that you're in any position to make stipulations," she said, laughing at his expression, and wondered why it was that she always seemed to end up being so amenable.

"Please don't nag me about the house," he begged, and she pulled a face at him.

"I won't, if you don't nag *me* about it," she retorted and he laughed softly, bending swiftly to brush his mouth against hers.

"Agreed," he said.

CHAPTER FIVE

NOEL WAS, Charlotte realised with an inward sigh, getting much too serious too soon. She liked him a lot, more than she had ever liked a man before, but she had far too much on her plate at the moment, with Blanestock to look after and restore, to want a serious romance to cope with as well.

"For someone you don't like," he told her one evening as they sat together on the edge of a low wall that surrounded the paved terrace, "you see an awful lot of him, it seems to me."

They were, of course, discussing Scott Lingrove and not for the first time Charlotte wished she had not let him know that she had lunched with Scott instead of quarrelling with him about the letter.

"I don't see any more of him than I can help," she told him. "I did go round to Wainscote that time, I admit, but usually it's he who does the visiting, not me."

"Keeping an eye on his property, I suppose," Noel said sourly, and she glanced at him curiously.

"Do *you* think of it as his property?" she asked, and he frowned.

"No, of course I don't."

She laughed shortly. "Well, it sounded very much like it, and Scott himself has no qualms about telling me he intends to get it, one way or another."

"And that wouldn't surprise me in the least," Noel said shortly. "I told you he doesn't like losing anything he's set his heart on."

"He admits it."

His earnest blue eyes looked at her anxiously for a moment. "Did you say as much to him?" he asked, and she realised that she had been indiscreet this time.

"I'm afraid I did," she confessed. "But you needn't worry, he took the opinion in his stride as he does everything else." She laughed softly when she remembered what else he had taken in his stride too, although it had infuriated her at the time. "He even offered to marry me to get his hands on Blanestock," she told him, and Noel stared at her aghast.

"Good God!" he said hoarsely. "He's sunk pretty low, hasn't he?"

Charlotte, now treating the whole thing as a bad joke, laughed again, and raised her brows at the opinion. "You think it's sinking low to want to marry me?" she asked, and he shook his head hastily.

"Charlotte! You know I didn't mean that—nothing *like* that. But I never thought he'd sink to the level of asking a girl to marry him just to get possession of a house. I wonder what Caroline Blythe would say if she knew."

Charlotte looked at him curiously, a sudden and rapid fluttering in her heart, although the change was quite inexplicable and without reason. "Who is Caroline Blythe?" she asked, and Noel shrugged. It could have been imagination that made her think the shrug was an uneasy one, but she thought not, and he did not look at her when he answered.

"The county's belle of the ball, until you came

along," he said. "And—and I heard that she and Lingrove were thinking of getting married some time soon."

"Oh, I see."

There was no earthly reaon why it should come as such a shock to her to learn that Scott was contemplating marriage. It had even passed through her own mind, only the other day, to wonder why he was still unattached. But she felt suddenly confused and not a little angry when she considered his attitude towards her. The lighthearted way he kissed her, although he had never made a pretence that it was serious in intent, had misled her, and she resented it.

"Anyway," Noel said, suddenly shaking off the subject of Scott Lingrove, "don't let's talk about him anymore. I came to see you, and you're a much nicer subject for discussion."

"Am I?" she said, and smiled, but the idea of Scott being on the brink of matrimony troubled her a lot more than she was prepared to admit.

"IT'S ME!" The face round the edge of the front door had a broad smile on its brown features and for a moment Charlotte almost responded to it, then she remembered that if he chose to forget his commitments, she had no intention of doing so.

"Hello, Scott." The greeting was so obviously without enthusiasm that he could not miss it, and raised a curious brow.

"Am I in the doghouse?" he asked. "And if so, what for?"

"Not at all," Charlotte replied, continuing on her way into the sitting-room with a stepladder.

"Here, let me take that for you!" He took the step-ladder from her despite a few murmured protests, and carried it into the sitting-room where he spread its wooden legs and leaned on it, one hand stroking his chin as he gazed at her thoughtfully. "Tell me, Charlotte."

She did not look at him, but moved him away from the ladder and dragged it over to the far wall where she carefully aligned it with a big gilt-framed painting. "There's nothing to tell," she said coolly. "Now please excuse me, I have something to do."

"So have I," he retorted. "But I came over here to ask you if you'd like to come for a little trip tomorrow. I can see now I shouldn't have bothered. You've got one of your uppity moods on, and I'm not in the mood to put up with you when you're like that."

"Nobody asked you to," she told him tartly, and wrung out a sponge in water before climbing the steps. "Now if you don't mind I'd like to get on with this."

He watched her for a moment or two in silence, and she wondered just what was going through his mind, and if he had any inkling at all why she was being so offhand. "I don't know why you don't get a proper firm to do that for you," he said at last. "You could damage it, you know."

"I won't," she assured him, rubbing gently at the frame of the painting.

"Charlotte, you—"

She turned, too hurriedly, to argue with him and her left foot slipped on the wooden step, sending her flying with a piece of the frame still in her hand. Her cry was instinctive and she knew he would say I-told-you-so even while she was bumping painfully down the rest of the steps.

"My leg!" she complained, trapped inelegantly between two slabs of wood. "Help me, Scott!"

He lifted her out of her predicament, carefully and quite gently, but he seemed far more concerned with the fate of the painting than he did with her leg. "Now you *have* spoiled it!" he declared, taking the piece of broken frame. "I knew you'd ruin it, mucking about with it like that."

Charlotte was too busy rubbing a painful leg to either see or care about the picture, and she glared at him reproachfully. "I'm more concerned about my leg," she told him. "Although you don't seem to think it's important, I do."

"You are a clumsy little devil," he told her. "I told you not to get up there."

"Oh—Oh, you and your precious picture!" Charlotte exclaimed angrily. "I could have a broken leg and you'd just ignore it, wouldn't you?"

He turned a brief, malicious grin on her. "Your leg isn't a hundred years old," he said. "If it was I might feel as concerned as I do for the frame."

"You inhuman, callous wretch!" she declared, and put out a hand for the sponge she had been using. "I wish I could kick you, then you'd know how I feel!" Instead she hurled the sponge at him and, quite by chance, her aim was unerring. It caught him full face as he turned towards her.

She was not sure whether she had intended it to find its target or not, but the look in his eyes gave her a curiously fluttery sensation in the pit of her stomach and she shook her head instinctively as he came towards her.

"That," he declared firmly, "was a mistake, Charlie Brown, a very bad mistake on your part."

"Scott!"

She backed away as best she could, but he followed her until she was brought up sharply by the opposite wall, then he reached out and pulled her across his knee, one foot resting on the edge of a chair. She felt the first hard slap but managed to evade the next one and stood with her back to the wall, daring him to come any closer, although he still held on to her arm in a grip like a vice.

"You've really got it in for me today, haven't you?" he said, a small tight smile round his mouth. "Tell me why and I might let you off the rest of that well-deserved spanking."

"I don't have to tell you *any*thing," she told him, her eyes wide and as appealing as she could make them. "I—I really have hurt my leg, Scott."

He did nothing for a moment, watching her and only half believing, then he let go her arm and, without a word of warning, scooped her up into his arms and carried her over to one of the armchairs. "Let me see," he said, and still sounded more resigned than sympathetic.

"It's my shin," she told him, resenting his tone. "I cracked it on the edge of the step."

There was already a red and puffy-looking patch on her bare shin and it promised to be a beautiful bruise by the next day, but the skin was not broken and he looked up at her suspiciously when she winced at his touch.

"Does it hurt that much?" he asked.

"Yes, it *does*!"

He smiled and straightened up. "Right! Doctor's for you—come on."

Charlotte stared at him in dismay. She had intended to impress on him that she was hurt as well as the picture frame she had been trying to clean, but she had no idea of going that far.

"That's not necessary," she objected. "It's only a bruise and—"

"I quite thought you'd broken it from the fuss you were making," he told her. "But if there's any doubt at all, I'll run you down to Doctor Waring's and let him look at it."

"It's not necessary!"

The hazel eyes regarded her steadily for a moment or two and she felt again that rapid and disturbing flutter under her ribs. "I suppose you think I'm the original hard-hearted Henry?" he said then, and smiled in the way that crinkled his eyes at their corners.

"I—I was thinking along those lines," she confessed, not looking at him, and he laughed softly and crouched beside her again.

"Tell me where the medical kit is," he said, "and I'll put something on it.'"

She found herself only too willing to let him take the onus on himself, but then she remembered why she had been offhand with him in the first place and determinedly shook off the lazy, almost sensual feeling he inspired and stuck out her chin.

"I can take care of it myself, thank you," she told him. "It's nothing much, I can manage."

Being crouched beside her as he was his face was lower than hers and after a moment's pause, he bent his head and looked up into her eyes, one finger raising her chin. "I wish you'd tell me just what dirty deed I'm supposed to have done," he said quietly. "This isn't anything to do with the house, I know, or at least I'm pretty sure it isn't. Now what *is* it, Charlotte? What have I done to make you so damned distant with me?"

"I—you—" She shook her head, avoiding the finger that held her chin. "Please don't question me, Scott."

"I think I have a right to know why you're being so shirty with me," he declared inelegantly. "Now talk, Charlie Brown, before I get really annoyed with you."

"You have no call to be annoyed," Charlotte retorted, unwilling to raise the subject of Caroline Blythe, whoever she might be.

He still crouched beside her and it was very hard to resist looking at him, meeting the curious and increasingly impatient gaze. "Charlotte." The voice was low and infinitely persuasive, and a warning bell shrilled in her brain, but still she said nothing and he used a hand to turn her face to him again. "What have you been listening to?" he asked softly. "Some tale some gossipy local's regaled you with, and which you're only too ready to believe?"

Charlotte raised her eyes at last and looked directly at him, and there was nothing she could do about the appealing, little girl look in them. "Who's Caroline Blythe?" she asked.

"So that's it!" He still looked at her for a long moment, then shook his head, a small tight smile just touching his mouth. "Damn Noel Chartres, he couldn't resist it, could he?"

"How—how do you know it was Noel that told me?"

"Oh, it has to be Noel," he said wryly, as he stood up, the fingers of one hand running through the thick hair where it lay across his forehead. "For reasons you needn't know about, Charlotte."

Charlotte got to her feet, her bruise momentarily forgotten. "You—you are—"

"What I am needn't concern either you or Noel Chartres at the moment," he told her briskly. "It seems to me that he's stepping out of line far too often lately, and mostly where it concerns me and my affairs. I don't like it."

There was a stern, autocratic ring to the objection and she wondered if she was included in his disapproval or if it was confined only to Noel. "I—I know it doesn't concern me really," she began, "but if you—"

"If you're worrying about my taking you out, you needn't," he assured her brusquely, and Charlotte stared at him.

"Are you?" she asked. "Taking me out, I mean?"

For a moment he looked at her curiously, then he smiled. "Didn't I tell you?" he asked. "That's what I came over here for. I wondered if you'd like to go to Scayswich one day."

"Scayswich?"

"The safari park—it's not very far from here." He laughed. "I gather from your expression that you've never heard of it."

"I haven't," she admitted. "is it a new one?"

"Fairly new," he agreed. "It certainly hasn't had its fair share of publicity yet, it only opened this year."

"Oh." She was not quite sure why she was hesitating, only that she was yet to be convinced that Caroline Blythe could be as easily dismissed as he seemed prepared to do. She could not altogether disbelieve Noel's version—that Scott was on the brink of marrying her, and it made her cautious. "I—I'm not sure if I—"

"Scared?" Scott suggested softly, and Charlotte frowned at the suggestion.

"No, of course I'm not," she denied. "I like animals."

"I felt sure you would," he said, his eyes fixed on her, waiting. She was weakening, she recognised ruefully, it was inevitable that she would, and seeing her almost sold on the idea, he smiled again. "It's very interesting," he told her persuasively. "And they have some lion cubs there too—little ones."

It was blatant seduction, Charlotte thought, and wondered at herself for allowing it. "Little ones?" she asked instead, and he nodded.

"Come and see for yourself."

He held her gaze for a long moment and she could feel her pulses racing wildly until she felt sure he must be aware of it. "Maybe I will," she said at last, and lowered her eyes.

"Tomorrow?"

She shook her head. "Not tomorrow," she told him. "I'm seeing Noel for lunch, and he's coming over to see me tomorrow evening too."

He pulled a face, one expressive brow commenting on such constant attention. "Is he?" he said softly. "He *is* dancing attendance, isn't he?"

She disliked the suggestion of sarcasm and frowned over it. "He—he happens to like me."

"Of course he does," Scott agreed, his eyes showing malicious amusement. "You're not only very beautiful, you're very rich, too."

Charlotte stared at him, then his full meaning dawned on her and she glared, enraged, her deep violet eyes glowing angrily. "That was spiteful and uncalled for," she told him crossly. "And what's more, if those implications apply to Noel, they equally well apply to you. And *you* were ready to suggest I marry you, just so that you could get your hands on Blanestock."

His laughter, she told herself, was no more than he expected, but she kept her own features determinedly straight and left him in no doubt of her disapproval. "But maybe it wasn't only Blanestock that I had in mind," he said softly, and in a voice so outrageously seductive that her pulses responded to it by thudding wildly as she hastily lowered her eyes again.

"Scott, I wish—"

"I wouldn't make remarks like that," he finished for her, and laughed. "I'm sorry, Charlie Brown."

"And *don't* call me Charlie Brown!"

He licked the tip of one finger and made an imaginary mark in the air. "*Three* black marks," he said, "I'd better watch my step or you'll change your mind about coming with me."

"I probably will," Charlotte retorted, then caught his eye and found herself smiling. "I don't think I like you," she told him.

"No?" He bent his head over her and, despite her previous anger with him, she was unable to resist laughing at his expression.

"I shouldn't have anything to do with you," she told him firmly. "you criticise me, leave me in agony while you fret over a picture frame, then try to spank me when I turn on you in self defence."

"Are you still in agony?" he asked softly, bending

much too close for comfort as he gazed down at her bruised leg, and she shook her head.

"Not now, but it would have been all the same to you if it had been broken, wouldn't it?"

"Not quite," he told her solemnly. "I can put stingy stuff on cuts and bruises, but I'm not good with splints and bandages."

"Then what would you have done?" she asked, out of sheer curiosity, and he grinned.

"Hauled you off to the doc's," he said. "But I'm glad you can walk, because there are acres of garden at Scayswich as well, and I'm sure you'd love them."

"I'm sure I would," she agreed, and looked up at him. "When *can* you take me to see your little lions?"

He sighed, rubbing the back of his head as he thought about it. "Bother Noel Chartres and his persistence," he said, almost as if to himself. "I can't make it on Saturday or Sunday. The season's almost finished, but if there are any stray visitors they'll come at the weekend, and Monday I have an appointment in Chedwell. How about Tuesday?"

Charlotte nodded. "Fine. Morning or afternoon?"

"Afternoon, if that's O.K." She nodded. "Good." He reached out and took her hands in his. "And Charlotte—don't arrange to see Noel Chartres as well, will you?"

Charlotte pouted reproach, but allowed him to retain his hold on her hands although she told herself she was only encouraging him, and her heart was rapping urgently at her ribs. "Of course I shan't," she told him, and he laughed softly.

"Of course you *might*," he retorted, then, before she realised his intention he put a hand behind her head and pulled it back with a handful of her hair, his mouth on hers, hard and purposeful. "Just so you don't forget," he said. "I shan't take second place again."

IT WAS a lovely evening when Noel came over to visit her the following day, and it had been Charlotte's idea that they should go for a walk. Noel had all a confirmed townsman's aversion to wide open spaces, despite the fact that he lived in a small town surrounded by some of the most beautiful and impressive scenery in Britain, and he had greeted the suggestion with a certain reticence that Charlotte could not fail to notice.

"Don't you like walking?" she asked with a smile, as she got to her feet.

"Oh yes, yes, of course I do," he assured her hastily, although so unconvincingly that she laughed and shook her head.

"I don't believe you," she said. "You look very long suffering about it."

"Oh no, truly, Charlotte, I don't dislike it that much."

She eyed him curiously for a moment before deciding. "I shall take you at your word," she told him. "It's such a lovely starry night I'd really love to go for a walk."

"Then you shall," Noel promised, his blue eyes as earnest as ever. "You're obviously a country lover, and I really don't object to the occasional walk, especially when the company is as delightful as mine will be tonight."

She appreciated the compliment with a smile, and went through to fetch a coat. "It probably isn't very cold," she said, "but I'd better have a coat."

It was, in fact, quite warm once they were walking, although there was a clear, cold sharpness in the wind that blew up from the valley below them on the other side of the road.

These enormous, rocky falls of landscape were something she found it hard to get used to. It seemed so awe-inspiring, almost frightening at times especially when one was driving at any speed, to find oneself on a road that fell away some two hundred feet or more on one side of the road and rose as high on the other. There were gaunt and straggly ghosts of trees and shrubs growing, even on the most exposed places and often in unbelievably precarious positions.

"Are you warm enough?" Noel asked as they walked along the winding road, their footsteps crunching on the loose grit, and Charlotte nodded. She wondered a moment later, with a smile he could not see in the darkness, if he had been hoping for her to say no, so that he would have a legitimate excuse for putting an arm around her shoulders. Experience had taught her to recognise it as an opening gambit and Noel, she thought, seemed to be in a particularly mellow mood tonight, and rather less reticent than usual.

"It isn't as cold as I expected," she told him. "In fact it's quite beautiful out here, isn't it?"

He looked down at the shadowy, moonlit valley on the other side of the road, bordered here by a safety fence, and was bound to agree. The stars were out in strength and glittered clear and bright over the dark hollow between the rocky walls, and above their heads. There was just enough wind to keep the clouds at bay too, and allow the heavenly bodies to display themselves in all their glory.

"It's lovely," he agreed.

Charlotte sighed deeply and with infinite satisfaction. "I can imagine how my Granny Brown must have felt at leaving all this to go and live in a town," she said. "it must have been awful."

Noel's good looking face turned towards her, looking shadowy and somehow older in the moonlight. "You've really taken to your new home, haven't you, Charlotte?" he asked, and she nodded agreement.

"I love it," she told him truthfully. "I think it's wonderful country."

"And nice people?" he suggested, and she laughed softly, looking up at him.

"And nice people," she agreed.

He ventured to put an arm around her shoulders at last, although it did no more than rest there lightly for the moment. "I'm glad," he said quietly, and with his customary earnestness, "because it means you'll be wanting to stay."

Charlotte smiled up at him, not averse to a little reticent romancing on such a beautiful night. "Oh, I *shall* be staying," she told him determinedly. "I told Scott so on Tuesday when I got that letter about the house."

"Oh yes, that letter," he said. "I forgot to mention it at lunch time. Thank heaven he didn't give away the fact that he knew you'd already been told about his wanting to buy the house. I quite expected he would."

"I'm not really *too* surprised," Charlotte said, a little surprised to find herself defending Scott, no matter how mildly. But it was quite true—to have betrayed Noel's indiscretion to his father would have been a petty and rather childishly spiteful thing to do, and whatever his faults, Scott was not petty.

"You like him, don't you?" Noel asked, and somehow managed to convey disapproval.

Charlotte said nothing for the moment, trying to decide just what she did feel about Scott Lingrove, and unable to come up with an answer. "I'm not sure," she told him at last. "I don't think I *dis*like him, but he's rather—I don't know quite. Overpowering is the word, I think. He's such a strong personality that trying to argue with him, or get the better of him, is rather like trying to stop the tide from coming in—it does no good at all."

"Like his wanting Blanestock?" he guessed, and she nodded. "You won't let him have it, will you, Charlotte?"

"Most definitely not!" She sounded so firm and adamant about it, that he could hardly believe her other than unshakeable.

"I'm very relieved." The arm about her shoulders was more confident now, and his fingers curved into the softness of her arm.

"I couldn't part with it now," she said. "I love the place, the countryside, everything. And everyone's been very good to me."

"Even Scott Lingrove?" he suggested, and she was not really surprised to detect a certain resentment in his voice.

"He *has* been very helpful," she was bound to agree. "Even if I do suspect he has an ulterior motive."

"Blanestock, you mean?"

She nodded, remembering that facetious suggestion that marriage would ensure his getting the house. "But forewarned is forearmed," she said. "I know he'll do almost anything to get it, so I'm not so easy to fool as I might have been. I even suspect that the proposed trip to the park is only another way of working things round to his way."

"Park?" He frowned curiously, and Charlotte nodded.

"Scayswich, I think he called it."

His frown deepened. "The safari park? Is he taking you there?"

Charlotte nodded. "Yes. On Tuesday." She looked at him curiously. "Do you know it?"

"I've been." He shrugged, apparently not very impressed by what he had seen.

"What is there to see?"

"Lions, giraffes, the usual things."

"It sounds intriguing."

"I suppose it is," Noel allowed, grudgingly she guessed, and smiled up at him.

"But you don't sound very enthusiastic about it."

He looked down at her, and so bright was the moonlight that she could see the rueful face he made. "Maybe because I wish I'd thought of asking you to go with me," he confessed, and hugged her close for a second. "I suppose it's no use hoping you'll change your mind?" he suggested.

"I can't, Noel."

"No. No, I suppose you can't."

He seemed so sunk in regret that she sought to bring a little more cheer to their mood. "Well, never mind," she said, looking up at the wonderful star-spangled sky and smiling. "I should have to go a long way before I found anything as impressive or as lovely as this, all around us. Just look at those stars—I feel I could reach out and touch them!"

"I can see some even brighter ones," Noel said quietly, his voice deeper suddenly, and throatily husky as if he fought with some uncontrollable emotion. He turned her to face him as they stood at the edge of the dark road, and Charlotte's heart thudded hard against her ribs when his face, shadowed by the moonlight, bent over her. "You're so lovely, Charlotte."

"Noel."

She was unsure whether she would have protested or not, but it was unlikely, she thought, for she had heard much the same words a number of times before, and she was not averse to hearing Noel say them. Indeed she lifted her face to him and smiled, the moonlight lending a dark shine to her deep violet eyes, and, after only a brief moment of hesitation, he kissed her.

It was a gentle, slightly reticent kiss, and there was nothing nerve-shattering about it, but the cool, starlit night made everything seem so romantic that she was prepared to be quite carried away by it.

He held her close for several moments after he had kissed her, and she could feel the heavy, rapid beat of his heart too, as if he felt far more than his kiss had revealed. Then he held her away from him and looked down at her almost anxiously.

"I hope I haven't been too—too premature," he said earnestly, so earnestly that Charlotte could not resist a smile.

"Who could possibly object to a kiss on a night like this?" she asked lightly, and he smiled, hugging her close for a moment.

"I don't want you to think I'm an opportunist," he told her, and she hastily dismissed Scott's veiled suggestion that he was possibly just that.

"Of course I don't think anything of the sort," she assured him, leaning back, her eyes deep and shining. "It's a beautiful night, Noel, and I didn't object in the least."

Thus encouraged, he kissed her again, this time with a little more fervour, and she wondered, as he released her at last, if she had given him the wrong impression of her own feelings. She liked Noel, she even found him more than usually attractive, but she was not prepared to commit herself any further at the moment.

He looked down at her again, and she could see how bright and glowing his eyes looked in the moonlight. "It *must* be a magical sort of night," he told her with a short laugh. "I feel like a different person. It must be you, lovely Charlotte."

"I expect it's the moon and the stars," she said lightly, looking across his shoulder to the tall, black rocks with the skeleton of a tree outlined at the very top of the sheer climb, against the starry sky. "There's an old dead tree up there, and it looked exactly like a hand." She gazed up at the sparse, thin branches sprouting from a knotted rope of trunk and spread out like gnarled fingers against the sky. "It's exactly like a big hand, full of stars."

He laughed, the first time she had ever heard him do so, and he kissed her lightly on her mouth. "That's a romantic notion," he teased, and Charlotte smiled.

"I suppose it is," she allowed, and wondered why she should suddenly think of Scott Lingrove.

CHAPTER SIX

"You don't have to look quite so much as if you suspect I'm going to throw you to the lions," Scott told her as they waited in the car to be admitted to the Scayswich Safari Park, and Charlotte looked at him through her lashes.

"I wouldn't put it past you," she said darkly, and he laughed.

"You are a suspicious little devil, aren't you?"

"Maybe," Charlotte admitted cautiously. "But you can't really be surprised if I see an ulterior motive behind everything you do."

"Why should you, for heaven's sake?"

"Because I think you'd stop at nothing to get what you want," she retorted, and again he laughed at her frankness.

"Well, if you really think I'd go so far as to feed a beautiful woman to the lions, you're way out in your estimate of me, Charlie Brown. Ask anybody who really knows me."

Charlotte studied him for a moment from beneath her lashes, taking advantage of his preoccupation with paying for their entrance and receiving instructions about staying in the car while they were in lion country.

It would not be easy to understand the man behind those rugged brown features, she thought. When his face looked stern, as it sometimes did, it was difficult to imagine it smiling as it was now, when he turned briefly to look at her.

"Does anyone *really* know you?" she asked, and he glanced at her again briefly.

"Huh-huh, a few people. A lot more *think* they do."

"Including me?"

He smiled at her again. "Maybe," he said. "Now look at the lions, not me—that's what we've come for."

The whole thing was even more fascinating than Charlotte had anticipated and she was thrilled to see that there really were some lion cubs. They were so irresistible that she felt like getting out of the car and playing with them.

"They're adorable," she cried delightedly. "Ooh, I—I could hug them!"

"You'd come off worst if you did," Scott teased, but the taunt was without malice, and he watched her with as much interest as he did the animals outside so that Charlotte, feeling his gaze on her, turned at last and looked at him.

"You told me to look at the lions," she reminded him, feeling horribly self-conscious, especially in such close proximity as the closed car enforced. "Why don't you look at them too?"

He laughed, a soft, deep sound that stirred her pulses. "You enjoy your view, I'll enjoy mine," he said, and spared a hand from the steering wheel to run a gentle finger down her cheek and onto her neck—a caress that sent a shiver down her spine and made her turn hastily away.

"Scott, please don't."

"You know," he said quietly, after a moment's consideration, "this is an ideal situation from my point of view."

"Oh?" She eyed him suspiciously, thankful that at least they were obliged by the rules to keep driving along.

He laughed softly, just keeping them moving, and experiencing no difficulty in using only one hand while the other lay on the seat between them. "A beautiful girl trapped in my car with me, and unable to run away no matter what I do, because we're surrounded by lions."

"There's also a car in front and two more behind us," Charlotte retorted, a pulse hammering wildly at her temple as she clenched her hands together. "And if it came to the point I don't know that I wouldn't choose the lions!"

"Oh, *would* you?" He put on a little more speed, though still staying within the specified limits.

"Also," Charlotte went on, feeling she had the upper hand for once, "you can't do much while you're driving a car, can you?"

The hazel eyes regarded her steadily for as long as he could safely take his attention from the quiet road. "If you'd care to make that a challenge," he said softly, "I'll accept it willingly."

Charlotte could feel the rapid and uneasy flutter of her heartbeat and the slightly dizzy sensation in her head as she looked at him before hastily lowering her eyes. "I came to see lions and giraffes," she told him. "There was no mention of wolves."

He laughed, as she might have guessed he would, then pointed ahead to where a house showed briefly among surrounding trees. "All right, Charlie Brown," he said goodhumouredly. "We'll look at lions and giraffes, then go and have some tea in that stately pile up ahead."

"That," Charlotte told him fervently, "sounds like the best idea yet!"

It was in fact quite a lot later when they finally got their tea, for Charlotte was reluctant to leave the animals and they drove over every inch that was allowed before going out through more gates and into the section of the estate that was laid out with gardens and lawns, like Wainscote was.

There was the inevitable souvenir shop near the gates, and she chose a small china model of a lion that seemed to her to be inordinately expensive, but for which her escort paid without hesitation or comment. She must, she told herself as she walked beside him carrying her gift, get used to ignoring the price of things and choose things instead by their appeal.

Tea was served in what had once been a large orangery, and Charlotte was thankful that, as it was the end of the season, there were very few people there. She enjoyed the feeling of luxury it gave her to sit there surrounded by glass walls and potted trees with a smoothly polite waitress serving them.

From Scott's smile as he watched her, he might have guessed at her feelings, and she felt the colour in her cheeks when she looked up and caught his gaze on her. "I wish you wouldn't watch me," she complained, albeit mildly, for she was feeling quite relaxed, almost lethargic in the warmth of the orangery.

He leaned his elbows on the small table, a movement which brought him much too discomfitingly close, and smiled at her. "Don't you like being watched?" he asked softly. "I'd have thought you were used to it."

"Not the way *you* look," she retorted, feeling her hands trembling and wishing he would not be so observant when he reached out one of his own and covered them.

"How *do* I look, Charlie Brown?"

"Don't use that silly name," Charlotte said breathlessly. "You know I don't like it!"

"Charlotte." He lifted her fingers and put them briefly to his lips, speaking softly, his eyes half serious, half amused. "You don't like the way I look at you, you don't like the name I call you, you suspect me of an ulterior motive because I ask you to come out with me." His lips brushed her fingers again lightly. "Why did you come with me, beautiful Charlotte?"

She gazed at him for a moment, disturbed to find that she could not answer such a simple question, then she withdrew her hand from his and picked up the spoon from her saucer to give her something to steady her hand. "I—I don't quite know," she admitted frankly. "Except that—I'd never been to one of these safari parks, and I wanted to see one."

"I see." He was smiling in a way that set her pulses racing and sent her gaze hastily downwards again. "Then why didn't you turn me down and ask Noel Chartres to bring you? I'm sure he'd have been only too willing to."

So he would, Charlotte realised. He had suggested that she might change her mind and she had had her chance then, but she had not taken it. "He's—he's been once," she explained, hoping it sounded like a good reason. "He wasn't very impressed."

"Oh, I see. And what about you, Charlotte? Aren't you impressed either?"

"Oh, Scott, you know I've loved it!" She was so anxious to assure him on that point that she reached out and touched his hand softly with her fingertips.

"Then I'm—"

She glanced at him curiously when he stopped in mid-sentence and saw that he was looking across the glass-walled room to somewhere behind her. Before she could turn her head to see what was drawing his interest, however, the object of it came across to their table and he got to his feet.

She was a tall, dark-haired girl, several years older than Charlotte, and not quite pretty but with a definite air about her that gave the impression of almost magnetic attraction. Blue eyes regarded Scott for a moment as if she could hardly believe what she saw, then she smiled and held out a welcoming hand.

"Scott! I don't believe it!"

"Hello, Caroline." His fingers closed around the proferred hand while Charlotte's eyes widened in surprise. It could be only one person, she felt sure. Caroline Blythe, the woman that Noel had told her Scott was probably going to marry—and yet the greeting was hardly that of lovers.

It was a friendly smile that looked down at Charlotte, and Scott hastened to introduce them. "Charlotte, this is a very old friend of mine, Caroline Blythe—Caro, my new neighbour, Charlotte Brown."

The friendly blue eyes were curious but not malicious. "Ah yes, I heard poor old Ezra Blackwell was dead. You're his family, I presume, are you, Miss Brown?"

"I'm all he had," Charlotte told her, quite willing to be friendly. "I wish I'd known about him sooner."

"Sit down and join us, why don't you?" Scott invited, and she cast a hasty glance at the other end of the room before sitting down.

"I shall be accused of slacking if John sees me," she told him. "Ann's away and I'm helping out this week."

"John is the owner of this stately pile," Scott explained for Charlotte's benefit. "Caroline's his cousin and in this lark everybody gets raked in to help, eh, Caro?"

The other girl laughed to hear it put so plainly but nodded agreement for all that. "You're so right," she said. "Don't ever be tempted to join the commercial stakes, Miss Brown, it's nothing but hard work—right, Scott?"

"Right," he agreed, then looked at the girl for a moment as if he was unsure whether or not to ask the next question. "When's the wedding to be, Caro?" he then asked quietly, and Charlotte held her breath.

Caroline Blythe's friendly blue eyes were hidden for a moment by lowered lashes, then she reached out with long, slim fingers and pleated the edge of the white tablecloth, as if she found the question as difficult to answer as he had to ask.

"As soon as Peter gets back from Germany," she told him quietly. "Next month."

"I haven't had a chance before," he told her, "but you know I wish you both every happiness, Caro."

"Thank you." She looked up at him then, and in those few seconds Charlotte felt herself horribly superfluous. "I'm very happy, Scott, and very lucky. I appreciate that most of all and I'm grateful. It's a blessing one of us at least had some common sense."

Scott's strong fingers covered her restless ones, and he smiled. "We both did," he said softly.

THEY WERE almost back home, much later than they had originally intended, because Charlotte had seen an old inn as they drove home and thought it looked interesting. The result was that Scott insisted on stopping and having a drink and a sandwich there. Consequently it was already dark as they drove along that same twisting, starlit road she had walked with Noel a few nights ago.

The moon had dwindled to a slimmer form now, and there were fewer stars visible than on that night, but it was still a clear and lovely evening, and she felt something of the same enchantment, except that now the attractive, friendly face of Caroline Blythe kept coming before her.

Her curiosity about the other girl was boundless, but she thought there was little chance of it being satisfied. Despite his matter-of-fact handling of the meeting, Charlotte suspected that seeing Caroline Blythe again had been both unexpected and disturbing to him.

As they drove along the last half mile, Scott suddenly turned his head briefly and glanced at her face with its preoccupied expression. "You're curious," he said softly, and with dismaying accuracy.

"What makes you think I'm curious about anything?" she asked, and he laughed shortly.

"Oh, come on, Charlie Brown, you can do better than that! Ever since we left Scayswich you've been wondering about Caroline, haven't you?"

It made her uneasy to be faced with admitting her curiosity and she shook her head. "I don't have to wonder about her," she said. "The—the situation spoke for itself."

He was smiling, she could see when she turned her head, it was evident even in the dim interior of the car. "I suppose it did," he allowed. "But I didn't expect to see her there, Charlotte, I promise I didn't."

His insistence surprised her, but she was gratified to hear it. "I don't imagine you did," she told him. "But I *have* been wondering about her for a long time, ever since—" She bit her lip hastily when she realised her slip.

"Oh yes, of course," Scott said quietly, after a moment's pause. "I'd forgotten you already knew about Caroline."

"I—I only—" she began.

"I forgot, Noel Chartres gave you the lowdown, didn't he?" he went on, ignoring her attempted denial. "Just how much *did* he tell you, Charlotte?"

"I haven't admitted Noel told me anything," she insisted, and he laughed again, the same short, humourless sound.

"You didn't actually deny it either," he told her. "And I know Noel Chartres as well, or better than you do. He had his own ideas about Caroline at one time too, but I don't imagine he told you that, did he?"

"Scott—"

"He just intended you should cold-shoulder me, like you did that day last week," he went on relentlessly. "And it damned nearly worked too, didn't it? You were riding such a high horse you nearly threw me out for no reason at all."

"I've always got a reason for throwing you out," she was stung to retort.

"I suppose he told you I was having an affair with Caroline and you took it as a personal affront to yourself. Well, you can see now that he was wrong."

"I—I didn't care either way," she said, unsure just what she was feeling at the moment. "I am—I *am* sorry, though, Scott."

She was not certain whether she was apologising or expressing sympathy, and neither, apparently, was he. "Why?" he asked quietly.

She tried to see him more clearly in the dim light, but the moon was temporarily hidden and the interior of the car was dark. "I mean," she said slowly and with infinite care, "that it was obvious, even to me, that there was—had been something—" She used one hand to convey a meaning she could not quite put in to words.

"I've known Caro ever since the first time I stayed at Wainscote, about fifteen years ago," he told her. "She's a nice girl, a friendly girl, as you saw for yourself." He seemed to be seeking just the right words as he drove along the road towards home and Charlotte made no attempt to interrupt him. "We saw quite a lot of each other during the last two years while Peter was away, and I suppose we—*I* let things get a little out of hand for a while."

"She was—engaged?" Charlotte ventured, and he nodded.

"Caro has been going to marry Peter, ever since the year dot. It's always been that way between them ever since school. But he's abroad a lot in connection with the family business, and Caro was here—so was I. Need I say more?"

Charlotte shook her head, seeing Caroline Blythe's predicament all too easily. With Scott Lingrove to console her in her fiancé's absence, any girl was likely to be carried away by the situation and probably make a fool of herself. Scott, she guessed, would be the one to see the danger of it before it was too late. Scott would always sense that sort of danger.

"She's—she's very nice," she said, and he nodded slowly.

"Yes, she is," he agreed quietly, and she was left wondering if their versions of nice were the same.

It was not possible from the car to see the old tree on top of the ridge. The handful of stars, as she had rather fancifully named it the other night, but she could imagine it out there, its gnarled fingers spread to encompass the bright glitter of stars, and she smiled.

"There are stars again," she said, almost to herself, and Scott turned his head briefly to look at her, smiling, she thought.

"There are," he agreed. "Do you go star-gazing, Charlotte?"

"Sometimes." She made the admission cautiously. "One seems so much closer to them here, somehow."

He laughed softly. "It's the wide open spaces," he told her. "No chimneypots in the way, or skyscrapers."

"Only a big, ugly old hand," she said, and saw him turn his head again curiously. "It's an old tree up on the top of the ridge out there," she told him. "It looks exactly like a big hand holding the stars in its palm."

"Very poetic," he said. "You must show me this handful of stars."

He was, she realised with a start, already pulling the

car into the side of the road, under the rocky overhang. "Now?"

"Why not now?" he asked, and opened his own door. "Come on, show me your miracle."

With a strange and completely inexplicable lilt in her heart Charlotte got out of the car, his hand under her arm, and turned to look back the way they had come, seeing the old tree, not quite so clear as it had been on the night of the full moon, but still visible and still giving the same impression.

"There!" she said, pointing upwards. "You see it?"

He looked upwards and across at the gnarled tree and she knew immediately that he was seeing it with her eyes. He turned his head and looked down at her and she could distinguish a smile touching his mouth as he spoke.

"It *is* a handful of stars," he said softly. "Maybe we should wish or something, hm?"

It was so unlike her impression of him that she could only stare at him for a moment, then she laughed softly, feeling a warm glow of pleasure that he was ready to share her flight of fancy to such an extent. "Why not?" she said, and closed her eyes to do just that.

She opened them again swiftly when his lips brushed gently against her closed lids, and her heart was thudding like a wild thing seeking to escape. He was looking at her in a way she found both exciting and disturbing, and she moved away from him after a second or two and walked back down to the car.

"Did you wish?" he asked when, after a moment, he joined her, and she nodded.

"It's been a lovely day," she ventured as he started up the car again and drove down the steep hill towards home.

He turned his head and she thought he smiled, although she could not be absolutely sure. "I've enjoyed it," he said. "I'm glad you did, despite your suspicion of me."

"I—I wasn't really suspicious," she told him, and he laughed softly.

"That's a fib, Charlie Brown, and you know it."

After such a pleasant day and then that few fanciful moments on the road just now, she felt disappointed that he was reverting to more or less normal, and she frowned her disappointment, even though he could not see it.

"I still don't like being called Charlie Brown," she told him, and he laughed again, the sound of it grating on her sensitive nerves.

He turned the car into Blanestock's overgrown drive and she looked down at the house in darkness, and for the first time slightly nervous of venturing in there on her own. "Isn't it time you got a man out here to do something to this driveway?" he asked as the tyres crunched over the weed-strewn gravel, and Charlotte turned her head and looked at him resentfully.

"I will if you give me time," she told him.

"You've been here almost a month now," he told her, unperturbed by her resentment. "That's time enough to have got something sorted out in the garden."

"I'll do it when I'm good and ready," Charlotte informed him. "I don't see why you should bother about it."

"Oh, but I do," he insisted with a laugh. "I don't want it looking too much like a jungle when I get it."

Charlotte drew a deep breath, seeing her earlier enjoyment banished for good by his raising the one subject they were bound to quarrel about. "You're not getting it, Scott," she told him quietly. "I've told you over and over, and I mean it."

He laughed, a soft, disturbing sound in the intimate confines of the car. "I shall still keep trying," he told her, and braked the car to a halt in front of the old house. "Come on, I'll see you safely in."

Charlotte did not wait for him to come round and give her a hand from the car, however, but swung the door open and scrambled out on her own, marching up to the front door with her key gripped in one hand, her chin set at a defiant angle to let him see that she was not to be easily pacified.

"I can manage on my own, thanks," she told him.

He stood beside her on the top step while she tried in vain to insert the key in the lock, and laughed when her shaking hands made a hopeless hash of it. "Give it to me," he told her, giving her no chance to refuse, but taking the key from her and opening the door with annoying ease. "I'm more used to it than you are."

She glared at him and snatched the key back, reaching in to turn on the hall light. "You think you already own it, don't you?" she stormed at him, more or less standing where she could block any move on his part to come inside. "Well, you don't, Scott, and you never will!" Big, dark violet eyes looked at him reproachfully for spoiling her lovely day, and she stood there in the yellow light with the key clutched in one hand and her handbag in the other. The knuckles of both hands showing bone white as she fought for self-control.

He sighed deeply as he looked down at her. "Here we go again," he mourned. "Back to normal."

"Well, it's your fault," Charlotte declared. "You *would* have to start on about the house."

"You're too sensitive about the wretched house," he retorted. "I was only teasing you, it's time you were used to it by now."

Charlotte shrugged. "I don't care. You've—you've spoiled everything," she accused.

"I don't see how!"

"You have! I—I had a lovely time and now you've gone and spoiled it all by being so—so nasty about the house."

He leaned easily against the frame of the door, one hand supporting his head, his eyes glinting in the light from the hall as he regarded her steadily. "The only thing spoiled as far as I can see," he said quietly, "is you."

"Oh, you—" She stared at him with brilliant, indignant eyes. Then she dropped the key into her handbag and fumbled for a second or two among the contents, at last bringing out the china lion he had bought for her. "You're *not* having Blanestock," she declared breathlessly, "and you're not bribing me with this or anything else. *Take* it!"

She gave him no opportunity to take it, but hurled the trinket as far away from her as she could, seeing it arc away into the darkness, then she turned swiftly before he could speak or move, and slammed the door shut on him.

She did not know what he would do, and told herself

she did not care. She was through being harrassed by Scott Lingrove, and from now on she would not even ask him into the house. She would certainly never, ever go out with him again—anywhere.

IT WAS nearly two hours since Charlotte had slammed the door on Scott, without even stopping to thank him for taking her on what had been a very enjoyable outing until the last few moments.

She would have been the first to admit that she had simply lost her temper and allowed it to make her behave with a regrettable lack of good manners. A good hot meal and a time curled up by the fire, however, had mellowed her and she was feeling much less murderously inclined towards him.

It was when she was ready for bed some time later that she thought of the lion again and she paused at the foot of the stairs. The thought of that exquisite little figure lying out there on the path made her frown, and she sighed at the prospect of searching for it.

She was not yet prepared to face Scott and apologise, but he need not know that she had gone out and rescued the model. He *had* been deliberately annoying and, even if she had misjudged him about Caroline Blythe, it was no excuse for his subsequent behaviour.

In thinking about Caroline Blythe, she wondered, too, if Noel had really been in ignorance of the true facts about her and Scott, or if he had deliberately misled Charlotte for his own reasons. Next time she saw him, she would tackle him with it, and find out.

She yawned as she looked at the front door, and glanced at her watch. She was always ready for bed much earlier here, and never had any difficulty in falling asleep, but she did not like leaving that little china lion out there all night.

It could not have gone very far, for she had been standing only just inside the front door, and she had never been a very good thrower. Shrugging off the voice of lethargy, she went across to the door and opened it, staring out at the darkness without enthusiasm. She almost had second thoughts too, when something moved out there, and made a soft, rustling sound in the wind-tirred bushes on the other side of the drive.

Shrugging off cowardice, however, she walked down the steps and across the crunchy gravel. It was difficult to even guess where it had fallen, for she had not even bothered to see it land, but hastily slammed the door before its donor had time to realise her intention.

After several minutes' searching she stood back, shivering in the chill, sharp wind and feeling a sense of hopelessness when she looked at the thick, tangled mass of shrubbery. It was like searching for a needle in a haystack and she might as well resign herself to losing it for ever, or else to looking again in the daylight.

Turning to go back into the house again, she put a hand to her mouth suddenly and her heart lurched crazily in fear when she saw a tall, dark figure standing in the lighted doorway. For a moment neither of them spoke or moved, then the intruder extended one hand, holding the small, shiny object she had no difficulty in recognising.

"Is this what you're looking for?" Scott asked quietly.

For several seconds she could only stand and stare at him, then she closed her eyes in relief, and moved forward, with her heart once more thudding wildly against her ribs and a strange tingling sensation coursing through her veins. He stood leaning on the door frame, his pose nonchalant and incredibly relaxed considering the hour and the circumstances, and she wondered dizzily if anything ever disturbed his bland self-confidence.

She reached for the figure of the lion, but he did not immediately relinquish his hold on it and instead moved his fingers to enclose hers in the same strong grasp as the figure.

"Thank you."

It sounded rather ridiculously formal, but there was little else she could say that would either ease that disturbing tension between them or sound as matter-of-fact as she wished it to. "You did want it?" he asked, still quietly, and she nodded, glancing up at him.

"I was looking for it," she admitted, and then suddenly wondered why he had been there. She could not see his car, but it was too dark to see anything much further along the drive, because the moon had hidden itself behind a heavy bank of cloud.

"I thought you might be."

"What—what are you doing here?" she asked, and he smiled.

"I got half way down the drive," he told her, "and suddenly thought you might have second thoughts about slinging your little lion away, so I went home and had a supper, then came back and picked it up off the grass where you'd thrown it."

"Oh!" She could, she realised, have asked him to have supper with her. It was the least she could have done in return for his frequent hospitality towards her, and for her outing. "I'm—I'm sorry I didn't ask you in for supper," she told him. "I should have done."

"Oh, I didn't expect you to do that," he told her, with a solemnity that was belied by the gleam in his eyes. "A young girl living alone has to guard her reputation. Especially when she has no guardian angel in the form of a housekeeper."

"I—I suppose so," Charlotte admitted.

For a moment neither of them spoke or moved, then he smiled slowly and lifted a stray wisp of hair with a finger that managed to make a caress of the gesture. His gaze was fixed on her mouth with an intensity that stirred her blood and made her feel slightly breathless.

"*Would* you have asked me in, Charlotte?" he asked softly.

She half shook her head, uncertain what she should say, but wondering at the sensation of light-headedness that possessed her. "I—I don't know," she confessed at last. "I suppose I shouldn't really, not while I'm on my own."

"People do gossip," he said, and reminded her of Noel's gossip about him and Caroline Blythe.

"They do," she agreed, and looked up then with a small, provocative smile just touching her mouth. "But since there was no one here to see, I could have given you a supper. Who would know?"

He stood for a moment, his lean tanned face shadowed by the yellow light from the hall, the thick thatch of fair hair roughed by the brisk wind, then he lifted her chin with one finger and gazed at her mouth with that same intense look as before. He carefully set the little china lion down on the sill inside the door and smiled.

"Who would know?" he echoed softly, and his

hands drew her closer, one spread out to cradle her head, the other holding her tight against him while his mouth came down on hers with a fierce urgency that was almost a hunger.

CHAPTER SEVEN

IT WAS DIFFICULT for Charlotte to accurately interpret her own reaction to that unexpected end of her afternoon out with Scott. Nothing, she felt sure, had changed at all really, even though he had refused to come any further than the front doorstep. Despite their vowing that it did not matter whether he came in or not, he had stayed on the outside, and his refusal had been accompanied by a laugh that was so loaded with meaning that Charlotte had reproached him for it.

She was the first to admit that he was a very attractive man, and he kissed her in a way that no one else had ever done, but she was prepared to believe that it was very likely a case of practice makes perfect, and she still did not altogether trust him.

He had quoted the Everslade family motto to her as Fortune Favours the Bold, and she was ready to accept that he believed it wholeheartedly. He wanted Blanestock and he meant to have it, one way or another—he had vowed as much. Seduction of its present owner could well be part and parcel of his determination to achieve it, although she could not still the bright little hope that it wasn't.

She saw him rather less during the next few days, and by the time the formidable Mrs. Borden was installed as housekeeper the opportunity of being alone with her was rather less. For one thing, they were no longer likely to sit in the kitchen having coffee, as they had done more than once in the past. The kitchen now was Mrs. Borden's domain, and ladies paid only occasional visits to consult about meals, etc., so she was given to understand.

It was not a state of affairs that Charlotte was altogether happy with, but she supposed she would get used to it in time. Scott now called at the front door, like any other visitor, and the impressive Mrs. Borden seemed to bother him not at all.

"Why don't you come in as you used to?" Charlotte asked him one day after Mrs. Borden had ushered him into the sitting-room.

The hazel eyes twinkled wickedly at her as he perched himself on the edge of an armchair, elbows on knees, hands together. "Because I don't want to lower your standing with the Duchess," he told her, using the nickname he invariably did for her housekeeper.

"I thought you didn't give a cuss for what Mrs. Borden thought," she retorted. "You said you didn't, and you urged me not to either."

"Ah well, I wasn't sure you'd taken my advice," he told her solemnly. "But if *you* prefer it, I can go back to sneaking in by the back door, although the Duchess'll probably have a nasty turn each time if I do."

Charlotte giggled. "I hope she does," she told him, maliciously. "She scares the living daylights out of me, I'd like to know she was having the vapours about one of her *'best'* people!"

Scott grinned, shaking his head over her honesty. "That sounds very catty," he told her. "I don't claim to be any more 'best' than you do, so stop being a little snob, Charlie Brown, before I'm forced to do something about it."

"I'm not being a snob," Charlotte denied. "I'm just seeing it from Mrs. B's point of view, that's all." She looked at him speculatively from under her lashes, then smiled. 'Will you really come in through the back door, Scott? Like you used to?"

He looked at her steadily for a moment. "For you—anything," he said softly, and she laughed, a light, lilting sound that betrayed the excited flutter in her heartbeat.

"Then do it," she told him. "Give her a shock next time you come."

He bowed his fair head in mock humility. "Your word is my command, madame."

"That," Charlotte told him bluntly, "I don't believe!"

MRS. BORDEN, Charlotte was quite sure, would not approve of people who rummaged around in the cellars, but she had long been curious about that dark and damp-smelling dungeon beneath the house. Exploring it while she was completely alone in the house had been rather risky, in case she had an accident, but now that she had the housekeeper to keep an eye on her comings and goings it was safe enough.

Accordingly she put on a fairly old dress one morning after breakfast and, waiting until the housekeeper was busy in the kitchen, opened the thick plank door and went down. She hesitated at the top of the steps and groped for the light switch she knew was there, flicking on the low-watt lamp.

There was an enormous number of cobwebs and no

doubt an occupant for most of them, a thought that gave her food for thought, for she was not very fond of spiders at the best of times. It smelled dank and very uninviting too, but she could see several large trunks down there in the gloom, and she was curious to know what, if anything, was in them.

She left the door an inch or so ajar and made her cautious way down the rickety wooden steps that shook alarmingly and made her wish she had not started. It would be even more precarious now to try and turn while she was part way down, however, so she went on, clinging on tight to the flimsy handrail.

The dampness was even more evident when she got to the bottom and she shivered in the dimly lit cave that arched above her head, festooned with cobwebs and alive with other, more worrying, sounds. It was to be expected that there would be mice down here, of course, she thought ruefully.

The trunks she was interested in stood, fortunately, quite near the light, so it was not necessary to move them at all, merely to pry the heavy lids open, a task more easily said than done, for the damp had long since rusted the hinges.

The first of the three, and the smallest, held what she immediately dubbed mementoes, and she handled them with a care that she would have given to her own precious trinkets. A locket and several rings, quite good pieces, and a little box with a silver clasp that she had some difficulty in opening. When she did manage to open it she stared at the contents in wide-eyed surprise for a moment.

There were seven or eight photographs and a small painted miniature, all depicting the same woman and none of them very old, so that it did not take Charlotte long to decide that the subject of them was undoubtedly Mary, Lady Everslade, née Bishop.

Evidently the old man, however bitter he might have been at his rejection by the woman he loved, could not bring himself to destroy her likenesses, and he had stored them down here in this damp, dark cellar, well preserved in their protective box.

She was a pretty woman, if her photograph was anything to judge by, and Charlotte gazed at them for some time, her mind busy with the idea of an old man so bitter about losing this nice, pretty woman that he had spent the last few years of his life in misery and loneliness. She would, she decided, give them to Scott and he could decide what should be done with them.

She managed, after much effort, to get the second trunk open at last, and she had just started rummaging through its contents, mostly papers, when she saw something that caught her eye. It was a handwritten document in a large scrawling hand and the signature at the bottom of it was in no doubt.

The letters stood out large and black even in this dim light and the name "Ezra Albert Blackwell" sprawled almost the width of the paper. It was a will of some sort, that much was obvious, and she had just noticed the date on it when a sound at the top of the steps made her look up sharply.

"Oh no!"

There was no mistaking the sound she heard. It was the snicking of the lock on the cellar door, and she was now a prisoner in that damp, cold place unless she could make Mrs. Borden hear her and open the door again. No doubt the housekeeper had found the door ajar and closed it without a thought that Charlotte might be down there. Such a thing would never occur to her.

Tucking the will she had just found and the photographs of Mary Bishop into the spacious pocket of her cardigan, she began a perilous climb back up those rickety steps. The door was very thick, but sooner or later the woman would hear her as she passed and let her out, though heaven knew what her reaction would be.

She had gone no further than the first three steps, however, when there was a loud and ominous creaking and she stopped, one hand to her mouth as the hand rail shook in her hold. Another step and the creaking became worse and, before she had time to cry out or jump for safety, the steps were wrenched away from the brick wall of the cellar and collapsed in a cloud of dusty wood on the stone floor.

It was debatable if the noise it made was audible in the house upstairs, for it made surprisingly little impact. It was too rotten, Charlotte supposed dazedly, as she picked herself up from the floor and gazed upwards hopelessly at the twelve or so feet of insurmountable space between her and the door into the house.

She stood there for several minutes trying to decide what was best for her to do. Shouting was the only course open to her, for there was no window in the cellar, nor even a grating and the more she thought about it, the more panic-stricken she became.

Perhaps no one *would* find her. After all, why should they think of looking for her in the cellar? Even Scott would give her credit for more sense than that, and Noel would not even think of coming down himself, let alone see Charlotte down there.

She shouted at the top of her voice, and shouted again, a hundred times, but there was no reply and she put a hand to her strained throat after a while, tears of frustration coursing down her dust-streaked face and the hopelessness of it.

It was when she looked at her watch, after a miserable two hours curled up against the wall where the stairs had been, that she realised that she was to have met Noel for dinner that evening, and her heart leapt hopefully. He would surely take some pains to search for her when she was not waiting for him, even if Mrs. Borden did not raise the alarm at her absence from lunch.

Bit it was obvious, when one o'clock came and went, that either Mrs. Borden had presumed her out for lunch, or was not even considering looking for her absent employer in the old cellar. She could hear nothing of what was going on in the house, the walls were much too thick for that, and she could almost imagine people looking for her within a few feet of her and never knowing she was there.

It was a situation which had all the ingredients of tragedy, she realised only too well, and she tried again, shouting at the top of her voice until it grated harshly in her throat and became no more than a thin croak. Then she leaned her hot forehead against the damp brick wall and wept unashamedly.

It seemed like days later when she heard, at long last, the sound of the rusty key in the lock above, and raised her head wearily. She must be imagining things, she thought, looking bleary-eyed at her watch again and seeing that only four hours had gone since her last desperate effort to attract attention.

The lights were on in the hall she could see, and she got to her feet, unable to shout as she wanted to, to tell them that she was there, instead reaching up her arms in a silent plea, and hearing Scott's voice, hushed with shock.

"My God, she *is* down there!"

She remembered little of what happened after that, but someone came down with a ladder and she was carried in a not very expert fireman's lift over a broad shoulder, then willing hands took her and helped her to stand in the bright warmness of the hall.

"Charlotte! Charlotte!"

The arms that held her tight belonged to Noel, she knew and he held her as if he would never let her go, until Scott's ever practical voice penetrated her fuzzy brain and even now made her frown.

"Don't just stand there," he ordered. "Get her to bed while I ring Doctor Waring."

"I was—" Noel began, but was curtly interrupted by Scott again.

"All right," he said, "*you* ring the doc and I'll take her upstairs." He wasted no time on words, but lifted Charlotte into his arms and strode across the hall with her, and on up the stairs with a red-eyed Mrs. Borden following meekly.

The housekeeper indicated Charlotte's room with one hand and opened the door with the other, then stood back while he walked across the room with his burden and put her gently down on the bed. For a moment he stood looking down at her in silence, then he shook his head. "You pie-eyed little nut," he said then, huskily, "you might *never* have been found, do you realise that?"

"I—I know."

There were no words coming from her, only a whispered croak, and he shook his head again, as if he lost patience with her. "Take care of her," he ordered the housekeeper, and the impressive Mrs. Borden bowed her head meekly and murmured compliance as he strode across the room. He turned in the doorway and looked back at Charlotte. "And you do exactly as the doctor tells you, Charlie Brown, or so help me I'll break your beautiful neck!"

He was gone, and for a moment the housekeeper looked at the closed door, then she turned to Charlotte and Charlotte had never seen her look so meek and contrite. Her eyes were red-rimmed as if she had been weeping, but surely the formidable Mrs. Borden would never do such a thing.

One bony hand clasped the other under her thin bosom and she looked for all the world as if she was about to apologise. "I—I didn't know you were down there in the cellar, Miss Brown, I swear I didn't!" she declared. "I *didn't* close the door on you on purpose, I swear it."

Charlotte wished she could have found enough voice to reassure her. It was like seeing some idol crumble to see a woman of Mrs. Borden's calibre so abjectly humble. Instead Charlotte reached out a hand and smiled as best she could to convey her meaning.

"I—I know I should have looked down there before I closed the door," the housekeeper went on, evidently feeling the need to reveal all, now that she had been encouraged. "But that horrible damp old place gives me the creeps, and I just closed it and locked it up quick without even thinking."

"Of course you did," Charlotte tried to say, but managed only a croak.

"I didn't mean anything, and I don't see that Mr. Lingrove has any call, or any right, to go dismissing me like that."

Charlotte's eyes conveyed her surprise, and she fought desperately to give that harsh croak some form. "Dismissed you?" she asked, and the housekeeper nodded, her hands twisting together miserably.

"He gave me my notice," she said. 'He was so angry he looked as if he was going to hit me first off when I remembered about the cellar door. Then he said if you *were* down there I was dismissed without notice or references."

Oh, did he? Charlotte thought, and had to admit being more intrigued than annoyed at the moment. She had yet to learn what Noel's reaction had been, but something a lot less violent she was prepared to bet on. Scott would not bother to conceal his feelings, not for anybody, and she had to admit to finding his rather emotional reaction rather gratifying even if it had completely demolished poor Mrs. Borden.

She smiled reassuringly at the woman and indicated that the notice of dismissal was hereby revoked, making the woman smile with unbelievable gratitude. "I'd better help you into bed, ma'am," Mrs. Borden told her, resuming some of her habitual manner. "The doctor'll not be long, I expect."

The doctor was not very long, and neither was he very concerned about the result of her fall and confinement. His main concern was the damage to her throat, but he even smiled about that as he looked down at her and fastened his case.

"It'll soon heal," he told her cheerfully. "Though it's bound to be painful for a while, and you mustn't talk, of course." He smiled at her. "That's not a very popular instruction with the ladies, I know," he added. "But it is the quickest way of getting your voice back, Miss Brown."

She indicated by signs that she would like to get up, but he shook his head. "Stay there for the rest of today," he told her. "Then see how you feel in the morning. this prescription will take care of your throat, the rest of your bumps and bruises will take care of themselves in good time."

He left her feeling much better already, and wanting nothing so much as to ask Scott what he meant by sacking her housekeeper without her permission. Only wanting to say things to him and being able to were two very different things, and she would have to content herself with looks and actions.

IT WAS TWO DAYS before even a glimmer of her voice came back and in the meantime Charlotte was obliged to put up with Scott's delighted baiting of her. She had resorted to poking out her tongue at him in desperation, and Noel, coming in at the crucial moment had been obviously horrified at the gesture.

"How are you, Charlotte?" he asked, handing her a huge bouquet of early chrysanthemums, and she smiled ruefully, one hand to her aching throat.

"Better," she croaked hoarsely, and wrinkled her nose in defiance when Scott put a finger to his lips.

"I never thought about bringing you some flowers," he said frankly. 'I suppose I could have, we've got plenty in the gardens."

"You *could* have," she echoed huskily, and laughed at his expression.

Noel looked at him meaningly, as if he expected him to get up and go, but Scott showed no sign of taking the hint, looking quite at home in one of the armchairs in the sitting-room.

"I—I was rather hoping you might feel like coming for a ride," Noel ventured, and she looked at him and smiled.

"I would," she told him.

"The damp air isn't good for your throat," Scott opined, and she raised a brow.

"How would you know?"

"Because it's common sense," he retorted. "And if you don't stop talking you're going to have a relapse anyway."

She ignored the jibe and instead smiled at Noel who sat, much less at ease, in another armchair. "I'd love a ride," she told him in a hoarse whisper. "Just as soon as I've put my flowers in water."

He smiled his satisfaction and looked at Scott in a way that left no doubt he considered himself the winner of that round anyway. "I'll get you a vase and some water, shall I?" he offered, and Charlotte smiled her thanks.

As soon as he was gone from the room Scott looked at her for a moment, then smiled knowingly. "You just have to go now, don't you Charlotte? Just to show me you don't have to take any notice of what I say."

"I don't *have* to," she retorted in her whispery voice. "You haven't any say in what I do, any more than you have in whether I sack my housekeeper or not."

"Ah, I wondered, if she'd tell you or not," he said, apparently unperturbed.

Charlotte looked at him curiously. It hurt more than she cared to admit, to talk, but she wanted to know from his own mouth what had made him dismiss the housekeeper so grandiosely.

"You had no right to do it," she told him, one hand to her throat. "And I can't think what made you think you had."

He grinned amiably. "I *didn't* think." he told her frankly. "I was so spitting mad that the damn fool woman had shut and locked the cellar door without even looking to see if you were down there first that I could have slapped her. Of course I didn't know then that little clever boots had demolished the steps and couldn't have got out anyway."

"At least I could have thumped on the door, though," she said. "But you really upset the poor woman."

"I know," he said with obvious satisfaction. "I'd never have believed that the Duchess was capable of tears."

Charlotte shook her head reproachfully. "You are a callous brute," she told him without malice, and he laughed.

"I suppose you and she are as thick as thieves now," he guessed. "You may not be what the Duchess considers the best people, Charlie Brown, but you're her friend for life now you've let her keep her job."

"She's not as bad as she gives the impression of being," Charlotte informed him, and again he laughed.

"Neither am I, believe it or not," he told her, and got to his feet, stretching lazily before he bent over her, his hands on the arms of her chair, his eyes only inches away from hers. "I suppose it's not a bit of use me telling you not to go out in this damp, is it?" he asked, and she shook her head. He sighed. "I thought not."

"You could try *ask*ing me," she suggested softly, in her husky voice, and he smiled, his gaze fixed intently on her mouth.

"I see." He was close enough for her to see the myriad of tiny lines at the corner of his eyes, and she could feel the warmth that emanated from him as he bent even closer until his mouth almost touched hers. "Then will you *please* not go out, sweet Charlotte?" he asked softly, and stopped her from answering by bringing his mouth just that little bit closer, until it was pressed down hard and firm over hers.

That would, Charlotte thought a moment later, have to be the time that Noel chose to return with the vase of water for her flowers, and she glanced up at Scott reproachfully before she turned to Noel.

Noel's earnest blue eyes had an angry glint in them that she had never seen before and his hands were tight knuckled round the heavy glass vase he carried, so that for one wild moment Charlotte thought he might either throw it or hit Scott with it.

Instead he looked at her and put the vase down carefully on a table. "Sorry if I chose the wrong time to come in," he said in a voice scarcely recognisable as his usual rather quiet one. "I didn't think I needed to knock first."

"Oh, Noel, please don't," Charlotte begged. "Scott was just going, that's all."

"Oh, please don't bother," Noel said, heavily sarcastic. "*I'll* go."

"Noel!"

She wished more fervently than ever that she had a voice to plead with, but it was no more than a harsh mockery of its usual self and growing less all the time, as Scott had warned her it would. Scott himself stood for a moment, his hands on his hips, then he looked at Noel and shook his head.

"Don't be a fool," he told him. "I *was* just going, as Charlotte said."

"Because you don't like being caught?" Noel asked harshly, and she saw the tightness that straightened Scott's mouth.

"I'd better go before this develops into a slanging match," he said quietly. "This is Charlotte's home, after all, and we *are* her visitors."

"I thought you considered yourself practically the owner now," Noel jeered, apparently prepared to throw all caution to the wind now that he had overcome his professional reticence at last.

For a moment Charlotte held her breath, while the two of them glared at each other, then Scott, without another word, strode across the room and out of the door, closing it with meticulous care behind him.

There was silence for a long, long minute and Charlotte felt as if she had been wound like a watch spring, only now releasing her tensed nerves in a sigh as she looked at an already contrite Noel standing beside the table still.

"Oh, Noel," she said huskily. "Why did you do it?"

He shook his head. "I don't quite know," he confessed. "I know I was insanely jealous when I saw him kissing you, but it was no excuse for behaving as I did, and I apologise, Charlotte, please forgive me."

"*I'll* forgive you," Charlotte told him willingly. "But I'm not sure Scott will feel so generous towards you."

"I don't—" he began, then stopped himself and shook his head, looking down at his shoes. "Yes, of course I care," he said ruefully. "And so will Father and Basil Clee if he starts complaining about me. Oh lord, I seem to have made a hash of things all round, don't I?"

Charlotte was already busy with her flowers, and taking it a lot less seriously than he was. "I shouldn't worry about Scott telling tales on you to your father," she told him. "He's unlikely to do that, and it's not all that much of an incident to worry yourself about."

The earnest blue eyes looked at her dolefully. "You aren't disgusted with me for making a fool of myself?"

"No, and I don't know that I'd call it making a fool of yourself, exactly. You certainly jumped to a wrong conclusion and made a couple of unfortunate remarks, but as far as I'm concerned, I suppose I should take them as a form of compliment."

"Charlotte!" He took her hands in his, regardless of the bloom she held, snapping its stem with the strength of his hold. "Oh, Charlotte, I was so afraid you'd be too angry with me to realise how I felt and why I said what I did."

"I realised," she said in what was left of her voice, and he raised her hands to his lips and kissed her fingers gently.

"I love you," he said earnestly. "And I want so much to marry you, Charlotte."

She wished more urgently than ever now that she had a voice. That she could tell him that she liked him a lot, but not quite that much yet. Instead that annoying croak threatened to disappear at any moment and leave her with no communication at all.

"I—I can't, Noel," she begged, the words only just discernible. "I mean I—"

"You need more time," Noel said, nodding understanding, but apparently undeterred altogether. "I understand, my dearest Charlotte, and I won't rush you into anything." He smiled and kissed her fingers again. "You told me once that you couldn't be rushed into anything, didn't you?"

She nodded. "Yes," she agreed hoarsely, "I did."

"Then I'll wait." He bent his head and kissed her mouth, but with much less passion than Scott had shown when he was trying to persuade her not to go for that ride with Noel, and she was a little annoyed with herself for comparing them.

CHAPTER EIGHT

CHARLOTTE saw nothing of either Noel or Scott during the next couple of days, and she wondered if Scott had taken Noel's remarks so much to heart that he had decided not to call so frequently in future. It was not like him to be deterred by anyone's opinion, but it was the first time since she had been at Blanestock that she had seen neither of them for two whole days, and she was not sure that she liked it.

She missed Scott, she was forced to admit, rather more than she did Noel, for he was a much more frequent visitor usually. Noel was very good for her ego, and made her feel very much the important lady of the manor, while Scott's effect was just the reverse, but she was prepared to admit, if only to herself, that she quite enjoyed their verbal exchanges at times.

Her throat was very much better, and she saw no reason why she should not venture out, although the weather was progressively more cold and wet as autumn grew older. This morning, however, it was quite mellow so far, and even a mere glimmer of sun was sufficient to entice her outside.

She walked out in the garden for a while, stopping to admire the work done so far by her newly acquired gardener, and thinking how much better the whole place would look next spring when she had everything better organised. She had told herself that Scott's remarks about the state of the grounds had had nothing to do with her decision, but she had hired a man to come and do the work only a couple of days after Scott had complained about it.

She stopped and had a few words with the gardener, and discussed the relative merits of various flowering bulbs, but those few minutes did not satisfy her need for company and she eventually rang for a taxi to take her into Chedwell.

It was while she was waiting for her transport to arrive that she remembered Scott's suggestion that she should learn to drive, and decided on the spur of the moment that if a reason was needed for going into Chedwell, it might just as well be to look at cars.

She was not, she felt, being too precipitate in spending money on a car, because the necessary settlements in connection with old Ezra's will were almost complete now, and the estate legally hers. Having a car would make her independent of either taxis or helpful neighbours, no matter how willing.

Once in Chedwell she debated for some time whether or not to try and see Noel and consult him about choosing a car, but since he had been absent for two days, presumably from choice, she did not feel inclined to force her company on him if he did not want it.

She wandered around for quite some time, and then stopped to look in the window of a car dealers, but there was such a bewildering array of vehicles for sale that she simply stared at them vaguely, unwilling to betray just how appallingly ignorant she was in matters mechanical. Her predicament, however, was observed by a young man in a dark suit, who saw in her rather more than the usual casual look, and came out from his wood and glass cage to ask if he could help her.

"I'm—I'm not sure," Charlotte told him.

Nothing averse to passing away a few minutes with an exceptionally pretty girl, the young man smiled. "Have you a car already?" he asked. "If so we have a very generous part exchange scheme."

"I haven't," she confessed. "I can't really drive yet although I have the basic knowledge of what to do."

"Oh, I see."

"I thought perhaps something—well, a bit *old* to start with," Charlotte explained. "Just in case I smash it up."

"Very wise," the young man agreed, and led her across to a display of second-hand models in various stages of preservation. "Maybe you'll find something here that takes your eye."

Not knowing the first thing about cars put her in something of a predicament, and left her at the mercy of the salesman, she realised, but she was prepared for that in the first instance. With something more expensive she would be more particular.

Her eye fell on an ancient model right at the back of the display, and she could not fail to see the look on the young man's face when she pointed to it. He was anxious to oblige, however, and she had no difficulty at all in persuading him to drive her out to Blanestock in it while he explained that it was taxed and insured until the end of the year. She would, she promised with a smile that dazzled him, pay for a taxi to take him back to Chedwell.

He left her quite reluctantly, having offered to help her with driving lessons, an offer she smilingly refused, but which nevertheless touched her. She confided her secret to Mrs. Borden, who looked rather less impressed when she saw the vehicle standing on the drive, but Charlotte was undeterred.

There was a wide gravel path at the back of the house as well, what had once been a ride from the disused stables, and she could drive the car down there and out into the fields. She could practise there to her heart's content with no one any the wiser, and without breaking any laws.

She had been a little dubious about the engine when she had ridden home in the car, but now, under her far from expert handling, it sputtered and banged quite alarmingly, crackling away like a whole fusillade of shots as she drove across the field.

Possibly the rough grassland was not the best kind of surface for the health of the car or for learning to drive, but at least she would be undisturbed, and it suited Charlotte's purpose.

Round and round she went on the perimeter of the field, changing gear to cope with the slope of the bottom half of it, practising every move over and over again while the little old car responded gallantly, if noisily. Feeling a little more venturesome at last, she decided to drive right down the length of the lower field, hanging on grimly to the steering wheel as she went down a steep gradient.

It suddenly occurred to her as she rattled on downwards that she was going much faster than ever before and was unable to do anything about it. Her eyes widened with dismay as the little car careered on down the steep hill, her foot on the brake pedal but having no more effect than to give it a sort of hiccuppy jerking progress.

There was only one thing for it, as far as she could see, if she was not to go hurtling to destruction down the two-hundred-foot drop at the far end of the field—she must steer the car into the dividing hedge to her right.

The car, seemingly, was bent on self-destruction and she had to fight hard to turn the wheel in the direction she wanted to go, gritting her teeth determinedly, and mentally uttering some very unladylike phrases. She managed it at last, however, and tore through the hedge at a rate that terrified her until she remembered to take her foot off the accelerator.

The ensuing silence fell about her like a soothing veil and she closed her eyes for a few seconds to enjoy it. But her enjoyment, as she might have guessed, was shortlived, for she heard a voice calling out her name and looked across the rolling parkland she was now on to see Scott galloping towards her.

It took her a moment or two to realise she was no longer on her own property but on Wainscote's impeccable parkland, and she sighed as she prepared an apology. Scott was riding the same big black horse she had seen him on before when she fell foul of him on his side of the boundary, and she wondered if he would be as easily forgiving this time, in view of their last parting.

He certainly looked stern and angry as he rode up to her, but that was an expression she had learned was not always indicative of his mood. While she waited for him to join her, she took time to admire the way he rode the great black animal. It was the first time she had really seen him riding and she found the grace and ease with which he sat and handled his mount quite exciting to watch.

She wore a hopeful smile as he came nearer, but he did not respond to it. "What the devil are you up to now?" he demanded as he reined in his mount and sat looking down his arrogant nose at her.

"Learning to drive," Charlotte ventured, meekly for the moment.

"On our land?"

"I wasn't *on* your land," she retorted, the meekness shortlived in the face of his obvious ill humour.

"You're on it now," he argued. "This happens to be Wainscote land, and you've ploughed up about six feet of it with that exploding juggernaut, to say nothing of damaging the hedge!"

"I couldn't help it," she explained, trying to keep her temper since she was so obviously in the wrong, even if it wasn't entirely her fault. "It was either that or go over the edge of a drop of about a thousand feet."

"What's the matter?" he asked sarcastically. "Can't you turn left in that thing?"

Charlotte blinked for a moment, realising for the first time that she could just as easily have turned to her left in the field she had been in as right into the hedge. "I—I didn't think about it," she confessed, unwillingly honest, and the hazel eyes surveyed her from his superior height, expressing all manner of uncomplimentary things.

"You're a hopeless little nut case, Charlie Brown," he declared bluntly. "And what on earth is that thing supposed to be anyway?"

"It's a car, of course," Charlotte retorted.

"You could have fooled me!" He lifted one leg in the stirrup and rested an elbow on the raised knee, studying her for a moment. "Why, oh, why do you always do things the hard way, Charlotte? You could have afforded a decent car, even to learn in, and I've already offered to teach you to drive. But no, Miss Charlie Brown—you have to go and lumber yourself with some useless old banger, and bash around in a field, spoiling the property and almost breaking your own neck in the process."

"Oh, stop laying down the law!" Charlotte complained. "I haven't hurt your blessed property, and the hedge will soon grow again. As for my neck, that's my affair and I'd have thought you would be only too glad if I *did* break it, then you'd stand more chance of getting Blanestock."

"How charming!" he said. "Do you really think I'm such an ogre that I'd want it that way?"

Charlotte looked down at her restless hands. "No. No, I suppose not," she admitted. "But you don't have to take it out on me just because you've crossed swords with Noel. Oh, I *know* why you haven't been over for nearly three days, but it doesn't matter to me one way or the other."

"Then why mention it?" Scott asked softly, and she glared at him reproachfully.

"I'll pay for the hedge and have the field—"

"Park," he corrected her.

"All right, *park*. Whatever it is, I'll pay for it."

"I see."

She sat there in her little car, feeling inexplicably tearful suddenly. Her throat hurt and she told herself that was the reason, but she had to admit that she had been hoping he would express some desire to resume his visits to Blanestock, and she was bitterly disappointed because he had not so far done so.

"I'd—I'd better go," she ventured, and he still did nothing but sit there and watch her.

"Are you proposing to drive *back* in that thing?"

"Yes, of course!"

"Then make sure you use the same tracks you; ploughed up on your way in," he told her, and Charlotte glared at him angrily, starting up the engine again with such a racket that the great black animal he sat skittered nervously. "Charlotte! for heaven's sake!" she heard him yell above the din, and she laughed as she drove round and back through the gap in the hedge.

Revenge was sweet and it would give him something else to complain about while she made her escape. A brief glimpse over her shoulder showed him still battling with the indignant and temperamental Satan, and she could not help the small malicious smile that touched her mouth as she changed gear ready to tackle the upward slope.

She had gone several feet on her way when she chanced another look back and this time her eyes widened in dismay. The horse stood more or less where she had last seen him, tossing his head impatiently, but there was no sign of his rider, and she remembered suddenly and vividly her own experience of lying under those flailing hooves.

"Scott!"

She braked noisily and inexpertly, and the little car rolled back almost as far as the opening in the hedge.

Charlotte got out, in such a hurry she did not notice a sharp edge that ruined a pair of new tights, snatching herself free impatiently and running back through the gap in the hedge.

He lay on the ground, crumpled into a heap that was frighteningly still. "Scott! Oh, Scott!"

She knelt beside him, tears rolling down her cheeks, her hands turning his head towards her so that she could see his face, then she lifted his head and shoulders and laid them gently on her lap. "Scott?" Her fingers gently smoothed back the thick fair hair from his forehead and she bent over him anxiously, willing him to open his eyes. "Scott, please look at me!"

There was no response to her plea, and she was crying in earnest now. She felt so helpless out here with no one to call on and with that great black animal watching her. She could see no sign of injury, but she was no expert by any means and he could well have several broken ribs, if not more serious internal injuries. Even a head injury would take some finding in that thick, rough thatch of hair.

"Oh, Scott darling," she pleaded tearfully. "I'm sorry. Please answer me, *please*, darling. I didn't mean this to happen! Please, Scott!"

He still lay, silent and unresponsive, supported by her knees, and she soothed gentle fingers over his forehead, her heart heavy and sickeningly cold in her breast. It was several moments, when she was beginning to despair of him ever coming round, before she noticed a faint but very definite twitching at one corner of his mouth.

"Scott?" The soothing fingers stopped their ministrations and she looked down at the brown face suspiciously, drawing back so that his head slid the few inches to the ground. "Scott, if you're—Scott!"

She shouted his name when he opened his eyes suddenly and reached out for her. He caught her off balance as she tried to move away and before she could do anything about it, he rolled over and pinned her to the soft turf with the hard, lean strength of his body. She heard him laugh, a soft, deep sound that reverberated through her, then his mouth came down on hers, hard and demanding, so that for several moments it did not even occur to her to fight him, even if she could have done.

Slowly and hazily then it began to occur to her how she had been tricked and she began to struggle, making angry little sounds against his mouth and wriggling desperately to escape. The moment, however, was of his choosing, and when he released her at last, smiling again, she fought herself free and slapped his face stingingly hard before scrambling to her feet and running as fast as her legs would carry her, back through the gap in the hedge.

"Charlotte!"

He called after her, but this time she did not look back, but drove the little car back up the slope, grinding gears and slamming down pedals in an uncaring fury. It bothered her almost as much to find that she was shaking like a leaf with some strange, blood-stirring elation, as with anger at being tricked so easily.

Whatever his reasons for staging that disturbing incident, he must be feeling pretty pleased with himself by now, knowing how frantic she had been when she thought him hurt and unconscious. Worst of all was the way she had responded to him in those first few dizzying moments when he had kissed her. No doubt he thought himself as good as owner of Blanestock now, his object achieved. And she cried aloud as she braked the car to a halt at the top of the slope and, dropping her forehead on to her arms, sobbed despairingly.

CHAPTER NINE

It was the following morning that a letter arrived asking her to call and see Philip Chartres as soon as possible, and Charlotte welcomed it as much for the opportunity it offered of possibly seeing Noel again as for the news that everything was at last finally settled about the estate. That must be the reason for the summons, she felt sure, although the letter did not actually say so, but hinted at urgent and important matters to be discussed.

She felt a lilting excitement in her heart as she read it, and decided that today was as good a day as any to go. She breakfasted and then telephoned for a taxi to come and fetch her and take her into Chedwell. She rather optimistically told Mrs. Borden that she would be out for lunch and smiled at her own optimism. If Noel was either not free or not willing to take her she would take herself and the housekeeper none the wiser.

She was puzzled and not a little hurt that Noel had been out of touch for so long. She had seen nothing of him since his exchange with Scott, but she was unwilling to believe that Scott had had anything at all to do with his absence. Usually he used every opportunity to speak with her, or visit her, and she could not understand why he had not rung and arranged the appointment, as he more normally would have done. Unless of course he knew nothing about it.

Philip Chartres rose from behind that same big desk that she remembered from their first meeting, one finger inevitably stabbing the ill-fitting spectacles more firmly into position on his nose. "Ah, Miss Brown!" He looked rather less affable and smiling than at their first meeting, Charlotte thought, and felt a sudden ominous coldness clutch at her stomach. "Please do sit down."

She sat, as she had done before, on the chair facing him across the desk, but his time there was no sign of Noel and she swallowed hard, suspicion again rearing its ugly head. Something was wrong, she could feel it in her bones, and it left her with a limp, panicky feeling inside.

Suppose some other family heir had shown up at last? Someone she knew nothing about and who, perhaps, had a better claim to Blanestock and old Ezra's fortune than she had. It was a prospect that would hardly bear thinking about, but nevertheless had to be faced.

"Is—is something wrong, Mr. Chartres?" she asked, and Philip Chartres gazed down at the papers in front of him for several seconds before he raised his eyes and looked at her over the tops of his escaping spectacles.

"I'm afraid matters have taken rather an unexpected turn, Miss Brown," he informed her pedantically. "We appear to have been rather remiss in leaving some stones unturned."

The rather annoyingly vague allusion irritated Charlotte, and she frowned her dislike of this obvious beating about the bush. "I'm afraid I don't follow your meaning," she said. "*Is* something wrong?"

Apparently Philip Chartres was still not prepared to come directly to the point, instead he leaned back in his chair, his elbows on the arms of it, his fingers steepled and his rather full lips pursed thoughtfully. "My son tells me that you had a most unfortunate accident last week," he said at last, and Charlotte's frown deepened.

"If you mean when the cellar stairs collapsed, and I was trapped down there," she said, "I'm quite recovered now, Mr. Chartres, thank you."

"I'm very pleased to hear that." The smooth, deliberately blank face betrayed nothing, but he nodded his head slowly. "Such a fall could have had much more serious consequences."

"It could," Charlotte agreed, tired of procrastinating. "I'm grateful for your concern, Mr. Chartres," she went on. "But I understood that you had something important to tell me."

"Ah yes, so I have, so I have." He smiled, a cool and distinctly non-humorous smile that set Charlotte's heart racing in panic again. "The law, so they say, Miss Brown, cannot be hurried, and I'm afraid the adage is true."

"If it's important and it concerns—if it concerns Blanestock, I have a right to know," she told him.

"Oh yes, yes, of course." The steepled fingers were lowered to the top of the desk and there tapped out a slow dirgelike rhythm that made her clench her hands tightly and feel like shouting. "While you were down in the cellars at Blanestock, Miss Brown, did you—er—find anything?"

"Find anything?" Charlotte echoed, frowning curiously. "I don't understand you."

Smooth, plump hands waved vaguely in the air.

"Did you discover any documents, papers of any sort?"

She thought for a moment back to those long, frightening hours she had spent in the cellar. So much had happened since then, although it was only a few days ago. "Oh yes, of course." She put a hand to her forehead, probing her memory. "Yes, I remember now. I was looking in some old trunks, cabin trunks or something of the sort—they were stored down there. In one of them I found various pieces of jewellery. A locket, rings, things of that sort. Sort of keepsakes—mementoes, and there were some photographs too." She bit her lip when she remembered those, for she had fully intended handing them over to Scott. She had no desire to see old Ezra's very private feelings for the now Lady Everslade become public knowledge. She must do something about them as soon as she got back.

"Anything else?" Philip Chartres asked, and Charlotte brought herself back sharply to more immediate matters.

"I believe there was a—a legal document of some sort," she said, frowning over the vague memory of it. "But I'd just found that when I heard the door being locked and I don't remember what I did with it." She thought for a moment. "Oh yes, wait a minute! It was a—" Her eyes widened suddenly and she knew all at once the reason for her being there. "It was a—a will, or something of the sort," she said slowly and warily. "I remember now. It was signed Ezra Albert Blackwell, I seem to recall, but I had no time to look at it properly before I heard the door close and I was shut in down in that wretched cellar. All I could think about after that was how to get out of there again."

"Naturally," Philip Chartres agreed quietly. "But you must have put that document into a pocket or something, Miss Brown—"

"I did," Charlotte concurred. "I remember now, I had on an old brown cardigan with big pockets and I stuffed the—everything into them."

"I have no knowledge of anything else," the solicitor told her, "but the document must have fallen from your pocket and my son picked it up, rather absent-mindedly, I imagine, in the circumstances."

"You mean—Noel took it?" She thought she began to understand at last, and the realisation brought her no comfort.

"My son must have put it in his own pocket on the spur of the moment," he explained, carefully and pedantically. "Intending, of course, to return it to you, but with one distraction and another I suppose it was forgotten until Saturday morning. He discovered it still in the pocket of the suit he had been wearing that day. Naturally, in the circumstances, he was curious enough to read it and realised at once the significance of it. Accordingly, Miss Brown, I wrote and requested a visit from you."

"I see." It was becoming more plain every minute, Charlotte thought wryly. She had expected to see Noel on Saturday, but he had not been near all weekend, and today, Tuesday, she had received the letter. "Where is it now?" she asked quietly.

The eyes behind those precarious spectacles had a shrewd glint as he looked at her across the width of the desk. "Where it should have been all the time, Miss Brown, in my hands."

"It—it *is* a will?"

He nodded, with evident satisfaction. "It's the only will, as far as we can discover, that Mr. Blackwell ever made, and we searched most diligently. While it isn't a proper, legally worded document it *is* sufficiently clear and legal to affect your own position, Miss Brown."

"I see." Charlotte's heart was somewhere in the region of her stomach and it felt cold and heavy as she anticipated further disaster to come. "You—you mean—I'm *not* the heir?"

"I'm afraid not, Miss Brown."

The words fell like a bombshell and it was quite clear to her now why Noel had not contacted her first about his discovery, given her some warning instead of being so legally proper and showing it to his father without even a hint to her. If the will affected her position as an heiress, she was obviously much less of an attraction than she had been.

She sought for words, knowing it was hopeless to even ask for a glimmer of hope, but unwilling to see it all slipping away from her. "But—but you advertised, you said there *were* no relatives! No one at all, you said so."

"And as far as we are aware there are no other relatives but yourself, Miss Brown," he told her, and Charlotte shook her head.

"Then how can—"

"One need not be a relative to inherit under a will, Miss Brown, as you will realise," he told her smoothly. "We advertised in good faith, under the impression there was no will, because Mr. Blackwell had seen fit to conceal it. And unfortunately for you Mr. Blackwell knew nothing of your existence. There is absolutely no doubt that the instructions given in the document you found in the cellar are Mr. Blackwell's last wishes and therefore must be carried out as he states."

Charlotte shook her head slowly, her eyes shiny with threatening tears, although she was determined not to cry. At least not until she was somewhere on her own, and then there would be bitter and self-condemning tears, for if she had not gone down into that wretched cellar the will would not have been found and nothing would have changed.

"Does that mean that—that I get nothing?" she asked huskily.

"I'm afraid so."

"I see."

"Of course we may be able to come to some arrangement with the new heir," Philip Chartres went on smoothly. "A reasonable amount, no doubt—"

Charlotte stared at him. "You mean, ask for some of the money?" she said, eyes wide.

"A small settlement, as the only relative. I'm sure something could be arranged, Miss Brown."

"I wouldn't dream of it," Charlotte declared firmly.

"Well, of course the decision is yours, my dear young lady, but I'm sure something could be settled if you should have second thoughts when you have had time to think clearly about things."

She merely shook her head slowly, feeling utterly and abjectly miserable and, as yet, unable to fully grasp the complete reversal of her fortunes since yesterday.

Also, she realised, her loss not only made her less attractive to Noel, but there would no longer be any reason for Scott to pursue her so relentlessly to make her sell Blanestock. Probably he would try the same tactics with the new owner, if it was a female, and that she was ready to admit was what she liked least about the whole thing. Scott's determined pursuit of her had been purely mercenary and at times had angered her, but she had enjoyed every exciting minute of it.

"I can't tell you how sorry I am, Miss Brown," Philip Chartres told her, and she could find it in her heart to believe him, but she could not easily forgive Noel for the way he had acted against her, and without a hint of warning.

She sat for a moment or two, stunned and unhappy, then she looked up at last, her eyes appealing. "Can I—may I know who *does* inherit?" she asked.

Philip Chartres considered the question for a long moment, then he shook his head and drew a deep breath as he pursed his lips. "I think it would be unwise of me to divulge that at the moment, Miss Brown, since the legal heir has not yet been informed."

"Oh! Oh, I see. I'm sorry, I shouldn't have asked."

"A natural curiosity," Philip Chartres allowed, magnanimously. "And now, Miss Brown, if you will kindly excuse me," he smiled, and the errant spectacles slid down his nose, "I have to see another client in a few moments."

"Of course." Charlotte got to her feet, still a little dazed, and not quite sure if she was living some appalling nightmare, or if it was really happening to her. "I—I suppose I must leave Blanestock right away?" she guessed, and felt that would be the hardest part of all. She had learned to love the old house and leaving it again would break her heart. For some inexplicable reason she found herself wishing that Scott was there to console her, and she bit her lip while the solicitor regarded her for a moment with a raised brow.

"I imagine the new heir will not be too adamant about that," he told her. "But it would be advisable, of course, to find alternative accommodation."

"Yes. Yes, of course."

She left the well-polished, old-fashioned office in something of a daze, so much so that she saw nothing and no one until she cannoned into someone at the corner of the corridor and hands reached out to grasp her arms and steady her.

"I'm so sorry!"

The voice was familiar, and she jolted herself out of her daze to meet Noel's earnest but undeniably discomfited gaze. "Noel!" He would have preferred to have hurried off without saying any more to her, she thought, but she was feeling hurt and angry as well as dazed, and she reached out and curled her fingers round his arm, keeping him there. Her eyes were huge and deep, and their violet colour was made dark by the emotions that churned chaotically in her. "Why, Noel?" she asked huskily. "Why couldn't you have told me?"

For a moment he looked shamefaced and embarrassed, then he shook his head. "It—it wouldn't have been ethical, Charlotte."

"Ethical!" Charlotte's face warmed to a bright, angry pink and her eyes blazed at him. "Neither was it ethical to warn me about Scott wanting to buy Blanestock," she reminded him. "But it didn't stop you telling me, did it?"

"Charlotte—"

"Neither did it stop you from making some very unethical remarks about your *very important* client at times, but I suppose it didn't matter quite so much then, did it?"

She knew she sounded bitter, and she was perhaps being a little unfair to attack him so bitingly, but she had lost Blanestock and old Ezra's fortune and nothing could persuade her that the knowledge had not influenced his behaviour.

"Charlotte, please!" He looked around uneasily, as if he feared someone might overhear them. "Look—I have to take these papers in to Father now, but—" he glanced at his wristwatch, "in ten minutes I shall be free. Will you let me buy you lunch?"

Charlotte hesitated, tempted to be rude to him and reject the offer out of hand, but instead she sighed deeply and shrugged. "If you still want to be seen with me now that I'm just a common or garden secretary again."

"Oh, Charlotte, please don't!"

"I'm sorry." She smiled ruefully. "Anyway, I can't afford to turn down offers to buy me a lunch now," she told him.

He did not bend his head and kiss her, however lightly, and she knew then that it was all over.."I'll see you in about ten minutes," he told her, and she watched him walk off along the corridor towards his father's office, wondering if he would really remember to have lunch with her or if some well trained member of her own kind would come and smile apologetically with a message of regret.

Charlotte looked across the table at Noel, her lashes concealing the speculative look she studied him with. He was very good-looking and very charming, although there was a less fulsome character to the charm, she was prepared to swear, then there used to be.

"What are you going to do?" he asked, raising the

question of her position for the first time as they drank their coffee.

"Do?" Charlotte raised a brow, and smiled at him wryly. "What else is there to do, Noel? I find another job and go back to being a working girl." She laughed shortly, but in fact she felt more like crying. "I didn't really have much experience of being anything else, did I?"

"I'm—I'm sorry."

She looked at him steadily over the rim of her coffee cup. "Are you, Noel?"

"Of course I am—you know how I felt about you."

"I also notice the past tense," Charlotte told him, and he shook his head.

"I'm sorry, I really am."

"But it was the rich heiress you were so fond of," Charlotte said softly, "not Miss Brown, secretary. Oh, it's all right, Noel," she added hastily, when he would have spoken. "I understand."

"I—I wish it could have been different, Charlotte."

Charlotte smiled wryly. "So do I," she said.

"I don't know what to say. I—I wish I needn't have found the wretched thing, if you hadn't dropped it after you were trapped in the cellar no one would have known anything about it and everything would have been all right."

"Yes. Yes, I suppose it would."

"And for Lingrove to have the wretched place after all, I—" He stopped then and stared at her, aghast at what he had done, while Charlotte in her turn looked at him with huge, unbelieving eyes.

"Scott?" Her voice sounded little more than a husky whisper. "Are you telling me that Scott is old Ezra's new heir?"

It made sense, of course, she realised when she really thought about it. Scott himself had told her that during those last five years after Mary Bishop had rejected him old Ezra had had no contact with anyone else much, beside him. It was logical that he should leave his home and everything else he owned to the man who had been his only friend during those last, lonely years.

"Oh, Charlotte, I—I shouldn't have told you. I didn't know if Father had told you who the new heir was, I just didn't think."

"It was very unethical of you," Charlotte told him unkindly. "But if I'd stopped and thought about it, it would have been the only answer, of course, unless it was—" She shook her head at betraying the alternative, but thought the old man would have been too fond of Mary Everslade, née Bishop, to have embarrassed her by making her his heir.

"Who else?" Noel asked, his eyes curious, but Charlotte shook her head, not to be persuaded.

"No one else," she told him.

"There was a rumour I seem to remember," Noel mused, not taking kindly to her refusal to disclose the other possible heir. "Something about a woman, but I don't remember much about it. I was only just starting in the job then." The earnest blue eyes that had once seemed so soulful when they gazed at her now regarded her with almost as much shrewdness as his father's had done. "*Was* there a woman, Charlotte? I'll bet Scott Lingrove knew—he was the only one who got near the old man in the last few years."

"There was someone," Charlotte admitted cautiously. "But she preferred to marry for love."

It was a deliberate jibe at his own attitude and Noel recognised it as such, his good-looking face flushing warmly while he looked down at his hands. "I suppose I asked for that," he allowed, and glanced at his wrist-watch.

"Now you have to go," Charlotte guessed, and smiled.

"Charlotte—"

"Please, no speeches or excuses, Noel," she begged. "I don't think I could take it, not today." She extended a hand which he took only reluctantly. "Thank you for the lunch, Noel, and for the good times. Goodbye."

"Please, Charlotte!"

"Goodbye, Noel!"

She got to her feet, gathered up her handbag and gloves and walked away without a backward glance, but her mind was already in another situation. It would be much less easy to say goodbye to Scott, especially now she knew he was the one who had dispossessed her.

CHAPTER TEN

CHARLOTTE did not quite know how she managed to stay at least outwardly cheerful until she got back to Blanestock, but as soon as the old house came into sight at the top of the drive she felt herself weakening. The irresistible urge to cry her heart out became too much for her, even though she knew the taxi driver was watching her curiously while she paid him her fare.

He was probably drawing all the wrong conclusions, but she was uncaring what he or anyone else thought by now. The tears just would not be resisted any longer and she did not wait for him to thank her for the over-generous tip before she ran up the front steps to the door.

She inserted the key in the lock and was immediately reminded of other, happier times when she had done just this same thing, when she had come to Blanestock for the first time as its proud new owner, foreseeing a rosy future stretching before her, and revelling in the extravagance of a taxi.

Again when she had visited the safari park with Scott and she had been so angry when they arrived home that her hands would not stay steady enough for her to insert the key. Scott had taken it from her and laughed at her as he so often did, so that she had hurled that beautiful little china lion he had bought her into the shrubbery.

She had been at Blanestock such a little time, but she had made herself so many memories in those few short weeks that the idea of leaving it was unbearable. By the time she reached the hall and took off her coat and gloves she was crying uncontrollably and she knew that the threatened storm was about to break at last.

An amazed Mrs. Borden watched in surprise when she dashed past her and straight on up the stairs to her room, with only a shaking head to answer her question about dinner. Basic needs like food were furthest from her mind at the moment.

Once in her own room Charlotte threw herself across the bed and gave herself up to the emotional upheaval that had been threatening her all morning. She wept without restraint for a very long time until she could cry no more and fell into a half-sleep that was sheer exhaustion.

There was nothing she could do to change things; it would be back to office routine for her as quickly as possible, for she had no more now than when she had arrived, she thought. A great shuddering sigh ran through her when she thought of the many plans she had had for Blanestock and its gardens. She had looked so far ahead, visualising how grand it would look by next summer, and now it would all come to nothing.

Blanestock itself would be looked after, of course, Scott would see to that, and it was her one consolation in an otherwise wretched outlook. Then the irony of it struck her suddenly so that she almost smiled, despite her unhappiness, as she lay there stretched across the width of the bed, her chin resting on her folded arms.

To think how she had so staunchly resisted all Scott's attempts to buy Blanestock from her, and now she was thanking heaven that it was his and not someone else's.

She had no idea how long she had lain there, she was too abjectly miserable to care about time, but she suddenly became aware of footsteps on the landing outside her room, followed a few seconds later by a soft, hesitant tapping on the door itself.

"Miss Brown?"

Charlotte pulled herself upright and looked at her watch, realising she had been there for much longer than it seemed. She rubbed the last vestige of tears from her cheeks and brushed down her crumpled dress, hoping her eyes were not too red-rimmed.

"Yes, Mrs. Borden? Come in!"

The housekeeper looked anxious, an expression Charlotte would not have believed her capable of only a short time ago. "I was wondering about dinner, Miss Brown," she said, and looked as if she would like to have said more, but years of training had taught her not to become too personal with her employer.

Charlotte gave a long, sobbing sigh that was quite beyond her control. "I—I don't think I'm very interested in dinner, Mrs. Borden," she told her, and the housekeeper looked at her curiously.

"Aren't you dining in, ma'am?"

Charlotte nodded. "Oh yes, I'll be in, but I don't think I want any dinner, not tonight."

The housekeeper hesitated, obviously with something on her mind, then she raised her brows resignedly and made as if to leave again. Apparently second thoughts decided her, however, and she did not even close the door but came back into the room again.

"I don't wish to appear forward, Miss Brown," she said slowly and carefully, as if she was acting out of character. 'But I can't help noticing you're obviously very upset and I wondered—" She hesitated, her usually stern features relaxed into anxiety. "Forgive me if I speak out of turn, but if I may say so, ma'am, you seem as if you need to talk to someone."

Charlotte blessed her for her understanding. "I think I do," she confessed, and got to her feet, walking over to look at her reflection in the dressing-table mirror. It was not an encouraging sight and she sighed again. Her eyes were swollen and red-rimmed and her cheeks puffy from weeping. Even her hair was untidy where she had been lying on the bed, and altogether she could understand the housekeeper's concern. "I do look a mess, don't I?" she said.

"You look very unhappy," Mrs. Borden opined.

"I am." She felt another threat of tears now that she was faced with the prospect of putting it all into words for Mrs. Borden's benefit, and she bit her lip anxiously, unwilling to indulge in another bout of weeping.

"Please allow me to be of service," Mrs. Borden offered again, and Charlotte was convinced that it was not mere curiosity that prompted the offer.

She rolled her handkerchief into a damp ball and held it tightly in her hands as she walked across to the window where she could look out at the breathtaking and awe-inspiring view. "I've lost Blanestock," she said flatly, seeing no other way of putting it.

"Oh no, Miss Brown!"

She turned and looked at the woman, knowing her regret was genuine and appreciating her sympathy, even if it did threaten her self-control. "I'm afraid it's true," she told her. "That's why I had to see Mr. Chartres this morning."

"I didn't realise," Mrs. Borden said, "and I'm very sorry to hear it, Miss Brown."

Charlotte laughed shortly. "I suppose it's a classic case of counting chickens," she said bitterly. "I was Mr. Blackwell's heir only because I was his only living relative, but there turned out to be a will after all, and Great-Uncle Ezra had never heard of me."

She was assuming that Mrs. Borden was familiar with the circumstances of her inheritance, for there was little went on in country houses that was not known to the staff of them. "I'm very sorry about it, ma'am," she said. "I really am."

Charlotte turned again to look out at that magnificent view that would soon be no longer available to her. "The worst part of it is," she told the housekeeper, "I was the one who found the wretched will—when I was down in the cellar."

Mrs. Borden blinked for a moment as if something had just occurred to her. "Did you have it in your pocket, ma'am?" she asked, and Charlotte turned again and looked at her curiously.

"Yes, I did. Why?"

It was Mrs. Borden's turn to sigh and she shook her head in regret for lost opportunities. "I saw it fall out of your pocket when Mr. Lingrove picked you up to carry you upstairs," she said. "If only I'd realised what it was!"

Charlotte smiled ruefully. "It wouldn't have made any difference, Mrs. Borden, you'd have been bound to hand it over eventually, wouldn't you?"

"I'm not so sure," Mrs. Borden averred firmly. "As

it was, Mr. Chartres had it in his hand before I could reach it, and I never gave it another thought until now."

"Neither did Noel Chartres, apparently," Charlotte told her ruefully. "He found it in his pocket at the weekend, and showed it to his father."

The housekeeper looked at her, shaking her head. "I don't know what to suggest, Miss Brown," she said. "I suppose there's no arguing with the law, is there?"

"There isn't," Charlotte agreed, and sighed again. "Oh, well, it was grand being a country landowner while it lasted."

"Mr. Lingrove—" Mrs. Borden ventured, and Charlotte shook her head firmly.

"Mr. Lingrove can do nothing about anything, Mrs. Borden, it's all over."

CHARLOTTE was very uncertain whether or not she was disappointed that Scott did not come over the following day. She would like to have seen him, she frankly admitted, in fact she could have cried on his shoulder, but with him being the cause of her unhappiness, however unwittingly, it would have made things very awkward.

She walked in the gardens during the morning, and sat in the sitting-room all afternoon, knowing that soon she must do something about moving out, but wanting to stay until the very last moment. Dinner was a gloomy, solitary meal and she felt restless and tearful again faced with a solitary evening too.

"I'm going for a walk," she told Mrs. Borden after an hour or so of moping about, and the housekeeper shook her head but said nothing to discourage her.

It was a cold night, but clear and bright with the moon about three-quarters full and the stars so brilliant they must surely forecast a frost. She walked along the road where she had walked with Noel, and where she had shown Scott the old tree that looked like a handful of stars.

A wry smile curved her soft mouth as she thought of it. She had held a handful of stars for a while, but now all she had were a few memories, not fully appreciated until now. She looked up as she got further along the road, where it rose sharply with the rocky sweep of the peak, and saw the old tree again with its fingers spread, black and stark and holding a scatter of stars like a handful of diamonds.

It was a romantic notion and she remembered how much more appreciative of it Scott had been than Noel. He had wished and encouraged her to, though hers had done her little good as it worked out. She would never be able to live at Blanestock for ever and ever now.

She was crying again, she realised when she could see the road only through a haze of tears that rolled down her cheeks and gave them a stiff, icy feeling in the cold wind. Never in her whole life had she cried so much as she had the past couple of days and it could do no good at all.

Impatiently she brushed a gloved hand across her eyes and swallowed hard, then a moment later turned her head sharply when she thought she heard a car coming along behind her. There were no street lights here and no way for a driver to see her until she was picked up in his headlights.

The sound died away, however, and she thought no more of that, but there were other footsteps crunching along the road behind her and she looked back over her shoulder, wary suddenly and uneasy. She had never met anyone else along here before, not on foot anyway, and it made her heart thud warningly under her ribs as she paused, wondering which way was best to go.

The cause of the disturbance came into view round the bend in the road at that moment, however, and she heard her own breath expelled in relief when she recognised him. The long easy stride and the light-coloured hair were unmistakable and she stood there with her hands clasped tightly together, waiting for him to come up to her.

He called out no greeting nor even smiled, but came right up to her and took her arm, bringing her to a halt and looking down at her for a long moment, the hazel eyes without identifiable colour in the moonlight.

"The Duchess said you'd come out for a walk," he told her then, without preliminaries, and he glanced up at the old tree. "Have you come to renew your wish?"

She was near to breaking point and his gentle jibe was almost too much for her. "It—it won't do me much good," she told him in a tight little voice that she scarcely recognised as her own.

He still held her arm and his fingers curled tightly. "You have to believe in it before it comes true," he told her solemnly, and Charlotte bit her lip.

"Oh, Scott, don't! You—you know I've lost Blanestock, don't you?"

He nodded. "I saw Philip Chartres this morning. I also saw that weak-kneed son of his, too, and told him what I thought of him."

Charlotte gazed up at him, seeing the stern set of his mouth and jaw through a haze of tears. "You—you didn't!"

"Indeed I did," he assured her. "When I learned about the will and that you'd been disinherited I expected him to be out here consoling you, but no—his lordship was no longer interested, I gathered."

She shook her head, hiding her eyes with a long sweep of lashes. "I—I wasn't really—I mean I—"

"I know you weren't in love with him," Scott told her confidently. "But he *was* supposed to be a friend, and he let you down when you needed him most. That's a pretty poor sort of friend, and I told him so."

Charlotte had a sudden and almost irresistible desire to giggle, despite her tears. It was not difficult at all to visualise the scene between them, or Noel's shamefaced admission, and she was suddenly lighter-hearted, even though nothing had really changed. Nothing ever seemed so insurmountable once Scott had cast his optimistic eye over it.

"Poor Noel," she said softly, only too ready to forgive him now. "He really wanted to marry a wealthy heiress, but I don't think I'd have ever married him."

"I'm damned sure you wouldn't," Scott assured her. "For one thing, bigamy's still illegal in this country, despite the permissive society."

She glanced up at him through her lashes, trying desperately to do something about the way her heart was skittering wildly and making it feel quite incredibly light-headed. "I've already told you I wouldn't marry *you*," she told him, wondering at her own provocativeness, and he laughed softly.

"It's your only chance of getting Blanestock back."

She said nothing for a while, and they stood there on the winding moonlit road like two shadows, quiet and unmoving. "Don't tease me about Blanestock," she told him at last, a husky sound to her voice. "Please don't, Scott. I love it, and I've cried for hours since old Chartres told me it wasn't mine any more."

"Poor Charlie Brown!" His voice was soft and his lips brushed gently across her eyelids. "The Duchess told me how you'd been crying."

She looked up at him, suspicious suddenly. "Mrs. Borden told you?"

He nodded. "I called at the house and you weren't there. The old girl was in quite a state about you, seemed to think you might do something drastic." His fingers again tightened on her arm. "I really am sorry about your losing everything, Charlotte. Please believe me, I wouldn't have had it happen that way."

"I—I know."

"I went to find you this afternoon," he went on, "but I got cold feet before I got to the door, and went back again."

Charlotte stared unbelievingly. "You? You got cold feet?"

"I was afraid you wouldn't see me," he confessed, to Charlotte's amazement. "Not after the way I pounced on you on Tuesday when you frightened my horse and then came back and cried over me. Then learning that I'd got Blanestock from you after all, I quite expected you to hate the very sight of me."

"How do you know I don't?" Charlotte asked, suddenly and gloriously unworried.

He bent his fair head over her and she could see the glint of laughter in his eyes, but something more besides. There was an expression there that stirred her pulses into such a wild state of chaos that she was not even sure where she was.

"Well, you were *def*initely worried about me when

you thought I'd been thrown by Satan," he told her. "And—well, let's see, shall we?"

He pulled her close, so close that she could scarcely breathe, one hand holding her head with the strong fingers twined into her hair so that she was held firm, and the other arm right around her waist and iron hard.

His mouth was gentle at first, then more urgent until she felt her head going round and round with the sheer excitement of something she could not altogether understand, and she clung to him tightly, her fingers caressing the rough nape of his neck where the fair hair grew just slightly curled.

"Scott!"

He laughed, and it tickled her neck where his face was buried in the softness of her hair, his voice muffled by its thickness. "I wonder what you'd have done if I'd done this the first time I felt like it," he speculated, and Charlotte drew back for a second to look at him enquiringly.

"And when was that?" she demanded.

The hazel eyes glinted at her in the moonlight and she knew he was laughing. "The very first time I saw you at the foot of the stairs at Blanestock," he told her. "I didn't really believe you were real, standing there. You certainly didn't look like a Miss Charlotte Brown."

"Oh?" She laughed softly. "What *did* I look like?"

"The most beautiful girl I'd ever seen," he said, and kissed her again until she was breathless. "How about that wish now?" he asked at last, and she smiled as she buried her head against his chest.

"I think it has a good chance of coming true," she told him. "But are you sure you want to—I mean I'm not an heiress now, you know. I'm only a—"

His mouth stopped the rest of the sentence as he had done when she had been about to denigrate herself once before. "I've told you before about that," he said sternly. "And my wife won't be an *only* anything."

Charlotte sighed and looked over his shoulder at the old tree, stark and black against the starry sky, its gnarled fingers full of glittering stars. "I can't think why I've been crying so much for the last two days," she told him softly. "There was bound to be magic in a handful of stars, wasn't there?"

Scott laughed softly and hugged her closer. "Bound to be," he agreed. "Especially when we were both wishing for the same thing."

FLAMINGO MOON

Flamingo Moon

Margaret Pargeter

To be asked for proof of identity astounded Eve Reston. She hadn't wanted to come to the Camargue in the first place. Now Raoul DuBare's hostile reception was the last straw.

But Eve was determined. She had come to see her cousin's baby and report back to her aunt and uncle—and she wasn't going away until she had. So she prepared herself for a long siege.

She was totally unprepared, however, for Raoul's proposal. What did he mean asking her to marry him when the elegant Amelie Troyat was so obviously entrenched in his life! Surely he couldn't be serious?

CHAPTER ONE

CÉLÈSTE HAD SAID not to come to the farm, and now that she was actually here, standing in front of it, Eve Reston began to wish she had taken her advice and stayed away. It probably wouldn't have strained the last remnants of her patience overmuch to have remained at the hotel a little longer in the hope that Célèste would eventually contact her. The DuBare ranch, or *manade*, as such places were called in the Camargue area of France, had a singularly formidable look about it, an air of distinct hostility which seemed to linger around its heat-hazed precincts. If there had been notices posted stating that strangers were unwelcome, Eve wouldn't have been at all surprised!

She had left her car beside a cluster of low scrub, a short distance behind her near the road. Why, she had no very clear idea as she certainly felt quite vulnerable without it, and half hidden as it was, it definitely wasn't handy for a quick getaway should the need arise. Maybe instinctively she had known the necessity for a more silent approach than a noisy little engine allowed.

The car she had hired from Mrs. Wood, the hotel proprietress, who had owned and ran the large establishment with the help of a competent staff since her husband died. An enterprising woman who also kept a small fleet of cars which she rented to guests who came without one.

Eve was aware that Mrs. Wood's curiosity was probably no greater than any other hotelier's would have been regarding a young English girl who appeared to do nothing but sit in her room all day.

"It will do you good to get out, Miss Reston," Mrs. Wood had remarked pointedly, coming into reception just in time to hear Eve inquiring about a car. "If you've come for a holiday you won't find much to entertain you inside the hotel, not during the day at any rate. I should drive into the countryside, if I were you, or down to the coast. You'll at least get a change of air."

Eve had smiled uneasily, conscious of Mrs. Wood's close scrutiny, the sudden flicker of speculation in the receptionist's considering glance. "I intend to," she hurriedly assured them both, "but I have," she hesitated momentarily before repeating in a nervous rush, "I have other business to attend to first."

Swiftly she turned away, in her haste almost snatching the car keys from the desk, anxious to escape the more pertinent questions which she sensed were hovering on the tip of Mrs. Wood's tongue. "I only expect to require a car for one afternoon," she had murmured before she fled.

Now, taking a deep breath in an attempt to still the agitated tremors that ran through her, Eve advanced a few more steps. There appeared to be no one about, no one to interrupt her first moments of reluctant surveillance as her wide-eyed gaze wandered nervously over a long line of buildings. Slung out, they seemed to be, on a dusty, limitless plain, thrown, as if by some careless artist, across a primeval landscape which stretched between water and sky.

She had only been here three days, but long enough to realise this was a remote land, a land of white horses and herds of cattle, of gipsies and cowboys. The latter she had heard referred to in the hotel as the *gardians* of the Camargue. A hard land it seemed to be, although, until now, Eve had liked what little she had seen of it, but there was something about the atmosphere of this ranch which filled her with a peculiar, intangible foreboding.

This house before her was presumably the residence of the DuBares, the place where Célèste DuBare had been born, the home that she had often spoken of with apparent affection at school but which she now seemed to regard rather in the light of a prison—a prison from which she seemed to imagine it was Eve's definite duty to release her!

Beset by numerous anxieties, Eve had allowed that Célèste, in making such assumptions, was probably right, but now she didn't feel so sure? Surely Célèste expected too much? She must have been more than a little crazy to imagine she could bring an almost complete stranger into her family circle and force them to accept her? Already her elder brother, the notorious Raoul DuBare, was hostile, and this before he had even met her. How could Célèste possibly hope that he might react favourably on finding her here, on his very doorstep?

Of course, she hastened to assure herself, it was entirely Raoul DuBare's fault that such a peculiar state of affairs existed. While her eyes remained fixed nervously on the expanse of low stone dwellings, a slightly mutinous change of mood firmed Eve's soft lips with an unfamiliar determination. It was, she considered, entirely because of him that there had been any estrangement between their two families, that he still after all this time appeared to hold her family wholly responsible for the events which had led up to it. To be able to tell him exactly what she thought of his outrageous prejudices had been one of the chief reasons why she had allowed herself to be persuaded to come here. There was a growing urge within herself to meet this man—a man whose forbidding arrogance had been conveyed so realistically both by his actions and in the one letter he had condescended to write to her aunt Mavis, Carol's mother.

It was this thought of her cousin that jerked Eve's mind back to Carol's baby, Michel, who was really the real reason why she had come. Célèste had declared it was her duty.

"Michel is your nephew," she had said, adding with incredible coolness. "Now that Carol is dead you have as much right to him as any of us!"

Which wasn't strictly true, as Célèste knew very well. Carol's parents had more or less adopted Eve when she had been eight, after her parents had both lost their lives in an accident. She had been George Reston's brother's child. "She'll be company for Carol," he had declared, and his wife had wholeheartedly agreed.

They had been so good to her that Eve had always hoped some day to repay them. Indeed, she had tried to do this almost from the very beginning. She had been a clever child and striving especially to please her aunt and uncle, she had worked hard, eventually delighting them by winning a scholarship to quite a famous girls' school. It had been there that she had met Célèste DuBare, a French girl whose mother had been English, and who still had relations living in Cornwall, not far from Eve's own home.

Célèste, who had only two brothers in France, spent many of her long vacations with these relations, and occasionally she had also stayed with Eve's family. "My brothers simply consider I am a nuisance," she had been fond of declaring emphatically. "They do not care for me."

Yet, for all her protestations, Célèste's younger brother, Dominique, had visited her regularly at school, and one Sunday Eve had taken them both home for tea. Eve's home, compared with that of Célèste's relations, was extremely modest, but Dominique had apparently found nothing displeasing about it. In fact it seemed that he found something about the small, semidetached house very pleasing as he returned again and again. But it wasn't until about two years later, when he eloped with Carol, that Eve really understood why he had visited so regularly.

Because they could think of no valid reason for such a furtive marriage, Carol's parents had been upset, but their natural dismay had been nothing compared to Raoul DuBare's fury. Over the telephone Mavis had been frozen by his icy disapproval. Célèste's visits had stopped abruptly and she had returned to France straight away. Here, on this very ranch, Raoul DuBare had made things so awkward for Carol that she had begged George and Mavis to wait a while before attempting to come to France.

Raoul had been the reason, Carol had tried to explain after her honeymoon was over, why she and

Dominique had been forced to elope. It seemed that Raoul had chosen a French bride for his younger brother, and in France, even today, many people still favoured such arrangements. In a way, Carol had generously declared, she quite understood, and time must be allowed for Raoul to forgive and forget. She had begged them to have patience.

But despite Carol's optimism nothing happened, Raoul DuBare being apparently unwilling either to forgive or forget. Carol visited her parents in Cornwall occasionally, but that was all. There was certainly never an invitation for any of them to return with her to the Camargue, a state of affairs which fretted George and Mavis so much they could often talk of little else.

After Carol's baby was born Eve, despite her fondness for them, had felt almost relieved when George, who was a civil engineer, went to Rhodesia, taking Mavis with him. Eve, at that time, had been in London studying to be a children's nanny, the one thing she had been really keen to do, so she couldn't have gone with them even if she had wanted to, but she had fervently hoped the change would do her aunt good and take her mind off Carol for a while.

Yet, unfortunately, George came to blame this very trip for the real tragedy when it struck. Carol, who had not been really well since Michel arrived, had managed to persuade her husband to take her for a short holiday to South Africa to see her parents, against, it was revealed later, Raoul's express wishes. This time it must have seemed to the superstitious that his anger had been justified when the plane carrying Carol and his brother had crashed into the sea with a loss of all life.

The shock had almost proved too much for George,

who foolishly blamed himself for the accident. At once, after hearing the news, he had collapsed with a heart attack and been in and out of hospitals ever since. Even now, after almost a year, he was not nearly well enough to travel, and Mavis wrote that his doctor had advised him to remain in Rhodesia, where at least she had plenty of domestic help. She had also, in that last letter, enclosed one which she had received from Raoul DuBare—a letter which had infuriated Eve greatly, and which she still remembered only too clearly.

In it he had assured Mavis, with more than a hint of cruelty, that he was more than able to take care of Carol's baby himself, and it would be better for all concerned if they continued to go their separate ways.

"A veritable tug of war would do the child no good," he had said, "and considering your husband's state of health no one would look on him as a suitable guardian. In my care he will want for nothing and have a better life than you could ever hope to provide, providing, of course, you do not seek to interfere..."

His last sentence had seemed to hold more than a measure of insidious warning. Stay away, it had implied, or else! And, at that particular time, there had seemed little else that any of them could do but to comply with Raoul DuBare's wishes. But inside Eve was still a smouldering anger, over a year later still as fresh as when she had first read his letter with its intimidating, forceful handwriting. One day, she had vowed, she would surely find a means of hurting him as badly as he had wounded her aunt and uncle, and poor Carol, whom he had scarcely ever allowed them to see!

Once her training had been completed, Eve had taken a temporary job in London, looking after the small son of a French business man and his wife. Carefully, she had saved her salary, hoping, when her job was finished, to be able to fly to South Africa to see George and Mavis, but before this could happen, to her surprise, letters began to arrive in a positive deluge from Célèste.

Eve had seen nothing of Célèste since she had left school, and now she wrote: "I wish to live in Paris. It was all practically arranged before the accident. After that, Raoul declared my duty was here, at the ranch. I must remain to look after Michel who, even now, is still a baby. Raoul appears to think I must share the responsibility of seeing he is reared correctly, and seems to take it for granted that I should willingly sacrifice the best years of my life. Our cousin Nadine assures me I am wasted here in the Camargue, and, while she is not nearly so strict as Raoul, would look after me well. Raoul appears to imagine I should be content with the Rallye and a few carefully chosen friends!"

The Rallye, Eve knew vaguely, was a sort of private group, formed by the mothers of the upper classes who regularly gave dances so that their daughters might meet only eligible young people. Eve's employers had mentioned it and Célèste had talked of it at school, but as Eve had never moved in such circles herself she had paid little attention.

It had been Célèste's next words which had utterly dismayed her. "You must come, Eve, and help me talk to Raoul. If I do have some responsibility regarding Michel, then so do you, and you must share it. You are his aunt, exactly as I am..."

After numerous attempts, Eve had replied as best she could, pointing out bluntly in the end that, as

Célèste must know very well, she had merely been Carol's cousin, so wasn't really Michel's aunt, and consequently would only be wasting her time. Raoul would never be prepared to receive her.

Back had come Célèste's next letter—furiously! "You must come! If you continue to refuse I will bring Michel immediately to England. Then the fire will be in the fat—or how is it you say! I will swear you invited me and Raoul will believe me. He will accuse you of persuasion and he will be very, very angry, and you do not know what my brother is like when he is angry, *ma chérie*!"

Recalling all she knew of him, Eve had no real doubts about Raoul DuBare's temper. Unconsciously she had shivered. It was as if the dark personality of the man had even then reached out and touched her.

Célèste had finished on a pleading note. "But you know I will only do this if all else fails. I beg of you to reconsider, *chérie*. Raoul is a man of many moods, if you caught him in a good one he might listen to you. You are almost twenty-two, more than a year older than me, and most attractive with your lint-fair hair and wide eyes. It is when you smile that I think Raoul will see in them that which he likes in a woman. So you must smile, Eve, and assure him times are changing and girls are not to be kept in absolute exclusion any more, that you are quite prepared to look after Michel for a few months while I enjoy a little freedom. After all, I cannot see how he can remain so rigid when he is so fond of his own amours! I know of more than one *mademoiselle—madame*..."

Célèste had rambled on so much in this vein that Eve had grown alarmed. She had no wish to hear about

Raoul DuBare's indiscretions, as she already despised him, but Célèste's obviously unbalanced attitude regarding her immediate problems filled Eve with apprehension. She might indeed be quite capable of arriving in London as she threatened!

And for all her resolve not to set even one foot on French soil, Eve's mind had clung uneasily to the problem of Michel. Was it desirable that a young baby should be reared by such people? Yet might it not be worse for him to live in possibly inferior digs in London—always supposing the arrogant Raoul allowed him to remain! Yet it wasn't until the third letter, when Célèste threatened to contact George and Mavis, that Eve felt left with no other alternative but to give in. Clearly, if faced with even an inkling of such a dilemma, George might again collapse, and Eve knew it was up to her to rule out the possibility of any such thing happening.

By return she had promised cautiously that she would pay a short visit, and immediately Célèste, as if anticipating her surrender, had sent a list of instructions. There was a hotel, a short distance from Les Saintes Maries, run by an English woman who had always rooms to spare at the beginning of the season. It was an ideal place for Eve to stay. It had the decided advantage of being both convenient and several miles from Célèste's home. Eve was to go there and Célèste would get in touch as soon as she arrived. On no account was Eve to try and contact her.

In spite of being inwardly almost terrified of such an undertaking, Eve had also felt an undeniable flicker of tense excitement. Previously she had had neither the time nor money for foreign travel—now she must find both, yet the prospect, while daunting, was not, she soon realized, insurmountable. Her recent job completed, she took a little of the money she had saved to buy material for dresses which she made quickly herself, then positively clutching her passport and a few small pieces of luggage, one spring evening she had caught a train from Victoria to Dover, then on to Calais, arriving several hours later in Paris. From there the remainder of her journey south had proved much easier than she had expected, and would have been, had she not had so much on her mind, very enjoyable.

The hotel she had found with difficulty, although, contrary to what Célèste had told her, almost all the rooms had been taken and, but for the intervention of Mrs. Wood, the proprietress, Eve fancied she might have been turned away. Taking compassion, it seemed, on Eve's rather panic-stricken face she had assured her she could have a room for at least a few days. Eve had thanked her gratefully, adding that she didn't expect to require it for longer than this as when it became convenient she was to stay with a friend.

But for three whole days Eve had waited in vain for Célèste. Strung up to a high degree of tenseness, she had scarcely dared leave her room for fear she should miss the girl should she telephone or arrive. On the fourth morning, beset by a wholly frightening despair, Eve rang the ranch in the vague hope that Célèste might answer. It was a risk she had felt driven to take. At first she had thought it was Célèste who answered, but when Eve spoke her name there had been only a short, sharp silence before a stranger, another woman, had informed her that Mademoiselle Célèste was not there.

Filled with alarm, Eve had quickly dropped the receiver. Where Célèste was she had no idea, but she was strongly convinced that something must have happened. There and then Eve decided she would no longer remain hiding in the hotel like some errant criminal or defenceless animal. She must go out to the ranch immediately and get this thing settled once and for all. Célèste obviously didn't intend to get in touch as she had promised, and, at that moment, Eve felt suddenly too incensed to even consider returning home without seeing somebody—even if that somebody had to be Raoul DuBare himself. He might be a force to be reckoned with, but so could she be on occasion, and he couldn't possibly eat her.

Without giving herself a chance to calm down, when it might have been possible she would have changed her mind, she had started out in one of Mrs. Wood's cars, and now that she had actually found her way to the ranch, the only hurdle left seemed that of having to knock on the door. Which proved the worst of the lot, now that her defiant temper had subsided a little.

The house looked shabbier than she had imagined it would be, a great barn of a place with solid stone walls and a heavy roof of straw beneath which small windows peered curiously. There was an overall shabbiness which Eve found in no way compatible with the DuBare image. Maybe Raoul DuBare spent his reputed wealth on other things?

Whipping up her already failing courage, she knocked louder than she might have done in other circumstances, and heard her thunderous rapping echoing inside, hollowly, as though the place was empty. She was startled by such a thought as she waited. Célèste must surely be around somewhere, especially when she was being forced to look after Michel? But when eventually the door did open, Eve found herself staring into the eyes of a stout, elderly woman—a woman who was definitely not Célèste!

If Eve was curiously bereft of speech the person in front of her was not. Swiftly she drew herself up, her black eyes darting over Eve's slight figure as if actively resenting such an intrusion. *"Que voulez-vous?* What do you want, *mademoiselle*?" she repeated, as Eve didn't immediately reply.

Quickly Eve tried to pull herself together, gulping on a deep breath. *"Je regrette..."* she found herself apologizing politely, trying to subdue a sharp resentment at the woman's tone. "May I come in?" she requested abruptly, "I have called to see Mademoiselle Célèste. I am a friend of hers." Cautiously, and only just in time, Eve withheld her own name. Perhaps, in remaining anonymous, she would stand a better chance of seeing Célèste.

The woman continued to stare suspiciously, her doubts not wholly alleviated, it seemed, by Eve's very good French. "You are not one of us, *mademoiselle*," she said at last. "We do not care for strangers here."

"But you are mistaken, *madame*," Eve cried, losing some discretion in a moment when she felt the door about to be slammed in her face. "I cannot explain to you, but if you would please tell Miss Célèste I am here I can assure you all will be well."

"*Mademoiselle*—I—" the woman was clearly still far from convinced as she blinked uncertainly.

Attempting, in a moment of insanity, to push an advantage she obviously didn't have, Eve interrupted wildly. "I should like, if Miss Célèste is not here, to see the baby."

"L'enfant?" Pinched lips pursed with disapproval in flabby cheeks, as for a startled instant the woman dropped her guard, allowing Eve to push past her into the house.

"Yes, the *enfant* Michel." Following up the move which appeared to make her position stronger, Eve spoke firmly. "I should like to see him at once. *Vous comprenez?*"

As the woman shook her head in a dumbfounded fashion, Eve felt instinctively she had made a mistake. Yet it would be impossible to try and change matters now. Besides, her head was so tense with nerves that anything she might say could only make matters worse, and she had no possible excuse for thrusting her way in here uninvited. "*Je regrette...*" she apologised again, distractedly, as the woman turned away.

If Eve had suspected she was about to be thrown out she was wholly relieved when, as if completely nonplussed, the woman muttered sullenly. "If you will wait here, *mademoiselle*, I will see what I can do."

Left on her own, new fears seemed to rush upon Eve from seemingly many directions. The whole thing, the very atmosphere of the place, her own stupidity in coming here, was frightening. Helplessly she gazed about her. It wasn't the sort of dwelling she had ever associated with Célèste DuBare, nor could she remember Carol describing her home in France like this, although she had always been reluctant to talk of it. The house was unusual, different from any farmhouse Eve had seen in England. A flight of stone steps led up to the first storey, where the family obviously lived. These ended on a sort of terrace and a door opened straight into the kitchen. This was a very large room, furnished with a long wooden table, flanked by benches and wood-seated chairs. There was a fire smouldering on a flat hearthstone in spite of the heat of the day, and from the chimney hung chains on which a large pot was suspended over the flames. The strong, appetising aroma suggested soup might be cooking. There were also, Eve noticed, inglenook benches on either side of the wide chimney, and while the whole conveyed an impression of rough comfort it seemed scarcely in keeping with the rich bourgeois.

Eve sighed, suddenly weary; this was a minor consideration. She was, after all, only in the kitchen, a room which the DuBares probably never came near. Where on earth was Célèste? The woman had been long gone. Renewed indignation flooded through her so that when the door behind her was rudely flung open she swung swiftly around, her face taut with a nervous anger.

But again it wasn't Célèste. It was a man who stood there regarding her from peculiarly light green eyes. Eve didn't think she had ever seen anyone like him! It wasn't that he seemed to loom over her, his expression hard and indifferent, seemingly as annoyed as her own... It was perhaps more in the way he stood, impassively, something that combined with the darkness of him and the clothes he wore. Startled, Eve's eyes took in the high-heeled leather boots, his wide-brimmed hat, so reminiscent of western cowboys. As he drew nearer her nostrils were assailed by the smell of warm leather and sweat and she flinched, as if instinctively defensive against the lightning effect the man had on her. Though obviously almost covered in dust his good looks were undeniable, yet because of the dust which seemed to cling to every determined groove of his body, Eve would have been hard put to even guess at his age. A lot older than herself, she thought, well into his thirties. Her heart lurched as she returned his narrowed, inquiring glance, feeling suddenly the impact of an intently sharpening gaze. And she didn't, not after those first few wholly depressing moments, need to be told exactly who he was.

Yet it was he who spoke first as his eyes ran coolly appraising down the whole slim length of her. "Good afternoon, *mademoiselle*," he said, his voice curiously stirring her already heightened senses. "What can I do for you? You are inquiring about my nephew, I am told?"

"Yes—yes, I am." In her confusion Eve omitted to return his greeting, or indeed to speak French. Before his intense masculinity her own gaze faltered and fell as wildly she tried to decide what she must do. Hadn't she promised Célèste she would not betray her? She drew a quick breath without realising it was quite audible. How foolish she had been to come to the ranch this morning! How could she have imagined there would be little risk of running into Raoul DuBare? He had probably known the very minute she had approached his land.

"I'm Eve Reston," she went on in a breathless rush. "My cousin Carol was married to your brother. She used to live here..." With some dismay Eve halted, realising she was giving needless explanations in a muddled fashion that would never impress the man before her. "You see, I know who you are," she managed to whisper, as Raoul DuBare stiffened.

His eyes, icy with anger, flicked her flushed cheeks, but there was no indication that her news startled him. Coldly sardonic, his fine sarcasm like a douche of cold water, he inclined his head. *"Mademoiselle,"* he said, smoothly, "I suggest you go no further, you would merely be wasting your breath. Such information as you have given is not impossible to find. Have you any proof of your identity?"

Eve's eyes flew to his blankly, already hating him. It seemed a twist of fate that she carried nothing with her; she didn't even have her handbag in the car, unfortunately having left it lying on the reception desk at the hotel. She had, in fact, become aware of this before she had gone very far and had almost gone back, then decided this would be silly as the receptionist must have noticed and it would be well taken care of until she returned. Did Raoul DuBare actually think she was an imposter, or was he simply seeking an excuse to get rid of her? What reason would she have for pretending to be someone she was not? "This is ridiculous," she said breathlessly, attempting to ignore his query, to treat it with the contempt she was sure it deserved.

His eyes glinted. He was not to be put off so easily. "You must carry something on your person?"

"No," the turmoil within her tightened her throat painfully. "But I am not a liar, *monsieur*, I do know your sister."

"So you would like me to think." He was looking straight at her, his gaze derisive. "Other would-be kidnappers have sought to convince me of the same thing."

"Kidnappers?" Eve's mind felt curiously disconnected with shock, and she was unable to turn away from the brilliance of those strange eyes. For a moment her voice seemed lost in her throat and she couldn't utter another word. Surely she couldn't have heard properly?

As if he read her mind with a devilish accuracy, his mouth hardened. "You heard correctly, *mademoiselle,* and I might add that the ingeniousness of criminals never ceases to amaze me. One would never imagine they would employ a girl with a face as deceptively innocent as yours. How did you get here?"

The abruptness of this last question cut like a scalpel through Eve's last remaining fragments of evasion. "By car," she confessed weakly.

"By car? I do not see any such vehicle. Where is it?"

"Oh..." Swamped suddenly by a cold apprehension, Eve stared at him aghast. "It's—I mean..."

"Yes—?" he chopped through the mumbled words sharply, malice in every hard line of him.

Eve caught her breath at his tone, yet was impelled by it to continue more clearly. "I left it a little way down the road, behind a clump of trees."

"Hidden!" Now she could see triumph shooting almost visibly through him, but it was too late to regret that she hadn't driven boldly up to the front door.

"It was because I was nervous!" There was a feeling she was caught somewhere in the middle of a nightmare, and only able to find answers which seemed to give the opposite impression to that which she sought."

"Or afraid of being caught?" he taunted, without giving her a chance to be more explicit, his own opinion obviously all he was prepared to believe. "You were apparently prepared for the necessity to escape quickly should the need arise. And your fears were no doubt justified, *mademoiselle.* Men frequently overlook the fact that a woman's nerve is not all it should be, and they very rarely possess the expertise to prove satisfactory accomplices in a scheme such as this. Your friends should also have considered that Raoul DuBare might know too much about women ever to be fooled by any one of them."

Eve spun on him in a fury, goaded beyond measure by his outrageous line of attack. So he knew all there was to know about women! She could quite believe he thought he did, but his mouth had too cruel a twist ever to have known tenderness. His affairs, she guessed instinctively, would be violent, in keeping with the terrain he lived in, subtly calculated to bring pleasure only to himself. A woman's feelings would be of minor consideration so far as this man was concerned. Convulsively Eve found herself shuddering as her wide-eyed glance clung to his hard features, not knowing quite where such intimate thoughts had come from, but willing to be convinced that they had been wholly prompted by his vicious, unfounded suspicions regarding her integrity. Small wonder Carol hadn't liked him!

Dazed, she passed a numbed hand across her gently perspiring forehead, trying to collect her scattered thoughts into some semblance of order. If, as he arrogantly declared, he knew everything about women, then he might easily have guessed how very little she knew about men. He was a stranger, an unknown quantity, whom a girl with so little experience would be crazy to tangle with. No doubt, if he chose, he could be as ruthless as this harsh, barren land. Yet how could she let his terrible accusations pass as though she had never heard him? Human nature was surely never meant to be as tolerant as all that!

"Monsieur DuBare," she found herself saying, coldly, "you simply can't realise the seriousness of your stupid allegations?"

The word stupid must have been a mistake, as immediately she had uttered it his jaw tightened savagely and he replied in a hard, tight voice, in no way inclined it seemed to take back a single sentence of what he had said. Indeed he went on, intent obviously to insult further. "Your friends have certainly slipped up this time, *mademoiselle*. You are too naïve to fool anyone!"

"Why, how dare you!" Eve felt herself quiver in an agony of futility. "I only wanted to see Carol's baby. Why should I want to kidnap him?"

His eyes went almost insultingly over her, in a way calculated to make her blood pressure soar. He laughed, but completely without humour, his lips curling contemptuously. "Money can tempt even the best of us, *mademoiselle*, but for those of low principles it can prove irresistible. A god—a factor to rule one's life."

Stung beyond measure, Eve cried recklessly, "What money could I expect to receive from you, *monsieur*?" Deliberately she forced her eyes to travel around the shabby living room before coming back to linger on his dusty faded shirt, a button of which was torn off at the neck to expose an expanse of brown skin. Yet to become suddenly conscious of all that bare skin, covered as it was by rough dark hairs, was more than she had bargained for, and her heart lurched in a frightening manner. She felt hot, breathless, incredibly nervy, as his strength seemed to hit her like a physical force, warning her that whatever else this man might be he was no weakling. Lowering her startled gaze quickly before it could betray her, she added sharply, "From the style of your house it's obvious you are no millionaire!"

He took a threatening step towards her, his hand reaching out to grasp her arm, his face hard with anger, as if her imprudent observation had proved the last straw. "*Mon dieu!*" he exclaimed, "one can at least admire a thief who acknowledges the blackness of his heart, but for one who pleads perpetually of innocence I have nothing but contempt."

Her face white, Eve tried to free her arm, but his fingers held, gripping with the remorseless cruelty of steel, and the taunting ring of his words seemed to explode in her ears. "Good heavens," she choked, "Michel can scarcely be safe with a man like you!"

His breath was warm on her cold skin as he brought his face oppressively within inches of her own. "I don't know quite what you refer to, *mademoiselle*, but I am asking you to leave before I lose both my patience and my temper completely. Then you might not escape so easily," he threatened.

"And if I refuse?" Above the clamorous beating of her heart which seemed to shake her slender body, Eve attempted defiantly to ignore his threatening tones. The only thing to do, she was convinced, was to stand her ground. This man would be too used to having his own way to appreciate grovelling in others. "You can't force me to leave," she challenged unwisely, as if discrediting his ability to do so.

His white teeth snapped together as he regarded her with black cynicism. "There you are mistaken, *mademoiselle*. I am more than capable of removing anyone from my premises. Perhaps you would care for a demonstration?"

To Eve's horror, before she quite understood his intentions, his grasp on her arm tightened, his other arm going hard around her as he almost carried her from the room. Ruthlessly he held her to him, taking her swiftly down the uneven steps that led to the ground, taking no notice whatsoever of her frantic struggles as he deposited her roughly on to the baked earth below. The totally uncaring thrust he administered as he released her caused her to lose what little balance she had left and land in an undignified heap at his feet. Into her dazed ears, a moment later, came the sound of the door slamming decisively—a crash which informed her indisputably that he had not even waited to see if she could pick herself up!

CHAPTER TWO

ALMOST CRYING with fright, Eve scrambled to her feet, only half aware of her torn dress and bruised limbs. Wishing fervently that she had been a man, able to rush after Raoul DuBare and punish him for his sins, she stared for a long painful minute at the stone steps up which he had disappeared, obviously quite satisfied that he was rid of his unwelcome guest.

A whimpering sob catching in her throat, Eve turned away, her temper deserting her as quickly as it had risen. Left in her heart was only an aching despair, a sense of frustration, a guilty conviction that much of what had happened might have been her own fault. That she must have managed Raoul DuBare badly for him to turn her out like this?

Yet her own fault or not she had never felt so horribly treated! Raoul DuBare was a positive monster, a brute, and she regretted that she had no means of conveying to him clearly exactly what she thought of his diabolical behaviour. But then he would only laugh. She could imagine that strong dark head thrown back, his wicked eyes gleaming, and the picture thus conjured up disturbed so strangely that she immediately put it from her.

Bitng sharply her full lower lip as her side hurt, Eve walked slowly back to the car, determined not to obey an urgent inclination to run. She wouldn't put it past the man to be still standing by the window, making sure she went. Her chin tilted, she tried to move steadily. She must show him she was not completely defeated—if he was really watching, which, casting foolish fancies aside, she very much doubted.

Inside the car it was hot, suffocatingly so, as she hadn't remembered to lower the window when she had left it. The seats burnt and she winced convulsively as tears of self-pity began to run helplessly down her flushed cheeks. She knew a terrible feeling of being totally alone and deserted, and an equally intense if irrational longing for the comfort of a loving breast to weep on. Attempting to pull herself together, she groped for a handkerchief, the only likely means, she told herself wryly, she might ever have of drying her tears. And if she was to return the hired car by lunch time she must get back to the hotel.

Turning quickly on the hardened track, she pressed her foot to the accelerator, heedless of the ensuing dust as she left the ranch far behind. A wind blew in a tormented fashion over land and Eve didn't care for it. It was the mistral, and she had learnt that with the exception of the summer months, there were very few days in the Camargue without it. Today it blew strongly, buffeting the small car, whirling the inevitable dust clouds across the horizon. There were other minor hazards, apparently, if in a more enticing form. Fresh water marshes, grown densely with reeds, a trap for the unwary. Or the more attractive but brackish lakes, *étangs*, where other dangers might lurk, but none of these, she decided miserably, could be worse than the human element, in the form of Raoul DuBare!

Try as she might to distract it, Eve's mind kept tenaciously returning to him—and Célèste. She had come especially to see Célèste and failed, and there seemed little more she could do about it. It was no use arguing with herself that she might have tried harder. If she went on like this she would only make herself ill. With a little effort she might even convince herself that Raoul might have been more successfully approached another way, but no matter how they had met such a meeting would have been doomed to failure.

Straight away she had sensed in him an antagonism which had not been wholly because of baby Michel. Eve's painful sigh of bewilderment was constricted. Babies such as Michel, from ordinary families, were surely in no great danger of being kidnapped? Raoul DuBare, in accusing her as he had, must be more than a little crazy!

Back at the hotel, Eve left the car keys in reception, and thankfully retrieved her bag before retiring to her room. Once there she sank down on to the edge of her bed trying to review the situation clearly. The morning had proved a complete failure, in the nature of a disaster, but something else disturbed her almost as much. Her money was running out. Gloomily she surveyed the contents of her handbag. There was only enough left to see her through another day or two, and then only if she economised on meals. A frown of apprehension creased her smooth brow as she counted her remaining francs. It had perhaps been foolish to come with so little, but it was all she had decided she could spare from the money she had set aside to go to South Africa, and Célèste had promised she wouldn't have to stay at the hotel for more than two nights.

However—Eve closed her bag sharply; it was no good crying over spilt milk. She had done enough of that already. She must arrange to leave tomorrow. This would at least give her a few more hours to think of a way by which she might still see Carol's baby. If it was at all possible?

Eve's head, as she sat there, began to ache, and the longer she thought about it the more confused she became. To her shame all she could visualise was not the baby, but a man's hard face, a proud, dark profile, the quivering reaction of her own traitorous body to the hurting strength of his arms. She merely had to close her eyes to hear the attractive vibrance of his voice which had seemed to strike some answering chord within herself, making contact as it had seemed to with every sensitive nerve. She would do better, she knew, to remember that his voice had had a volume of bitterness in it, and that his eyes had held cold cynicism, all too clearly reflecting his opinion of women on the whole. And the utter indignity of that last scene!

It wasn't until she was about to tidy herself before going out to find a cheap snack rather than indulge in an expensive lunch that the idea came. Not a very original one, or exciting, but because the arid regions of her mind seemed incapable of producing another, she snatched at it. She might find herself a job.

Desperately she tried to think if there was a French equivalent of the English employment bureau and failed. Again a frown drew her feathery brows together doubtfully. How did one set about getting work in a foreign land? She couldn't remember whether she would require a work permit or not. Some regulations, she knew, had been changed. Maybe the best thing she could do was to ask Mrs. Wood, who seemed always so willing to advise her guests. Quickly, without stopping to change her soiled dress, Eve rinsed her hands and rushed downstairs.

It was almost three o'clock and the hotel was quiet, many of the visitors being down on the nearest beach or gently snoozing beneath mammoth umbrellas on the hotel lawns. Mrs. Wood was in her office as Eve hoped she would be. There was no one else around apart from her secretary whom she dismissed to reception when Eve asked tentatively if she could have a private word with her.

"Now, my dear," she said briskly, as the door closed behind the girl, "what can I do for you? Sit down."

Eve hesitated, her face suddenly pale, scarcely aware of being watched closely as she took the chair Mrs. Wood indicated. "I'm sorry," she began in some confusion, with an apologetic glance after the disappearing secretary, "I really didn't mean to interrupt you like this." She continued in a rush when Mrs. Wood told her not to worry, "The thing is, Mrs. Wood, my affairs here haven't worked out quite as I expected, and I should like to find a job. It's just that I don't really know where to start and wondered if you could help me?"

If Mrs. Wood was surprised she didn't show it, although she didn't reply immediately. But her sparse lashes flickered as her glance rested curiously on Eve's slightly torn dress, and her eyes narrowed a fraction. "I rather got the impression," she said, "that you were here to meet a friend, a boy-friend, perhaps. Someone who's let you down?"

Eve flushed, momentarily startled, in no way prepared for such an unexpected contingency, though, regarding her present position introspectively, who was she to quibble? Wasn't she in an extremely awkward position? False pride could have no place in her life at the moment. Yet, it came to her instinctively, because the DuBares were involved she must be cautious. The Woods had been in the district five years, they must know the DuBares or, at least, of them. It might not do to be too indiscreet in that direction. So ignoring a natural desire to confess the truth, she managed to merely nod her head evasively, hoping that Mrs. Wood would probe no further.

Mrs. Wood didn't. Eve's pink cheeks and hastily lowered lashes convinced Mrs. Wood that her guess had been accurate, and she was too busy to waste more time. "I'm sorry, my dear," she said, "but these things do happen. And now you would like to stay a little longer, in the hope perhaps that you might be eventually reunited with this young man? Well, you say you would like work, but are you trained for anything, dear?"

Quick relief overcoming a faintly indignant, if ridiculous tremor at Mrs. Wood's swift disposal of her affairs, Eve found herself agreeing almost eagerly and acquainting Mrs. Wood with a few details of her training. Whatever else she was prepared for it hadn't been Mrs. Wood's delighted exclamation.

"Why, you might indeed be the answer to my prayers!" the woman smiled, her gaze resting with renewed interest on Eve's face. "I usually employ a nurse, you see, as many of my guests have children and they welcome someone who will take them off their hands occasionally and keep an eye on them in the evening when they're out, or even simply dining in the hotel. Unfortunately the woman I've employed for the past two years has been called urgently back to England as her mother is very ill, and I'm actually looking for someone suitable to take her place. She hopes to return in a week or two, and, as she's so good, I promised to keep her job open for her, for at least a while, but if you would care to have it on a short term basis, then it's yours."

Minutes later, as she almost flew back to her room, Eve found it difficult to believe it had all happened. With an efficiency which Eve had found rather frightening, Mrs. Wood had completed a few details, her brisk businesslike manner proving instantly why her hotel was such a success. She was delighted, she said, with Eve's qualifications, her satisfaction being obvious when she learnt that, as well as French, Eve also had a passable fluency in German and Italian, languages having been one of her favourite subjects at school.

"As we get quite a lot of visitors from these two countries," Mrs. Wood explained, "this will be useful." She had dismissed Eve then, after telling her she could start right away, the sooner the better.

Eve had agreed, very willingly, promising to begin that very evening, without completely realising exactly what she was taking on.

During the days that followed, however, reality caught up and a little of her new optimism faded as she found herself having to take sole charge of numerous small children. There seemed little consolation in reminding herself that she was still in the Camargue, and because of Raoul DuBare's attitude had not been forced to return home immediately, without any hope of ever seeing Michel again.

Her new job Eve found interesting but very hard work, which wasn't, when she stopped to think, very surprising, as the hotel was a large one and most of the guests appeared to have their families with them. Sometimes she found it difficult to make up her mind who was the most demanding, the children or their parents. The latter apparently expected her to fetch and carry for them long after their offspring were in bed. Comparing this with her first position in London, Eve realised that there she had had very little to do. Yet here she had too much, and her gratitude towards Mrs. Wood changed rapidly to a rather wry cynicism, which fortunately she managed to keep to herself. It could, she was aware, prove a blessing in disguise that she was left with little time to brood over the DuBares, being usually too exhausted to spare them more than the occasional passing thought. If she did get round to thinking of them her mind, too tired by the chatter of small, excited tongues, refused to come up with anything new. On her day off, she resolved, she must try to get out and explore the area, then the answer might present itself as to what she must do.

It was on the following Tuesday morning, just before she was about to take a group of small children to play in the paddling pool, that she received another shock. She had gone with a parent to collect an inflatable ring from a car and was on her way back alone when to her utter amazement Célèste drew up. She was driving a small, bright yellow car and, although Eve could only stand and stare at her speechlessly, Célèste didn't seem in any way abnormally affected by the sight of

Eve, her only concession to bewilderment being in the glance she directed at the collection of toys clutched in Eve's hands.

"Hello, *chérie*!" she laughed, her eyes crinkling with a sudden merriment as she wound down her car window and leaned out. "Don't tell me you intend all those for Michel? He is not yet of an age, *chérie*, and he has enough."

"For Michel?" Indignantly Eve stopped in her tracks, her own glance widening. Really, for sheer arrogance these DuBares took a lot of beating! Here she was, almost exhausted after a week of worry, not to mention work, and all Célèste could do, after keeping her in suspense all this time, was to giggle and pass some ridiculous remark. "Really, Célèste," she managed at last with uncontrollable bluntness, "you do have a nerve!"

"Why, how do you mean?" the girl inquired absently, to Eve's disgust not even yet displaying a hint of remorse as, after her first few flippant words of greeting, she chose to glance about the car park furtively as if scared someone would see her.

"Look, Eve," she rushed on nervously, not waiting for Eve to answer, "I think it would be better if we talked somewhere else. I don't wish the so busy Mrs. Wood to see us together. She has the ear of my brother, that one."

"It was your idea that I stayed here in the first place," Eve reminded her, resentful that Célèste was avoiding the fact that she was a week late, that no apology was forthcoming. "And the so busy Mrs. Wood, as you call her, happens to be my employer, so I can't do what you ask even if I wanted to."

"Eve!" For the first time Célèste seemed to look

at her properly. "But what is the matter? *Je ne comprends pas*—I don't understand."

Coldly Eve stared at her. "You appear to forget that I've been here over a week. I had to do something when you didn't turn up."

"A week?" Célèste threw up her hands, her little squeal of dismay very French. "But, darling, you distinctly stated you would arrive today!"

"I said the first of the month."

"No, Eve, you said the ninth!"

"Listen," Eve began fiercely, "I made a special note of the date, the day and everything. I couldn't possibly afford to make such a mistake. Have you my letter?"

"I'm sorry, *chérie*." For the first time Célèste had the grace to look slightly ashamed. "You see, Raoul came across me reading it just after the post had been. I was forced quickly to put it in the fire and immediately he imagines it is from my boy-friend whom he does not care for. But I could swear you said the ninth."

Eve sighed deeply, restraining her growing impatience, fully aware that so far as this went Célèste was quite probably speaking the truth. In the best of circumstances she had never been able to memorise properly, but Eve couldn't understand why she hadn't, in this one instance, been particularly careful. Or was it that Raoul DuBare struck the same fear into those he loved as he did strangers? Remembering his cold light eyes, Eve found no difficulty in believing it.

"I came last week," she repeated in a more even tone, feeling it pointless to argue further. "I waited for three whole days before going out to the ranch."

"You came to the ranch?" Célèste's eyes were

like startled saucers, and for a moment she seemed to forget the need to leave the hotel quickly as she gazed incredulously at Eve's taut face.

In a stony voice Eve replied, "Yes—and your brother threw me out, literally! But I didn't see you."

"Mon dieu!" Célèste's exclamation was a hoarse whisper. "You must have been crazy ever to contemplate such a thing! I have warned you before about Raoul. And to arrive at the ranch, just like that. You are an *imbécile*! What day was this, you say?"

"Wednesday..." beneath such an onslaught, Eve's pale cheeks flushed with anger.

"Wednesday...*mercredi?* How was it I did not see you? I was at home all day. And how do you mean, he threw you out?"

"You don't have to disturb yourself," Eve assured her bitterly. "It hurt, but then I suppose you're quite used to seeing visitors treated in this fashion."

"But I'm not! I can't think how...Look, Eve," Célèste, a frantic frown on her narrow brows, glanced about wildly. "Look, darling, we can't talk here. Mrs. Wood does know Raoul, occasionally she hires our horses, and she is always relating, or trying to relate, some little tittle-tattle. Raoul does his best to avoid her, of course, but it is not always possible. She has the determination, you see, and Raoul is a man women like. I'm sorry everything has been—what do you call it—mixed up, but if the fault was mine, and I suppose it will be, then you must forgive me. But you must also agree to meet me somewhere and discuss what is to happen next."

"But your brother?"

"Oh, if only you had waited!" Célèste gave a despairing little moan. "Now Raoul is upset and everything will take much longer to sort out. We must reach a solution, but not here. You must come with me at once."

Such audacity! Eve shrugged indifferently, not in any way impressed. With that hint of imperviousness as she spoke, Célèste reminded her too forcibly of her brother, and a violent dislike of Raoul DuBare restrained her from agreeing too readily with Célèste's suggestion that she should go with her now. Besides, she couldn't just walk out. She wasn't free to do so. Mrs. Wood might have her faults, but she had provided a job when Eve had been desperate and Eve had no intention of letting her down.

"I can't possibly get away," she told an agitated Célèste. "You must wait until I get time off, and, as I've only just started, I don't know when that will be."

"But you are entitled to time off, *chérie.*" Taking not the slightest notice of Eve's protests, Célèste named a small village some distance away along the coast. "I shall meet you there tomorrow. This will enable you to make the necessary arrangements."

"I don't know." Illogically Eve began to reconsider, wavering in spite of herself. "Mrs. Wood does appear to imagine I've had words with a boy-friend, and I didn't exactly correct the impression."

To her surprise, Célèste's gay laughter pealed out. "Oh, Eve," she cried, "Raoul would be flattered!" Then, just as swiftly as she smiled she frowned, as something suddenly occurred to her. "If Raoul threw you out, it was surely not because he knew who you are? You can't possibly have told him!"

Again Eve felt her cheeks go red, and hated herself for feeling guilty. "I suppose I did in a way," she heard herself admitting reluctantly, "but I'm not certain he quite realized. He seemed to imagine I was there at the instigation of a gang, all set to kidnap Michel. This, I gathered, was what infuriated him."

"Kidnap Michel—you!" Célexste stared at Eve disbelievingly. "But yes," she added mysteriously, "I do see. We did have a little trouble, but so far as you are concerned, it still doesn't make sense."

"What do you mean?" Eve asked jerkily, glancing swiftly at her watch. The children would be tired of waiting.

"I'm sorry, Eve, I can't explain now. There is no time." From the corner of her eye Célèste caught a glimpse of Mrs. Wood's searching figure. "Here comes your so good employer, no doubt wondering if someone has kidnapped her new slave. Meet me tomorrow at three, *chérie*. You must!"

Flooded with a kind of angry frustration, her cry of protest lost beneath the noise of an over accelerated engine, Eve watched as Célèste swung the small car swiftly around and disappeared, thus avoiding a curious Mrs. Wood. That she had left without offering even one constructive suggestion filled Eve with despair.

It was with some reluctance that she did eventually ask for a few hours off next day, pretending not to notice Mrs. Wood's disapproving expression as she agreed. Eve was quickly learning that there was a great deal of difference between being a hotel guest and an employee. Her room had immediately been changed, the one she occupied now little more than a cubbyhole with one tiny window half way up the wall, which opened only with the exertion of a great deal of pressure. Her meals, naturally, were not the same, nor had she expected them to be, but the size of the portions were often so meagre that she frequently felt hungry, even though her appetite was normally small.

"It is just her way." Other members of the staff shrugged off Mrs. Wood's meanness indifferently. "In some things Madame is generous—in others, just the opposite. It can be better to eat outside, or take extra food to one's room."

But this cost money, Eve knew, and she still didn't seem to have enough to spare. Resigned, she remained silent.

During the next weeks she managed to meet Célèste occasionally. The other nanny whom Mrs. Wood employed didn't return and Eve decided to stay on at the hotel a little longer, at least until she had seen Michel. She thought it advisable to write to Rhodesia and explain where she was, though she skipped several details, and when Mavis replied, full of gratitude, asking eagerly about her grandson, Eve felt forced to renew her determination to see him, despite Raoul DuBare's attitude.

The first time she met Célèste they talked, among other things, about Michel, Célèste endeavouring to explain how he had almost been kidnapped.

"It was while Carol was out shopping in town. I was with her. A woman managed somehow to get into the house and Marie, our maid, actually caught her carrying Michel out. She said afterwards it was because she had lost her own baby, which might have been true, but the woman was a stranger and there were rumours of a gang. However, nothing was proved and she got off with a fine, but Raoul has been fussy ever since. He just won't allow Michel to be taken from home unless he is well guarded."

Eve gazed at her in bewilderment. "But why should anyone wish to commit such a crime?"

"Money, usually," Célèste shrugged. "It happens all over the world. In France we are perhaps fortunate that such occurrences are rare. It is, as Raoul says, an international curse, projected by greed. Nevertheless, he won't take any chances."

Which might excuse his rude behaviour in a way, although it still seemed ridiculous that he had suspected herself. "If I went with you to the *manade*, and you introduced me yourself, then surely he would see sense?" Eve insisted.

"Not where you are concerned," Célèste replied nervously. "I have a great suspicion that he actually did realise who you are, because he has taken to lecturing me again about your family. So, for the moment, I dare not do anything!"

Eve tried to remain patient. "But you must have had some plan when you contrived to get me here? You can't possibly have brought me all the way to France for nothing? After all, Raoul's dislike of my family is not altogether a new thing."

"I had nothing definitely arranged," Célèste confessed, lightly, much to Eve's disgust. "I felt sure something would occur to me."

Célèste's plans had always been like mirages in the desert, Eve recalled bitterly; she might have known!

"Actually, I have thought of something," Célèste surprised Eve by continuing, if with some hesitation. "There is a shallow lagoon, some miles away from our house, on the far side of the *mas*. We used to play there as children, Dominique and I. Sometimes Raoul came too, but then he was older. Our father built us a large hut for picnics and such and Raoul has always kept it in repair. It is a place where many rare birds are breeding, and occasionally I take Michel. The lagoon is not deep and he seems old enough to watch the birds and play a little by the water. To this Raoul does not object."

"You mean," Eve's face lit up eagerly, "that I should meet you there, you and Michel?"

"I will do my best," Célèste promised, "but you must be careful. There are mudflats, ditches of brackish water which you won't be familiar with, and if any harm should befall you I should never get to Paris, I'm afraid."

It might have been amusing, if her sense of humour had still been intact, to realise that Célèste's concern was entirely for her own plans. Yet Eve couldn't deny a small thrill of anticipation as she set out on her next afternoon off. After all, although this plan of Célèste's might prove crazy, anything was better than languishing at the hotel.

Célèste had given her clear instructions which she found fairly easy to follow. First the autobus to a certain point, then to follow a track to another point from which she should find it possible to see Célèste's car parked in the distance. The only thing to watch out for, Célèste had said, was perhaps a *gardian* rounding up cattle or horses, but it was unlikely that Eve would meet anyone that afternoon as most of the men were working on the other side of the ranch.

Bearing in mind Célèste's vagueness regarding the actual location of places, Eve wasn't greatly surprised to find the lagoon much further away from the road than she had been led to believe, and was both hot and irritated long before she reached it. But once there she did, to her relief, find Célèste, and the baby.

They were sitting outside the hut, Michel, now over a year old, playing happily while Célèste thumbed carelessly through the pages of a fashion magazine, taking little notice of the child by her side. For a moment Eve paused unseen, strangely moved as she watched soberly her irritation fast fading. He was a small, dark baby—a DuBare, not a bit like Carol until one noticed his eyes, which were large, and as warmly brown as hers had been. Eve felt her breath catch with a still aching sadness, a resentment against a fate which decreed that Célèste, who had no real interest in Michel, should be here instead of the mother who must have loved him dearly.

There came the noise of some laughter to her right, causing her to turn swiftly. Further along, shadowed by the tall grass which bordered the lagoon, were two men. They appeared to be elderly, their faces brown and wrinkled, creased in idle contemplation as they played cards, scarcely glancing at Eve as she stood apprehensively staring.

"It is all right, *chérie*, don't worry," Célèste, having looked up and seen her, called gaily. "It is only old François and Pierre from the *mas*. Raoul would never let me come here alone, but these men owe loyalty to me as well as him. They see nothing I don't wish them to."

"Indeed!" Eve spoke sharply as she advanced, not at all happy about the situation in spite of Célèste's assurances. To have said these men gave her loyalty after her brother might have been nearer the mark, Eve suspected. However, there was nothing she could do but let it pass, and hope fervently that it might be at least partly true.

"Come and meet your nephew," Célèste cried, her eyes indifferently amused on Eve's troubled face. "I have no great feelings for so young a man, as you will know, but you will admit he is a darling, *n'est-ce pas*?"

But before Eve could reach them, or even had time to speak to the baby, to her horrified dismay there came the sound of a recklessly driven vehicle. Even Célèste's bright smile faded as the scream of heavily applied brakes pierced loudly through the overhanging trees, followed by the crash of a car door which must have rocked it on its hinges. "Raoul!" Célèste started up, clutching Michel to her, blank surprise chasing the expression of supreme self-confidence from her small face. "Oh, no!" she whispered, gazing helplessly at Eve. "It can't be!"

But, unfortunately, it was. Striding through the scrub he came, around the corner of the hut, his face darker even than Eve remembered it. He looked positively dangerous, his mouth drawn thinly, and beneath his narrowed eyelids his light eyes glittered.

"*Mon dieu!*" he almost spat at his sister. "So—when my back is turned this is how you repay my trust! Take yourself and the child back to the house at once. As for you, you scum," he called with cold fury to the two old men, "I will deal with you later, and do not hope I will forget."

"And you, *mademoiselle,*" the ice in his eyes blazed to a burning anger when he allowed his glance to rest for one scorching moment on Eve's white face. "You I will deal with immediately, as soon as I have seen my disreputable young sister on her way!"

"Oh, but, Raoul—!" At last Célèste seemed to find her tongue although she had obviously no clear idea as to how she might put things right. Her stumbling voice and frightened demeanour betrayed this. "I don't think you should judge Eve too harshly. She only is interested in the baby."

If Célèste had hoped to improve matters she had only succeeded in making the situation worse. The colour of controlled displeasure tautened Raoul DuBare's skin, leaving it marble-like in appearance, a coldness which caused Eve an inward shudder. "Of that I have no doubt," he agreed icily, "but I beg of you, Célèste, go now, before I completely lose my temper. I do not wish to have to speak to you again!"

His temper! Eve's own anger, supplanting a little of her apprehension, raised scorn. Must he always be threatening people with the loss of a commodity he had too much of ever to run short of? Just in time she restrained herself from uttering her irrational thoughts aloud. The effort to hang on to her dignity was almost beyond her, yet she managed somehow to stand stiffly while Célèste drove away with nothing more than an apologetic glance over her shoulder, the delicate implication that it was now up to Eve to make Raoul see sense. Clearly Célèste would be of little more help.

Her soft lips compressed, Eve turned warily to the man who stood, hands on hips over his skin-tight trousers, immensely tall in his leather boots. Her fair hair was swinging, blown by the wind across her eyes, hiding, she hoped, the sense of shock she experienced at the closeness of his presence. It was the same nerve-jerking sensation she had known before and, while she didn't understand it, it aroused vague fears which she found no easier to interpret. And because this surfeit of emotion seemed in some way to instigate a warning she tried, if unconsciously, to be sensible.

"Won't you please listen to me, Monsieur DuBare?" she said. "I think," she added, greatly daring, "that you should. You can't possibly go on ignoring facts, or hope to change them by doing so."

His eyes skimmed her face, not one whit relenting, and for one dreadful moment Eve felt he toyed with the notion of throwing her into the lagoon, and her own eyes flew with startled apprehension to the dark, reed-bound water.

"I should like to, *mademoiselle*, very much," he assured her softly, with deadly accuracy reading her thoughts.

Eve swallowed painfully, trying to ignore the threat behind his words, choosing instead to repeat what she had just said, "Won't you please listen?"

She was not prepared for the way in which his mouth thinned with contempt. "So you would beg, *mademoiselle*—or bargain. Are you not able to make up your mind?"

Colour flamed, fanned by the taunting inflection in his smooth voice, to paint her pale cheeks vividly. "I seldom resort to the first, *monsieur*, and never with you would I consider the second. It is not a case of being unable to make up my mind. I merely seek a logical solution."

His hard lips continued to curl. "And as you naturally suffer from the inherent stubbornness with which one automatically associates your race you won't take no for an answer. You are stubborn and pig-headed, and yet you expect me to be tolerant. Very well then, *mademoiselle*, I will consent to five minutes, no more. But it is I who will do the talking," he finished enigmatically.

Without waiting for another comment he grasped her arm, the same arm which his forceful grip had bruised before, and where the marks of his fingers had long lingered. "Come," he said coldly, "we will go into the hut. A little shade might help you deliver the speech you appear to have prepared in your head so diligently."

"More quickly, you mean?" Eve gasped, knowing herself unheard as he thrust her almost rudely into the large wooden building only yards from where they stood.

If she had envisaged the inside of the hut at all she would have given it average proportions as there was nothing about the roughly hewn exterior to suggest the spaciousness and comfort she would find within. The floor was covered with cool green tiles and scattered rugs of a thick luxurious fur. There were small, glass-topped tables set near chair units deep with cushions, the material which covered them silken, obviously expensive. Soft glowing colours, reminding one of semi-precious stones, showed up intensely against the matt white paint of the walls, and across the windows hung curtains of the finest voile, shading delicately from creamy-white, yellow, pink and peach through to cyclamen.

It was beautiful, remarkable, a veritable oasis in a desert. Rather like an Eastern harem which someone had planned with care. And that someone could only have been Raoul DuBare. Not for the first time, in the short while she had known him, Eve felt her senses spin, and when she wrenched herself from his grasp and turned to face him she experienced all the terrors of a small, trapped animal.

CHAPTER THREE

For several minutes as Eve stared at Raoul DuBare the atmosphere seemed charged by an almost tangible distrust. Silence reigned, an uncomfortable silence, while Eve's thoughts raced alarmingly, her uneasiness quite clear to see. What did she really know of this man with his darkly compelling looks, his piratical manner? The trace of remoteness about him she found in no way reassuring. Rather it imbued a peculiar resentment that one so tall and solidly built should also contrive to possess such an air of elegance, denying as it did to his rough checked shirt and serviceable attire any claim to be the possessions of an ordinary worker.

Nothing stirred; the faint sound she heard could only have been the irregular thumping of her own heart. Outside there came only the occasional call of a bird, which seemed to emphasise their isolation, not detract from it. A shiver ran through Eve in spite of herself as his eyes went over her, lingering on her hair, as if considering its pale fairness, the damp, curling tendrils which had escaped the shining coil at her nape. Here was a man to notice, a man able, when he chose, to promote fear! Yet, as she met his assessing gaze, Eve was determined not to be browbeaten.

With impatient despair she tried to rally her wandering thoughts to decisive action. Such an opportunity as this might never again present itself, and here she was without apparently a word to say.

"I am waiting, *mademoiselle*," he prompted, his eyes narrowed now on her hesitant face. "If I allowed a mistaken sense of generosity to persuade me to hear you out, don't be tempted to try me too far. My patience is limited and I am a busy man."

"But I don't have a great deal to say, *monsieur*," she protested hurriedly. "I only wish to insist that you don't continue to ignore the fact that I am Carol's cousin."

"I wasn't aware she had one," he stated impassively.

Eve started. Had Carol given this impression? It was difficult to believe and, even if for some unknown reason she had, there was surely evidence of her husband and Célèste. "Well, Carol's parents adopted me, but I really was her cousin, not her sister, and Carol always considered me one of the family. But then I've told you this before."

"Indeed!" he gave the black-browed rejoinder more than a hint of incredulity. "You'll have to do better than this, I'm afraid."

He spoke in almost perfect English, with only the slightest intonation, otherwise Eve might have thought she hadn't heard aright. Was it possible that Carol had been forced to play down the actual size of her family in order to avoid Raoul DuBare's displeasure? "*Monsieur*," she found herself exclaiming, "I can't really fathom your determination to ignore plain facts, especially when you must know I can easily produce papers to prove my identity. Even if," she added deliberately, remembering another day, "I don't always carry such documents with me. Also, your sister knows me, and if you had spared her a moment she would have told you so. We were at school together—she stayed often at my uncle's house. It's not as if she had never seen me."

His head came up, emphasising the taut line of his implacable jaw. "So you keep saying, *mademoiselle*," he taunted softly, "and yet she fled like someone with a guilty conscience. I wonder why? I also wonder, *mademoiselle*, if you are who you say you are, what exactly you hope to achieve in coming here at this late hour."

His question, coming as it did unexpectedly, reduced Eve to a state of some agitation, and, in faltering uncertainly, she made another mistake. Célèste hadn't yet given permission that her part in this affair should be disclosed. "I wanted to see Michel," she replied, deciding swiftly this was the line to take. "My uncle, as you must know, is still an invalid in Rhodesia, and both he and my aunt worry about the boy as they are unable to visit. Not even you, *monsieur*, could insist that it is unnatural for them to be anxious about their only grandchild. So I, before going out to join them, agreed to at least try and see him."

The glint in his eyes deepened dangerously as he studied her tense face, watching how the colour came and went beneath her flawless skin, giving her a curiously young, untouched look. Yet there was in his eyes, as they wandered to her delicately curved lips, a narrowed consciousness that here was no child but a woman, if an unawakened one.

"And if I refuse to let you see him?" he murmured almost absently, as if his mind explored other, more interesting possibilities.

For no reason at all, beneath his calculating glance,

Eve's pulse jerked, causing her to assert more firmly than she intended, "I must have some rights. Acting, as I should be doing, on behalf of Michel's grandparents, I'm quite sure I have, I'm also fairly sure there is nothing really much you can do about it, in spite of your fine talk!"

"You are impertinent, *mademoiselle!*" For one awful moment as his anger surged, Eve thought she had gone too far, but instantly he reverted to cool control, a sneering scorn. "Whatever rights you or your family might imagine you have, I could sweep aside very quickly! Believe me, *mademoiselle*, I have gone into this matter very closely. Michel's place is here on the ranch where, when he is of age, he will inherit considerably—all that his father possessed, and more than probably, much of mine. No one you could name could offer so much or look after his interests so well. And let me warn you, *mademoiselle*, I am not a man to be threatened, not unless you are prepared to risk some form of retaliation."

Whatever did he mean—retaliation? There was that in his face which suggested many things quite clearly. Eve felt her breath catch strangely in her throat and annoyed herself by taking a defensive step backwards. Not wholly aware of what she was saying, she cried, "But you might have a family of your own! Even now you might have one?"

The phrasing of her sentence was so muddled as to be easily misconstrued. Again his eyes glinted. "So you don't even know if I am married!" Triumph rang suavely. "If you were familiar with my family then surely you would know this."

"Of course I'm aware you aren't married!" Eve

flushed, choking suddenly with the impatient, futile rage Raoul DuBare seemed able to arouse so easily, a rage, which after only two meetings, seemed to bring her to a state of hitherto unknown recklessness. "And now that I've met you," she cried, tears of despair almost blinding her eyes, "I can well understand! I don't believe you have it in you to lead a normal married life! You're too full of ice! There's no understanding or tenderness in you anywhere. If you were to hold a girl in your arms you wouldn't know how to love her!"

Suddenly aghast, she trailed off to an almost indistinguishable whisper on her last three words. But he had heard all right—his face went hard and his eyes glittered, and she had never been so close to a man in such a cold fury before. In that crazy fraction of time, as he stood staring down at her, she would have given anything to have taken back what she had just said. On top of everything else to practically accuse him of being less than normal must seem the final insult. Whatever had made her utter such a lot of nonsense? She had no idea where such thoughts had come from—only a fool would ever think of Raoul DuBare as a celibate bachelor!

Something, not an intentional apology, escaped her cold lips unconsciously. "I'm sorry," she gasped, her cheeks stained red, her heart fluttering, "I..."

Sharply he gave her no time to finish. Her voice faltered, cut off in mid-sentence as his hands snaked out to grasp her shoulders, to pull her ruthlessly into his arms with a sureness and economy of movement that confirmed all her half formed doubts. There was a sensuousness, even in the touch of his hands, which Eve could not but be aware of as he held her to him.

His body was like steel, tough, and as he dragged her closer, the buttons and belt of his clothes pressed almost forcibly into her soft skin, hurting her. But her despairing wince went unnoticed as his hand went tightly to her slender neck, tilting her trembling mouth to meet his as his head came down.

Eve had never been kissed before, at least not like this. She supposed she had led a singularly chaste life, perhaps because she had been an unusually fastidious child, more interested in her immediate family and books. Mavis and George had never actively encouraged her to seek many friends of the opposite sex, being stricter with her than they had ever been with Carol, and Eve had always tried to please them by devoting herself firmly to her studies. In her dreams she had always imagined a man's arms would be wonderful, an experience she might cherish, but Raoul DuBare shattered such an illusion. His mouth on hers was unbelievably cruel, bruising her soft lips while she writhed and twisted in his arms in a desperate, unsuccessful attempt to free herself. Helpless, she was forced to endure his embrace until he chose to release her.

Yet for a moment, before he did so, she was still from sheer astonishment or something like quicksilver ran vividly through her. His arms held her tightly and with a kind of shameful confusion she became aware of the response of her body to every urgent nerve in his. It could only be that he sought to punish, but when he lifted his head she could scarcely find the strength to push him away.

Surprisingly his expression had changed slightly, a hint of speculation softening the derisive lines of his face as he stared narrowly from her dazed eyes to her bruised, quivering mouth. "You are still of the same opinion, *mademoiselle*?" he queried savagely.

"Opinion...?" Eve's voice came weakly. Through the peculiar tumult in her head she was not sure she had heard correctly. "What opinion, *monsieur*?" she breathed, with the trembling air of one bemused.

"Do you deliberately misunderstand, or do you wish for even greater proof that I am a man?" he taunted dryly. His words which should have shocked, raised instead a pleasurable, if wholly puzzling excitement. Deliberately enticing, he played on her young nerves with an experience he made no attempt to hide as again he lowered his dark head.

Eve couldn't turn away, even while conscious that in spite of a curious inclination to follow the dictates of her fast throbbing heart she must resist him. She was no child any more and, instinctively, she knew this man knew it. She merely lacked the experience which her traitorous body suddenly longed for, a knowledge of men which might have made her infinitely more exciting to someone like Raoul DuBare. As it was, she realised hazily, the situation could be fraught with danger. The lengthening shadows and fragrantly scented air of approaching evening played insidiously on the senses, doing nothing to assist her in her effort to pull herself from his arms.

His grasp on her cotton-clad shoulders tightened as he felt her resistance lessen. "You make a very rewarding novice," she heard him whisper, as his lips caressed the smooth fairness of her temples, exploring the soft curve of her cheek. "I can be gentle, *ma petite*, should the need arise."

"*Monsieur*...!" Swiftly, as the taunting softness of

his voice smote her, she tore herself resolutely away, convulsively ashamed of her over responsive body. Raoul was almost a complete stranger; that she had gone to school with his sister could be no excuse. Lost for further words, she stared at him, her blue-green eyes wide. Any claim to dignity she had possessed must be lost for ever, yet surely no humiliating scene need be prolonged to the extent of becoming painful. Somehow she seemed to have lately acquired the unhappy knack of getting herself into awkward situations, but no one, she felt sure, could have foreseen this. "*Monsieur*," she tried again, "you must excuse me. I will return to my hotel."

His white teeth glinted as if he took pleasurable satisfaction from her strained, slightly haunted expression as she stared into his face. "And you, *mademoiselle*," he remarked, with a coolness she envied, "must discontinue telling me what I may or may not do. That I have found a way of silencing your eloquence very considerably is something I intend to keep in mind."

"I'm sorry—there were things I had no right to say." For an instant Eve's thick lashes flickered as she felt the apology tremble involuntarily from her lips. Did he have to stand there looking so wholly superior, his eyes, like a light flame, licking over her, missing nothing, carelessly cynical.

His head inclined the merest fraction, autocratically, as if he accepted her humbled gesture as his due. "I will take you back to your hotel, *mademoiselle*, if you would be so kind as to tell me where you are staying? I'm afraid I have no idea."

And he had never tried to find out. After their first, stormy encounter at the ranch he must have considered himself well and truly rid of her, otherwise, she guessed with sudden conviction, he would have made it his business to discover her whereabouts. Somehow, unpredictably, the knowledge hurt. "There is no need to take me anywhere, Monsieur DuBare," she stressed his name deliberately. "I found my way here. I can just as easily find my way back."

"You would enjoy thinking even less of me should I let you?" he taunted.

Again her colour flared in creamy cheeks. "*Monsieur*, I've said I'm sorry."

"Not very convincingly."

"And you're a man who must have his pound of flesh twice over!" she cried impetuously.

One black eyebrow rose sardonically. "Don't quote your bards to me, *mademoiselle*, I am not in the mood!"

Eve noticed he still refrained from calling her anything else but *mademoiselle*, which seemed to emphasise his suspicions, each time he uttered it, of her true identity. Nervously filled with an odd trembling resentment, she turned from him, making for the door. "I will accept your offer, *monsieur*," she acquiesced, without meaning to, subconsciously desperate to escape. "I forgot to ask the time of the returning bus. I intended to ask Célèste."

He followed her from the hut before answering, turning the key in the lock before thrusting it deep into his pocket as if something about the building irritated him. His shrug as he turned to her again seemed suddenly very Gallic, warning her forcibly that he was alien, not one of her own countrymen, but she felt too strung up to let it bother her. Maybe he was recalling other more amorously rewarding episodes in the hut beside which her own reluctant responses compared unfavourably?

"Célèste," he was grunting, "would merely have told you that there was no guarantee that the bus would return, and then left you to find out for yourself. It would be well, *mademoiselle*, that you do not expect too much of my sister."

Was that a threat—or a warning? There was no telling. Glancing despairingly at his hard profile as he expertly drove his heavy vehicle through the dense scrub, Eve was intensely aware of how little she really knew of this man who had just kissed her so roughly. She disliked him, and everything and everyone to do with him! Impulsively her mind made numerous decisions. None of them—neither Célèste, nor George and Mavis—could expect more of her! She couldn't bear to stay here any longer; she would tell Mrs. Wood.

The vehicle sped—driven violently. She had a good excuse, if one was needed, as they bumped madly over the uneven ground, not to make any comment on his sarcastic statement. There was, anyway, no point in discussing anything with Raoul DuBare any more. His mind had been made up long before she had ever arrived. Her feeble persistence hadn't changed one thing, only annoyed him and strengthened his resolve to keep Michel away from his mother's family.

Mulling over this sullenly, Eve was surprised to hear him say just before they reached the hotel, "Carol's father...Has he recovered at all from his heart attack?"

"Not really, *monsieur*," she replied stiffly, unable, because her head felt so numb, to reconcile his remark with his persistent refusal to acknowledge that she was Carol's cousin.

Yet he went further, if rather obviously against his will. "They have not yet returned home?"

Still stiffly, Eve murmured, keeping her eyes determinedly on the road, "The doctors don't advise it—besides, they can't afford to risk it, not at the moment."

"I do not follow."

Eve sighed, her brow troubled in spite of her resolve to present an indifferent front. She said reluctantly, "They like it out there, and, if England had an adverse effect on George's health, they couldn't afford to return."

"I see..."

Something calculated in his words caused her to glance at him with sudden suspicion. It was as if he deliberately probed for information that pleased him. Yet how could this be? Then almost as if he read her thoughts and wished to banish them from her mind, he attacked deviously, as she indicated vaguely towards the hotel.

"You may complain about a lack of money, *mademoiselle*, but you appear to be doing yourself very well!"

"How do you mean?" Again she floundered uncertainly, bewildered by his changing tones.

"Living here," he waved a sarcastic hand towards Mrs. Wood's large, modern establishment, "how many weeks?"

"Almost four."

"Mrs. Wood's hotel is not the cheapest, being almost first class."

The implication was suddenly quite clear. Eve's skin prickled with angry resentment as he drove swiftly into the car park and, before he had quite stopped, she wrenched open the door and jumped stumbling on to the tarmac. It made no difference that he watched her untimely flight with dark eyebrows raised, nor that Mrs. Wood, on one of the never-ending promenades, was coming around the corner, her eyebrows elevated almost as high as Raoul DuBare's.

"Thank you, *monsieur*," Eve gasped as her breath choked. "What you point out is no doubt true, but you may be sure I won't trouble you again—and that when I go I will leave no debts that might sully, even indirectly, your illustrious name!"

"*Au revoir, mademoiselle*," he returned grimly, as with an indifferent lift of his hand to Mrs. Wood he drove away.

"And what were you doing driving with Monsieur DuBare?" Mrs. Wood pounced almost before he was out of sight.

In vain Eve tried to hide her hot cheeks. She could see quite clearly that Mrs. Wood felt rather slighted because Raoul DuBare had not stopped to speak and, now that he had gone, Eve had no wish to discuss him. Nor did she want Mrs. Wood to know she knew him or any of his family. "He merely gave me a lift," she forced herself to prevaricate. "I missed the bus."

If she had hoped to divert Mrs. Wood easily she was doomed to disappointment. Mrs. Wood's eyes and wits, sharpened by many years in business, saw through her small subterfuge. "Raoul DuBare," she persisted suspiciously, "does not make a habit of picking people up, especially strange girls. I do hope, my dear, you haven't been indiscreet? I must think of the reputation of my hotel."

To Eve's chagrin she felt her flush deepen, until she felt an expression of guilt must be written all over her. It was little use trying to convince herself that Mrs. Wood's unfortunate phrasing was entirely responsible for the warmth in her cheeks. What, she wondered unhappily, would Mrs. Wood have thought could she have known what had happened in the hut by the lagoon? But there were some things Eve had no wish to recall, not even to herself. "I can assure you, Mrs. Wood," she managed, "that Monsieur DuBare is in no way interested in me!"

Partly mollified by the vehement emphasis in Eve's tones, Mrs. Wood's doubts appeared to leave her, and when she continued it was with a surprising archness. "You see dear, he is a man with a considerable reputation regarding the fair sex, and I do feel in some way responsible for you. You couldn't have known this, of course, when you accepted his offer of a lift."

"I wouldn't know, naturally," Eve replied shortly as, in an attempt to escape, she turned to walk away. In spite of herself a flicker of dry humour smote her. Mrs. Wood seemed to imply that Raoul DuBare was a kind of highwayman, laying in wait for unsuspecting victims by the roadside. She wondered curiously what he would have made of such an exaggerated impression, and shuddered to imagine the sarcasm of his indifferent comments. "I don't think I shall see Monsieur DuBare again," she added, deliberately.

Mrs. Wood walked with her, obviously, even while satisfied her fears had proved groundless, not willing to be diverted. "He's reputed to be well off, certainly he's a man of some property, but apart from this, his looks and personality make him much sought after."

"But I'm not in the least interested in Monsieur DuBare, Mrs. Wood!" Of a sudden the drama of the afternoon combined with Mrs. Wood's tenacious attack caused Eve's voice to tremble. "I hadn't the faintest notion that he's wealthy."

"Just because he rides with his own *gardians* and often wears the same rough clothing, people are apt to be misled. They say he can work harder than his men when he takes it into his head, but this shouldn't hide the fact that he's equally experienced when it comes to women."

Uneasily Eve stared at her employer with barely concealed astonishment. It didn't seem possible that Mrs. Wood was more than a little interested in Raoul DuBare herself, and Eve couldn't help wondering what it was about him that attracted women so helplessly. "Why hasn't he married," she asked scornfully, "as he's so popular?"

Mrs. Wood shrugged. "He's apparently not in any hurry. There is an heir, of course, his late brother's son, so he possibly feels there's no urgency in that direction. A Frenchman, more than many others, sets great store by a son and heir, so eventually I expect he will get around to marrying and having a family of his own. There has been a rumour about a girl who occasionally comes and stays."

"I see..." Eve said thoughtfully.

"You must excuse me, dear." Mrs. Wood's secretary was waving, and business must always come first, even before the fascinating DuBares. Mrs. Wood ran, leaving Eve gazing unhappily after her.

Later that same evening there was a telephone message. It was Célèste, although she didn't give her name until Eve picked up the receiver. For one awful moment Eve had thought it might be bad news from Rhodesia, but instead of relief she knew only anger that she should be made to suffer even momentarily through the DuBares again. "What is it?" she asked coldly, her voice clearly unfriendly as she resisted the impulse not to speak to Céleste at all.

"I had to ring, Eve." She apologised briefly for her part in the fiasco of the afternoon, before having the audacity to add, "When you come to know Raoul better you will realise he is not too bad."

"I don't want to listen while you sing your brother's praises," Eve retorted, feeling she'd had more than enough from Mrs. Wood.

"Please," Céleste cried shrilly, apparently alarmed, "don't ring off. Raoul has had to leave for Paris—an emergency has blown up. I must not see you until he returns, he says, but when he comes home he will arrange to bring you here, to the ranch. He is prepared, he told me, to discuss certain things, although he would not divulge exactly what."

"I'm afraid," Eve said stonily, "I won't be here."

"Oh, please, *chérie*," Céleste begged, "do not go away, you must not! I don't know what you said to Raoul, but you seem to have made quite an impression. He has been strange all evening, as if he has much on his mind. This might be just the opportunity we are looking for to arrange something for Michel."

"I'll think about it," Eve answered tonelessly, and, without giving the girl a chance to say anything more, she quickly replaced the receiver. Her few words had been deliberately misleading. She had no intention of going within miles of the ranch ever again. Wild horses, not even Camargue ones, she reflected with a mirthless grin, could drag her within miles of the place! She intended to leave at the end of the week. If she had still been a guest she would have left in the morning, but, as things stood, she did owe Mrs. Wood some sort of notice.

But unfortunately Mrs. Wood considered Eve owed her much more notice than a few days. When Eve tentatively announced that she must return to London almost immediately she met with icy displeasure. Mrs. Wood was furious and made little attempt to hide her anger. "I simply can't allow you to walk out on me like this," she exclaimed. "And it's not as if you have another job to go to. You must stay until the end of the month," she commanded, dismissing Eve from her office with a decisive wave of her hand.

Perhaps she was right, Eve reflected gloomily. As an employer, Mrs. Wood must have certain rights, and she did have her hotel to think about. In her position she wouldn't be given to quoting untrue facts which might easily be refuted. "Very well," she shrugged, giving in unhappily, but realising there was no other thing she could do.

During the next week Eve worked extremely hard, and if she had her suspicions that Mrs. Wood deliberately found her more to do than was necessary she proudly made no protest. Mrs. Wood might shout and bully, but Eve determined to keep her dignity intact. Yet there were days when she felt almost weighted down beneath the sheer number of children she was expected to supervise, and when the rest of the staff whispered that she was being "put upon" she found it difficult not to succumb to their obvious sympathy. To keep a stiff upper lip had never seemed harder, but what other alternative did she have? And, as Mrs. Wood had so ruthlessly pointed out, she had nothing really to return to. In spite of all the hard work she was probably wiser to stay. Her salary, though not generous, was good. If she saved most of it by doing without the extra meals she had got into the habit of buying outside, the small nest-egg she would consequently acquire would come in very useful when she did eventually return to England.

It was then, just as she began to imagine hopefully he had forgotten about her, that she heard from Raoul DuBare. It was in the form of a brief note from Paris. In it he said he was returning to the ranch and would see her next day. It was signed with equal abruptness—DuBare, and Eve stared at it in some dismay, wondering apprehensively why even the sight of his dark, masculine handwriting had the power to accelerate her heartbeats. It was almost as if he had appeared in person, actually confronting her. Why had he chosen to write? Of course, while he could have more easily contacted her by telephone initially she would not have answered herself and other people would have known. This, she was convinced, he would not want. Yet a note was merely a note, there was nothing to stop her from pretending she had not received it. It would do him no harm to discover not everyone was ready and willing to obey him, and he must know as well as she that there was absolutely nothing left for them to talk about.

Much later in the day she was still reassuring herself that she didn't have to go, scarcely aware that the note she had stuffed in her pocket was almost worn to fragments by constant re-reading. It didn't seem possible, in the face of such resolute determination, that she should find herself on the following afternoon clinging to the seat of a recklessly speeding bus on her way to the ranch.

Fortunately it was her regular evening off. Mrs. Wood had asked her to work, but for once Eve had been adamant, even daring to say she was going an hour earlier than usual—a statement which had met with such a frigid reception that in the frozen silence she had managed to escape before Mrs. Wood had had time to question such a frivolous disregard of duty. Eve knew instinctively that she would never have got away had Mrs. Wood had the vaguest idea where she was going to.

It wasn't until some time after the bus set her down that Eve discovered she was much further from the ranch than she had thought. Distance, in such a wilderness, she realised must be deceptive. On her first visit she had hired one of Mrs. Wood's cars and had seemed to reach the ranch quickly. When she had met Célèste at the lagoon it had been almost completely in the other direction. Now she found the vast plains curiously frightening, the size of them dwarfing her like a small dot in a seemingly limitless region of scrub and water. She had travelled a good way from the hotel, some twenty miles, she guessed, but otherwise she had little idea exactly where she was. To her right she saw water buttercups spreading like white carpets across sheets of water, and on her other side, windswept steppes, covered with salt grass. She shivered, concentrating on the dry land rather than the marshes where she remembered Célèste once mentioned wild boar lurked. Noticing the reeds, the thick clumps of bulrushes, she could quite believe it.

The sun was hot, too hot for comfort, and with it the inevitable mistral was blowing which bothered Eve even more than the heat. Fortunately the rough road was well marked so she couldn't get lost, but with each step she became more and more convinced she had been crazy to even think of coming here. Even to think of Raoul DuBare filled her with a painfull confusion, a growing certainty, where he was concerned, of her own vulnerability.

One heel was badly blistered and her thin cotton dress clung damply to her skin long before she reached the ranch-house and wearily climbed the now familiar steps, the extra effort required to do so making her feel quite peculiar. Possibly Raoul wouldn't be in and she would be forced to wait in the warm kitchen until he condescended to appear. Already she fancied she knew him well enough to be able to foretell clearly how he would treat her.

Eve knocked, and, contrary to her expectations, the door opened almost immediately, and a dark, pleasant-looking young woman appeared. Eve spoke in French, imagining it would be quicker, and was rewarded by a swift smile.

"Ah, yes, *mademoiselle*," the woman nodded, as Eve asked for Monsieur DuBare, "he thought you might come here. I am to take you to him at once. My name is Marie," she concluded sedately.

"But why shouldn't I come here, is this not where he lives?" Eve asked with surprise, as Marie stepped outside, closing the door quickly behind her. Marie merely shook her shining black head, beckoning that Eve should follow.

It was difficult to argue with the temperature so high and feeling as she did. It was all she could do to walk back down the uneven stone steps without tumbling to the bottom in an undignified heap. Not for the first time that afternoon Eve deplored the fact that she hadn't come by car. Quite easily, if she hadn't become obsessed by the need to save money, she could have hired one, and could now have returned to the hotel until she felt better, or at least to some not so distant spot until she had managed to pull herself together.

At the bottom of the steps Marie paused, glancing doubtfully back over her shoulder at Eve's pale face, then, as if deciding that all Englishwomen must look like wilting violets, she continued on around the corner of the building, making for a thick clump of trees a short way off. There was poplar, Eve noticed, and ash, some elm and alder, all fully in leaf. She was astonished to find such luxuriant growth here in an area which seemed mostly covered by low scrub. Through the trees, as they drew nearer, she glimpsed a house, a long, low structure painted in a beautiful clean white, set in the midst of gardens gay with flowers, again in direct contrast to the arid countryside around them.

Eve found herself blinking as she entered the imposing front door. Mrs. Wood had not been exaggerating; Raoul DuBare must indeed be a man of some substance to run a place like this! In direct contrast to the warmth outside the interior was tiled and cool and, as Marie directed her into a drawing room she noticed the eighteenth-century French furniture, the Chinese porcelain, Samarkand rugs. She longed suddenly to sink into one of the deep sofas, draped with furs. The sensuous luxury beckoned almost irresistibly, and it was only by concentrated effort that she remained on her own two feet. Marie said, "I will go now and seek Monsieur

Raoul," but Eve scarcely heard her leaving, and was startled, a few minutes later, to find him standing by her side.

"So—you have arrived," he said smoothly, his keen glance flicking her closely, his voice dry—as if he never, for one moment, had doubted she would come.

For an instance Eve made no response. She was too sensitive. Already she had realised the futility of resenting this man's ability to bruise and deflated. Glancing at him swiftly, her eyes darkening, she strove to keep her face in the shadows, that he might not read the quiver that ran across it.

"You have the evidence of your own eyes, *monsieur*," she tried to lace her own tongue with some of his light sarcasm, "but I believe I was extremely foolish to come..."

Abruptly he cut in, "That, Mademoiselle Reston, will remain to be seen. I in turn could be regretting that I sent for you, but once you are gone I must be satisfied I am rid of you completely. I do not intend, at some future date, that my conscience should suggest I made a mistake."

Eve felt nothing but scorn for his enigmatical statement. "It is good to know you have a conscience, *monsieur*, whichever way it works, but not that you consider it the only reason for dragging me all the way here!" When she considered all those endless miles in the sun she could cheerfully have hit him. But her soft vehemence spoke for itself, as did the tenseness of her slight body, the smouldering heat in her wide blue eyes.

He shrugged, apparently discounting anything she might have suffered. "I regret, *mademoiselle*," he bowed slightly, dryly, "if I have caused you any inconvenience, but I have only just arrived from Paris myself, having been unavoidably held up. As a matter of fact I was about to ring your hotel to tell you that I would send a car when Marie told me you were already here. I know, of course, that you have your own car, and while I agree it is quite a distance, you had surely nothing else to do."

Eve ignored this with difficulty, not willing to give him the satisfaction of knowing how far she had walked. He had called her by her actual name, even though he had quickly reverted to the more anonymous *mademoiselle*, which must be a sign that he half believed her story.

If only her head would clear, then this last interview might be made to justify all the humiliation she was suffering in coming here today. Everything about this man seemed, for no sensible reason, to be becoming too personal! This was merely their third meeting, yet he appeared to have the power to hurt her in a deeply disturbing way.

Eve's fraught emotions whirled, and, in flare of unconscious despair, she wished fervently to escape from him. Michel's fate must be dealt with promptly. "Please," she begged, agitation quickening her tones, "what exactly did you want to see me about?"

CHAPTER FOUR

EVE'S QUERY, put so nervously, hung between them tentatively for several seconds before Raoul answered. "You must know, *mademoiselle*, that I wished to see you about Michel. There could be nothing else."

Eve flushed, in spite of an all-prevailing numbness. There was in his voice a slight insolence which she found difficult to assimilate. He surely didn't imagine she had hoped there could be anything else? That she had expected an apology for his uncouth behaviour when they had last met beside the lagoon? Men like Raoul DuBare, she sensed instinctively, never apologised for kissing a girl, not even as he had done. "I am quite aware, *monsieur*, there could only be Michel, but just a short while ago you refused to discuss anything about him. I'm simply curious to know why you should change your mind."

"Let me put it this way," he drawled suavely, "you have already condemned me as a brute, and long before a certain—er—incident occurred, but I put it to you that your own manner of approach has been far from straightforward. If you are who you say you are—and I have more reason now to believe you are speaking the truth—then I think you owe me some sort of explanation—as to why you arrived on that first day as you did, the veil of secrecy you chose to draw over your initial approach."

With an air of slight desperation, Eve hedged, still reluctant to implicate Célèste. "Would anything have made any difference?" she remonstrated. "You've always refused to see me."

"You probably don't realise," he said curtly, "that once an attempted kidnapping was conducted in almost exactly the same manner. A woman, not an English one, forced her way in here when Michel was but a few weeks old. It was only because of Marie's vigilance that she did not succeed."

"But surely—" Eve whispered, as shock ran through her.

"Perhaps," he continued, interrupting without apology, "you can imagine how I felt when you appeared!"

"But I did tell you," Eve protested, unwilling to accept what she was convinced was only half of the truth, "and you had only to ask Célèste."

"Yes," he nodded grimly. "In fact I have consulted my sister, but she has been almost as devious as you."

Quite helplessly, Eve sat down. He hadn't asked her to, and, conscious of what seemed a deliberate omission, she had been determined in spite of a feeling of faintness to stand, but of a sudden her legs just refused to support her. "Please," she whispered, her eyes dilating strangely with terror, "I must return to the hotel. I feel terrible—my head..."

For fully a minute he took no notice, remaining where he was, a few feet distant, his dark gaze narrowed cynically on her lightly perspiring face. "I suppose," he taunted dryly, "this is all part of the act. Now that you feel you have established your identity, you announce that you are ill, possibly hoping to gain an invitation to stay until you are quite recovered."

"Why, you fiend...!" Through a hazy whirl of colour which danced confusingly before her eyes Eve was unable to see the calculating sneer on his face, but she knew it would be there. How could he ever imagine she would wish to stay when she would have given anything to have been able to get to her feet and walk out—and never come back! She couldn't even find the strength to continue her involuntary attack, her few furious words petering out as another wave of sickness hit her. "Please, *monsieur*," she pleaded, aghast, "you'd better get someone to drive me back to the hotel, otherwise I won't be responsible. It must have been the sun."

"The sun?" he rasped. "How could that be?"

But Eve was past answering. Unable to stop herself, she sank back, letting herself be enveloped in the depth of the sofa, her head slipping to one side, drunkenly, her face paper-white against the soft green velvet.

"*Mon dieu!*" he ground out, beside her in one stride, his fingers swiftly on her wrist, his head blocking out the light. His fingertips on her pulse seemed almost professional. "*Mon dieu!*" he repeated, "what have you been doing with yourself?"

"I walked too far, I think," Eve forced herself to reply through shaking lips as the room whirled in a most peculiar fashion about her. She bit her lip hard, knowing that all of a sudden her eyes were full of over emotional tears. "Please," she begged, with a slight movement of her head, "won't you just take me home?" Home, at that moment, was not the hotel, nor even London, it was the small town where she had grown up. She had a sudden longing for it.

He naturally thought she meant the hotel. "No, not

there," he exclaimed, unexpectedly curt. "Obviously, although Mrs. Wood's establishment is good, the air there must not suit you." His eyes swept her slight figure. "You look as though a slight breeze would blow you down. When did you last have anything to eat?"

"This morning," she muttered, scarcely daring to speak for fear the nausea overtook her. "I shall be quite all right, *monsieur*, if you would only do as I ask."

"And who is going to look after you?"

Eve ignored the savage emphasis in his voice, just as she hoped she hadn't heard aright when he shouted loudly for Marie. Her eyes, enormous, like rainwashed blue skies, fastened on him despairingly, and she couldn't control the trembling unhappiness which shook her limbs. Why wouldn't he listen? The expression on his face was so cynical she could have cried. Why didn't he just throw her out when he wasn't duty bound, or inclined, to do anything else?

Then suddenly there was a glass in his hand and she found herself hauled up against his hard male frame, and he forced her to drink while Marie hovered. His hand came firmly behind her head and the brandy stung her lips, making her choke. Wildly she tried to turn away, the fineness of her hair spilling over his wrist like silk, shaken, even while feeling so ill, by a primitive determination to resist him.

She might well have been a small child wrestling with someone of infinitely more experience. He controlled her feeble struggles by merely tightening his grip on her slender shoulders while he swiftly instructed Marie, "Mademoiselle Eve appears to be suffering from exhaustion as well as the sun. We will put her to bed and see how she feels in the morning. The Blue Room, I think. The colours there are cool and she might feel a certain affinity which might help her head."

How did he manage to insert so much hidden mockery into a simple statement? Marie, with an anxious if slightly bewildered smile, was gone in an instant, presumably to turn down the bed, and Eve knew a moment of blind, unreasonable panic. Illness was no excuse; she must not be persuaded to stay in this place, with this man. "No, no!" she cried, attempting unsuccessfully to sit up so he might see she was not in need of such attention. "You can't be sure," she added weakly, "I'm suffering from exhaustion."

As she had half expected, he took not the least bit of notice. "Isolated as we are in the Camargue," he grunted, "a *manadier* must be knowledgeable about such things—a layman's knowledge, if you like, *mademoiselle*, but one that not many of us could manage without. Besides, *le docteur* is a busy man, we do not call him unless necessary. My men often consult me first before the doctor. This is why I venture to conclude that you are merely suffering from some kind of exhaustion and require chiefly rest. As I have said, we will possibly be able to judge better in the morning."

When I might well be dead, Eve thought, curiously contradictory. She winced, touching a hand to her temple. It was pounding abominably, burning hot too. She felt vaguely sorry for herself and oddly resentful that he should sound so coolly unsympathetic, even while he offered a bed.

"Stop fighting," he ordered, suddenly decisive, as if her odd murmurings of protest irritated him beyond endurance. "I have had a busy day and, as yet, can see no end to it. Come."

Was it her imagination or was there actually a thread of tenderness in his voice on that last word, or was it simply in his arms as he lifted her, a normal but impersonal compassion as he carried her from the room? Even to be lifted brought back the terrible dizziness and she found herself clinging to him in an aching, suffocating silence, wholly grateful for the cool smoothness of his elegant town suit against the heat of her cheek.

"Marie," she heard him speaking, but in such rapid French it was impossible to follow. She was dimly aware that the woman came with them upstairs and was assuring Raoul earnestly that she had found a suitable negligé for Mademoiselle and would most gladly help her into bed.

"And do not argue, Eve," he said lightly, as he strode into a bedroom and laid her carefully on soft cool sheets. "You're in no condition, and you'll soon feel more comfortable if you leave everything to Marie."

When he took his arms away Eve felt strangely lost and unconsciously clasped hot fingers on his sleeve as if to detain him. "I'll be back," he fixed his dark gaze on her, his face enigmatically grim as he noticed how the whiteness of the pillow almost matched the colour of her face. "In a few moments," he promised, releasing her slim hand.

He was. She was scarcely between the sheets before he returned, in his hand a glass of water and some tablets. "Two of these will enable you to get a good night's rest," he said, and Eve was helplessly ashamed to find herself submitting meekly to his firm administrations. She swallowed the tablets as if anxious for the oblivion they might bring, so that she might no longer see how his coolly assessing glance swept over her.

It was an effort to speak through the throbbing pain in her head, but she did manage to say hoarsely. "In an hour I shall probably have recovered, at least enough to go back to the hotel. Mrs. Wood will be wondering where I've got to. Perhaps Marie would be kind enough to wake me up?"

"You won't be going anywhere this evening." Raoul DuBare retorted, Eve's persistence obviously irritating. "As for the good Mrs. Wood, I shall see to it personally that she is informed of your whereabouts. Naturally she will be worried to lose one of her guests, but it is a simple matter of picking up the telephone. I will see to it at once, so you might relax, *mademoiselle*."

Eve's eyes, too large for her face, stared up at him in dismay. He must not be allowed to contact Mrs. Wood—she must find the right words to stop him. But already the sleeping pills were at work, her lashes drooped, too heavy to lift again, even slightly. There was a somewhat muddled plan in her mind as to what she must do. She must ask Marie to find Célèste—she must ask Célèste to deter her brother from ringing Mrs. Wood. She must... but whatever else it was Eve knew as, with a wholly indifferent disregard of her efforts to stay awake, sleep overtook her.

It was morning before she woke, and to her surprise found Célèste perched on the end of her bed, appraising her pensively.

"Oh, good!" the girl exclaimed, when Eve opened her eyes. "I thought you weren't going to, ever. Do you know what time it is? It is after midday, *chérie*. You have almost slept the clock around."

Momentarily Eve couldn't remember a thing. She hadn't the faintest idea where she was or what Célèste was talking about? Then, because she hadn't been actually hurt in any way, it all came rushing back. The humiliating way she had almost collapsed into Raoul's arms and how he had ignored her struggles and carried her here and doped her ruthlessly with sleeping tablets when she had dared to protest! At least, in the light of her rising annoyance, this construction seemed reasonably correct. Gingerly she felt her head with nervous, exploratory fingers. The ache was still there, but only dully, the nausea was gone. Yet she still felt strangely tired in spite of sleeping—what had Célèste just said, almost the clock around?

Surely not? Aghast, she tried to sit up, while Célèste watched her feeble contortions with a kind of detached interest. "Raoul is right," she observed aloud and with faint astonishment, "you are quite attractive when you are not all starched up. That nightgown, *chérie*, never can I recall you wearing anything like it. Even your cotton dresses always managed to appear—how is it you say, old-fashioned."

As she digested what she presumed were Raoul DuBare's remarks, Eve felt her cheeks flush scarlet, and exhausted by a surge of dismay she collapsed again against her pillows. Rather incredulously she glanced down at the brief wisp of satiny material which Célèste referred to as a nightgown. Had Raoul DuBare really seen her like this? As he had put her to bed, he must have done, but it didn't bear thinking about! She swallowed a nervous lump in her throat, beset by an odd trembling.

"This nightgown, Célèste, as you must know, is

probably yours, and I have never been able to afford very much in the way of clothes. You must be aware that a student is usually hard up, and besides, it has never mattered much how I dressed. I've always tried to be tidy."

"Which at your age should not be something to boast about, Mademoiselle Reston."

Through Céleste's small squeal of laughter, Eve's eyes swung to collide with Raoul DuBare's as he stood in the doorway and her breath caught raggedly in her throat at his sheer vitality. He was dressed this morning in a pair of casual but well tailored cream trousers which he wore with a cool silk shirt, a cravat knotted with careless elegance circling his brown neck. She was struck anew by his absolute physical presence, the almost tangible strength of the man, because there was something physical about him, a prevailing masculinity she had never encountered in one of her own countrymen. Helplessly she shuddered. Her instincts had warned her, had they not, on their first encounter to be wary, but what possible defence did a girl have against such a dynamic personality? Yet she did try, when at last she found her voice, to assert herself a little.

"I don't think you have the right to criticise my appearance, Monsieur DuBare," she exclaimed.

"Not under normal circumstances," he agreed mildly as he moved into the room, "but you must admit that since you arrived circumstances have been far from that."

"Which does give him a certain licence," Céleste added gaily, before Eve could speak.

"That will be enough from you, *chérie*," Raoul

warned his sister, although his voice retained its prevalent mildness.

He turned again to the girl in the bed, studying her narrowly, his gaze wandering without haste from the ruffled strands of her pale hair to where the slender straps of her diaphanous attire clung transparently to her slender shoulders. There was an odd flicker in the back of his dark eyes, something Eve had noticed before—dislike, perhaps, but it was enough to cause her heart to begin hammering relentlessly at her ribs, and make the blood go rushing through her body. It brought a hectic flush to cheeks still too lacking in colour, a wild resentment that this man could have such an effect on her, and defensively aware of his intent regard, she gathered the white coolness of the sheet tightly around her.

Raoul saw the flush which painted her smooth skin and misconstrued it. "I didn't wish to disturb you until you felt better, Eve. There are things I would rather leave until another day, but I can see that until we have certain matters cleared up you will not rest as you should."

He glanced swiftly to Célèste. "You may make yourself scarce until Eve and I have talked, but first you can bring her a shawl, something she might wear until such a time she does not feel it necessary to cover herself up."

Eve had never felt so confused before. His audacity was almost unbelievable! She tried to raise her eyes to look at him steadily, only to find his green ones looking down at her, a glitter in their depths that made her quake inwardly. Even the smile which just touched his hard mouth was not the least humorous. There was something calculated about it, oddly menacing which in no way steadied her racing pulses.

Inside her moved a desire to spring out of bed, if only her legs had not appeared to be held down by leaden weights and her head still too fuzzy to direct a clear course of action. Célèste had rushed to do his bidding in a whirl of sweetly innocent alacrity. Between the two of them she might have little chance of surviving if she didn't watch out!

The bedjacket arranged, Célèste retreated with what she seemed to imagine was an encouraging smile, but one which Eve couldn't for the life of her return. The girl, like her brother, appeared, singularly lacking in conscience. Hadn't it been Célèste who had got her into all this trouble and who, from the look of things, was not willing to lend even one hand to help her out!

Wordlessly Eve stared mutinously at her own hands while Raoul drew forward a chair and placed it beside her. "Do you feel better now, Eve?" he inquired, disregarding her silence, the slight sulkiness which emphasised the wide curves of her mouth.

"I'm not sure," she responded reluctantly, not sure if he referred to the bedjacket or her health. She decided on the latter. "I think I should feel better once I was up," she suggested pointedly.

He merely shook his head. "In a few minutes Marie will bring you a light lunch and straighten your bed, then you must rest again until this evening. Only then, if you feel well enough, may you get up, perhaps for dinner."

"You can't keep me a prisoner here!"

"No?" His smile was slight and this time faintly

mocking as he glanced around the charming room. "There are those women, my dear, who have enjoyed being kept prisoner in a bedroom, but I will promise that you may come down for your evening meal if you in turn will promise to do as you are told until then."

Why did he have always to taunt her inexperience? Obviously the women he knew had a sophistication to match his own and wouldn't be troubled by inhibitions such as hers. Desperately she tried to keep her mind on other things. "I am not an invalid," she insisted stiffly, "nor can I guess why you should choose to turn me into one, *monsieur*."

"Raoul..." he corrected, gently but firmly, his eyes glinting as her slight body visibly flinched, her curved breasts tautening sensitively against the sheet as though his hand had touched her. "Especially as you are my guest."

"I can't believe..." Shaken, she moistened dry lips by biting hard.

"That a leopard can so quickly change his spots?" he suggested swiftly.

"I was merely going to say something about a change of tune," she rebuked him. "It is only a few short days ago that you were advising me to leave the country."

"It is not always a woman's prerogative to change her mind," he countered smoothly, "and I am not suggesting you should stay indefinitely. For some weeks perhaps, so that you might get to know your nephew. As you are my sister-in-law's cousin it might seem remarkably strange if we continued to address each other formally. Have you not observed how I have begun calling you Eve?"

She deliberately ignored his last remark, sure that he wasn't a man to worry in the least as to his friends' opinions. "I'm sure you would survive such a contingency," she said sharply, in no way reassured by his suave explanation. "Besides," she added slowly, her hesitation not unmixed with alarm, "I am not free to stay even if I wished to. At least," she amended, "not until the end of the month."

He viewed such ambiguity with raised eyebrows and Eve felt the colour which flooded her cheeks guiltily and put a hasty hand up to hide it, her eyes lowered swiftly rather than meet his.

"You don't have to explain," he said severely. "You see, I went to the hotel myself last night, after I had made sure you would be no more trouble until this morning, and I talked with one of the staff before consulting the good Mrs. Wood."

"Mrs. Wood...!" Shock hit Eve hard and she could only stare speechlessly.

"Yes," his reply came bluntly, "but, as I have just said, before she appeared I spoke to her secretary, who was not reluctant to answer a few questions."

"You mean you tricked her into discussing my private affairs!" Acutely miserable, Eve stared at him, her fears not proving groundless when he came swiftly upright, resorting to his old savagery as he attacked her curtly.

"Did you seek to humiliate me by working like a slut in that establishment!"

His hard words stung and hurt and started the pain in her head again, but if her cheeks paled dramatically he was not, at that moment, disposed to notice. "You're being quite ridiculous!" she gasped, her own temper rising. "I won't stay here to be insulted. I am not—what you just called me!"

"I wonder!" His eyes narrowed on her curved and generous mouth. He might easily have said "you kissed like one", and Eve felt herself go hot and cold by turn as she thought she read his mind. Then suddenly his speculative glance was veiled as if he deliberately restrained himself and he briskly inclined his head. "I apologise, Mademoiselle Eve. But why did you do it? *Tiens*," he exclaimed, "that room! Was it money?"

"No, no. Of course not!" In her haste to convince him she used too much emphasis which was her downfall.

"Oh, but of course!" HIs wits were sharper than hers. "Didn't I hear you say yourself a student has often no money for clothes? The secretary said it was merely your second position. You did not have any money!"

"I stayed for the experience..."

"Do not be so stubborn," he advised softly. "You cannot hope to hoodwink me so easily. You wished to leave at the end of last week, I was told, but Mrs. Wood forced you to stay on. That room where you were expected to sleep! A barren square, with a box-like window. And all those hordes of demanding children! Small wonder you are suffering from exhaustion. If nothing else I was satisfied that it confirmed my initial diagnosis."

"And lost me my job! You don't understand," she cried, "it could be some time before I find another." The mental picture of him sweeping ruthlessly through Mrs. Wood's hotel was enough to make Eve gaze at him in horror as she visualised all sorts of repercussions. "I think you have been impertinent, *monsieur*!"

"If so, it was only for your own good," he contradicted. "It would appear, Eve, you were so determined to see your nephew that you were willing to put up with any inconvenience. Such self-sacrifice should not go unrewarded."

Eve's fingers clenched into damp palms. "Just what did you have in mind?" she asked stormily, not unaware of a certain suaveness in his tones. Her stomach muscles went tense with nervous suspicion. Why was he so devious?

He considered her for one long unhurried moment before rising abruptly to his feet, as if her fluctuating colour and heightening tension warned him that she hadn't yet fully recovered her strength. "There is nothing, I must repeat, for you to worry about any more. I have seen Mrs. Wood and arranged everything. You will not be returning to the hotel; she has no further use for you and your salary will be paid until the end of the month. Marie has already unpacked your belongings which the good secretary kindly collected from your room, and I shouldn't advise you to quarrel with such arrangements. Now, all you have to do is to forget the whole business and rest. Maybe tomorrow, if you feel up to it, we can select an itinerary which might please you for the remainder of your stay."

Afterwards Eve blamed Raoul DuBare entirely for her continued exhaustion, the peculiar lethargy which she didn't seem able to shake off until next morning when she woke to find she had indeed slept the clock around, starting from after the light lunch which she hadn't found possible to eat the previous day. This morning, however, she felt better, really better, and though a little hazy about the time, was able to appreciate that her head no longer ached and the curious inertia she had known had almost left her.

She lay for a moment, pleasantly drowsy, subconsciously unwilling to allow the events of the last weeks to intrude on her aura of blissful unawareness. Then, with a reluctant sigh, she jerked herself back to reality and swiftly left the bed, running to the window. Below her lay the gardens, and she gazed on to green lawns and cool arbours, to wide borders, gay with flowers. Through a thick hedge of trees she thought she could glimpse blue water which might be a swimming pool, secluded and pleasant within the cool shadows of the high-walled boundaries. Although beyond this she could also see a narrow stretch of the arid, scrub-covered terrain she was coming to know, the immediate grounds were luxuriant, advertising no shortage of money, but rather a plentiful supply of it. How Carol must have loved it here, with such a beautiful house and numerous willing servants to look after her... Remembering the mistake she had made, if inadvertently, on her first visit, in thinking that Carol had been forced to live in other, not so palatable accommodation, Eve went almost hot with embarrassment.

Unhappily confused, Eve turned back to her bedroom, and recalling what Raoul had said about collecting her clothes she went to the wardrobe and found her dressing-gown. It was old and shabby and didn't really complement Célèste's glamorous nightdress, but this latter she meant to discard as soon as she had washed. Her face flushing slightly, she regarded the short row of her clothes which Marie had arranged neatly at one end of the commodious wardrobe. The cotton dresses, most of which had been run up quickly on a borrowed sewing machine in her digs, hung limply, without either cut or notable style, something which had never worried Eve unduly until now. Frowning slightly, she turned aside, choosing instead a pair of old jeans and a casual shirt that she had worn around London on her free weekends. If Raoul DuBare found her shabbiness not to his liking perhaps he wouldn't be long in packing her off home, and while such a thought should have cheered, it brought with it only a surprising touch of depression.

Making the most of the limited time she suspected she had at her disposal, Eve opened a door opposite that which she knew led out on to the corridor and found a bathroom, complete with bath and shower. Quickly she slipped out of her dressing gown and turned on the shower, glancing wistfully towards the bath, imagining the pleasure of a long luxurious soak in water scented from one of the range of exquisite looking toiletries which lined a glass shelf on the mirrored wall. Who had chosen them? she wondered. Had it been Célèste, or had someone else left them there? Some woman, perhaps, one whom the master of the house knew intimately? Someone with elegance and beauty, sophisticated enough to make full use of the superb, expensive perfumes to be found in those wonderful glass-stoppered bottles.

Nervelessly held, she stared through the sparkling rivulets of water which soaked her hair and shoulders before running over her slim body, the trend of her thoughts suddenly tightening her skin painfully, darkening her blue eyes. Why did she have to think of Raoul DuBare like this, a man who clearly only considered her a nuisance? It didn't seem possible, and her mind shied away from admitting it, that she had never felt the same since he had kissed her. His cruel treatment of her had, she assured herself, increased in no small way the hatred already in her heart. Why then did the thought of him with other women bring such sharply exquisite pain?

Flinching instinctively as if from a physical blow, Eve, in a desperate effort to thrust him from her mind, grabbed a thick towel and dried herself ruthlessly as she sought to regain a slipping composure. She was twenty-two, time she grew up a little and learnt to take men like Raoul DuBare in her stride—not to act like some lovesick participant in some modern tragedy who, after one brief embrace, was again longing to commit herself to the arms of a man who, with his undoubted knowledge of such matters knew all too easily how to arouse a passionate response. It was all a matter of simple experience, she decided bitterly, firmly closing the bathroom door.

She was dressed and busy tidying her room when Marie arrived.

"*Ah, bon, mademoiselle*," she exclaimed, smiling at the sight of Eve's much improved appearance. "You look better, there is now colour in your cheeks. You slept and slept and I was afraid you would not wake up, but Monsieur Raoul assured me you would, all in good time."

"I feel a fraud," Eve smiled ruefully as she thanked Marie for looking after her, and Marie glanced at her as if pleasantly surprised, as though she wasn't too used to appreciation from many of their visitors. "Mademoiselle is too kind," she murmured.

Mademoiselle could go down for lunch, Marie continued, but only if she felt recovered enough to do so. Otherwise she could have it here, in her room.

Reluctant to cause any more inconvenience, Eve drew a deep breath and replied that she would go down, but first she must see Mademoiselle Célèste.

Suddenly Eve knew this was imperative before she met Raoul again. She must get things straight. It had been Célèste, in the first place, who had insisted she came here, and it was Célèste who must tell Raoul this, otherwise he might not believe it. "Please, if you can find her, would you tell Mademoiselle Célèste I must see her at once, Marie," she said.

Célèste came eventually, looking sullen. "What a fuss you do make, Eve," she grumbled, as Eve tried patiently to explain what she wanted her to do. "Does it matter who asked you to come? After all, the main object was that Raoul should receive you. But now that this has been achieved why implicate me? He would only be furious with me!"

"But don't you understand?" Eve almost pleaded. "He thinks I've more or less wormed my way in. I'm convinced that, although he has issued a short invitation, he secretly despises me for it."

Célèste glanced at her, suddenly taunting. "Surely, Eve, you are not over concerned as to what opinion my brother should have of you? Don't you think he deserves to be deceived a little after the way he has treated you? And don't you think also that you owe me a little loyalty, a little silence? After all, I have sacrificed almost two years—two most important years of my life—to your cousin's child."

Which happened to be true in a way, Eve conceded, whichever way one looked at it. And while Eve could point out that Carol's parents had been barred from the child this had not been Célèste's fault. Perplexed, she watched, momentarily at a loss for words, as Célèste wandered to the window, pausing to tap restlessly on the narrow wooden frame before turning to face Eve again.

"You see," she continued, her small, piquant face petulant, "Raoul bullies me. I must obey his every command. When Dominique was alive it was not too bad, although he too must do as Raoul dictates. He must stay here and look after the ranch while Raoul enjoys himself in Paris with his *petite amie*. I have always been afraid of him, Eve, and you must remember it is I who shall have to live with him after you have gone."

In spite of the warmth of the day Eve was conscious of chill. "But I thought you were going to Paris almost at once?"

Célèste flipped her small hands regretfully. "Cousin Nadine has been called to New York. Unfortunately she will be there for several weeks."

"So it is not really necessary for me to stay?"

"Oh, but yes, it is!" Célèste exclaimed eagerly. "She will be back—and if everything goes well here... You understand that Mrs. Wood at the hotel told Raoul you are a trained children's nanny and this has aroused his interest."

"I see." Eve shivered, feeling strangely colder. So it was this information which had prompted his invitation to stay, not her personally, as a woman. This of course, she hastened to assure herself, she would not want, but she hated to think she was being considered merely in the light of a possible employee. Exactly how she might be expected to fit in here as a trained nurse she had yet to work out. Apart from Célèste, Raoul surely already had adequate professional help, and only now was Eve beginning to realise how impossible it would be to stay on at the ranch by herself.

"Eve!" the girl was exclaiming loudly. "You sent for me, post-haste, and now I am here you sit dreaming, and Raoul does so dislike being kept waiting for luncheon. I presume you are ready?" Her dark eyes swept Eve's denim trousers insolently. "I am not sure he will appreciate what you are wearing, *chérie*."

"I'm quite sure he will never notice," Eve retorted coolly, rising quickly to her feet, unwilling to explain the precarious state of her finances, wondering, at the same time, why she should allow these DuBares to hurt her so. "I will at least remain a little while," she agreed reluctantly, "but I refuse to make any promises."

As it happened, Raoul did not arrive for lunch. Marie explained that he had been called unexpectedly to the other side of the ranch and would eat with his men. "Always there is something," she grumbled, as she served the delicious light meal. "Always these *gardians* imagine he can solve every problem."

"They are busy with the herds," Célèste supplied further details without apparent interest as she greedily attacked her lobster. "They are checking the calves before branding. Dominique used to let Jules, our chief *gardian*, get on with it, but Raoul must go himself and see."

Had Carol taken any part in this intriguing activity outside the house, out on the wide open spaces of the marshland? Eve wondered, knowing herself, even after such a short time, to be full of an eager curiosity regarding the workings of the ranch. Perhaps Carol had learnt to ride and acquaint herself with the herds of black bulls and wild horses, but glancing tentatively at Célèste's absorbed face she was aware that this was not the moment to ask.

Afterwards Célèste left to visit friends. "Michel has his meals in the nursery and will now be having his rest, but I suppose you might visit him later," she said before she went, but not apparently feeling any necessity to take Eve there herself.

Finding there was no one around after Célèste had gone, Eve resisted the temptation to seek Michel out right away, wandering instead into the garden. For the first time since she had come to France she felt lonely, strangely shut out from this wildly primitive area of the Camargue. Or was it that she still felt a little tired, and would have been wiser to have retraced her steps and gone to her room? Only if she was really well could she ever hope to take all this in her stride. Yet, after sleeping for so long the previous day, another siesta didn't really appeal and, in spite of the increasing warmth of the sun, she continued to explore the gardens, her pale face soon glowing with mounting interest in all she found there.

CHAPTER FIVE

THE GARDENS, Eve found, were beautiful, even more so than they had appeared to be from her bedroom window and she spent a pleasant hour walking around them. Yet in spite of her pleasure a sense of frustration prevailed, as there were so many plants and birds she didn't recognise. There were wrens, a robin and goldfinch, but she found it impossible to name many more. Among the plants there were those which she had seen in English gardens, but, as with the birds, there were a lot she didn't know. She made a mental note to ask Célèste about them when she returned.

As she had suspected, there was a swimming pool hidden away in the walled part of the garden, but it was with some difficulty that she found the narrow door which led to it. It wasn't locked and once through it she halted in some amazement. The pool was long and wide and paved inside and outside with translucent blue tiles which reflected the colour of the water and changed with every faint ripple on the surface to a shimmering, iridescent green. On the opposite side of the pool to where she stood there were changing rooms, and outside these, placed at intervals on the tiles, were numerous chairs and small tables.

Quite a place, Eve decided, recovering her breath sufficiently to wander to one of the chairs and sit down.

She felt suddenly tired and glanced with unconcealed longing at one of the comfortable garden loungers, but to stretch out on it might give the impression, if anyone caught her, that she was making herself too much at home. Resisting the temptation, she stayed where she was, but the heat of the sun and soft wind which moved through the branches of the nearby trees had an hypnotic effect, and she was almost asleep again when Raoul DuBare found her.

Startled, Eve jerked herself upright. Must he make a habit of approaching her on silent feet? She hadn't heard a thing—it had only been instinctively that she had known he was there. Like a reflex her pulse had suddenly quickened, warning her in a peculiar, unpredictable way. If there was a single thought in her head it was one of relief that he hadn't found her in a more indolent position. Blinking uncertainly from drowsy blue eyes, she looked up at him as for a moment he towered over her before dropping negligently to the seat opposite.

"I wondered if I should find you here," was all he said.

The brevity of his greeting aroused odd feelings of guilt. "I'm sorry," she began, "I'm probably trespassing."

Rather abruptly he shook his head, as if impatient with such a suggestion. "Marie thought you were in the garden, and if you like it here by all means stay, but I think you would have been better advised to have gone to your room for a proper siesta. You are still looking too fragile, *mademoiselle*.

"I'm quite fit, really," she protested, with an effort speaking lightly, his voice with its momentarily caressing note affecting her strangely.

"You must take it easy for several days," he persisted, as if she had never spoken. "If you don't wish to remain in your bed you can come out here. Eventually a short dip in the pool would do you nothing but good. It would bring back—what is it you say in your country?—the roses to your cheeks."

"Thank you," she murmured, trying to remove her gaze from his darkly handsome face, unable because of a peculiar constriction in her throat to reply in any other way. "Célèste went out," she managed eventually, as he continued to examine her cheeks in lazy silence, "but I haven't been lonely, *monsieur*. I have enjoyed your garden."

"It is pleasant," he acknowledged.

She persevered. "This swimming pool...?"

"My father built it, several years ago," he enlightened her idly, "when I was a boy. Dominique enjoyed it and so did Carol occasionally."

It surprised Eve that his words brought more pleasure than pain. It was comforting to know Carol had been happy here, and she felt curiously disinclined to challenge Raoul about it at this moment.

"Yes," she nodded, "Carol would. I enjoy swimming myself. So does Célèste."

"Why do you always bring Célèste between us, *mademoiselle?* Do you regard her as some kind of protection?"

Eve stiffened, the brightness of the day suddenly fading before the returning mockery in his tone. Rising to her feet, she moved with swift agitation, a slender shape against the sun-flecked water. "You enjoy teasing me, I think. To begin with, it seemed, you wished only to dispose of me by fair means or foul. Now—"

she hesitated, her face flushing with confusion, at some loss to describe accurately the way he chose to treat her now. The thread of gentleness alarmed rather than reassured, the transition from cool enmity too sudden to ring true. This outward show of benign civility could be part of a deliberate course of action, planned deviously to succeed where brute strength had failed in ridding himself once and for all of Carol's family. This man, she realised despairingly, would always be one step ahead. It was up to her to be wary, not to allow a few soft words to weaken her defences, yet how could she accuse him of duplicity on the evidence of the past two days? The flush of embarrassment in her cheeks deepened as, unable to find the right words to continue, she began to walk quickly away.

"*Mademoiselle!*" His voice caught her like an arrowhead between the shoulders, bringing her headlong flight to an abrupt halt. "Come back at once," he ordered, and she didn't know how a man's tones could carry such command yet be so low.

Curiously unable to follow her own inclinations to disobey, she found herself doing as she was told, even to resuming her seat, aware, as she did so, of his downward glance of satisfaction. The glint in his eyes sharpened. "Do you always leave your sentences unfinished, Eve, or was it simply that you wished to spare my feelings? I shouldn't have thought you lacking in courage, whatever else."

"I promise you won't find that, *monsieur*," she retorted shortly, seeking to convince him of a virtue she was not sure she possessed, but unwilling he should guess. "I'm sure your feelings are too tough to be dented by any words of mine. I'm not sure why I felt a desire to leave the garden, nor why I changed my mind and didn't do so."

His hard mouth quirked, as if he understood that her little explanation was quite ridiculous. "I am used to being obeyed, Eve," he purred, taking her acquiescence wholly for granted. "You will find it easier to remember."

"Not so painful, you mean?" She had never intended referring to an incident she fancied would have been better forgotten, if only for her dignity's sake, but impulsively it had slipped out.

"So...?" his eyes raked her. "Explain yourself, *mademoiselle*."

The blood beat hot in her temples, even to think of it, and her tongue felt paralysed, but afraid that he should notice even a twinge of apprehension, she lifted her chin defiantly. How dared he pretend she had no cause for complaint! "On my first visit here you must remember how you almost threw me down those steps? I was hurt—bruised!"

In a second as his gaze met hers it sharpened to a frown. "You were? I didn't realise. But," he shrugged sardonically, "I do recall that I was furious."

"You were that all right!"

"Hush, *mademoiselle*," coolly restrictive, his eyes slid over her, "you are too sensitive, and perhaps this makes you too responsive. There is a fragility about you which might arouse a devil in a man. To a small degree I still consider my behaviour was excusable, but I am not a brute. I am sure I didn't deal too harshly. These bruises you speak of?"

"I still have them faintly." Carried away by a consuming flare of indignation, Eve pushed up her sleeve to where the smooth young skin of her upper arm still showed a shadowed mark.

His eyes dwelt on the bare skin thoughtfully, and though he murmured softly that he was sorry, Eve sensed instinctively that he was no such thing. That the infliction of pain, in her case, was something he had enjoyed, and might still do, should the need for further chastisement arise. From a distance she heard him add, "It appears I owe you an apology, Eve."

Her breath curiously uneven, Eve dropped the subject as if it burnt. "I believe so—yes, but I would much rather have a few straight answers, *monsieur*."

"To what?" His dark brows rose.

"Regarding the way you treat my family, for a start."

"And I suggest, Eve," he objected suavely, "that we leave such a discussion for the time being." As she sought to protest his hand went out to cover her nervous fingers firmly, giving emphasis to his next words. "I can't think any useful purpose would be served by dissecting the past until we know each other better. On our future relationship so much could depend, so you must have patience, *mademoiselle*. If you are to stay here for a week or two then it is possible to leave things as they are at present. If I have been over-hasty about certain matters then I do not wish to make the same mistake again."

So he admitted he had been wrong, but like a tyrant was not prepared to dwell on his misdeeds! Swiftly, as if stung, Eve jerked her hand from under his, a release for her taut senses. How conveniently he wrapped up years of irrational behaviour like a bundle of scrap to be thrown lightly aside, the riddles he talked merely a means of setting up a camouflaging confusion. Bitterly she stared at him, at his dark face, knowing a desire, stronger than any she had ever known before, to hurt. Yet, even as she stared, there washed over her a finely ground frustration. How could she ever hope to wound anyone so impervious? For all his plausible words he left her in no doubt he held the whip hand. If she were to protest too much, make too much fuss then, just as easily as he had given it, he could withdraw his invitation, and she had yet to meet Carol's baby.

"As you like, *monsieur*," she agreed aloofly, her coolness giving, she hoped, a clear indication that while she was being forced to ignore the past it was not so easily forgotten. "And," she added, with unwonted sharpness, "as my time is limited, I should like to meet Michel as soon as it can be arranged."

If she had expected to annoy him a little with this last observation she was doomed to disappointment. He looked merely amused by the outrage in her eyes. "I do believe I like you better when you forget to be the demure nursemaid, my dear. Too much sweetness can be cloying. On occasion you have a refreshing tartness which I enjoy. Carol could never defend herself as you do."

Should he not have said Carol was no fighter? If Carol had been fond of having her own way she had usually succeeded in getting it by other means. Yet what right had Raoul DuBare to sound so critical? Active dislike against the man stirred. "You forget, *monsieur*, Carol and I were only cousins, and she was always gentle."

Of course," there was in his voice an unfeeling restraint as he rose to his feet, drawing her up with him. "You wish to see the child? I will take you to him myself, but as you are still too thin and pale I do not want you to wear yourself out—not again. You may stay with him for a short while and then go to your room and rest. Tomorrow, if you wish, a little longer, but only in easy stages, *mademoiselle*."

Restlessly, Eve flinched, reluctant to agree he could be right, that it was possible. Her breathing still came painfully, even her pulse behaved erratically, too aware of his steely fingers beneath her arm as he led her from the garden. She was also aware of an increasing need to oppose him. "I promise not to do anything foolish, but I cannot rest for ever, *monsieur*."

Eve had often wondered exactly how she would feel about Carol's baby, should she ever get to know him. Her present work would have been impossible had she not been fond of children en masse, and the one individual child whom she had looked after in her first job had presented no problems. He had been a particularly placid boy, very easy to manage. For Michel she hadn't expected to feel any immediate attachment such as a grandparent or real aunt might have done, and she was surprised at the way her heart went out to him when she and Raoul entered the nursery and found him weeping. His whimpering cries could in fact be heard as they walked along the wide corridor towards his room, and Eve was quick to note the dark frown on Raoul's face as the cries rose in volumes of sheer rage, a crescendo that subsided pathetically to defeated, hiccuping sobs.

"*Mon dieu*," he breathed, pulling open the closed door, "can there be no competence anywhere when my back is turned?" His voice rose angrily as, after one comprehensive glance over Eve's head, he stepped back into the corridor. "Marie!" he called, his mouth grim.

It was within seconds of Eve scooping the baby up that a rather scared young girl came running along the passage. "I am sorry, Monsieur DuBare," she gasped, breathlessly, "but Marie is too busy—*le diner, vous comprenez, monsieur?* And I must help with the preparation which she tells me is more important than *le petit.*"

"Nonsense," Raoul declared curtly, glaring at the girl, "You may go and tell Marie that the child is more important than any meal! I will be down to have a word with her immediately."

"*Bien sûr, monsieur,*" the girl bobbed, Eve thought ridiculously, as she backed frantically from the room, her small face nervously reflecting her alarmed reaction. "I will tell her, *monsieur,*" she cried earnestly as she disappeared.

Still furious, Raoul turned on Eve's disapproving stare. "And you can take that—what-is-going-on-here? look off your face, *mademoiselle.* Michel is not neglected, it is probably a case of having too many people attending to him, one half of whom are always supposing the other half is in the nursery, while in reality there is often no one there at all. Michel is almost two and it will do him little irreparable harm to yell a little. It is the incompetence I find irritating."

Eve stared at him stoically as Michel clung to her like a limpet, not wholly aware yet that she was a stranger, indifferent, it seemed, to anything but the comfort of her rescuing arms. "I haven't had time to wonder anything of the sort, *monsieur,*" she replied stiffly, as she held the baby close. "Michel, as you say, is almost two, but a young child can suffer perhaps even more than a baby from too great mixture of affection and neglect. Children of any age need to feel secure."

"And I do not require a lecture on child psychology," he said savagely, continuing unfairly. "I will not have him turned into a milksop, *mademoiselle.* If he is mollycoddled too much he will never make a satisfactory *manadier.*"

Michel's cries had ceased, as if Eve's gentle authority had dispelled his fleeting fears. Possessively triumphant, she cradled him to her and across his head fearlessly met Raoul DuBare's narrowed, speculative glance. In yet another way he was no doubt telling her that he would never let Michel go, but suddenly she didn't care. That he was irritated by the situation seemed clear. There might be room for optimism yet if she trod warily.

"I will stay with him, *monsieur,*" she replied, coolly ignoring his taunt. "He appears to need changing. I am sure you can't object if I do that?"

"Just for one half hour, *mademoiselle,*" his eyes glinted darkly as he nodded briefly. "Then, if you are not in your room, I will come and conduct you there myself."

He would be quite capable of it, she thought, startled, as he left abruptly, after a swift word with the baby. Michel, to her surprise, had responded happily, holding out his chubby arms as though he was not in the least apprehensive of his formidable uncle. She had been further astonished when Raoul had laughed and tossed his nephew almost to the ceiling, and it had been when he had held the then gurgling child for another moment that she had noticed the resemblance, as she had seen it before. Michel was truly a DuBare.

"You like children?" Raoul asked, the next evening, as they had drinks before dinner. Célèste was not yet down, as it was still early, but Eve had been restless in her room and unable to stay there any longer.

"I would scarcely be a trained nanny did I not," Eve answered, staring down at her drink, blaming the dullness of her reply to a lack of confidence in her appearance. How much better she could have faced Raoul DuBare if she hadn't felt so dowdy. Strangely enough, in the hotel it hadn't seemed to matter. There, when she had been on her own, the plainness of her attire had helped her to remain inconspicuous, but now she wished fervently that she had possessed a prettier dress. The one she wore this evening was, she realised unhappily, a mistake, and that might prove a kinder description than the one Raoul DuBare had in mind, judging from his expression! The dress was cotton, a stiff material which tended to crease each time she sat down, and the peculiar shade of green did nothing for her particular colouring. At best it was respectable, and tenaciously Eve tried to cling to this assurance, pushing all thought of something more glamorous, a little smarter, from her mind.

Raoul's eyes, she was well aware, were quite frankly assessing the cost of her entire wardrobe. Faintly resentful she flushed, not used to a man's close scrutiny although she knew his to be wholly objective, a mere curiosity regarding her unfashionable appearance. This she was prepared to tolerate, but not that he should speak outright. An Englishman wouldn't have done, she felt sure, but Raoul was different.

"It is as well your figure is naturally good, *ma chérie*, otherwise that dress—! *Mon dieu*, where did you get it!"

She had expected a few more polite remarks regarding her career, and her eyes flew open wide with a sparkling resentment as they met his. "I made it myself, *monsieur*," she choked, "before I came to France."

"Otherwise you would have chosen something more flattering," he quirked. "I find it difficult to be captivated by what you have on. It is obvious, Mademoiselle Reston, that you are not skilled in the art of dressmaking."

"I have never pretended to be," she retorted stiffly, the indifferent tilt of her chin designed to hide a growing sensitivity to his criticism, and not willing that he should have any knowledge of her recently born desire for something nice, a longing which she hazily supposed might have been aroused, stupidly, by the sight of a few decorative jars in a bathroom. Raoul DuBare, she tried to convince herself, had nothing at all to do with it! "Nor am I very interested," she added coolly.

Idly he continued, rocking back on his heels, his teeth glinting white in a smoothly calculating smile, clearly doubting the truth of her brittle little statement. "If, as you declare, you are indeed one of the family, then you must not resent a few honest remarks from one of its members. I personally prefer women to be chic, *ma chère*, but perhaps your boy-friends rank among today's young revolutionaries who do not consider it the thing to be well dressed?"

Innocently she fell into the trap, although she wasn't aware of it at the time. "I have no special boy-friend, *monsieur*. I have devoted myself to my training."

His eyes smouldered with a momentary satisfaction. "And you have only just finished this?"

"No, I held one position before I came here." She didn't know why she felt so reluctant to give him this information about herself, unless it only seemed to make her more vulnerable.

He took a considering drink from the glass held contemplatively in his fine-boned hands. "You look too young, *mademoiselle*."

"I'm almost twenty-two."

"So old? Forgive me, you look about seventeen—I find it difficult to believe you are older than Célèste. And you so happily devote yourself to other people's children, while being old enough to have a family yourself?"

His eyes added many things, while his face remained a polite mask. Stung by a sudden warm confusion, she answered ingenuously, "One has to acquire a husband first, *monsieur*."

"Ah, an old-fashioned girl!"

Eve squirmed, furious with herself, and even more at Raoul DuBare's sardonic tones, but she refused to be drawn further. Biting back a sharp retort, which might only have bounced off his tough exterior, she said instead, "Your nephew is a good child, *monsieur*. I enjoy being with him."

There was silence for a moment, and she felt annoyed by his lack of interest when he said, "He is a good child, yes, well content with his lot, and I should like him to remain so, but I suggest we leave the nursery for the evening, *ma chère*. It is a time when babies, if they are well, should be tucked up in bed and forgotten."

Which might be an easy matter in a place like this where there were numerous servants to keep an eye on them, she wanted to retort, but somehow dared not, some part of her still wary of this man's reactions. Yet she couldn't resist what was probably a pertinent remark. "Some fathers only manage to see their children in the evening, *monsieur*."

"And I should wish only to see my wife. You must allow that men can differ, *ma chère*, and pray do not begin to waste your abundant sympathy on a metamorphosed wife. If ever I acquire one I shall see to it personally that she has, at this hour, no thought left in her head for the nursery."

A wave of indiscernible feeling swept over Eve, though she willed her face not to reflect it. "It is possible," she whispered stubbornly, "she might not share your views."

"She would soon forget such independence and become compliant, *mademoiselle*. I should soon teach her that these hours are to be enjoyed in a different way."

Strangely Eve shuddered almost visibly as she stared down at her trembling fingers, something she seemed to be doing in his presence with increasing frequency. She suspected he deliberately set out to shock a little her so-English susceptibility. Yet surely he had some English blood himself? "You had an English mother, had you not?" she murmured, as if talking to herself.

"My dear *mademoiselle*," he said smoothly, obviously quite clearly following the trend of her thoughts, "It was Dominique and Célèste who were thus blessed. Were you not aware that I am merely their half-brother, wholly and completely French?"

"So," she chuckled, "naturally you don't approve of Englishwomen. Now I begin to understand!"

"*Mademoiselle*—" he began, but didn't finish the sentence.

Eve's eyes fell before the impatient glint in his, and never before had she been so pleased to see Célèste. Yet she appreciated her presence more than her remark.

"You are looking quite hot and bothered, Eve," she laughed. "Don't tell me Raoul has managed to ruffle your so tenacious dignity?"

Eve's flush deepened even while she managed to smile carelessly. Célèste, dressed as elegantly as her brother, contrived to make her more conscious than ever of the plainness of her dress, and she was relieved when Raoul interrupted abruptly, relieving her of the necessity of replying. "Where have you been all day, Célèste? You seem to forget we have a guest, one who is supposed to be your special friend."

The girl laughed lightly. "But you forget, Raoul, our visitor is not here solely to see me. You surely don't begrudge me the little freedom Eve's presence here allows? If you must know I've been to Marseille to see Amélie. I could," she continued airily, "have stayed longer. Amélie did ask me to, but I knew you would only make a fuss."

Eve felt Célèste was somewhat surprised when he didn't, even now. He simply shrugged and inquired, "How is she?"

"Oh, very well." Célèste too shrugged as they all went in to dinner. "She was so interested in *la demoiselle anglaise*." Wickedly she grinned at Eve. "Madame Troyat is so attached to Raoul that she must know of everyone who comes near him. I assured her, *ma chère*, she had nothing to fear from you, but already she is making up her mind to come and look you over."

Unsure of her own reactions, Eve blinked, feeling Raoul's dark gaze on her head as she sat down, wondering why her heart should grow so cold at the mention of one Amélie Troyat. Madame, Célèste had said, which surely meant the lady was married?

"Madame Troyat is a widow," smartly astute, Célèste enjoyed a little drama, "but not such a very old one, *ma chère*, and she likes Raoul so much!"

"That is enough, Célèste." Raoul spoke sharply this time. "Amélie has always been a good friend, but haven't I told you before, it is too far to go to Marseille by yourself."

"But I am not an infant, Raoul," Célèste exclaimed crossly, choosing to ignore his level glance. "Besides, when Nadine returns I shall probably go to Paris, which is much further afield."

"You would do better to settle down and marry André," Raoul rejoined shortly, "as I should have insisted you did years ago."

"You forget, Raoul, I am not yet of age, and not ready to oblige you by settling down with one so dull as André. And it is no use getting annoyed, because you can't force everyone to do as you command."

"*Mon dieu*...!"

Eve continued with her dinner without being really aware of what she ate as she listened uncomfortably to the terse interchange of words. She was quick enough to realise that Célèste deliberately hinted at Raoul's attempt to force Dominique to marry one of his own countrywomen. But might Dominique not be alive today if he had obeyed. Glancing up, she met Raoul's enigmatic eyes and knew he had been about to reply in this vein, but for some reason changed his mind.

Not out of consideration of Eve Reston's feelings, surely, Eve thought with disbelieving surprise.

"Never mind," he said, looking quickly back at his sister, "it is clear you can't escape to Paris or anywhere else just now, so you must content yourself for a while."

"Only for a while." Célèste's consent was given grudgingly. "In the meanwhile you might perhaps consider Eve as a suitable nanny for Michel, or better still, there is always the so obliging Amélie, who, if you were to ask her nicely, might be willing to be both nanny and wife."

Why did Célèste's impertinent little speech stay with her, Eve wondered, all through the night? Even when she woke, at frequent intervals, it was still on her mind. Eve knew, from past experience, that Célèste when she chose could be absurdly indiscreet, yet Eve hadn't thought she would have dared to go so far with her brother. Raoul's reaction to Célèste's taunting observation had not been apparent. He had merely grinned, a swiftly sarcastic smile which Eve was sure had not reached his eyes, being mainly for her benefit. In another place, with other people, Eve might have thought the situation amusing, but somehow, here at the DuBare ranch, the humour of it evaded her.

Who exactly was this Madame Troyat, who Célèste declared would make such an excellent wife? It must, of course, be time Raoul married. He was about thirty-five but looked much older, with an authority and sophistication far beyond that meagre span of years. How was it, then, that the thought of him with a wife seemed strangely abhorrent? It could only be a form of pity for the girl who would eventually find herself in such a position.

It was still quite early next morning when Eve decided she could stay in bed no longer. Rather than toss and turn, even on such a well sprung mattress, she would go outside and enjoy the delightful early freshness of the gardens. Quickly she showered, putting on a fresh shirt and pair of jeans, brushing her unruly hair into some semblance of tidiness but not bothering with any make-up. She didn't, she considered, studying her glowing complexion, look as if she needed it this morning, and for the first time in days she realised she was beginning to feel really well. At her face in the mirror she grimaced wryly. So much for the lotus-like existence she had been leading! It wouldn't do to get too attached to such idle luxury, otherwise the sudden transition back to a life of toil was going to be unendurable!

Raoul surprised her by being at breakfast when she ran down. Usually, Marie had told her, he was gone long before this time.

"Do you ride, *mademoiselle*?" he asked, his gaze more approving than the evening before as it rested on her blue jeans which, though not expensive, hugged neatly the tender curves of her figure.

Confused, Eve glanced at him while making a great ado over the pouring of coffee. For some unknown reason she found it difficult to drag her eyes away from him this morning and inwardly jeered at herself that she should be surprised he looked exactly the same. Had she expected to find him changed overnight just because she had discovered he wasn't half English? But even that much had been a sort of bond, bringing with it, as it had, the comforting reassurance that he wasn't altogether alien. Now she felt she could not be sure of anything, and it didn't help that it was there in his eyes, the hard satisfaction of knowing that once again he had confounded her.

He had asked if she could ride, and already her silence was irritating him. As his dark brows rose impatiently she flushed and said swiftly, "Yes, *monsieur*, I do, but hardly, I think, like one of your *gardians*."

"That, *mademoiselle*, is nothing to be ashamed of. Our *gardians* are a race apart; one would not expect you to be immediately as good as they are, but you will learn. Our horses might not be quite what you are used to. I will, however, accompany you to begin with, so there is nothing to be afraid of either."

"Thank you, *monsieur*," she replied demurely. "I can assure you I'm not afraid, although, as you say, your horses will almost certainly not be what I've been used to. I was taught at school, where some of the girls had their own ponies, which, alas, I could not afford, and the horse I rode there was old. A darling, of course," her eyes, momentarily reminiscent, softened, "but often I longed for an animal with a greater urge of speed."

"Don't worry," he said softly, his eyes on her small, vivid face, "you will find that here. I promise you, *mademoiselle*, you have the ability to reach greater heights than you have ever known, if you leave it to me."

Was it simply her nonsensical imagination that whispered that he was not merely referring to riding? Her breath caught as she felt his very personality drawing her closer. Yet it was this total reliance on him, on which he deviously insisted, that she resisted. The warm blood beating blindly in her temples, she stirred too much sugar into her coffee and was aware of his eyes viewing her unsteady hand with a glint of near satisfaction. "Is Célèste coming with us, *monsieur*?" she asked.

"No." Just that.

Eve had forgotten that he had accused her of using his sister like a piece of armour plating. Now Eve held on to her like a lifeline. Even so, she had no clear idea where her next question came from, as it was a subject she was striving to avoid. "You said Célèste is only your half-sister, *monsieur*? Does that mean that Dominique was..."

"My half-brother also? Yes," he supplied, as she paused uncomfortably. "I must confess I am surprised you did not know?"

"Carol never said... Not that it can matter," she added hastily.

"But now you feel, *mademoiselle*, I am a stranger?"

He had guessed, but only partly. He couldn't know how her quickening heartbeats, when he looked at her intently as he did now, proclaimed him no stranger.

"I can assure you, *mademoiselle*," he went on, when she made no reply, "a man is a man, no matter what his nationality. It is merely that an infusion of foreign blood can occasionally, bring minor problems."

"Such as Dominique's desire to marry an English girl?" she challenged, resentment returning.

"Not necessarily that, although he was convinced there must be immediate compatibility because of it."

"And you didn't—you don't agree?"

"Not with every detail of his theorising, Eve." Raoul's eyes considered her steadily. "It is more, I believe, an inherent relationship with his country which might be bred into a man. Dominique's mother was English, a daughter of one of your own aristocracy, whose ideas as to how land should be managed were quite different from our own. In another part of France, perhaps, her plans might have been put to practical use, but not here in the Camargue. One has to be almost born in a district like this to understand it."

"And she tried to instil her ideas into Dominique?"

"Exactly, and possibly naturally, but while she was alive he must listen to widely diversifying views from both her and our father, so it was not perhaps to be wondered at that he grew up as he did."

"I didn't know him too well, *monsieur*."

"No," Raoul's sigh went deep as his lips compressed. "He was, in many ways, an admirable young man, but always indecisive. He wished to manage the ranch, but invariably when I returned from Paris, I would find chaos in even the most simple of things. Then he would decide he must run the family business in Paris, but this too defeated him when it came to making decisions on his own."

"Couldn't he have worked under you?" Eve ventured to suggest.

"Ha!" Raoul's smile was suddenly sarcastic again. "It was here that your famous British independence came in! He wanted something more than this. At the same time he possessed a certain generosity of spirit which allowed him only to confess his own limitations. He and Carol were happier when away on vacation, but alas, I found it difficult to be in two places at once."

"Your business in Paris is important, *monsieur*?"

"It is," he said briefly, "but I now have an extremely competent manager who has little doubt that he can supervise me as well as an excellent staff. However, it is a great comfort to know the whole thing won't collapse beneath the first crisis when I am not personally on hand. The Paris business is important, Eve, but this is my life."

Eve found herself considering all he had told her when, minutes later, they walked out into the cool morning air. The nights were still chilly, the approach of summer still slow, but as soon as the sun rose above the ground mist, sending its first probing rays across the awakening land, a pleasant warmth would be spread everywhere. Raoul had risen abruptly from the breakfast table, as if already deciding he had said too much, and had granted Eve only enough time to snatch a light jacket. He had impatiently forbidden her to go near the nursery.

"Michel can do without you this morning," he had said firmly, adding enigmatically, "You will probably see more than enough of him in future, and he will not fade away, *mademoiselle*, should you neglect him for a few hours today."

She had glanced at him doubtfully, then given in without further argument, even while her conscience whispered that she was not here for her own pleasure, but for the sole purpose of getting to know the child.

A trace of bitterness in Raoul DuBare's expression kept her strangely silent. His dry, indifferent tones over breakfast had not fooled her completely. She had seen it in his eyes—he had cared about his young brother, possibly as much as Carol's family had cared about her, and this could be another, perhaps the most important, reason why he felt he must rear Dominique's son on his own. The important factor was whether or not he was right.

CHAPTER SIX

BEHIND THE HOUSE, away from the acres of luxuriant greenness of the grounds and gardens, lay, in Eve's opinion, the real Camargue, and not having been far from the house since she had arrived she now felt alive with a growing curiosity. Something inside her craved to get out and see as much as she could of the district before she left, probably for ever.

Raoul again wore a brightly coloured shirt with a broad-brimmed hat and produced a similar one for Eve to use. "The sun can become too hot," he smiled, showing her how to secure it. "You must not risk ruining that beautiful English complexion."

His eyes lingered for a moment, his fingers beneath her chin tightening slightly as his gaze wandered, as if contemplatively, to her pink curved lips. Slowly he took his hand away, but it was only when his eyes released her that Eve could move.

"Thank you, *monsieur*," she said, her voice a mere whisper which he might not have heard.

Everywhere there was silence, they appeared to have the place to themselves. Surely she remembered Célèste saying a lot of men worked on the ranch, but when she asked Raoul where they were, he explained that, even at this early hour, the *gardians* had long since gone. He did show her show her the bunkhouse where they lived. "Many still live in small clay houses with thatched roofs," he told her. "Traditionally these face south-west away from the prevailing north-easterly mistral which blows down the Rhone valley."

Eve was relieved the men were all at work when Raoul helped her to mount. "It is three years since I left school," she confessed, rather shamefaced as the horse fidgeted and she clung rather than sat in the saddle.

This time Raoul seemed genuinely amused. "So," he grinned, "we have here a hardened deceiver! It is three years since you last rode. Is that what you are trying to tell me?"

Numbly she nodded, apprehensive although she felt no actual fear, her only doubts being her ability to manage the small but mettlesome animal beneath her.

"Just relax," he said mildly, with a quick glance at her tense face. "You have quite a good seat, even though you may be no expert, and I am here to see you come to no harm."

Just a few brief words, yet like a rare wine they flowed warmly through her. What sort of man was this, she wondered, who could, almost in the same breath, both frighten and enthrall, fill one with a rare sense of reassurance? She would be less than human if she failed to appreciate his kindness. It was the other side of him which made her cautious.

Surprisingly, before they had gone far, Eve realised thankfully that her old skill was returning, and she was in fact able to relax, even to the extent of hoping Raoul would be willing to answer a few questions.

"Yes, certainly," he obliged. "The famous white horses still exist, if their numbers have dropped considerably. Many breeders now cross the white Camargue horses with Arab strains, but that does not mean that the pure-bred Camargue horse is threatened with extinction."

Raoul himself was riding a beautiful pure-bred Arab which he had told her he had imported from North Africa. It was much larger than the white Camargue horse she rode, which was only around fourteen hands. "I think I like this one better," she said shyly, reaching forward to pat its neck.

Raoul, to her surprise, was willing to expand on the subject when, after a gentle canter, they slowed to walk carefully along the side of a freshwater marsh. "Each year," he said lightly, "many tourists come here hoping to catch a glimpse of the wild herds of white horses, some even hope to ride them across the wide expanses of the Rhone delta. In a way, I suppose, it is yet another instance of man's fascination with something whose origins are ancient. Once, in the north of your country, I visited your famous white Chillingham cattle. Of course our horses are more numerous, and their origins uncertain, but their traditions go back to Roman times when Julius Caesar replenished his cavalry with Camargue horses and the area was named after the Roman senator, Annius Camar, who was proconsul of this region. Since then tides of invaders have swept across this corner of Europe, all leaving something of themselves. The Romans followed the Phoenicians, to be followed centuries later by Attila the Hun with his Mongol hordes. Even today the *gardians* use a supplementary rein similar to the Mongols'. It lets the rider lead without pulling the horse's mouth, and this increases the animal's agility. Then from the nomadic Saracen and Moorish horsemen who followed the

Mongols we have the iron head that tips the seven-foot pole the Camargue cowboy uses to control his cattle. It is of ancient Saracen design, a half-moon set between two sharp iron horns."

Eve had listened, fascinated by everything he told her. Now, as he paused, she asked, unconsciously eager, "Are there any herds of white horses actually to be seen, or are they now so rare as to be hopeless to look for?"

His eyes glinted at her heady excitement. "If I were to tell you we are approaching one such herd now, *mademoiselle*, what would you say?"

"That I could scarcely believe it," she breathed, her eyes daring him to tease. "Many visitors at the hotel never succeeded in finding any."

"Because they didn't know where to look," he replied more soberly, "but at this time of the year, when the foals are due, it is as well the herds prefer to hide themselves as, unless approached with caution, and with someone who knows them, they could be dangerous—the stallions, especially."

"Yes, *monsieur*," she said, and didn't see him smile, a little ironically, at her so meek reply.

"You said," she persisted, anxiously smiling, "you might know where to find some of these white horses?"

He grinned. "As you are obviously willing to be unusually agreeable in return for such a favour, how could I refuse?"

"I'm always trying to be agreeable," she said uncertainly, wary of something she couldn't pinpoint unless it was the slightest hint of a threat in his ambiguous voice? No matter...What was one small step in the dark if it meant the chance of seeing the famous white horses? With a childish trust, after he had tethered their mounts, she put her hand into the one he held out and allowed him to lead her through the trees.

The tamarisk thicket ran alongside the marsh, and the thicket with a stretch of dry grass beyond was part of the grazing ground of a herd of about forty horses. "This is one of their favourite spots," Raoul spoke quietly, as they saw the horses in the distance. "They can graze over several square miles, but they are most often to be found here."

He would not allow her to approach too closely, but even through a protecting screen of branches she could see reasonably clearly. Barely conscious of Raoul DuBare standing behind her, she stared at the powerfully built beasts. It was an unforgettable experience. A few of the foals had obviously not been long born, and were making their first tentative, unsteady steps on legs far too long and spindly to support them satisfactorily.

"Soon," Raoul told her, "they will be strong enough and run like the wind. Until then they have always the protection of the herd."

"But the foals are black," Eve frowned, the glance she flashed at Raoul full of disappointment.

He nodded lazily, yet she was quick to notice the expert surveillance in his eyes as he looked the herd over, something that convinced her that this trip today had not been entirely for the benefit of one curious English girl. Her disappointment went suddenly deeper, flickering to a slight pain, but was just as quickly forgotten as he explained that nearly all of the foals were born black with a white patch on their foreheads. "At about eight months old," he went on, "they lose this coat and by the time they are about four years old their colouring will have changed to pale grey, before it turns to its final white."

"You know a lot about them—I suppose naturally, as I expect you own some of them," she tacked on swiftly, realising that, having spent his life here, her first statement he might consider—ridiculous.

If he did he gave no indication. His eyes had gone back to the herd, as though her question had evoked no irritation, but was one he had heard many times before. "Contrary to what many people imagine," he said, "today's wild horses of the Camargue are not really wild at all, neither in species nor character, but because they live wild the whole year round they often go for weeks without seeing a human being. The herd you are looking at now is a family one, made up of stallions, mares and foals. On this stud farm I have about a hundred mares, on others this number varies, and we all have our own brands."

Eve's interest was growing. Inside, she felt a nebulous, mounting excitement. The horses were grazing along the reedbeds, moving leisurely through the shallows. Across the marsh flamingoes skimmed the water, and the golden rays of the sun melted into the blueness of the surface, throwing back its reflections to the sky. Her whole body seemed, in some hitherto unknown fashion, to come alive, flooded to a new, singing awareness of this amazing land.

Not sure how to cope with this disrupting effect, she caught Raoul's arm impulsively, seeking for words to subdue such tumultuous feelings. "Can't we go nearer?" she almost begged, her blue eyes clinging insistently to his silvery-green ones. "You must know the horses if you own them, so surely it wouldn't be too dangerous?"

He smiled gently, his glance holding hers deliberately before he answered. "They don't know you, *ma chère*, that is the trouble. It can take a long time, often weeks, before the horses get used to the sight and sound of someone, before they are ready to accept. There is no danger, as I told you before, if one uses a little common sense and remains at a distance. If you were to live here, now, I would bring you every morning and introduce you properly. Does not the idea appeal to you, *mademoiselle?*"

"You are teasing me again, *monsieur*," she rebuked him, colour flushing beneath her skin because suddenly, inappropriately, what he suggested, even idly, sounded attractive. She must remember that she could neither stay, nor come back to this delightful spot, and that no soft word, spoken meaninglessly should be allowed to tempt her imagination. As if stung she quickly removed her hand from his arm, and, after another swift glance at the meandering horses, turned away.

"It must be about noon," she murmured, "shouldn't we be getting back home? Célèste will be wondering where we are."

His sardonic glance left her face to note the sun, directly above the umbrella pine under which they stood. He ignored her reference to Célèste, but he did nod his head. "We must, in fact, be getting back to our horses, *ma chère*. The stallions often resent the presence of a strange horse, and while they have seen mine quite frequently, they do not know yours."

Eve noticed he had no comment to make about her unfriendly withdrawal. It was almost as if he understood the complexity of the emotional bewilderment which seemed to hit her better than she. His strange green eyes beneath their thick fringe of dark lashes merely flickered, as if unable to restrain a faint hint of satisfaction—something, she fretted distractedly, she fancied she had noticed before. She tried, this time, to respond coolly. "You have given me a great deal of pleasure this morning, *monsieur*. I shall not forget."

"Don't worry, I know the score." His white smile suddenly glinted devilishly. "One of these days, *ma chère*, I shall send the account. One only hopes you will find it possible to settle."

Why had he always to leave her with too much to think about? It could only make her dislike of him stronger to treat her this way. To mildly threaten reprisals, to pretend she was in his debt, when, apart from a reluctant and sometimes debatable, courtesy, she had had nothing from him at all. He had insisted she went with him this morning, it hadn't been anything she'd thought up herself! It was utterly absurd that he should think she ought to be positively overflowing with gratitude.

His hand on her wrist as he drew her quickly back through the tamarisk hurt slightly, and it was as if he deliberately intended it should, because when she tried to pull away his grip merely tightened, sending small spearheads of lightning through her veins. "Stop struggling," he ordered tersely. "I'm simply guiding you through the marshes. Maybe it might be better to let you drown, but I am sure if I did, your so serious little face would probably haunt me for the rest of my days."

Yet later he did take a few minutes to congratulate her on her horsemanship. "You are really very good, *mademoiselle*. With a little more practice you will soon be an accomplished performer, a credit to us all." His eyes had mocked her doubtful expression, yet he seemed to be watching her with a keen absorption, almost as if he was unable to make his mind up about something which faintly intrigued him.

Whatever it was, Eve knew what seemed to be a nearly physical relief when they reached the ranch. A promising novice or not, to her utter mortification she found her limbs so stiff she was scarcely able to stand. Nor did it seem to help the aloof little front she had contrived over the last hour that she should have to clutch wildly at Raoul DuBare while trying to regain some balance. "I'm sorry, *monsieur*," she gasped, furious with herself.

"If I were a suspicious man, *mademoiselle*," he answered, poker-faced, "I might begin to imagine you couldn't bear to let me go." But his hands held her, steadied her, and she closed her eyes abruptly against the darkly dominant charm which seemed to reach out and embrace her even while he only held her lightly to him.

When she opened them again she was rock-steady on her feet, the tremors only inside her. "I'm sorry, *monsieur*," she repeated, her gaze going no further than the hard cleft in his chin. "You must know it is because I am unaccustomed to this particular form of exercise."

"Of course, *mademoiselle*," he agreed smoothly, as his hands fell away, "but we will make a rider of you yet, *ma chère*."

Swiftly he unsaddled her horse, smacking it lightly on the rump, explaining, as Eve watched it run away, "A true Camargue horse is never stabled. In winter, when we do not use them so much, they run free in herds like the others."

"It is a good life," she whispered, involuntarily.

"It is," he agreed, "both for man and beast, but," his eyes ran intently over her flushed cheeks, "I think you have had enough of the great outdoors for one morning. This afternoon you must rest. You are still too fragile, *ma chère*."

But that afternoon another visitor arrived at the Mas DuBare, as the ranch was locally known. Madame Troyat drove up in her car from Marseille shortly after lunch, and Eve saw at once that she was extremely attractive. Darkly vivacious, she immediately annexed Raoul, who had seemed inclined to linger over coffee—which was quite unusual, according to Célèste.

Amélie Troyat swept in as if she was very familiar with the place indeed, and as she was obviously welcome it mustn't, Eve concluded, matter that she hadn't let anyone know she was coming. Célèste had said Amélie was curious about Eve, but surely this didn't justify a special visit? Amélie's eyes did flicker narrowly in Eve's direction, but apart from this one brief surveyal Raoul appeared to have all her attention.

It wasn't until some minutes later when she was settled by his side that she stared coolly back at Eve again. "Célèste mentioned your visit, Mademoiselle Reston," her eyes examined derisively Eve's faded denims, her slight, girlish figure. "I must admit to being curious about poor dear Carol's family. You are merely a sort of cousin, I believe? Nevertheless, it is interesting to meet you."

Amélie's expression said directly the opposite. She might well have declared aloud that she considered Eve a plain little nobody. Eve felt her skin prickle with a kind of subdued rage. Madame Troyat was apparently regretting that she had rushed all the way here in the heat of the day when there had actually been nothing to worry about—certainly nothing to threaten her so obvious hopes of capturing Raoul DuBare for herself.

You're welcome to him, and in you he might just get what he deserves, Eve felt like shouting, while at the same time being more than a little dismayed by the unprecedented force of her reactions. It surely didn't matter so much how Madame Troyat cared to insult her, Eve would soon be gone.

Because she was secretly ashamed of her own anger, Eve managed to smile weakly, but her resentment grew again when Raoul intervened sardonically, as though the matter was of no great concern. "Mademoiselle Reston is merely here for a few weeks, *ma chère*, so you probably will not see much of her. She has come to visit my nephew in order to take a first-hand report of him to his grandparents in Rhodesia."

"I see..." Amélie was speaking in rapid French, possibly unaware that Eve spoke the language. With a further contemptuous glance in Eve's direction, she added, "But is all this necessary, Raoul? You have always been so against it."

Raoul shrugged, it seemed indifferently, unashamedly, Eve decided bitterly, noting how he laid soothing fingers over Amélie's hand which reposed on his knee. "There are extenuating circumstances, *ma chère*, these one must allow for. Carol's father is ill..."

Could he always manage to explain everything away so smoothly? A few seconds later, Eve managed to escape, still seething, still feeling the coolly taunting flicker of his eyes. Stumbling slightly, she had mumbled something about taking Michel to the gardens.

Célèste followed her to the nursery. "You must not take offence at Amélie, Eve, *ma chère*. She is merely warning you off. I suppose it is natural, when, ever since her husband died, she would like Raoul."

"She has no reason to imagine I could in any way endanger her plans," Eve retorted stiffly, "but perhaps it is a pity your brother gave the impression that I'm here on a long visit."

Célèste's light laughter turned just as quickly to a frown, as she turned from a studied inspection of her face in the ornate mirror which hung on the white painted wall. "But you will stay, Eve," she begged, "if Raoul asks you?"

A short while ago Eve might have given in resignedly, now she wasn't so sure. A kind of panic smote her, throwing her into a whirl of confusion, reducing her voice to a strangled whisper. "I simply can't make any promises, Célèste. Besides, I don't really believe Raoul meant what he said. He was, more than likely, provoking Madame Troyat a little, to make her jealous, perhaps, although I can't think she would ever feel like that about me."

"Because you imagine you are plain?" Célèste's frown turned to laughter again. "But you are not so very plain, Eve. In fact, at times you can look quite *belle*!"

Beautiful! Eve sighed. She could never be that! "Madame Troyat didn't appear to think so," she said dryly, and with some spirit. "Her expression left not a thing unsaid!"

"And that, when she knows nothing of what has been going on," Célèste giggled gleefully, as though secretly not so enamoured with Amélie as she had made out. "How would she react, I wonder, if I were to tell her you have been out on the marshes with Raoul since dawn? That he has shown you his precious horses, an honour he bestows on few. Not even me, this morning!"

Eve gazed at her remorsefully. "I'm really sorry about that, Célèste. I did think about you, but Raoul gave me no chance..." Haltingly her voice trailed off, and she didn't notice how frequently she was beginning to use his name.

Célèste had, and her glance sharpened with a flicker of complacency. "I did not wish to accompany you, not this time," she tacked on hastily. "It cheered me so much to know Raoul begins to accept you. Didn't I tell you he would, *ma chère*? I can see Paris looming nearer each day!"

Eve started uneasily. Célèste was happy, full of a gay optimism, yet something was wrong. A whole lot needed carefully going into before Célèste could go to Paris or anywhere else. However, there was perhaps some elderly relation already waiting to come should Célèste really manage to get away. Some person Eve knew nothing about. She shrank from mentioning a chaperone to Célèste, well aware that the girl might only laugh, might simply point out cruelly that such a person was scarcely necessary, that people would never credit that there could be any liaison, improper or otherwise, between Eve and Raoul DuBare. Somehow Eve had expected the house to be swarming with relations. Many of the stories she had read about France seemed to imply that dozens lived under the same roof, and hadn't she heard Carol complaining about so many people being underfoot?

It was all too confusing. Eve's smooth brow wrinkled with a fretful anxiety, and she felt her heart heavy with unknown dread, an instinctive feeling of disaster, worse than anything she had ever known.

Michel, a contented enough baby, had been playing at their feet while they talked. Now, Eve scooped him up, holding him to her as though the warmth of his small, nestling body could dispel all her fears. She made no further comment about Paris, instead she asked Célèste if she wouldn't come with them to the garden. There, she half hoped to find a way to talk to Célèste rationally, to suggest there could be problems regarding her plans in a sort of roundabout fashion.

But, as usual, Célèste had made other arrangements. "Darling," she cried, "I am sorry...! I am obliged to spend an hour with Amélie, then André is arriving to take me out. He positively begged, and as it is also a chance to gain Raoul's approval how could I refuse? If Raoul thinks I am in love with André he will not mind my going to Paris because then he will be sure I shall come back. The garden will still be there another day."

Michel was not a baby, in the proper sense of the word, any more. He was almost two, and toddling, although he seemed to prefer sitting on the floor, but this, Eve had been quick to suspect, was possibly because he spent long hours confined to the nursery where he had numerous toys but little chance to try out his legs on the highly polished surface. And while it would have been ridiculous, with all he had, to allege that he was deprived in any way, Eve also suspected it was easier for one of his many nursemaids to simply leave him to his own devices, a quick glance through the nursery door being enough to ensure that he was taking no actual harm. It was perhaps regrettable, Eve reflected, that he was too placid a child to object. Raoul was busy, and having too much to do would imagine that as Michel was quiet, all was well. Man-like, he would not understand that Michel might well benefit from a more varied routine than he had at present.

Quickly Eve gathered up a few things and carried the boy into the garden. On her way she stopped only to tell Marie where she was going. Marie, whatever her faults, always insisted on knowing where Michel was. "*Bon, mademoiselle*," was all she said, preoccupied with her never-ending baking, but she did smile, and produced a rosy apple for *"le petit gosse"*.

Michel, Eve had discovered, loved the garden and, since she had begun taking him there, his small limbs were already growing brown. He quite often got dirty, more like a boy. Now she watched as he toddled around chasing the brightly coloured butterflies which fluttered on gauzy wings just out of reach of his chubby fingers. The air was heavy with the sweetly astringent fragrance of thyme and rosemary, the wild rosemary blossom which crowded the outer reaches of the garden, a delicate pale-blue haze against a rich green background. Eve breathed the scented air deeply. It was blossom time and everywhere the dark masses of shrubs and trees were smothered in brightly coloured flowers such as were rarely seen in the usual suburban garden at home. The profusion of colour she looked at was spectacular, and the glittering wings of the birds and insects which flitted in and out of the branches even more so. It would be so easy to become addicted to living in such colourful surroundings. By comparison London, even in May, was going to appear quite drab once she was home.

Michel, tugging urgently at her jeans, interrupted her wistful dreaming. Guiltily she picked him up, reproaching herself for neglecting him as much as his other nursemaids as she pretended to examine the bright yellow flower he had found. It was rather like a daisy, but she could tell him no more, yet it seemed a step forward that he had brought it to her so confidingly. He was just beginning to talk, and because he only spoke French, Eve occasionally found it difficult to follow his babyish ramblings. She was trying to explain to him in terms he might just possibly understand how a flower was made, while he in turn was laughing happily and doing his best to pull the bloom to pieces, when Madame Troyat arrived.

Amélie gave the impression that she was merely wandering in the garden passing the time of day, yet she seemed to walk across to them so purposefully that Eve felt an immediate twinge of apprehension at her rather exaggerated surprise.

"I had forgotten," Amélie smiled, "about your intention to come out here yourself. And how is your poor cousin's baby today?"

Too quickly she bent to poke at Michel with long, sharp fingers, and with a small nervous whimper he shrank back against Eve. He had been wholly absorbed with his daisy and Amélie's approach had been too abrupt. Then, to Eve's dismay, he began crying in earnest as Amélie continued to stare at him closely with darkly malacious eyes.

"One can see at a glance," Amélie said coldly,

"that he lacks discipline—haven't I told Raoul a hundred times! Of course he agrees with me, but he is too busy, poor man, to do anything about it. A young baby needs a firm hand, but alas," she shrugged, "at the moment I have no authority. However, very soon this may be altered."

With difficulty Eve bit back a sharp retort, not being able to think of one good reason for Madame Troyat's obvious antagonism. Madame Troyat's whole manner she found intensely irritating. However, she conceded grudgingly, perhaps the woman meant well? Some people always managed to make themselves appear in a bad light, while at heart they were full of good intentions. Amélie's manner was probably unfortunate, and Eve knew she could not but agree that children did need a certain amount of discipline.

"But Michel is young, yet," was all she replied, as the baby clung tightly to her. "He didn't expect to see you and simply received a little fright. A very young child often acts instinctively—he hasn't yet learnt to reason."

Faintly mollified, Amélie appeared to relax, even to smile again, this time charmingly, at Eve's anxious face. "So I stand chastised, *mademoiselle*," she laughed lightly. "I quite see you and I are adults, and must not allow the whimperings of one small, spoilt child to drive us to a frenzy. I have been wondering," she went on, "if Raoul would not let you take Michel to live with his *grand'mère* in Rhodesia. How much more convenient for everyone this would be."

A few weeks, even days ago, such an ally and such a proposition would have delighted Eve; now, she wasn't so sure. There was a hollow feeling inside her where a growing elation should have been. "Monsieur DuBare would never consider such a proposal," she said unthinkingly.

Amélie's glance narrowed keenly as though something amused her. "Monsieur DuBare?" she repeated softly. Then, "He can be so stubborn, that one, Mademoiselle Reston. Michel must have his poor father's share; Célèste, the idle wretch, must have a dowry. It is as well, is it not, he is a very rich man, otherwise what would there be left for his poor wife when he takes one!"

"That is none of my business," Eve retorted coldly, while longing to ask if it was any of Amélie's either. Yet why should the idea of Raoul being married to Amélie fill her with alarm? Amélie was an attractive widow and would undoubtedly make him an eminently suitable wife. It was not for her to bother her head about such matters.

Hazily she became aware of Amélie speaking, and that while her voice was still soft, it also seemed to hold a thread of threatening violence. "Just make sure it continues to be none of your business, *mademoiselle*, then we shall have nothing to quarrel about! And as for taking the child with you when you depart—well, you think not, but I should advise you to wait and see!"

Startled, Eve stared as Amélie whipped around, walking off as swiftly as she had come. "Whew!" she found herself exclaiming soundlessly. Madame Troyat was undoubtedly a force to be recognised, having no compunction when it came to issuing ultimatums, leaving Eve in no doubt as to what happened to those who stood in her way. All too clearly Amélie was determined to become Madame DuBare. Michel had stopped sobbing and scrambled from Eve's arms in almost the same instant Amèlie had gone, and Eve sighed. Raoul would never part with his brother's only child, that she instinctively knew, but what sort of á childhood would Michel have if his uncle married someone like Amélie Troyat?

SEVERAL EVENINGS LATER Eve came down to the garden by herself to sample the delights of the pool. The afternoon had been hot, unduly hot for the time of year, and after playing all morning with Michel, she had fallen asleep in the cool confines of her room. She had been quite annoyed with herself when she woke up and found it was quite late. She was also very stiff, as she had gone to sleep unintentionally, sitting in the armchair by the east window where she had only intended staying for a minute to escape the sun.

About to scramble into a dress for dinner, she had suddenly remembered that both Raoul and Célèste were out and she had told Marie not to cook anything hot, that she would just have a snack in the kitchen. Hastily she had put her dress back in the wardrobe before running downstairs where, to her delight, Marie had already arranged an assortment of cool salads on a tray with a bottle of wine.

It was Marie who suggested she took her meal into the garden, and had a swim. "One of the boys will carry your tray for you, *mademoiselle*," she said, smiling. "You will enjoy your *diner* better when you feel cooler, you will see."

The idea had suddenly appealed to Eve enormously. She hadn't yet swum in the pool as Célèste never seemed to be at home to accompany her and she had felt curiously reticent about using it on her own. But there would be no one around at this time of the day, no chance of Raoul discovering her unexpectedly, as he was not expected home until late.

So she allowed herself to be persuaded and, after murmuring a word of breathless thanks to Marie, rushed upstairs for her bikini and a towelling wrap. In the pool she had dived and swam until once again she was tired. Now, drowsily replete after enjoying her meal, she was ashamed to realise she could very easily go to sleep as she had done just a few hours earlier. The air was still and warm, the shadows gathering as the light began to fade. Even the piercing cries of the birds had dropped to a murmurous twittering, and the last busy insect retired for the night. Soon she would have to retire as well, but right now she couldn't seem to manage the effort to move. Her recliner was the last word in comfort, padded softly with cushions and boasting a huge fringed umbrella overhead. Idly Eve wriggled bare toes, while scarcely conscious of any movement at all, only aware it was a long time since she had felt so relaxed.

It was perhaps because of this, when she lifted her heavy eyelids to find Raoul DuBare gazing down at her, that she knew such an instant resentment. A twin feeling of flickering excitement she ignored, concentrating on her loss of pleasure in a losing struggle to create a sort of invisible barrier. Why must fate turn him up like this? During the last few days she had seen a lot of him, too much, in fact. Had it been totally unreasonable to hope for a breathing space? He was too swiftly decisive ever to need one, but Eve felt her own more vulnerable defences shaking. "Good evening, *monsieur*," she said weakly, gathering her wrap, for no reason she could think of, more tightly about her.

His eyes taunted the shaky fumbling of her fingers, his dark brows rising derisively. "You feel a sudden chill?" he asked, his voice threaded with ironic concern.

His sarcasm hit her, scattering for ever her mood of tranquility. "I didn't know you would be home so early," she challenged him foolishly.

"Obviously not, but there is no need to act as though you have committed a crime in bathing in my pool. Or is it something else, Mademoiselle Eve, that disturbs you?" His eyes still mocked as his glance swung to the remains of her cold meal, the almost empty wine bottle. "If I'd known you were celebrating, I might have joined you instead of eating by myself on the way."

Uncomfortably Eve flushed; his teasing glance was so pointed she couldn't pretend not to understand. "The night was hot, *monsieur*. It is only a little light wine—and I doubt," she added, with a kind of frantic daring, "if you dined alone."

He laughed at her pertinent observation. "No," he confessed, "I did not. At least, an old acquaintance joined me for coffee, which was not so amusing as it might have been here, with you."

"Oh..." Eve's thick lashes fluttered on her hot cheeks; perhaps she had deserved that! He wasn't to know her silly query had been prompted by confusion rather than curiosity. With concentrated effort she turned her gaze away from him, attempting to find distraction in the beauty of the garden, but dismayed to find her view still blocked by Raoul's image, seemingly indelibly imprinted on her mind's eye.

As if acknowledging the hopelessness of her own endeavours, she looked nervelessly back at him, wondering rather desperately what it was about him she was fast becoming unable to resist. He might have had a busy day, there could be no doubt about that, but he still gave the appearance of being alive with a sort of devastating energy, his eyes brilliantly alert, not missing a thing. He was a man whose dynamic personality would always be one step ahead, anywhere in the world. What chance would a girl like Eve Reston have of beating him at his own game, or any game at all, come to that?

Moodily lost in a whirl of uncertainty, Eve's eyes clung to his well laundered shirt, the immaculate distinction of tailored silk. He had obviously bathed and changed since returning home, having discarded his town suit in favour of a pair of more casual slacks. He looked cool and remote, but he was, she was quite aware, all man. Very masculine, which was undoubtedly the way he was made, but he was also dangerous, this she knew only too well, and prayed silently that, while he might sway her senses, she could still retain enough coolness of head to see him objectively.

As he so obviously waited for her to finish, or to make some further comment, she said faintly, "I don't think you would find me amusing for long, *monsieur*. As we have so little in common it is often difficult to find anything to talk about."

CHAPTER SEVEN

IF EVE HAD HOPED to confound him by such an obviously discouraging observation, she clearly failed dismally, as his eyes again flickered tauntingly. "You English set great value on the lengthy conversation, do you not, my dear Eve? In France we can often think of better ways of passing the time, especially at this hour of the evening."

Now she knew he deliberately teased, and would have liked above all things to have been able to get up and simply walk away, but it seemed as if his eyes deliberately pinned her to the soft cushions of the recliner and it was all she could manage to retain even a modicum of dignity as colour flared wildly beneath her skin. "I am not familiar, as you know, *monsieur*, with the way a Frenchman's mind works," she muttered crossly, "and it can scarcely matter as I shall soon be gone."

Without warning he dropped down beside her, on the edge of the wide recliner, facing her, his voice full of a menacing smoothness. "The wine had perhaps made you a little reckless, *mademoiselle*. I must have a word with Marie."

"No, please." He was so close if she put out a hand she could touch him. "I didn't mean to sound impertinent, *monsieur*."

"But you do," his mouth hardened, "all the time. What exactly do you hope to gain by these imaginary battles you fight, or is it that you hope a lot of smoke will conceal the exact amount of the fire?"

"You talk in riddles, *monsieur*!" she cried, trying futilely to edge away from him as his hand snaked out and caught her, holding her, regardless of her brief struggle. "Why should I have anything to conceal?"

"Perhaps you are right," he shrugged, suddenly indifferent, although his hand did not leave her arm. He merely relaxed slightly the steely grip of his fingers, as if not willing yet that she should escape him. His hard glance examined her face, the satiny, rose-flushed skin, the wide, apprehensive blue eyes, before dropping consideringly over her bare graceful limbs. "You are young, *mademoiselle*," he sighed, "at the moment uncommonly appealing, but, contrary to what you believe, we do have something to talk about, something we do have in common, and which I'm afraid we must discuss. I imagined this would be as opportune a moment as any."

As Eve's apprehension deepened, he continued. "We had a letter from my father's cousin, Nadine. She is on her way home and wishes for Célèste to go to Paris to stay with her for a while before they both return to New York."

"I see..." Eve's voice grew cautious as she sensed the looming danger.

"You are surprised, *mademoiselle*, by this news?" Raoul's eyebrows rose slightly.

"In a way," Eve flushed beneath his sceptical expression, and she added unintentionally, "but I have always known of Célèste's desire to go there."

"Always, *mademoiselle*?"

Eve stirred uneasily, hit by an utterly confusing conviction that they were nearing some sort of crisis, yet how could she think clearly when his fingers were shooting small flames up her arm in a wholly inexplicable way? "I've known for a while," she amended unhappily.

"So, Miss Reston," he went on, acknowledging her retraction narrowly, "we are confronted with the problem of Michel."

"Oh, yes, *monsieur*." For one horrible instant she had imagined him about to challenge her half-truths; instead it seemed, surprisingly, he was willing now to speak rationally of Michel's future. "Of course," she said eagerly, "Célèste could not be expected to sacrifice her whole life to the child. It's as well you are prepared to be sensible."

Something, a derisive flash of anger, flickered in the depth of his eyes. "That could, in this case, be questionable!" he drawled enigmatically.

"I'm sorry, *monsieur*, that was unfortunate. What I meant was..."

"I feel sure I know very well what you meant," he interrupted coolly. "You imagine I will be willing to part with the child, that I will allow you to take him?"

"Not necessarily." Eve's voice trailed off as she drew a deep breath, impatient that he could so easily confuse her. "You might have plans of your own." He could have decided to marry Amélie, or there could be others only too willing to oblige, especially if he was as wealthy as Amélie reckoned he was. Apart from this it was surely not impossible to find satisfactory help.

"I have plans, yes," he was saying, pausing, watching her expressive face closely, reading clearly the muddled trend of her thoughts. "I have known of Célèste's unrest for some time, but until you arrived a solution eluded me."

Rather desperately Eve stared away from him. She might have known he had seen through Célèste's too elaborate contrivances, but he couldn't actually be admitting he found her ideas feasible? "You mean...?" she began, with a painful hesitation.

"I mean, Eve," he again cut in firmly, "or rather, I am suggesting, that you knew something of my sister's attempts to enrol you as a nursemaid."

Bright colour stained Eve's cheeks and she felt guilt must be written all over her. "There was nothing definitely arranged," she faltered. "My aunt and uncle were very anxious to have news of their grandson."

"So you just came, hoping to see him, and suffered all kinds of reprisals because of it? Such devotion to one's infirm relatives ought not to go unnoticed, *ma chère*."

But it hadn't been altogether like that! Eve felt like crying. Hadn't she only come reluctantly, resenting wildly the conscience which had seemed to drive her here? This, and the wholly alarming fear that Célèste would carry out her threats and bring Michel to London, was almost entirely responsible. She was no self-sacrificing heroine as perhaps Raoul appeared to think, yet how could she explain this without implicating Célèste? But she was in fact searching for a suitable way to confess when his next words drove all such thoughts from her head.

"I have decided, Eve, it is not merely a nurse I must look for but a wife."

Heavens! For a moment she was startled, before the

surprise inside her seemed frozen cold. "A wife!" she whispered, paling clearly as a shiver ran through her.

"Why not?" he demanded, as she stared up at him.

"But of course, *monsieur*," realisation dawned. "A nurse, a young one, anyway, would require a chaperone perhaps... Madame Troyat..."

"Go on," he murmured sarcastically, as she faltered, "you were saying?"

"Oh, please," she gave him a scared glance, "it was only that Madame Troyat also said a wife would be the best thing. She was speaking generally—you understand? Someone who would see to it that the nurse looked after Michel well." She dared not tell him of Madame's other plans for Michel—there was such a lot she was too frightened to tell him, his anger could be harsh.

"So," he drawled dryly, "I am to be saddled with both a wife and a suitable nanny, two people when it is probably only necessary to find one."

"But Madame Troyat..."

"We will put the good lady to one side for the moment, Eve, although she may yet be necessary. She is indeed a most admirable person, but it is you who I am asking to consider this position. I am asking you to be my wife."

"*Monsieur*, please!" she felt herself go white. "I don't imagine," she gasped, "you are serious, but I don't somehow appreciate your little joke!"

"It is no joke, *ma chère*." His mouth curved ironically, as he looked down at her numbed face. "Do not look so completely disbelieving. This is not an entirely new idea, something unheard of. Men have been marrying with the same purpose in mind throughout the ages. In finding someone with your training, who suits my purpose admirably, I have been more fortunate than many others, shall we say."

Eve had a strange feeling, as she listened to him, that she was sinking in water so deep she could never hope to reach the surface again. That she was drowning, but perhaps in oblivion she might rediscover some kind of sanity. Now, as her eyes widened on his hard, handsome face, she realised he meant every word he uttered. And yet it did not seem possible.

Unconsciously she moistened dry lips. "Apart from my own feelings, *monsieur*," she said, "are you willing to sacrifice all hope of marrying someone you love in order to benefit a boy who isn't even your own son?"

"Oh, I would find compensations, *mademoiselle*, never fear. There is much which might be arranged."

"Maybe you are thinking of divorce, in a few years' time, when Michel is older?"

"A Frenchman quite often does not marry until he is older, *mademoiselle*, but when he does it is for the rest of his life, usually."

"But...!" Eve's breath seemed driven from her body, and as she spoke a wild flush returned to her cheeks. "But, if it was not a proper marriage, *monsieur*?"

His eyes were enigmatically veiled. "One crosses all these hurdles as one comes to them, *ma chère*. There is always a solution, and not always the obvious one. At the moment, as I think you must agree, the child is the important consideration."

He talked in riddles, terrible, heart-accelerating riddles. "What you suggest is of course impossible," her voice gathered a little strength and confidence as she tried to thrust all thought of it from her. "You could easily find a suitable nanny and some elderly relation to act as a chaperone. I would myself be willing to stay on a little while longer in these circumstances."

"Then you will leave," he commented dryly, "and once more the child will be at the mercy of change. And the elderly relation who is free to come, whom I could possibly endure in the house, does not exist. So you must think again, *mademoiselle*."

"I'm sorry," Eve replied stiffly, in no way convinced.

His broad shoulders lifted, the muscles moving smoothly beneath his thin shirt. "So am I," he shrugged.

Eve glanced at him apprehensively. It was merely a polite rejoinder, his tone holding no obvious regret, as though, in his opinion, in spite of what she said, a satisfactory outcome was simply a matter of time and patience. She would have liked to escape, but his hand still held her arm and he made no attempt to release her, and when he began to speak again she could only wait submissively to hear what more he had to say.

"Take a few days," he instructed coolly, "to think about it. Think also of the relief your uncle and aunt will know should you change your mind. Your uncle's heart, Eve, would surely benefit accordingly."

"I don't need to think about it," she insisted stubbornly, refusing to be blackmailed in this fashion.

He went on as if she had never spoken. "Then perhaps if you still refuse I must ask some more obliging lady. Someone with a tender, loving heart, such as Amélie Troyat, who I suppose would look after my nephew almost as well."

"I'm sure she could, *monsieur*," Eve retorted sharply, through a disquieting surge of dismay. Yet he mocked her so openly with his eyes that temper licked along her own veins so that she must retaliate. "You are a fool, *monsieur*, to imagine a liaison between the two of us would work out. We have nothing in common!"

Hard anger flared visibly in his eyes and his fingers tightened. "We are not incompatible."

"That I cannot believe, *monsieur*!" Hysteria, rising from tension, rose chokingly. He did not like it when she called him a fool, she could see. It was a raw flick to his pride even if he could control his anger better than she. "You are not only foolish," her voice rose wildly, "you are stupid, stupid..."

It was enough! He didn't attempt to disguise his contempt, the rare impatience that flickered through him at her reckless words. "You talk too much," he said sharply, "it is you who is being stupid, I'm afraid. Don't you know better than to provoke a man in this fashion?"

Her fingers clenched to stop her hands from shaking. "That wasn't my intention," she assured him quickly, as coolly as she could, "I was simply trying to convince you that what you have in mind would never work in a hundred years!"

"Really?" In other circumstances there might have been grim humour in his voice at such a forthright exclamation, but whatever it was it wasn't strong enough to dissolve his prevailing anger. His jaw hardened abruptly, and she felt the movement of his hands against her skin as they slid round her, behind her shoulders, almost lifting her from the recliner.

Then the warmth of her body was in his arms and he was saying roughly, "Must you always have proof of everything? There is apparently only one way to help you make up your mind."

Sheer, primitive alarm shot through her as she tried to pull away from him, but he merely followed up her ineffectual struggles, bending over her until she was stretched tautly against the lowered back-rest, her eyes, wide and distressed, never leaving his face. "Don't," she whispered, her voice a low cry in her throat, but he came right on, not stopping until he was crushing her to him, feeling the futile protest of silk and flesh under his hands and her mouth trembling piteously beneath his.

His arms held her to him with the same unrelenting strength she had known once before and there was no gentleness in his kiss, which was clearly meant as a punishment for daring to defy him. Yet the harsh shock of it evoked a bewildering response within her, something that seemed to hold her in a fearful void where all rational thought deserted her.

She wanted to push him away, but instead she clung to him, and when momentarily he lifted his head, her lips were soft and seeking against his, and the sweetness of her parted mouth seemed to loosen something in him which he could not subdue. He saw her eyes blurred with emotion and felt her hands move behind his neck, and there seemed nothing but a great silence, holding them immobile, locked together.

There was a danger around them that deepened, almost uncontrollably, and as if sensing this the man drew back slightly while Eve's head whirled and the blood pounded painfully in her ears. Quivering, she could not lift her heavy lashes to look at him, but she could feel his gaze, his breath on her hot skin, his fingers threading her tumbled hair, gripping the silk strands of it as she breathed eratically.

"*Mon dieu!*" she thought she heard his voice softly, "but I could love you..."

Then his lips were on hers again, crushing them this time with a demanding question in his, an unwillingness to take no for an answer. She felt his broad shoulders pinning her down, and sensation tore along her veins, racing madly through her heartbeats, as he swiftly swept aside the belt of her loose robe, his hands brutally frank on her bikini-clad body.

When next he raised his head she wasn't so inarticulate, she did manage his name. "Raoul," her voice was a shaken whisper, the sureness of his touch proving an almost intolerable stimulant.

"Would you still say we are not compatible?" he persisted, drawing an audible breath as she lay quivering in his arms.

Numbly she tried to answer, to nod stubbornly, but nothing happened. There was only her heart thudding into his, and she was vaguely aware there was nothing but the silk of his shirt between them as he began kissing her passionately, his caresses hard with barely restrained desire as they recognised the urgency within her and was more than able to satisfy it. And Eve found herself only clinging and clinging.

Then suddenly he was standing some feet away from her as Célèste came running, calling, into the gardens. "*Tiens!*" Eve heard him exclaim. "Can there be no peace anywhere!"

It was almost dark, Célèste but a dimly definable

figure, but Raoul turned, walking purposefully towards her—so obviously to give Eve an opportunity to adjust her robe that as reality returned, a flush of pure shame seemed to cover her completely, but when they returned together, Célèste chatting vivaciously, in Raoul's green eyes as they surveyed her still lingering distress there was not, so far as Eve could see, one flicker of sympathy—or regret!

For some time after the incident by the swimming pool Eve seemed to live only half aware of the world about her. Every sensitive part of her seemed to be steeped in a kind of agony, inducing awareness of her own weakness. Even her normal colourful energy seemed depleted, as though Raoul had, in some devious fashion, drained it away from her, and the usual daily routine with Michel was almost more than she could manage. There was a lassitude within her impossible to fight; it even seemed reflected in her appearance. Her eyes when she watched Raoul DuBare, when she thought herself unobserved, were wistful, shadowed with a puzzled confusion which held her mouth taut. It was only when she remembered his kisses that her pink lips unconsciously softened to a quivering awareness that not even a determined coolness of manner could disguise.

She couldn't seem to find any of the right answers. There were so many things to be done, yet the effort to organize her thoughts constructively brought only pain, something she fled from instinctively. There was Célèste to be informed about her return to London—a date to be definitely fixed for it. And the problem of Michel's future to be decided on, this in a way that might at least partly satisfy his grandparents in Rhodesia. Yet, as the days evolved into weeks, she came no nearer to the making of any of these apparently simple decisions. At times she thought almost frantically that it was as if Raoul stood in the background, ironically contemptuous of her obvious inability to take this last decisive step towards freedom.

She wasn't sure how much he had guessed merely by kissing her, but, if he was as knowledgeable about women as he was reputed to be, he had probably found it easy to judge how little she knew about men. Just how difficult she would find it to keep him at a distance should he really try to storm her defences she did not know? At night she could only bury her hot face in her pillows, quivering with humiliation when recalling how eagerly she had responded in his taunting arms. There was all the time the frightening conviction that he was simply watching and waiting, well aware that his experienced caresses had acted like a drug, for which, so far as Eve was concerned, there was no known antidote, no means of resistance. Nor did it do anything for the last remaining fragments of her confidence to realise it would be foolish to stay and even to try to fight a battle in which she would so obviously be the loser.

If Raoul had loved her it might have been different, but his proposal had been accompanied by no such declaration—Eve shuddered, recalling his businesslike tones. Why did he want to marry her? Of course an arranged marriage, especially one directly linked up with his family, would not seem so strange to him, the structure of French family life being strong. More and more, during the few weeks she had lived here, Eve was coming to realise this. Dominique's child was part of it, and Raoul was apparently convinced that by marrying Eve there would be no further risk of Michel being removed from his care. On top of this there must be the added assurance of her impeccable training, the fact that she had already worked with a French family, all of which would give added defence against the claims of others in Michel's future.

Perhaps if Eve could have looked at it from the same unemotional point of view it could have been easier, but certain things, she was finding, hurt too much. Amélie Troyat seemed always to be visiting, sometimes staying overnight, and always to be found near Raoul. Occasionally Célèste and Eve went up to bed leaving the two of them deeply absorbed in conversation.

"She is out to get him, that one," Célèste giggled derisively as they climbed the stairs. "Do you think, Eve, she will succeed?"

"She might," Eve managed, with commendable indifference, considering the sinking feeling in her tummy. "Your brother appears to be fond of her. He certainly seems to find her company stimulating. He must at least like her a lot."

"Oh, as to that," Célèste shrugged carelessly, "I should not be at all surprised if he is at this very moment making love to her. But as for marriage—that, I imagine would be quite another thing!"

But would it? Eve wondered, abruptly bidding Célèste goodnight and closing her bedroom door. Why was it whenever she thought of him married to another woman there was only pain? Amélie must be suitable in every way, as well as being, it was plain to see, entirely willing.

It was Amélie's attitude towards Michel that caused

her the greatest doubts. Clearly Amélie had no great love for him, even though she might pretend a delightful affection when his uncle was around, but it wasn't until Eve came upon her unexpectedly again, in the gardens that she realised Amélie might actually dislike the child.

One of the young girls employed in the house, had taken him there to play, a daily routine that Eve had managed to establish, and even Marie now insisted on it when Eve wasn't there. Eve had, that morning, been out riding with François and Pierre, the two old men she had met on that momentous day beside the lagoon. Her riding had much improved and she loved to go out in the early morning, but Raoul insisted she never went alone, ordering the two old men of the *mas* to accompany her whether she liked it or not. In fact Eve found their company very agreeable as, once they got to know her, she found them very willing to talk about the Camargue, François in particular proving a veritable fund of knowledge.

Now she was back, after spending some interesting hours watching the herdsmen working with the herds of bulls. There had been a sick animal and they had had to ride out to the pastures to bring it home. The bull had not, to Eve's way of thinking, looked as if it had much the matter with it, being morosely uncooperative and complaining.

When she asked François about it he had merely laughed, eyeing her doubtful face indulgently. "He is just like a man, *mademoiselle*, who is not ill enough to be anything but bad-tempered."

Le maître was away that morning, the men said, so Eve had allowed herself more time than usual, not anxious for once about running into him. It was fairly easy, she had discovered, by staying in her room a little longer, to avoid him at breakfast, and by lunch she usually felt more able to face him without visible tremors.

She hurried not into the garden. Michel was getting to know her, to like her, to like her beside him. At last she was beginning to represent something in his small world—someone who would laugh with him when he felt like being silly, someone to cling to when he was hurt or felt sad. At the same time, knowing she must one day leave him, Eve was wary of making him too dependent, a fine balance which, with so young a child, was not easy to achieve.

Long before she reached him she heard him cry and momentarily she stopped in dismay before hurrying on. It didn't seem the sort of whimpering wail he usually made when he suffered a little fright. This had been a high scream of rage. Then, around the next corner, Eve drew up sharply, her whole being flooding with rage. Amélie was there, holding Michel, shaking him, screaming with temper, and the child, Eve could see, was terrified. "Stop it—let him down!" Eve heard her own voice raised high as she reached them in a flash, almost wrenching Michel from Amélie's grasp. She didn't bother to speak in French, though knowing Amélie spoke very little English. If Amélie didn't understand what she said, Eve knew her expression could not be mistaken. "You're despicable!" she cried, holding Michel's trembling body to her. "Surely nothing could justify your shaking him like that!"

"He broke my necklace!" Amélie returned angrily. "He just wouldn't let go!"

"He couldn't be expected to understand..."

"He is old enough!" Amélie cut in contemptuously. "And don't pretend that in your country no child is ever chastised. My own sister is married to an Englishman and she tells me..."

"All right—I'm sorry, *madame*," Eve's voice was suddenly flat, as she tried to control herself. Perhaps, as Amélie implied, she was making too much fuss. It wasn't really a crime to shake a child when it was naughty, only Michel was so young. Surely he could have been forgiven on those grounds alone?

Suddenly, as Eve stared at her in bewilderment, Amélie's rage seemed to leave her and she subsided rather like a pricked balloon. "I'm sorry, too," she almost gasped, "I know I should not have lost my temper, but I swear I did not hit him. I'm sure he is making a great deal of noise unnecessarily."

Eve nodden numbly, there seemed nothing else she could do, but she was unable to rid herself of the suspicion that Amélie did not like the child, was not fond of any kind of children, which perhaps explained the fact that she had never had any of her own. "I'll take him back to the nursery, *madame*," she said, "if you will excuse me."

In the nursery Michel soon calmed down. Eve saw quite clearly he hadn't been actually hurt in any way, that he had simply had a bad fright, and in a few minutes would be none the worse. Her own apprehension was something quite different. If Raoul married this woman how would Michel fare? It wasn't a new thought, but, until this morning, and this incident she had just witnessed, the full implications had never struck her forcibly. Amélie was beautiful, well bred, and, when she liked, charming. No one would ever believe she had a slightly unstable streak, that she might not be a person who should have charge of a small child. It wasn't after all, an easy thing to ascertain. Eve herself was unwilling to misjudge her, even after witnessing two of Amélie's hysterical scenes.

"The child has been upset, Eve?"

Startled from her reverie, Eve swung around to find Raoul surveying her sombrely from the doorway. She had imagined him in Marseille, where the *gardians* had said he was going. He must have returned early. How much had he seen? "It's nothing, Raoul," she answered distractedly, glancing again at Michel's sleeping form. The heat and fright had tired him and she had put him in his small cot bed to rest. Now he slept soundly, his round face placid once more although the tear marks remained on his cheeks. "It was nothing," she repeated, unaware that the crumpled tear-wet state of her blouse perhaps called for something more by way of explanation.

Raoul's mouth thinned as his eyes went over her, quickly assessing her dishevelled appearance. "Marie said Amélie had taken him to the gardens."

This explained the absence of the girl who usually looked after him. "I think the sun must have tired him, *monsieur*," Eve answered, avoiding a direct reply as best she could.

His eyes dwelt on the colour which lightly stained her creamy cheeks. "I see," his glance was narrowly reflective. "He appears to have been crying—perhaps he did not want to come indoors so early. A trained nurse can occasionally be too much of a disciplinarian, my dear."

"But it wasn't like that..." she began, then stopped, words trembling on the tip of her tongue, words she could not utter. First it had been Célèste, now Amélie! Yet did she owe either of them loyalty? She thought not, but how could she change her own nature? If she was to betray them she would only feel miserable and, besides, what proof had she, and how was she to know if Raoul would believe her? "I mean," she stumbled bleakly, "I was sure he had been out long enough."

"Because he was enjoying himself with Amélie? I did not believe you would be rude to my guests. She was most upset."

"*Monsieur*...!"

"Yes?" his voice was darkly ironic. "Have you not the grace to look ashamed? The expression of a sullen child does not become you."

"You have no right to judge me," she tried to glare straight into his curiously light eyes. "You like to condemn me out of hand!"

His white teeth glinted though not, she thought, in amusement. "I do not forget, Eve, you have granted me no rights whatsoever, to date. But there are others, my dear, who would not be so reluctant."

"Someone?" she choked furiously. "A certain lady you don't wish me to offend?"

"You could say that," his smile was very white, amused, faintly cynical. "But do not let it agitate you, *ma chère*. You are hot enough by all appearances without adding to your discomfort."

Indifferently, it seemed, while she fumed, he put out his hands, drawing her to him. "Occasionally I find you infuriating, little one, at the same time I do not like to see you like this." His hand went, before she could move, to her hot brow, brushing back the clinging tendrils of damp hair, his fingers stilling effectively any protest she might have made if words hadn't eluded her. She saw in his face an impatient male tenderness mixed with a cool deliberation. "Do you have to get yourself in such a state over one small child?" he muttered sardonically. "Don't you think it's high time you began to waste some of these so intense emotions on a man?"

Her eyes deepened and darkened like the blue of the sky before night and she could only stare at the strong column of his throat, aware that by doing so she found none of the self-possession she sought, only a quivering reluctance to beg him to release her. He was undoing the top buttons of her shirt, his knuckles digging into her soft skin as he slid his hands under the stiff collar, easing it back. His fingers lingered on her smooth young back and he didn't withdraw them.

"*Ma chère*," he spoke with low emphasis, his eyes directly on her slender young figure, "must you always wear such exhausting, inhibiting clothes? *Mon dieu*, if you belonged to me I would burn the lot of them and buy you a few wisps of material in which you would look wholly enchanting!"

Colour swept again into her face, catching her breath sharply, making her eyes brilliant. "But I do not!"

"Not yet... but I might presume it is just a matter of time before you arrive at a decision?"

"—I've always told you..."

"I remember everything you told me, *ma chère*, but words are very rarely the whole of it." His breath was on her cheek as his free hand touched the racing pulse at the base of her throat, his insinuation so pointed she could not pretend to misunderstand.

"How I hate you!" she cried, feeling herself a stone's throw away from total disorientation, almost unable to restrain her own arms from going up around his broad shoulders, her shaking mouth from searching for his. Desperately, puppet-like, she stared at the faint stripe in his white shirt, willing herself rigidly from doing any such thing.

His hold tightened on her, hurting for another minute before suddenly he let her go. "You'd better go and change for lunch," he mocked, "if you're still determined to play it safe. Shall I see you to your room? The house is very quiet."

"There is no one around," the glinting devil in his eyes seemed to add, "and, although you may pretend, I shouldn't so much as wager two cents on your resistance!"

And he could be right, Eve admitted, terrified for the first time in her life by a man's taunting obvious thoughts as she turned and fled.

In her room, all the time she scrubbed her hot face and searched for a clean shirt, she tried to keep her mind closed to all thoughts of him. How dared he mock her so sarcastically? He couldn't really want to marry a girl after talking to her like that! What he had said was bad enough, but that which he had implied could be even worse. Was he simply expressing, she wondered wildly, his general opinion of women, or was it just herself? Perhaps she deserved it—his apparent disrespect? He must have guessed she lingered here not merely because of Michel. Shivering with alarm and confusion, Eve thought of the way she seemed always to respond in his arms. Might he not be excused if he imagined she would settle for a—less permanent relationship? It wasn't difficult to recall how hardly he had proclaimed he hadn't a drop of English blood in him. A wholly decisive man, and how little she knew of him. He would demand—no, take, more than she would be prepared to give, and daily the danger mounted. It was up to her to make the effort, to prove once and for all that she really had the strength to turn her back on him and go.

Amélie didn't come in from the gardens until Marie sounded the old-fashioned gong for lunch, merely going to the downstairs cloakroom to rinse her hands and not appearing in the dining room until everyone else was seated. It might appear she had been unwilling to confront Eve again, or had simply waited, with supreme confidence, for Raoul to annihilate her.

Eve noticed throughout the meal how Amélie's eyes gleamed spitefully as they wandered frequently from Raoul to herself, noting, with obvious satisfaction, that they rarely addressed each other. Raoul's solicitude regarding Amélie's comfort was something Amélie took so clearly for granted that, on more than one occasion with Amélie simpering at him, Eve ground her small white teeth almost audibly. Pain stabbed and she flinched while perversely glad of it, hiding as it did a worse type of hurt, and a flicker of jealousy which, of course, she disowned.

Altogether, Eve was glad when it was over and she was able to excuse herself. The men had told her when she had left them that morning they were breaking some of the young stallions later in the day, and she did not want to miss such a sight. Not that she particularly cared for the idea of wild horses being tamed in this fashion, but she supposed it was necessary for the good of the herds. The herdsmen, she knew, were superb, and would never treat an animal cruelly. Women, she supposed bitterly, remembering Raoul DuBare's treatment of herself, would be quite another thing!

She lingered with Michel until almost four, then, leaving him playing happily with his two young nursemaids, she ran down to the sheds where the *gardians* were already busy. Eagerly Eve climbed on to the top of some high wooden railings to watch. Young stallions of about three to four years old were caught in the marshes and brought back to the *manade* where they were handled to get them used to people before being ridden for the first time. It was hard work, sometimes dangerous, as the animals seemed instinctively to know they would never again have the same freedom and rebelled accordingly, their hooves flying out wildly at anyone who got in their way.

The mistral had been blowing for several days now, and it was hot and dusty, but Eve didn't care. The dust was the worst part of it, clinging as it did to her clothes and hair, getting in her eyes, half blinding her. Yet somehow the discomfort went unnoticed, surrounded as she was by numbers of excited horses, and equally excited men. Horses are creatures of habit. They liked familiar, well worn tracks, known grazing grounds, a regular pattern of activity, and object when this pattern is broken. All this Raoul DuBare had explained to *her* on one of the rare occasions when he had taken her out—excursions to be treasured but not dwelt on too deeply. Exactly how an animal's instinct works was still a mystery, he'd said, but a horse's perception was infinitely more sensitive than man's. In thick darkness a horse could find its way home without any difficulty, while anything new or different on its path would immediately arouse its suspicions.

François, Eve's faithful shadow, was giving a running commentary on the proceedings, encouraged perhaps by her animated expression. She listened fitfully, her whole attention diverted when one of the herdsmen, riding a working horse, brought out a young, unbroken stallion on a leading-rein. She watched closely as the man worked carefully to get the wild horse used to the saddle, holding her breath almost painfully as the horse reared, trying to get free.

"You are interested, *mademoiselle*?" At first she absently assumed it was François who had spoken, until the different timbre of voice broke through her absorption. She didn't need to turn to see who was standing behind her. Her pulse leapt even while she kept her eyes fixed steadily in front of her. Fervently she had hoped he wouldn't be here and, for a short time, she had felt completely relaxed because he wasn't, but she might have known he would arrive.

"Why, *monsieur*," she heard herself saying blankly, "You seem bent on startling me today..."

CHAPTER EIGHT

IMMEDIATELY SHE HAD spoken Eve flushed. That sounded naive, but did his brows have to shoot up so sarcastically? She let out a faintly stifled breath that had nothing to do with the dust, aware that he waited for some kind of explanation. "I had nothing planned, *monsieur*," her voice faltered. "I came on impulse."

If anything his brows rose higher. "You don't have to make it up as you go along, child," he rebuked ironically, "spare me that! If you had mentioned that you wished to come here today I would have brought you myself."

Eve gulped, fixing an unfocused look on a point somewhere beyond his shoulder. "I cannot tell you everything, *monsieur*, we are not on those kind of terms. Besides, you were talking with Madame Troyat, so I imagined you had other plans for this afternoon."

He ignored this, but his mouth tightened at the corners as he looked at her. "Why can't you be your age! Must you always act like some crazy child, sitting in the dust as if it was sand on the beach! What you really need is discipline, and one of these days, when my patience is at an end..."

His voice was low, and Eve did not need to glance at him again to know he was furious. Recklessly indignant, she retaliated, "You sound just like a disapproving parent, *monsieur.*"

"A while ago it was Raoul!"

Her lashes flickered, this time uncertainly. "Only because you startled me."

"Now you choose not even to look at me!" As if conscious of other ears listening, he spoke in savage undertones, something about her obviously driving him beyond sufferance.

Surely her lack of elegance should not offend him to this extent? Eve's blue eyes clouded curiously as, as if compelled by his anger, they turned apprehensively back to him, her glance clinging with a sudden, startled surprise to his checked shirt. She hadn't noticed he was dressed like one of his own men, and obviously not for pleasure. It couldn't be that he intended riding one of those snorting, infuriated animals himself?

"Eve!"

As her expression grew trance-like with dismay, his sharp tones jerked her upright. "I'm sorry," she gasped, her voice containing now only the shadow of a shaky defiance, "But I am looking at you as you requested, *monsieur*, if it was necessary?"

"*Mon dieu!*" he countered, missing completely the fears which beset her, in his apparent desire to shake the life from her. "You parade in front of my men in a pair of jeans so tight they leave nothing to the imagination! You sit on a fence like a young boy, not caring what the dust and dirt does to your skin! If you were mine, *mademoiselle*—"

"But I am not!" Eve cut in, feeling it was a point to be immediately emphasised, her heart thumping again at his sheer male arrogance.

"Not yet!"

"Monsieur. . . ?" His chief *gardian* approached him, seeking advice, and Raoul turned abruptly from Eve, dropping her arm, though not his dark scowl, and she stared after him compulsively, every nerve end tingling as if with shock, as he walked towards the horses.

"Stay there and don't move until I am finished," he commanded curtly, obviously indifferent as to whether the men heard or not. "I will not be long, then we shall return to the house."

Mutinously numb, Eve gazed after his tall, dark figure. He towered way and above most of his men and was also much heavier built, although he moved with a litheness which matched even the youngest of them, and was clearly, in every way, supremely fit. Unconsciously her fingers crept to her arm, where his hand had touched her, remembering how he had held her before lunch. It wasn't sensible to wonder if he liked the feel of her body close to his. With his hard masculinity perhaps any woman, not necessarily any particular one, would do.

In minutes his long stride took him away from her, to the other end of the huge enclosure, where she lost sight of him amidst the general mêlée of animals, dust and men.

The first horse she saw was saddled and walking quietly on the leading-rein. Now it was time for someone to try and mount him, and this wasn't accomplished immediately. Eve drew in her breath sharply as she listened to the encouraging calls of the *gardians* as the first man succeeded in staying in the saddle and both horse and rider disappeared in the ensuing swirl of pounding hooves and dust. The stallion's frenzied body flashed through the air as he tried every trick to unseat the man, but the exuberant *gardian* won. It was a clash of wills, a battle of strong temperaments, the outcome foreseeable if not to be taken for granted.

It was a ritual, born of necessity, that the young stallions should be broken and learnt to tolerate the saddle, as no one in the Camargue rides a mare, these being kept for breeding. After today's session the stallions would be gently and patiently schooled until they were ready to be mounted normally. The mutual respect between the famous *gardian* and his horse was something one was instinctively aware of.

Raoul, to Eve's relief, because she wanted to stay a little longer, remained where he was, and when one of the stallions managed to throw two men he mounted it himself. Eve felt herself tremble and her hands go slack with perspiration on the rails as she watched, unable, for a moment, to conceal the depth of her fear. She had been aware of Raoul DuBare's good horsemanship, and she could see how he was superb, but it didn't stop her from shaking, from being suddenly terrified for his safety. The animal, having already triumphed over two men, was quite confident of getting rid of a third and reared and bucked with this clearly paramount on its mind. Impossible...! The men laughed and cheered, relaxing after the first few traumatic seconds when it seemed that victory might almost be within reach of the infuriated horse. Eve's heart was in her mouth, which seemed uncommonly dry, when a short time later Raoul stepped down, as coolly as if he had merely been out on a leisurely excursion. *Le maître* was obviously a hero in the eyes of his men, indifferent while she had been fraught with anxiety about a danger, which for him, hadn't seemed to exist.

But the danger, it seemed, was there, not for Raoul but for herself. Another of the young horses managing to throw its rider, broke free from the lead rein, and, before anyone could move, charged wildly at the wooden fence on which Eve was perched. It all happened so swiftly she couldn't afterwards recall a thing. One minute she was sitting comfortably, gazing bitterly at Raoul DuBare, the next, she was lying flat on her back, a canopy of slashing hooves flying over her.

She couldn't be hurt, although the breath seemed to have been completely knocked from her body. Backwards she had been flung, every part of her jarred with the unhampered force of her fall, a small scream of frightened surprise echoing faintly from her lips. She hit the hard ground with a softly audible thud, and lay, momentarily unable to move, a slender, crumpled heap against the dry, arid earth, the fragments of broken railings scattered all around her.

"*Mon dieu!*" From a distance she heard Raoul's furious exclamation, and tried to open her eyes immediately so as to assure him she was only—the word stupidly eluded her—winded! It couldn't be more. At least, nothing to justify the way in which his hands were going ruthlessly over her, probing, it seemed, every bone of her body. Then he was picking her up, holding her to him with a force which she unhappily suspected might be doing more damage than her actual fall.

He was shouting to the men, his language only fit for the ears of the unconscious, so for a moment she considered it advisable to retain this appearance. He sounded like a man very near the end of his tether, but it was enough to lie limp, for once letting his anger flow unanswerably over her.

"And you," she heard him hiss in her ear as he carried her towards the house, "you may open your eyes. I am assured the damage is not irreparable. You deserve to hear everything I have to say for sitting on that rotten fence. *Mon dieu* I need my head examined for allowing you to remain there, but must you always be in some kind of trouble, *mademoiselle*?"

"I'm sorry," she whispered, her voice weak, not from the injuries he so rightly wouldn't allow her, but she had received a fright and felt badly shaken. His rotten fence, as he called it, had been quite high! All she needed was the consolation of his arms, just for a few more minutes, even if he felt no actual sympathy. His heart thudded into her through the blue and black check of his shirt, and she caught the dusty, perspiring heat from his body. Insanely she wished suddenly that the house was miles away. Her fall might have taken all her breath, but it had also seemed to remove all her resistance, leaving her trembling, unable to hide her devastating emotions. "Oh, Raoul," she moaned, pressing her hot face frantically against his broad chest.

"Be still," he ordered grimly, obviously thinking her wandering in the mind. "You could have hurt your head. *Un docteur*..."

"No, no," she cried, fully aware of his instant rejection, "I don't need a doctor. You can let me down, I can walk."

But, all at once, they were at the house, and Amélie was there, the sharpness of her glance, the suspicion in her face too apparent. Eve caught her glance and there was hate in it, warring with a patent disbelief.

Amélie's laughter came shrill as she saw Raoul

lowering Eve gently down to the sofa. "Good heavens," she exclaimed, "whatever has Eve been up to now?"

Raoul didn't answer. He took no notice of Amélie at all as he gently swept Eve's fair hair back from her pale forehead. "Am I to be always doing this?" he murmured enigmatically. "Will you never learn to look after yourself?"

Eve stirred beneath the piercing scrutiny of his eyes as they searched her white face, but before she could speak, Amélie intervened again. "Would someone mind telling me what has happened to Mademoiselle Reston? Does she have to have all your attention as well as your sympathy, Raoul?"

"She was knocked from the railings on the fence. Quite easily she might have been killed," Raoul retorted, sharply abrupt as he went to pour brandy.

"So," Amélie's eyes were spiteful, "what else would you expect of one so foreign to our ways! Who would flaunt herself from such a position in front of all your men! Surely you haven't forgotten Carol?"

"That will be enough, Amélie!" Raoul's voice was rough as he thrust the brandy into Eve's hand instead of administering it himself as had obviously been his intention a moment ago. He appeared to dismiss Amélie's vindictive accusations curtly, but Eve saw from his slight frown that there was something he had indeed overlooked.

With a great effort she managed to get to her feet, welcoming Marie's timely appearance in the doorway. "If you will excuse me, Raoul," she said hastily, feeling slightly sick, "I think I'll go to my room."

Marie went with her, on Raoul's orders, while he

stayed with Amélie, staring steadily down into the glass Eve had given him back and surveying the untouched contents moodily. It was nothing, Eve told herself stolidly as Marie helped her upstairs, and, if she felt hurt, she couldn't altogether blame Amélie. It was plain Raoul had been fed up with her behaviour, by what he had said as he had carried her in. This would be his way of making doubly sure she didn't attach to his small act of chivalry any of the wrong conclusions. And it was also clear that he sought to allay any suspicions Amélie might have by not bothering to escort Eve even so far as the drawing-room door.

Eve's head ached for the rest of the day, but after a good night's sleep she felt a whole lot better, apart from the persistent ache in her heart and limbs. The soreness of her limbs was only to be expected, she smiled wryly, when Marie, bringing her early morning coffee, asked how she was. Eve didn't mention the condition of her heart.

Raoul hadn't come near her again the previous evening, but had instructed Marie to bring her a light meal upstairs to save her the discomfort of coming down for dinner.

"*Le maître* is always so thoughtful!" Marie had explained, and while obviously wondering why Eve hadn't immediately agreed with her, had put down her reticence to her fall.

How could Eve possibly have told her, that for one short visit from *le maître* she would gladly have forfeited a thousand dinners! But then Marie might have understood no better than she did herself.

A few days later Raoul went to Paris, the direct sequence of a telephone call from his manager. He would be away, it seemed, overnight. "It would seem I am not so dispensable after all," he shrugged dryly, as he said goodbye at breakfast, before departing.

He had apparently addressed the three of them, but his eyes had lingered fractionally longer on Eve's glistening fair hair, the paleness of her cheeks as she made a great ado of stirring her sugarless coffee. "You look as if you could do with some fresh air, *ma chère*," he had suddenly frowned. "I have told you before I will not have you wearing yourself out over the child!"

"Of course not, *monsieur*," was the most she could manage, feeling, in some peculiar way, more like weeping than wishing him a gay farewell as Célèste was doing, or getting up from the table and kissing him tenderly, as Amélie was doing.

"Nothing from you, Mademoiselle Reston?" he had teased sardonically, pausing beside her chair.

"Goodbye, *monsieur*. It might be different if you were going away for two years," she had retorted, trying desperately to match his light raillery while bright flags of colour touched her cheeks. Deliberately she had striven to show complete indifference, yet she could not bear to look at him in case he should read the true state of her feelings—her despair at the apparent pleasure he had derived from Amélie's warm caress.

Later Célèste went out and, after lunch, Amélie suggested that she and Eve visited the Etang de Vaccarès, a vast lagoon of some seventeen thousand acres which formed part of the famous Camargue nature reserve.

"You must see it," Amélie enthused, adding sweetly, "before you go home."

Eve hesitated, and seeing it, Amélie rushed on,

"Didn't Raoul think you needed fresh air—to get out? And I quite agree with him, *ma chère*. Your pale face irritates him! On the lake there are flamingoes which nest in colonies on the small islands. You will love them, they are such a wonderful sight!"

In spite of Amélie's dramatic enthusiasm, Eve felt a strange, unaccountable reluctance. Yet hadn't Amélie been extremely pleasant all week, and especially this morning? So much so that Eve was convinced she had imagined Amélie disliked her. It probably wasn't possible, or fair, to judge someone on the evidence of one or two isolated incidents, and Eve had no wish to appear vindictive. No one knew better than herself that, where feelings were involved, it was all too easy to suspect the worst of others.

The idea of exploring the nature reserve, or at least some of it, was tempting. Once, she remembered, Raoul had mentioned it. He had, in fact, promised to take her there himself, but she doubted if he would really find time. Time, for her, she knew, was running out. It might be better to take a chance with Amélie.

"But what about Michel?" she hedged uncertainly, feeling torn in two directions.

"But what about him, *ma chère*?" Amélie mocked gaily at Eve's anxious expression. "Marie will do everything necessary—she loves the child. Besides, as it is so hot and Raoul is away, I have told her not to cook dinner, that something cool and light will do, a simple snack, so that it doesn't matter when we get back."

Knowing she had run out of excuses, Eve agreed, joining Amélie in her small car outside. Now it had been decided, Amélie was in a hurry to be off, assuring Eve that it was unnecessary to take jackets and, as she had already arranged everything with Marie, there was no need to do anything in that direction either. As Raoul would wish, all Eve had to do was relax.

North of Arles the Rhone divides, its twin streams flowing into the sea across a broad plain. There is always something eerie about a delta. The river has lost its momentum, running sluggishly until the estuary opens and there is a clash of opposing forces as the sea challenges the crawling streams. In turn the river attacks, pushing muddy streamers into the clear, sparkling waves. Here, too, the earth is unstable, fought over by both river and sea. Mud covers the sand in varying depths, to be washed away in the next rainstorm, and dunes which are moulded one day are swept flat by the mistral the next.

West of the Petit Rhone is an area of small lakes and sand dunes, and to the north is a district of vineyards, rice fields and orchards. Here sheep are grazed on the drier pastures while the bulls and horses are reared on the marshier parts. It was the *taureaux* and horses which kept the marshes from being overgrown with the dense reeds.

Amélie, when she chose, could be an interesting companion, being remarkably well informed. As they went along she explained that the major part of the huge Etang de Vaccarès was prohibited to the general public. So, too, was the other native reserve, Les Impériaux. Hunting was not allowed in this area, neither was fishing, except to a few professional fishermen from Les Saintes Maries de la Mer.

Raoul, she said, along with other landowners, still owned and controlled much of the area in between, and this was chiefly used for hunting and the grazing of the semi-wild bulls and horses. Although these places were not in the actual reserves they bordered them, and, because birds and animals rarely recognise boundaries, were almost as good. Indeed, in these boundary areas, where the animals were more or less used to the presence of people, it was often easier to approach them more closely.

The fresh-water marshes in particular provided nesting grounds for thousands of different birds, from the bittern to the purple heron, the water rail and many songsters. Wherever the marshes were heavily grazed by bulls the reeds were thinner, and here could be found terns and stilts along with many ducks and waders in the winter.

"But one must be careful," Amélie laughed. "These swamps are also ideal for our old friend the wild boar, of whom it pays to be wary."

Amélie drove swiftly along the winding roads, and on other stretches where no roads appeared to exist at all and obviously required skilled concentration.

Eve bit her lip as she stared about her. This part of the countryside was not familiar and seemed isolated and lonely. "You're sure you know where you're going?" She glaced at Amélie, trying to speak lightly, reluctant that the woman should suspect she was nervous.

"Of course, *ma chère*," Amélie answered impatiently. "My late husband, you know, was a great friend of Raoul's. He was also a keen ornithologist. When we were first married he used to drag me around these spots almost every weekend, until sometimes I could have screamed with boredom! I'm afraid I used to study the area more than the birds."

And she had thought Amélie overflowing with enthusiasm! Eve felt more confused than ever. It didn't seem to help either, that she soon lost all sense of direction. As the sun grew hotter the small car soon seemed to resemble an oven, and she couldn't restrain an audible sigh of relief when eventually Amélie stopped.

"Phew!" she exclaimed, laughing ruefully as she almost fell from the car, feeling sticky all over from the enervating heat.

Amélie merely shrugged, her eyes appraising on Eve's hot face. "The sun does not bother me," she replied coolly. "You see, *ma chère*, I am used to it, having lived here all my life."

Meaning I haven't, I suppose! Eve got the message loud and clear, although she bit back a sharp retort. In a way, Amélie was probably right, and it couldn't be a subject worth quarreling over! And it was a bit late to begin doubting her wisdom in coming here with Amélie today. It might be better to try and suppress a too vivid imagination! Amélie would never dare harm her, Eve felt sure.

The car was parked and locked on a piece of dry ground before they set off along the side of a swamp. Amélie, Eve was forced to admit before they had gone very far, was a wonderful guide. She seemed to possess a boundless store of sharp energy and soon had found numerous nests. As it was spring the air was alive with the sound of birds, and soon the loneliness of the terrain wasn't so noticeable any more as Amélie named various species, pointing out the wonderful construction of some of the nests. One in particular, that of the whiskered tern which built a floating one of bulrushes and sedge stems, intrigued Eve a lot.

It was much later when Amélie discovered she had forgotten to bring the picnic basket, that they hadn't so much as a flask of fresh water, let alone tea! They had reached a point bordering the edge of the lake, or *étang*, as lakes were called here, when Amélie decided she could go no further without a drink.

"It is all my fault!" she wailed charmingly, when they returned to the car and found what had happened. "*Tiens*, and I am parched!" she exclaimed.

"Well, it won't have to matter." Eve was feeling parched herself, but had no intention of complaining. Anyone could make such a mistake. "It might be better," she conjectured, "to simply go home." In fact she had a sudden, inexplicable longing to do so.

But Amélie wouldn't hear of it. "It is scarcely four o'clock," she cried. "There is still so much I have to show you, especially when, as Raoul has told me, you are soon to be leaving us for London. You must wait here. I will return to the *mas* to collect our tea. On my own I will go much quicker and should be back within half an hour, no more."

With a regrettable flicker of relief, Eve gazed after the departing car. Amélie just wouldn't take no for an answer, declaring adamantly that as the fault was entirely hers she couldn't object to the bother. Eve hadn't persisted, her desire to return to the ranch fading before an even stronger wish to remain where she was and brood. It was not the first time Amélie had related Raoul's remarks, yet always the hurt seemed fresh. Maybe Amélie did do it deliberately, with a touch of exaggeration, but somewhere, Eve frowned, there must be a glimmer of truth. Whatever, it might certainly be advisable to see what she could while she had the chance, and it was strangely soothing, in spite of her former apprehension, to sit here alone.

Eve settled beneath a rather ragged-looking white poplar, the nearest large tree she could find, and prepared to wait. Amélie had told her not to explore on her own, and for once Eve didn't feel like disobeying. The heat seemed to have made her quite tired and she yawned, content to watch a distant group of flamingoes taking off from the lake, the red feathers under their wings, which were hidden when folded, like a brilliant flash of flame against the sky.

Afterwards, Eve never could remember the exact moment she fell asleep, but she always remembered how stiffly uncomfortable she felt when she woke over two hours later. How apprehensive she was when she reealised she was still alone, there being no sign of Amélie with the picnic basket. For a few moments she sat where she was, frowning, trying to ponder constructively on what might have happened. Was it possible that Amélie, driving as she did, had met with an accident? It was now—Eve glanced again at her slim wrist—after six o'clock, and Amélie had been gone since four. There could, of course, be other explanations, if one had time to think them out, but one or two things seemed very clear. If Amélie had had an accident then it was highly improbable she would be back, but unless she was unconscious she could surely have told someone about her? The men from the ranch would have been here very quickly. But, so far as she could see, there wasn't a soul in sight.

For another half hour Eve waited, before deciding

she must walk. It seemed too obvious that Amélie, or help of any kind, wasn't coming, and it seemed senseless to stay here until dark. Wryly, as she rose to her feet, Eve glanced down at the place where she had been sitting. She didn't think she would ever forget these thirty minutes—the silver trees, the lake and flamingoes; the bare plain and, in the distance, a faint line of white horses grazing towards her. It helped, by concentrating on them, to overlook the peculiar trickle of fear which crept down her spine, making her tremble.

Briefly she hesitated, having little idea of her exact position or of the general direction she should take. The air was still warm, but her skin felt clammy and cold as she became slowly aware what it must be like to spend the night here in the open, alone. There was, she saw, with great relief, the marks of Amélie's car tyres, but though she followed these for what must have been the most part of a mile they eventually faded out as she reached drier ground.

Nevertheless, trying to use some common sense, Eve trudged on, keeping the sun determinedly on her right as she went along. The initial shock at being deserted in such a wilderness had faded yet taken its toll. Her hair was damp, clinging to her cheeks, and perspiration had soaked her thin shirt, which was now crumpled and dirty. Her jeans and shoes were soaked in mud from falling into a swamp, and wide-eyed she surveyed them, feeling only a half hysterical relief that Raoul DuBare, with his fastidious fault-finding, couldn't see her now.

It seemed to come to her only slowly that all about her was growing quieter. As night approached the birds ceased singing, there was only the rustle of wind in the tops of the pines. The treetops were glowing with the rays of the setting sun and the glinting light moved from leaf to leaf, dancing between the branches before subsiding into the olive-green canopy of shrubs and thick undergrowth. Then she was aware all around her of new noises and sounds, of shadows detaching themselves from the dark reed tunnels among the marshes and turning into hungry, searching creatures bent on foraging for food under the protection of the oncoming darkness. It was then, to her horror, that she heard what seemed to be a grunt, and remembering what Amélie had said about wild boars, she took to her heels and ran, spending what little breath she had left in one last despairing race to escape what she imagined could be a relentless pursuer.

Needless to say nothing did actually chase after her, but it was perhaps just as well that the noise had sent her off in another direction, as it was only after she had forced her way through a heavy clump of shrub that the *gardians* found her.

They assured her that they had never for a moment doubted they would, although relief mingled with disbelief on their faces as Eve burst into sight. Célèste did tell her later that they had all been terribly worried, especially as Raoul hadn't been there to direct them, and they had not immediately found her where Amélie had sworn she would be.

"The danger," Célèste said, "of being lost in the Delta comes not so much from being attacked by wild animals as from the possibility of falling into one of the numerous lakes or swamps."

Most of the *gardians* had searched for her on horseback, but two of them came in trucks, and it was into one of these that the men gently put Eve to drive her home, trying, she could see, not to look too closely at her bedraggled appearance. Fortunately, apart from this, she seemed none the worse; at least she wasn't fainting all over the place, as she had thought she might when her control had seemed to be slipping—when, for one awful moment, she had decided no one would ever find her again. For the first time in her life she had felt numb with fear as she had visualised a devilish pursuer in the scrub. Death, she remembered thinking, could be relentless, but could surely never overtake her like this!

Her face felt sore where deep scratches had cut the white skin, and when she touched the red weals with exploratory fingers she winced, glad again that Raoul wasn't here to see her. He was in Paris, thank goodness. Yet contrarily her flicker of relief brought no real comfort. He would be back!

When she found her voice sufficiently to ask the men what exactly had happened to Amélie, they looked peculiarly evasive, muttering something about engine trouble, which to Eve's dazed mind sounded just about right. No reason for them to reply in such uncertain tones, or, when they concluded that she was too spent to hear, to whisper together so apprehensively about *le maître*. Nothing of what had happened was their fault—anyone's fault, really, so what had they to worry about? Hadn't they rescued her, and wasn't Raoul hundreds of miles away. And, before he came back, she might even be as far away from this terrible place herself.

It was Célèste who eventually told her exactly what had happened. Amélie, it seemed, shortly after she had left Eve that afternoon, had developed a fault in her engine and had decided to make for Les Saintes Maries. The garage there, she had felt sure, would be able to sort out the trouble quicker than they could at the ranch. But it had been several hours before she had even got there, and a while longer before a mechanic diagnosed dirt in the petrol tank and pronounced that he could do little about it that night.

"So it was almost dark, you see, before Amélie rang here asking us to go and fetch you," Célèste said anxiously. "I think she blamed herself for not finding it possible to let us know sooner. I think she said it was a case of acting for the best and nothing turning out as she'd expected!"

And she could say that again! Eve thought wryly, as she surveyed her mutilated arms and face in the mirror next morning. Amélie hadn't, in fact, arrived back until after Eve the night before, and she had been full of commiseration, none of which, to Eve's weary ears at least, sounded particularly sincere. Amélie's story was too plausible. If there had been dirt in the engine, wouldn't it have troubled them on the way to the reserve earlier in the afternoon? It didn't seem possible—and certainly wouldn't be probable; she had deliberately put it there herself so that Eve might be forced to spend the night alone on the marshes, but Eve shivered, knowing suddenly beyond doubt, that what she suspected was true.

Yet why should Amélie Troyat do such a thing? Had she quite ruthlessly wanted to drive a girl she disliked out of her mind? Eve shuddered, remembering her own terror, wondering wildly if it could have happened. That Amélie should constructively plan such an occurrence surely indicated some degree of derangement. No wholly sane person would ever think of such a thing!

Agonisingly, all through the night, while her bruises and sore limbs refused to let her rest, Eve thought of it, and long before dawn pushed tentative fingers across her windowsill she knew what she must do. She might have misjudged Amélie, but she couldn't afford, for Michel's sake, to give her the benefit of this doubt. Raoul must not be allowed to marry Amélie, as he had indicated he might if Eve kept on refusing him. If Amélie really was unstable, then might it not be almost criminal to allow her any part in Michel's future, especially when the way to prevent this was clearly indicated?

As if to confirm her suspicions, Amélie came to her room first thing the next morning, suggesting lightly but firmly, "Don't you think you would be wise to go home immediately, Eve? Your face is scratched, but not too badly, nothing to stop you travelling. I could quite easily accompany you as far as Paris today, which would certainly guarantee your escape from Raoul's anger when he returns."

Her heart suddenly cold, Eve laid aside the small hand mirror she had been holding and stared at Amélie in confusion. So Amélie was determined to be rid of her after all—and today! She was certainly a woman of some decision, was Amélie! Dryly Eve swallowed, feeling a great necessity to gulp the tea Amélie had dropped sharply on her bedside table, but dared not. It could be poisoned! Half hysterically she giggled softly at her own humour.

Amélie, seeing only the hectic spots of colour on

Eve's pale cheeks, sought deviously to press her point. "You could never stand up to Raoul's anger, *ma chère*. His wealth makes him arrogant. You are too small and vulnerable."

Eve blinked in some confusion, sobering right away before the flaring speck in Amélie's eye. "I know he is impatient of accidents, *madame*, and I realise I have had several since I came here, but none of them, especially this last one, was my fault. Well, not exactly..."

As her voice trailed off Amélie countered sharply, "But if you hadn't insisted on going to the game reserve—"

"But I didn't!" Eve's eyes widened with bewilderment. "It was you who suggested it, you know that."

"But no one else does, and who will believe you?" Amélie's laughter was spiteful. "Raoul is too aware of my dislike for any part of the countryside, the reserve, with all those thousands of screaming, highly colourful birds, especially. And he knows better than most that I am not to be persuaded to do anything I would not enjoy."

"He wouldn't believe you!"

"He very probably would." Amélie's black eyes snapped. "And then you would also be a liar, as well as a nuisance, *ma chère*."

Eve felt stunned, also slightly sick with a great upsurge of foreboding. If she had been seeking for confirmation regarding the state of Amélie's mind, didn't she have it now? All the evidence she needed—if she only had to convince herself. Nothing else must be important, all her personal inclinations must be clamped down on. Carol, Dominique, her uncle and aunt would never forgive her if she let Michel down now.

For one distraught moment she closed her eyes against the inevitable. There was a chance, if a slim one, that such a decision might never have to be made, that Raoul might believe Amélie and consider this latest escapade of Eve's unforgivable and wash his hands of her. Involuntarily she flinched against the confusing pain of such a possibility, tremors which went shattering through her dismissing coherent thought. In such an event she could only make one last attempt to make alternative plans for Michel.

Amélie moved, sharply impatient, her eyes glacial on Eve's hesitant face. "Well, *mademoiselle*," she prompted, "are you deaf as well as blind?"

"I'm sorry," Eve whispered, her nausea strangely deepening before the insolence in Amélie's voice, "I'm afraid I can't go home today, *madame*. Raoul might, as you say, very easily be furious, but whatever else I may be, I hope I am not a coward. I must stay and see him."

CHAPTER NINE

EVE, understandably, was a little late in coming down for breakfast that morning and was surprised to find Célèste in the hall, already dressed to go out.

As she heard Eve on the stairs, Célèste glanced upwards with an unusual air of startled embarrassment colouring her smoothly made-up cheeks. "Oh, hello, *ma chère*," she said brightly, obviously pushing aside her confusion. "Amélie tells me you are fully recovered, so you won't mind if I go with her to Marseille. We are to collect her car from the garage in Les Saintes Maries. She is waiting outside for me now, and asked me to hurry."

"Yes—well, fine. Go ahead." Eve's lips felt strangely stiff. It seemed an effort to speak carelessly, as though Célèste's desertion didn't matter. Somehow everything was an effort this morning in spite of the fact that she must be relatively unscathed from her ordeal. It brought some small relief, however, to know that Amélie was going, although Eve doubted it would be for long. In another way her going didn't seem to make sense—hadn't she threatened to tell Raoul the wrong story? It seemed unlikely that she had had second thoughts and changed her mind.

Célèste, gathering up her handbag, soon enlightened her. "Raoul rang and Amélie answered, before I came down. She has explained about yesterday, but she didn't say what he said. He has a conference this morning, so will not be home before this evening or maybe tomorrow. But do not look so worried, *ma chère*, he can't be angry!"

But he was angry, furiously angry, and he arrived home in the middle of the afternoon, when Eve least expected him.

"Célèste told me you had a conference," she gasped, as her bedroom door was rudely thrust open and he strode in unannounced.

She was lying on her bed, fully clothed in one of the shapeless cotton frocks from her wardrobe, to which, after Raoul's dry criticism, she had taken an inexplicable dislike, only wearing it now because it was cool against her burning skin. Fervently she wished he hadn't found her like this, but the hot sunshine outside had made the scratches on her face sting, forcing her indoors, and somehow it had seemed Raoul's sudden appearance put her in a fine fret and she clenched her hands hard to stop them trembling.

"What happened to your conference?" she tried again, as he made no reply to her first query.

"*Mon dieu!*" It appeared to have taken him several seconds to find his voice, and he swore roundly, not beneath his breath, as his eyes blazed over her torn face, her sore young body huddled helplessly against the pillows. He rapped out an oath which was only surpassed by his glowering expression. "You talk of conferences, *mademoiselle,* but leave me with no peace of mind to concentrate. The moment my back is turned you seem all set to commit suicide, and I am forced to rush home to survey the damage!" Ruthlessly he sank down beside her on the bed, his hand going out to sweep the tumbled gold curls from her face. "*Mon dieu!*" he repeated, "if you had set out deliberately to ruin your beautiful skin you could not have done better!"

"It was scarcely my fault, *monsieur.*" His close proximity made her voice weak and she lay very still, aware of an urgent need to placate him before he added to the damage she had already sustained.

Coldly he continued to regard her. "Did I not promise to take you to the reserve myself? As a member, I have access to every part of it. But no, you must assert your insane independence by going yourself, by begging Amélie to take you. My patience," his jaw clamped, "is at an end! I refuse to spend my entire future quoting parrot-like, 'you might have been killed'! From this moment onwards, *ma chérie*, you will not so much as move until you have my absolute permission!"

"But it wasn't like that..." Near breaking point, Eve gazed at him, Amélie's words returning triumphantly to haunt her—"he will only think you are a liar". Could she risk this—would it not perhaps be better to let things slide? After all, no crime was involved, and matters might merely be made worse. Yet somehow there was in Eve the most fervent compulsion to protest, even though Raoul's darkness, his cold purpose was most intimidating, doing nothing to encourage a plea for understanding.

"You tell me how it was like?" he ground out sarcastically as she paused. "Then you will no doubt feel better, which is more than I can ever hope to do."

His ambiguity was beyond her. It was his tone of voice that prompted her to continue recklessly, "To go to the reserve wasn't my idea. You might recall saying, before you left yesterday, that I needed fresh air, and after lunch, Amélie suggested we went there."

"Eve!" His green eyes darkened coldly to jet, and she knew immediately she had made a mistake. On his face was no sign of the trust she had hoped for, only suspicion, an almost tangible longing to shake her. "I wish," he was suddenly taut, "you could lose this rather stupid habit of lying to me. Amélie would never dream of going near the reserve. It is too tied up with memories of her husband. She dislikes it intensely."

"Then there is nothing more to be said, *monsieur*," Eve's face went white, the shock of his incredulity worse to bear than any physical pain she was suffering. "You must surely be congratulating yourself that you discovered my true character in time."

"Before I married you, you mean?" His eyes were like diamond slits in the hardness of his face.

"Exactly." Gloriously defiant, Eve annihilated all her former resolutions. Never, never could she marry such an arrogant man!

His voice was smoothly suave. "But you mustn't let it bother you, *mon amie*. I intend to iron all such deception from you, if necessary with a heavy hand. You are young enough to learn. *Mon dieu*, you won't know yourself when I am finished!"

She flung at him her furious retort, "I like myself as I am, *monsieur*!"

"*Monsieur*," he mocked cruelly, his eyes contemptuous of her spirited protest, before his expression changed abruptly, and it seemed in spite of himself, as again his frowning glance rested on the livid marks on her otherwise smooth white throat. "I must have a look at those scratches," he went on, somewhat curtly, "so you can stop acting like an outraged child and oblige me by being still for a moment. Marie informs me that you refused to allow her to send for the doctor!"

"Well, it wasn't necessary..."

His mouth thinned. "But I, *mademoiselle*, will arrange that he shall come immediately, should I feel it necessary."

Eve squirmed sullenly, trying not to flinch as he began to examine her face very thoroughly, her hand clenched tight when once he probed too closely. Yet his fingers were infinitely gentle, his movements deft, and she could find no real cause for complaint. It was when he saw the deeper weals on her shoulders that his fingers stiffened as though he would have liked to hit her. "And you got up, this morning," he rasped, "and went down to breakfast, telling everyone you were well!"

"I suppose Amélie assured you she would not have left if she had thought otherwise?" Eve choked, almost breathless with an unhappiness she didn't understand and hating his seeming indifference.

"One more word," he ground out, the hardness of his green glance cold on her lacerated skin, "and I will add to your pain where it hurts most. Naturally neither Amélie or Célèste would have left if they had known. Now if you will make some endeavour to relax I will dress these wounds properly, before ringing the good doctor."

"I wish you wouldn't, Raoul," she begged, her eyes fixed pleadingly on his, not really surprised when he refused.

"There may be some infection, *ma chère*, as you must with your training know. Only a doctor can deal with that!"

It seemed hours later, but was actually just after eight o'clock, when Eve, bathed and dressed, joined Raoul for dinner in the cool dimness of the dining-room. The doctor had arrived and given her an injection, but declared himself unable to improve on Raoul's initial treatment. He had examined her so thoroughly that she suspected Raoul's implicit instructions, then, with Marie looking on, had informed her that with a little care she should soon heal, that she was indeed a very fortunate young lady.

If she sensed undertones of another meaning apart from her health, the doctor's suave countenance gave no clues. She had no clear idea what he was on about until she took coffee with Raoul in his study later in the evening. When he told her, without a fraction of hesitation, they were to be married in a few days' time.

"I have been making all the necessary arrangements in Paris," he said coolly, apparently oblivious of Eve's speechless stare. "We will be married there but return here immediately, as Nadine and Célèste will leave the same day on a six months' tour of the States. Afterwards, *ma chère*, we will be away on our own vacation, a belated honeymoon, if you like."

Eve's eyes widened and she felt dizzy and grasped the cup she was holding until her knuckles shone white. He had been extremely considerate over dinner and she had come down not knowing quite what to expect, the recollection of his total disbelief in her integrity clouding her imagination as a forerunner of escalating disaster. It was no comfort to learn that her instincts had not been wrong. "You go about things in a very high-handed manner," she whispered hoarsely.

Firmly he eased the fragile cup from her taut fingers, his dark eyes narrowed on her shocked face. "Otherwise," he emphasised, "we should never get anywhere. We both know what we must do for Michel and an impossible situation is fast developing, one which I hope to deal with very quickly once we are married. There comes a time when it is necessary to take action, Eve."

He talked in riddles, as usual, and her mind was too numbed to sort it out. Hopelessly, in spite of all her former resolutions, she knew what she must do, but what about him? Uncertainty flickered, distress turning her pupils to an almost intense blue. "You are willing," she asked nervously, "to sacrifice all hope of marrying someone you love?"

He said, very crisply, his eyes glinting with a kind of devilment, "Don't you visualise any romance between us?"

"I don't think so," her heavy lashes swept her cheeks as she faltered, not daring to let him so much as glimpse at her despair. "You would not find me very exciting, *monsieur*."

His mouth quirked. "You might surprise me."

The need to be completely honest drove her beyond her normal discretion. "I don't think I have a passionate nature..."

"You have some evidence of this?" There was still the touch of amusement, the indication that he refused to take this matter seriously.

Unhappily Eve was beginning to wish she had never said anything, but once started, what else could she do but go on? "I've never had a serious affair, *monsieur*, and I have had the opportunity, but you see I have never felt particularly amorous."

"And what if I told you I am willing to take a chance?"

"I wouldn't wish you to feel cheated."

This time his voice came very smoothly. "I do not anticipate such an event."

Immediately she went taut, something moving convulsively in the pit of her stomach. She felt all sorts of things about him instinctively, but this was one thing—the ability to find the right words to express such feelings, quite another. "What you are saying, *monsieur*, seems to suggest that you imagine a normal marriage. Or perhaps that you expect to seek some sort of distraction elsewhere?"

His eyes scorched her face with their cynical amusement, and he appeared in no way impressed by her obviously painful endeavours to have everything straightened out between them. His light laughter flicked her lazily as he drawled, "And why should I go to the trouble and the often considerable expense of keeping another woman when I will have a young and beautiful wife, who is probably only lacking a little careful tuition?"

His teasing was the last straw. Her face scarlet with mortification, she cried, "You must give me time!" In a breathing space anything could happen, a reprieve had been won in less.

His eyes narrowed comprehendingly, but he merely said, "Just so long as you don't ask for a written guarantee, *ma chère*. You British are very keen on your guarantees."

"But you are a man of your word?" Feebly she clutched at anything.

"Usually, but do not try me too far, *petite*. I might also be something rather beyond your experience."

What did he mean? He was French, of course, which did not necessarily mean he disliked all English girls, although he had disapproved of Carol. "You didn't like my cousin did you, *monsieur*?"

His lips thinned impatiently, although he replied evenly enough. "I can't see how that odd little question has any bearing on the present situation, Eve, and I don't think it would profit either of us to discuss either Carol or my brother. I will see to it that their child is well looked after, but they can't, unfortunately, have any part in his future."

Unhappily Eve stared away from him. So he intended marrying her with the mystery of Carol and Dominique like a blank wall between them? Which only implied that he didn't altogether trust her? And, come to that, in other ways perhaps the mistrust was mutual. Would he really find it possible to give up all his girl-friends—especially Amélie? Eve found herself doubting it.

Suddenly, as her eyes returned widely to his, he pulled her decisively to her feet. "Come, *ma chère,*" he ordered lightly, "you've had enough drama in the last few days without adding to it. I'll see you to your room, otherwise I fear you might collapse on the way up—you have an air of fine exhaustion."

Somehow she found it impossible to argue, to find so much as a whisper of protest as, with his hand protectively beneath her arm, Raoul halted outside her bedroom door.

"Now," he said, his mockery cancelling the solicitude of a moment ago, "say goodnight like a good girl. There is always tomorrow."

Without giving her a chance to protest, he bent his dark head and kissed her, his lips crushing hers hard. It was only briefly, but the touch of that ruthless mouth was enough to send a blaze of fire shooting through her, bringing chaos to her emotions.

"Goodnight, *chérie*," she heard his voice coolly following her, as, anything but coolly, she wrenched herself free and fled into her room.

THEY WERE MARRIED, as Raoul had promised, five days later, the ceremony brief, in the same church where he told her his parents had been married almost forty years before. It was all very quiet, with only Célèste and Nadine and an old friend of Raoul's, a man of about the same age, who seemed quite taken with Eve and embarrassed her by declaring emphatically to Raoul that he was marrying a beautiful *jeune fille*. She wasn't surprised to learn later that he was a member of the old French nobility—such sophistication and elegance would have been impossible to place elsewhere.

The day before the wedding she had travelled to Paris with Raoul and Célèste and the two girls had stayed overnight with Nadine. Eve was still not quite sure exactly how Célèste had taken the news of the impending marriage, but Raoul had given her little opportunity to air any definite views, if indeed she had any. In Raoul's presence she had hinted rather sharply to Eve that there had been no necessity to carry their little charade so far. And to Raoul she had protested that Amélie would be heartbroken. But before she had got any further Raoul had whipped her curtly into his study, to deliver, Eve had little doubt, a lecture. While she could sympathise with Célèste's bewilderment she had felt oddly grateful for the ensuing silence when Célèste, obviously enthralled with the prospect of America, had held her peace.

Only once, that Eve knew of, did she relate to the subject again. "I never thought," Eve heard her say smugly to Raoul before they went in to the reception, "that when I sent for Eve to come to the Camargue it would turn out like this!"

But there had been no time for Raoul to reply, or to even suppose he had heard properly, and, in the next champagne-drinking, congratulation-filled hours, no opportunity for him to question Célèste, if he had been inclined. Célèste's mood veered so changeably that Eve saw, not for the first time, she would always need a steadying influence in her life, and, fond as she was of her, Eve felt strangely thankful she would be away for six months.

It seemed inconsistent with her relief that the ceremony was over to feel a curious reluctance when she and Raoul left Paris to return home later in the afternoon. She would have liked to have lingered, but Raoul wished only to get back.

As he heard her low sigh, his lips moved in a slight smile. "Paris is really for lovers," he said, clearly reading her thoughts, "to be enjoyed to the full. But," he added, enigmatically, "I promise you will see it another day."

Eve bit her lip, looking down at her lap, a demure and attractive figure in her cool silk dress. It was a dress which had cost more than she had dared to think about, and, though it had been purchased in a hurry the previous morning along with several others, fitted her beautifully. She tried, but failed dismally, to keep her thoughts away from the fashionable boutique she had been taken to. "The leading couturière, the most expensive in the city!" Célèste had whispered, proceeding to reel off the names of some of its famous clientele before Raoul had growled at her to shut up.

It would have been sensible to have shown how humiliated she had felt, having scarcely enough money to pay for the shoes she had been married in, yet for a little while she had found it possible to be completely captivated by the ankle-length, frothy white dress which Raoul insisted she wore in church. There was also a collection of equally suitable gowns which had been sent this morning for her to take home.

And that hadn't been all. In the late afternoon there had been a lengthy visit to the luxurious salon of a famous beauty house where she had been gone over, it seemed, from head to toe, everything possible being done to turn her from a passably pretty girl into a raving beauty. Certainly Eve had found it rather difficult to recognise herself afterwards—all the gleaming, satiny skin, the enchantingly pure curve of a sensuous mouth, a fluffy fall of ashen hair, fingers so delicately tinted as to give every appearance of not having done so much as a day's work in their life. Yet every bit of her ironic self criticism had been forgotten before the glittering appreciation in Raoul's eyes as she had walked towards him up the aisle.

"You look wonderful, *chérie*," she had thought he had said, but wasn't sure she had heard him correctly above the frantic beating of her own heart. "Beautiful..."

It was late when they arrived back at the ranch and there was no one about. Even the nursery, which was on the other side of the huge house, was quiet. Tactfully, Marie had laid out a cold meal in the dining room, and, after wishing them every joy, she discreetly withdrew, but not without a glance of complete approval at Eve's flushed, embarrassed face.

"She only presumes you are covered with a very proper confusion," Raoul teased softly, as he removed her coat. "But that is nothing to what you might expect tomorrow," he smiled. "It is not every day that *le maître* is married. The *gardians* will have a feast and no doubt celebrate accordingly. I might even get a little drunk myself, *ma chère*, if you continue to look at me as you do now."

Hastily Eve removed her wide-eyed gaze from his grave face, excusing herself quickly to go and wash her hands. A few days ago it had all seemed comparatively easy, but now she was beginning to realise that her difficulties might only just be starting. Raoul had hinted that there would be celebrations. Did he forget they had married simply for the sake of the child? She would liked to have reasserted this point, but somehow she dared not, something intangible in the man himself stopping her. It almost seemed beyond her to carry on even a normal conversation.

Swiftly she ran upstairs. The journey had been hot and tedious, and she felt a sudden longing to freshen up completely, to find an old pair of more comfortable shoes for her aching feet. To her utter surprise, when she pushed open the door to her room it was empty. The furniture had not been removed, of course, but the bed was stripped and bare and the wardrobe stood open—bereft of all clothes.

As she stared apprehensively, her heart thudding uncertainly, she heard Raoul's footsteps coming up behind her. "You are naturally with me now, *ma chère*," he said coolly, his hands forcibly on her shoulders as he paused with her, surveying the room.

If Eve felt in his fingers some urgency transmitting itself into her soft flesh she ignored it, holding herself rigid, determined to resist the wild impulse to turn and fling herself wholly into his arms. Also to be curbed was the very real possibility of traitorous senses turning all this into some old-fashioned melodrama. A little common sense was all that might be required—to remain sane.

"I would rather have stayed here, at least for a little while longer." She tried to speak evenly, but her words didn't come out that way.

If he was aware of her agitation he took no notice. His hands merely tightened. "Perhaps you would, Eve, but I do not wish that we should become the objects of amused speculation, as would surely happen if you remained here."

"But you promised!" In spite of her resolve to be sensible her voice rose, as she wrenched furiously round to face him.

His eyes narrowed darkly at her obvious temper. "I made no promises about anything," he said quietly, "least of all about this."

"Just because we never had time to get around to it, but I should have thought it was understood!" she flashed bitterly. "Anyway," she stepped hastily backwards, "whether you approve or not I refuse to move! And, as I feel very tired, I don't think I'll come down again, so I'll say goodnight!"

It was a mistake to get hysterical, to goad him. Immediately she spoke she knew that, but she wasn't in any way prepared for his reactions. Like steel bands his arms went around her, scooping her up, scattering the handbag she was carrying and its contents across the floor as he turned with brute force, crushing her to him as he slammed the door and strode relentlessly along the wide corridor outside.

Eve became aware that she was screaming, half choking against his hard chest, and the more noise she made the more livid he became, clasping her so tightly it hurt. Then, when she seemed almost to have lost all breath, she felt herself released, flung down, or rather hurled, on to something soft—a bed.

"Goodnight, *madame*!" His voice, like a hard living flame, seemed to scorch her. "I no more wish for an unwilling bride than you obviously wish to be one. I can assure you you will not be disturbed here!"

Eve gasped, but before she could speak, if she could have found the words to do so, he had turned and was gone, the door rocking on its hinges emphatically behind him.

Next morning she wasn't sure it hadn't been all a nightmare, but during her first awakening moments when she saw she was completely alone, she slowly realised it had actually happened, her memory wasn't just playing tricks. Raoul had been completely infuriated, and now must be wholly antagonised, something she had never honestly intended should occur, and even now could not clearly understand how it had come about.

Unhappily her glance travelled around the room she now occupied. She must be in Raoul's private suite on the west side of the house, where she had never been before. Her bathroom door stood open, but there was another door, obviously a communicating one which she hadn't dared try the previous night. In case, she recalled thinking wildly, he was on the other side!

No doubt, she hazarded, her glance lingering, that would be his bedroom. Or maybe it was just a dressing-room and she was actually in the bed Raoul usually used. It was large enough and on the dressing-table was laid out what appeared to be a masculine set of brushes. A feeling of something very like shame ran through her, along with a definite quiver of misery as she considered, in retrospect, her own questionable behaviour. There could have been no real need to act as she had done. When they had first arrived home Raoul had not seemed as if he was preparing to be unreasonable. Now she had alienated him completely, he would probably not even be willing to be remotely friendly. And could she blame him? She might justifiably resent his mistrust of her, but had she not exaggerated her own attraction in imagining he wanted her as a man would normally want his wife?

Confused, and not a little embarrassed by her own racing thoughts, Eve scrambled out of bed, and after having a quick shower ran downstairs. Marie, for some reason, had not brought coffee, and Eve suddenly longed for some. Her suitcases had been left inside her bedroom door, although she had no idea how they had got there. Someone must have entered the room silently when she had fallen into an exhausted sleep just before dawn. From an array of new, expensive dresses Eve chose a soft, round-necked cotton, which was cool and hid the now almost faded evidence of her adventure in the nature reserve.

At first she did not look for Raoul, instead she sought Marie in the kitchen.

"But it is in the dining room, *madame.*" Wryly Eve noticed the new, fomal address, but let it go.

"I..." she stammered, suddenly aware of Marie's openly curious stare, "I—I missed my early morning cup and didn't want to go straight in for breakfast."

"*Le maître* said neither of you might want any this morning," Marie said bluntly, reaching consideringly for the coffee pot, her meaning so clear that Eve felt herself go hot all over.

How dared Raoul give such an order! How dared he, she kept repeating, silently furious as Marie's eyes went slowly over her. Swiftly she assured the woman she had changed her mind about the coffee and ran out into the gardens.

If Raoul had accused her of contriving to give the servants food for thought, it was apparent that he didn't think twice about committing the same crime himself. During that first day and the next she scarcely saw him except at mealtimes, when the conversation on both sides could only be described as cool, studiously polite. Occasionally he was attentive enough, to allay, she supposed, speculation. The *gardians* had had their day of celebration which Eve concluded, unbearably, neither she nor Raoul had enjoyed very much. She had scarcely drunk anything herself and Raoul had remained stone cold sober.

IT WAS this prevailing coldness that frightened Eve most, his ability to remain completely detached while she worked herself into a fine if incomprehensible fret of unhappiness. Her own private hell which grew almost past bearing. She lost a little weight, her inner turmoil reflected in a loss of appetite and a growing conviction that Raoul was beginning to mean more than she had ever thought possible.

It was this knowledge which she refused to face that prompted her to seek the isolation of the vast steppes on the third afternoon after their return from Paris. She had spent most of the day with Michel, already loving the boy and confident she had his affection in return. Eve hadn't been altogether surprised that Michel's grandparents approved of her marrying Raoul, because, she suspected, they would imagine this ensured Michel's future. But they had also, she knew, been overjoyed when Raoul had asked them to visit whenever they liked. It would seem that everything could end happily in this direction, if nothing else.

Raoul had been gone since lunch—something to do, he had explained briefly, with the next day's festivities in Les Saintes Maries de la Mer. He had not asked Eve to accompany him, and suddenly, after tea, she could bear the confines of the house no longer on her own. She would go riding; it seemed an age since she had been out on the little horse she usually rode. There was an eagerness inside her to have the wind wild on her face, through her hair, anything which might remove the increasing lethargy of the last few days.

Even to think of it made her feel better and she ran quickly upstairs. She would have to change into something suitable—the dress she was wearing certainly wouldn't do, but it wasn't until she reached her old room that she remembered her old clothes had disappeared. When she had mentioned this before to Raoul he had merely said he had instructed Marie to burn them, which had annoyed Eve so much she had been unable to make any comment, but surely he must have realised she would need something to ride in? Frowning, she stood before the empty wardrobe wondering what to do. There was just a chance Marie might not yet have got around to disposing of them, especially her jeans.

In the kitchen Marie glanced at her dubiously. "They are still in the old laundry, *madame*. I'm afraid I forgot all about them."

Or more likely, Eve thought, Marie had intended giving them to some of her numerous relations, as there was nothing actually wrong with the clothes, except their cut, and the French were extremely thrifty. She felt Marie's eyes on her as she triumphantly rescued her jeans.

"Gracious," she exclaimed disapprovingly, "you are going to look shabby, *ma chère*, after the smart clothes you've been wearing!"

Eve ignored this, simply grinned like a young child as she clasped her trousers happily to her and, after thanking Marie, flew back upstairs. That had been easy! Off came the new expensive dress which made her look so appropriately elegant. With careless hands she let it drop to the floor before donning the somewhat faded, definitely untidy-looking short-sleeved shirt and slacks. They were comfortable and familiar and in them she felt free, curiously untrammelled by the tenacious threads of a marriage which wasn't really a marriage at all. Now she felt almost herself again, a carefree young girl belonging to no one. Outside she could hear the shrill, exultant cries of the birds, and in her heart was a sudden, exhilarating excitement, an echoing response to their free, wild song. The evening stretched before her, enticing her out to seek the solace, the soothing atmosphere of those lonely places for which the Camargue was famous. With any luck she should be back before Raoul.

Almost dancing she whipped around, to find to her dismay that he stood in the doorway, the very man she had hoped to avoid, staring at her. Her eyes widened darkly as a visible quiver went through her. How long had he been standing there?

She had heard nothing of him coming in—hadn't expected he would be home. Hadn't he told her he would probably be quite late, after dinner? He must have been in the bathroom which she knew he made use of at the other end of the corridor as he wore only a white towelling robe belted loosely around him, and his hair was still damp from the shower. He must have caught sight of her as he had been returning to his room, and Eve's nerves jerked painfully with a brilliant terror.

Trying desperately to beat down such frantic feelings of despair, her lips moved in a travesty of a casual smile. Did he have to look so utterly furious? Her heart, which only a few moments ago had been sailing gaily among the white clouds she had glimpsed from the window, dropped somewhere in the region of the boots she had not yet had time to put on. She had known herself to be afraid of him, but not how much!

It was plain to see he was mad about something, his green eyes glittered like daggers. "Where were you going," his voice cracked like a whip, "dressed like that?"

So that was it! Helplessly, scarcely realising what she was doing, Eve blinked down at her crumpled jeans. "I..." she had to swallow twice, "I was simply going for a ride."

"I refuse to allow you!"

"Oh, but..." Instinct warned her it would be wiser to offer some sort of explanation, to beg him to understand, but an inherent fear of rejection held her back. How could she hope to appeal to his better nature when he obviously didn't have one? Yet in spite of a consuming indignation, she had the grace to feel slightly ashamed when her evasive glance fell to the carelessly discarded dress and slip on the floor.

He stepped over the threshold, the first time he had ever entered her room since that first disastrous night when he had flung her with such supreme indifference on to the bed. "You are not," he repeated tersely, a clear-cut determination in his mouth and chin, "going anywhere in those clothes!"

"But," her voice worked at last, and her eyes, intensely blue, clung to his face, "I was only going riding, *monsieur*."

"*Monsieur!*" he muttered some violent exclamation, his face black. "After three days of marriage you can still call me that?"

She felt a little shiver of fear. She had known it was a mistake, but from habit it had just slipped out. "It's nothing," she muttered sullenly, "to make a fuss about, but if you must have an apology, then I'm sorry!"

Such a reluctant expression of penitence was ignored. "I will give you two seconds," he said, the undertones of violence in his voice, "to get out of those unspeakable clothes, or I will remove them myself. It shouldn't be too difficult!"

CHAPTER TEN

STUNG BY momentary shock, Eve flinched, her dazed glance flickering uncertainly before returning to his face, seeing the strength and purpose bred into it. Once he had spoken, he wasn't a man easily swayed from his word, but he mustn't be allowed to think she was so easily intimidated. "You wouldn't dare!" she whispered emphatically. Too wholly on the defensive to be completely aware of the danger, she backed away from him, but he only advanced nearer, further into the room. Totally isolated as they were at this end of the great house, there was only silence as they stared at each other, tension beating, with almost tangible force, between them.

Desperately, as a panic she couldn't pinpoint rose within her, Eve glanced swiftly over her shoulder, measuring the distance to the bathroom door. Could she make it? She did manage a yard or two before he caught her—and then with an exclamation that scorched her already burning ears! Ruthlessly, as the moaning sound of the mistral rose outside, and clouds darkened stormily the evening sun, he dragged her to him, his hold inflexible as he gripped the top of her shirt and ripped, doing the same to her jeans. Upside down she seemed to go, the fury in his hands lending them strength, along with a surprising deftness, as he

removed the offending garments and flung them re-
morselessly across the floor.

"Why, you beast!" Half sobbing in her fury, she tried to turn in his grasp to strike him. "I hate you, I hate you!" she cried.

He pinned her pale, slender hands with one of his, rendering them ineffectual as his glance slid devastatingly over her. "And so, *ma petite rebelle*, it will not matter how I treat you, you cannot dislike me more. But, *mon dieu*, I will only put up with so much!"

The heat of his anger burned into her, and before she could stop him he turned her to him, wholly into his arms, his eyes blazing down at her while the leashed look on his face stilled her to sheer breathlessness and fear fluttered like a wild thing through her breast.

Her breath came in a short, distressed little gasp. "You're hurting me!" She pushed back against him, tears glinting with temper on her dilated pupils. "You're a brute!" she cried, unable to keep the tremors from her voice as his hand moved over her. He was formidable, utterly ruthless, someone she scarcely knew.

"*Insolente!* You are greatly in need of a lesson, *madame*. It is time you learnt you can't have everything your own way!" Ruthlessly he crushed her to him, his hand beneath her chin, exploring the soft hollows of her throat as he forced her mouth up to meet his, the fierceness of his assault parting her bruised lips, striking a living flame right through her.

In one last sane instant Eve tried to resist, to fight free of the burning excitement which the hardness of his lips aroused within her. But Raoul refused to relent. He was all force and passion, stilling her feeble protests until, lost in a labyrinth of emotion, she ceased to struggle. Under his touch her shrinking disappeared, and there was only the feverish insistence of her blood pounding in her ears.

"I'll never let you go..." His mouth lifted fractionally, his voice dark as his lips came down again, this time their pressure easing slightly as his hands probed the bareness of her skin through the ragged remains of her shirt. Eve moaned, turning in his arms, closer. Her heart was beating too fast, sensation hitting her in great waves, carrying her along on a tide of incomprehensible desire. Everything about her seemed to fall away, all her surroundings, even her own being whirling like a bursting dam about her ears as he drew from her slender body an ever increasing response.

"Raoul..." She wasn't wholly aware that she was sobbing his name, her lips moving numbly under his as she felt herself spinning out of control, her senses merely a roaring void in her ears. Her groping fingers touched the hard, smooth texture of his cheek, going slowly around his neck as she clung to him, her body going softly boneless against his.

"Raoul..." Tremors were attacking her limbs. Somewhere she was floating and he was lifting her, carrying her, but she had no knowledge of where he was going.

"Be still," she heard his voice, thickly impatient. "I don't wish to hurt you more than I must..."

"Raoul—please..." Was that her own voice trembling wildly before the passion in his?

"We are married, *mignonne*." The pressure of his mouth and hands deepened, and was the last thing she seemed to hear, other than her own cry a little later before everything faded to unconsciousness.

The next day she went with Raoul to the festival in Les Saintes Maries de la Mer. She hadn't really wanted to go, but he had insisted, and it seemed she had no will left in her now to defy him. All morning Raoul and his men had been cutting bulls from the herds. These would be taken by lorry to the bull ring but brought back again afterwards and released to the herds. Bull breeding in the Camargue was directed at producing good *cocardiers*, bulls for the sport known in that area as the *course libre*, and animals bred for this could prove quite profitable for their owners.

The town itself was full of gipsies from all over Europe who gathered there each year on the twenty-fourth of May to attend Masses. Added to this, or mixed rather incongruously in with it, Eve thought, were the stirring songs, the celebrations in the streets, the bullfights where the ensuing dust seemed to mingle with the heavy scent of incense from the high altar. There was much to stare at, much to hold the attention of even the most jaded palate, but in spite of attempting determinedly to enjoy herself she was far from succeeding. To keep her mind wholly on the vivid entertainment all about her seemed impossible. She could only think of Raoul DuBare and his lovemaking, which in his case had nothing to do with love at all. Her own headlong response was something she tried in vain to forget. The night had been an experience she must somehow contrive to put from her.

The noise and gaiety that filled the little town seemed to be at an ever-increasing momentum. As she wandered through the crowds Raoul was never far from her side, remote yet curiously watchful, as if fully aware of her continuing lassitude and always ready when she occasionally stepped heedlessly into danger. It was late afternoon when the paleness of her face obviously prompted him to suggest they should seek some light refreshment, then return home. He would take her to a hotel.

"Your old friend Mrs. Wood's establishment will do very well," he said, "and it will be quiet as it is out of town."

Eve glanced at him woodenly, having no great desire to go there. "It doesn't matter," she hedged. "I'd rather not, if you don't mind."

"Oh, but I do, *ma chère*," he replied thinly. "If you must insist on wearing the air of a martyr then I must do something to cheer you up."

Unhappily Eve refused to let him see how much his words hurt her. How could she ever have been crazy enough to imagine he might ever grow even remotely fond of a wife he had only chosen for convenience! He would look after her as he would any other investment, as part of his property, that was all. Towards her was always courteous, but suddenly this was far from enough. She wanted more.

Feeling it not worthwhile to protest further, she sat passively beside him as he drove swiftly to the hotel. Once there she felt relieved to see it was quiet, most of the guests still being in the town and not yet back to dress for dinner. Raoul ordered tea, a request, Eve mused, which wouldn't be too popular in the kitchens where, at this hour, they were no doubt preparing a celebration evening meal. Studiously, as they sat down, she kept her eyes averted, not needing to look at him to be aware of his faintly arrogant air of distinction, his undeniable good looks. How had she ever come to love a man like this? And love him she did—if it was something in the nature of an unwelcome shock to face the revelations of one's own heart! Previously her dislike had seemed to act as a sort of invisible reflector against the penetrating impact of his personality, but now, realising how she really felt appeared to remove all her defence mechanism and her subsequent vulnerability could only lead to further unhappiness, she was convinced.

Eve sat very still, her head bent slightly, allowing her fair, soft hair to fall over her cheek, hoping to hide her young despair. "You may pour," Raoul suggested when their tray arrived, and her hand went automatically out to grasp the teapot, shivering to hear him add, "You've had very little all day, *ma chère*, and last night you did miss your dinner."

Did he have to remind her? She had a feeling he did it deliberately, and it wasn't entirely one missed meal he was thinking of. "I don't happen to be very hungry," she replied as evenly as she could.

His glance, wholly encompassing, was full of restrained irritation, as though her silent distress was beyond him. "Don't worry," he said with seemingly cool indifference, "your appetite is sure to return."

Defensively she lifted her heavy lashes to glance at him mutinously, not caring for his sarcasm. "It wasn't my fault—" she began, only to be cut off abruptly as none other than Mrs. Wood bore down on them. Eve's breath caught uneasily. She had seen nothing of Mrs. Wood since she had worked at the hotel, but had always felt guilty about leaving as she had, in such haste.

But Mrs. Wood was obviously in the best of tempers, the presence of her former nursemaid, magically transmitted to the extremely enviable position of Madame DuBare, not affecting her adversely at all. Not on the face of it! "Ah, *m'sieur, madame*," she cried gaily, in the nature of a fully airborne balloon, "but how nice to see you!" Beaming, she wished them every happiness, expressing every hope of seeing more of them in the future. "And I also hope," she appealed, smiling at Eve coyly, "you can persuade your husband to open his riding stables again, dear. Nowadays I go elsewhere, but I miss the Manade DuBare very much."

Eve glanced at Raoul uncertainly, seeing that he merely shrugged. Vaguely she remembered hearing something about this from Célèste, but couldn't recall anything definitely, and it didn't appear that Raoul was interested.

As if sensing this, Mrs. Wood rushed on, "This wasn't why I approached you today, *m'sieur*. It was actually about Madame Troyat." As Raoul's eyebrows rose slightly, and Eve's heart jerked painfully, she continued, "About two weeks ago she came in at this time and stayed on to dinner, and, I'm afraid, left her cigarette lighter. It is here," she drew it out of her pocket, "and it appears to be a good one. See, it has her initials. Well, the next morning, when I rang your house, I was told that she and your sister had already left for Marseille, and the next thing I knew your household was in Paris for your marriage, so I decided to leave it. I thought perhaps Madame Troyat might return to collect it herself..."

Mrs. Wood talked for a few more minutes after passing to Raoul the elegant, gold-coloured lighter, then left them with a bright farewell and another fervently expressed wish about the riding stables. Dully

Eve looked at the gleam of gold metal turning idly in Raoul's hands. It would merely serve to remind him of a woman he might have married, someone better able to match his demands than she. Before she could stop herself she said, "You were very fond of Amélie...?"

"Fond!" The exclamation in his voice suggested she had understated, but curiously he said no more, just continued to frown contemplatively at the lighter.

Suddenly she didn't want to think any more about Amélie. "This riding school?" she queried.

"It wasn't my idea," he replied swiftly, obviously not concentrating on what she was saying, "It was one of my brother's. It can be quite a profitable sideline with summer tourists, but I'm afraid I'm just not interested."

"No, of course not." Why were they conversing politely, like a couple of strangers? She took too quickly a gulp of hot tea, almost scalding herself.

"If you will excuse me, *ma chère*, I will be back in a moment." Rising abruptly, his own tea apparently forgotten, Raoul left her without waiting for a reply.

All the way back to the manade Raoul was preoccupied, not talking very much, and Eve decided, the knowledge haunting her, that he was still thinking of Amélie. Even so, she was quite unprepared when, on arriving home, he said quietly, "I have to go out again, *ma chère*."

"Out—again?" Startled, she swung around to face him as he held open the vehicle door, his hand politely beneath her elbow as she climbed down. "You mean, back to Les Saintes Maries?"

"No." His eyes were hooded, enigmatic, as he held

her bewildered gaze. "If you must know, I am going to Marseille, and I may be late. Don't wait up."

Marseille? Oh, no, not that! Tears suddenly stung Eve's eyes as she stared after him. His jaw had been terse, and he had looked at her as if he was already regretting not only his marriage but the subsequent turn it had taken. If he had wrung from her all the response he had hoped for the previous night, he obviously didn't like her reactions today. Whatever he had expected she had no means of knowing, and this must be his way of showing his disapproval. His way of demonstrating clearly that if he had turned briefly from Amélie it had only been a temporary deflection, a moment of madness, not to be repeated. This evening, he must be confident, Amélie would greet him with open arms!

Unhappiness lending an air of extreme exhaustion to her taut young face, Eve ran upstairs, almost forgetting in her misery to look in on the nursery, but Michel was by this time fast asleep. For a long moment she lingered, looking half enviously at his smoothly unconscious face before going to tell Marie that Raoul would not be in for dinner. She pretended not to notice as Marie glanced at her sharply. That Marie should even guess where he had gone would prove the final humiliation!

The remainder of the evening stretched long and dismal before her, and it was only just after ten when, unable to settle, Eve decided to go to bed with a book. In Raoul's study she had discovered a wide selection and chose a detective story, anything which might take her mind off her own problems. Yet, after a shower and the usual routine tasks necessary before retiring for the night, she still felt too restless to climb into bed, and for a moment lingered by her favourite spot at the window. A huge white moon sailed across the skies and, as she stared up at it, it sketched the poignant planes of her face in a transparent glow, highlighting the shadows, turning to silver the loose strands of hair where it touched. But, above all, it seemed to accentuate her solitary figure, bestowing a loneliness which she was almost beginning to feel deep down inside her.

Beyond the gardens, across the vast plains, the wind drifted softly with all the promise of an early summer, but, as on other nights, all was quiet. No voices of birds, no mistral washing wildly through the tops of the pines, only the faint hum of a wandering insect as it threw itself heedlessly against the glittering glass of the window, attracted by the soft flicker of light. There was so much about this part of France that was attractive, so much she liked, could learn to love, even as she loved the man who owned this large bit of it, given the chance. Tremulously Eve sighed. Before it had all seemed so easy, but she must have been a fool ever to think it really would be. How could she stay here now, loving Raoul the way she did, even for Michel's sake? The difficulty of hiding her true feelings might be, she conceded, an impossible task, and she dwelt despairingly on Raoul's acute embarrassment should he ever guess exactly how she felt about him.

So deep and hopeless were her thoughts that she didn't hear Marie's tentative knock until she tried again, this time louder.

Eve, thinking for one heart-stopping moment it was Raoul, hastily grabbed her white silk robe with its unmistakable stamp of Paris and slowly opened the door.

Her pulse rate dropped to normal again as she saw it was only Marie—she might have known Raoul would never knock.

Marie was beset by her usual anxieties! "Oh, *madame*," she cried nervously, "I wonder if you would mind looking at the child. He won't stop crying, I think he might be ill, and as *le maître* is—er—still out?"

"Of course." Without pausing to satisfy Marie's curiosity about *le maître*, Eve followed Marie quickly down the corridor. It wasn't the first time since she had come here that Marie had sought her advice in the middle of the night, but for once Eve almost welcomed the diversion. It would quite probably be nothing serious, the young nursemaids had probably been indulging Michel too freely again, but Marie, excitable by nature, always seemed eager for reassurance.

Once in the nursery she found, as she had suspected, that Michel was suffering from a persistent pain in his small tummy. Swiftly she gathered him up, soothing him quietly before administering a small dose of something she kept for such occasions, to relieve it. It was only a matter of minutes before, cuddled closely in her arms, he went to sleep again.

"I'll stay with him a while longer," she promised, sending Marie off to bed, together with the young nursemaid who slept in the adjoining room. As she laid the boy gently in his cot he turned over on his side, contented, and she doubted if he would wake again that night.

Carefully she turned his nightlight low and sat down in a chair by his side. Here she must have fallen asleep, as she woke with a start a little while later to find to her dismay Raoul standing by her side, watching her intently as she struggled to find her bemused senses. "I must have forgotten where I was," she gasped, but he merely smiled.

"Come, *ma chère*," he said softly, bending over her. "You must tell Marie she must manage herself occasionally when the child cries, but there is no need for you to stay any longer."

So he had guessed what she had been doing. "He had only a small pain," she explained, "nothing serious. However, Marie wasn't sure. I intended staying only a few minutes..."

"And you fell asleep? No matter," he shrugged, bringing her to her feet, guiding her stumbling footsteps from the nursery, his arm gentle but firm around her narrow waist. "The child is all right now and we have much to discuss."

"Raoul!" Outside the door, at once wholly awake, she pulled back from his arms, too conscious of the thinness of her robe, the diaphanous quality of the nightgown underneath. How could he expect her to behave rationally when he had only just returned from Marseille, from Amélie? "I don't think we can have anything to talk about," she exclaimed bitterly, her eyes huge in her white face. "At least nothing that couldn't wait until the morning."

"Shush, *ma chère*," his voice soothed as his dark gaze slid deliberately over her slender figure, his grip on her waist tightening against her urgent struggles as he took her completely into his arms and kissed her hard. His hand moved slowly to her nape, threading through her ruffled hair, holding her passionately to him until she became completely acquiescent against him, his power over her no longer disputed.

Her lips throbbing, her body ablaze with a kind of feverish fire, Eve was scarcely aware of how she reached his study. She couldn't seem to fight him any more, nor could she count on any inclination to do so, common sense not seeming to function even slightly when up against an attraction such as his. "Raoul!" From somewhere she tried to assert a small measure of independence, only to find herself pushed authoritatively down on to the wide velvet sofa, his hands lingering momentarily on her slim shoulders before he bent to switch on the electric fire. Again he took no notice of the wild note of entreaty in her voice.

"Stay there," he commanded, leaving her to pour drinks, and bemused, Eve watched his every movement, staring at the back of his dark head, loving him too much, yet fully conscious that such one-sided emotion could bring her no happiness.

"Here, drink this, you are too pale, *ma chère*." He was back by her side, placing a glass in her shaking hands, guiding it with his to her mouth, watching intently until she took a small sip. He dropped down beside her as she sat like a very fragile, curved statuette, unable, for some reason, to take her eyes off him.

Rather too quickly he half emptied his own glass, as if endeavouring to retain an equilibrium he felt was slipping. "Darling," it was the first time he had called her that and her skin tightened electrically, her cheeks colouring. Dropping her head to hide such rushing confusion didn't help. He noticed instantly, and his fingers went out to gently touch the vivid tide of it and stayed caressing beneath the vulnerable angle of her chin. "Eve," his voice deepened, "you know where I've been this evening?"

"Yes," she drew a painful steadying breath. There was nothing to be gained by pretending not to. "You went to visit Amélie, and I think I know why."

"You do?" He paused for one obviously baffled moment, his glance keen on the slight betraying quiver of her lips.

"Yes..." It just had to come out. "You wish you had married her instead of me. Probably you've been to tell her so. There can be no other explanation."

"Enough!" his voice whipped, his hand on her face tightening almost cruelly before relaxing again. "I'm sorry, *ma chère*," her intensely anguished expression acted as a brake, "but of course you must be thinking something like this. It is natural, yet nothing was further from my mind."

"You mean you don't love her?"

Smiling slightly, he shook his head. "There is only one girl I love, my darling." His fingers tensed, tilting up her chin, forcing her to look straight at him as he asked very softly, "Can't you guess? From the moment I saw you..."

"No—Oh, Raoul!" Her voice came on a funny little gasp as he drew her forcibly to him, kissing her fiercely, as if glorying in the joy of her helplessly yielding body.

Minutes later he lifted his head. "I love you," he said, "but before I tell you how much, we must talk about tonight. All the doubt between us must be cleared up, otherwise you will continue to fret. Do you recall, *ma chère*, when Mrs. Wood gave me Amélie's lighter she also said when Amélie had left it? Something occurred to me almost immediately, but, to make sure, I checked up again with Mrs. Wood while you finished your tea. Amélie had arrived at the hotel around five o'clock on the very day she had left you in the nature reserve. When she was supposed to be on her way back here to seek the forgotten picnic basket."

"You mean...?" Eve flinched, her slight figure drooping as that dreadful experience came rushing back to her.

"I mean," he went on swiftly, "that all the time she has been lying. That while she was supposedly nursing her car off the reserve all the time she was at the hotel!"

"You're quite certain?" To Eve it didn't make sense.

Raoul's mouth thinned decisively. "After checking with Mrs. Wood I rang the garage where she left her car. The proprietor told me, *ma chère*, there was almost more sand in Amélie's petrol tank than the whole of the Sahara. Too much ever to have got there accidentally, and certainly more than would have allowed her to travel more than a very short distance. Of course he had no idea of the true circumstances, and I didn't tell him. *Mon dieu*," Raoul ground out, "and to think I didn't believe you!"

Her head came back against his shoulder, the tension inside her easing slightly. "I would never lie to you, Raoul."

"Darling," his fingers played through her ruffled hair, tenderly, "I've been a brute and must beg you to forgive me. It was Amélie who told me a tissue of lies, but it was actually my concern for you that made me so furious. This afternoon, as I pieced together what had really happened, I'm afraid I saw red. I was compelled to go and confront her personally—it would never be possible to pin Amélie down over the telephone, *petite*. I was so absolutely livid. To think she had endangered your life, spending that evening in Mrs. Wood's hotel in order to give you a fright! And, on top of this, she confessed everything when I found her in Marseille, and wasn't in any way repentant, even when I told her that what she had done could easily have been construed as a kind of premeditated murder."

"Oh, no!" Eve's eyes flew to his, startled. "I think she would only intend giving me a fright. Something to make me hate the Camargue and hurry back to London."

"Even so she couldn't have guaranteed your safety. She must certainly be a little mad. I will never have her back here!"

"I think," shuddering, Eve swallowed, trying not to exaggerate, "I think she could, on occasion, act very irresponsibly."

"Unbalanced?" He halted narrowly, an odd unexpected note in his voice. "Was this why you decided to marry me, *ma chère?*"

Inconsequently, Eve tried to avoid a direct answer. "Poor Amélie," she sighed. "She had no idea I'd ever worked for Mrs. Wood, or even stayed in her hotel. If we hadn't gone there today..."

"Eve—I asked you a question." There was a wealth of male purpose behind his voice.

"Yes," Eve answered evasively, "it was on my mind at the time."

"And since then?"

Her heart beating suddenly too fast, she turned a delicate profile to him. "Since then, Raoul," she confessed, frantically, "I've been fighting a losing battle, trying not to face the fact that I loved you. Then last night..." her breath changed as emotion shot through her, accentuating her extreme pallor.

"Yes?" he prompted, his hand sliding over the silk of her shoulder lightly, but enough to break the sharp sense of discipline which held her.

She turned up her face, knowing he didn't have to force her to surrender. "Last night," she whispered tremulously, "I realised how much..."

Silently he held her to him, his heart striking into her with force, his lips warm against the throbbing nerve at her temple. "Before I kiss you, *mignonne*, because I may not be able to stop, there are still one or two things left to say. On our wedding day, Célèste said something about sending for you. I'm afraid the manner of your arrival here was no longer important. It was something I had long put from me, certainly something I hadn't the time or inclination to think about on my wedding day. But was that also true, my darling. You let me think you had arrived completely uninvited. To protect Célèste you chose not to say anything?"

"Yes." There was in Eve a fine recklessness, compelling her to confess all. Perhaps, if Raoul really loved her, he had to hear it? "Célèste threatened that if I didn't come she would bring Michel to London. Unfortunately, when I did arrive she had mixed up the dates. I had her letter, but she had lost mine and hadn't made a note of my arrival. This was why I came here. My money was running out and I felt it imperative to know what had gone wrong. She had especially asked me not to telephone, in case..." Her voice trailed off, unwilling to implicate Célèste any further.

"In case," Raoul supplied, with a wry flicker of humour, "I found out. And I suppose," he added, still wryly, "in retrospect I couldn't really blame her. And, when you did come, I couldn't get rid of you quick enough."

"You threw me out, literally." The reproach in her voice was audible.

Raoul's laughter was low. "So you once said, *madame*, and again I apologise, but perhaps you don't understand how desperate I was to be rid of you. Immediately I caught sight of you I sensed you were a threat to my peace of mind. Not that I was wholly convinced you actually were whom you said you were, but how could I welcome you after protesting so much about Carol? Then the next time I saw you and held you in my arms I knew I could never let you go."

Through the uneven beating of a feverish pulse she forced herself to ask, "You never told me why you never liked Carol or her family."

In his voice was a half impatient tenderness. "It was nothing really personal, *ma petite*. Perhaps you were not aware that Dominique was already betrothed to a French girl when he ran off with your cousin. Can you imagine what I, a mere man, was left to cope with? The weeping of a distracted, deserted fiancée, a necessity to calm and appease irate parents. I may have overreacted, but the fact that my brother, whom I relied on a lot, didn't return for almost two months did not help. *Mon dieu*," Raoul smiled, "but I was ready to hate the lot of you!"

"But Carol?" Eve protested.

Raoul's smile faded and he sighed, "Oh, we got on very well, my darling, eventually, but she did little to help Dominique settle down. Always they were off somewhere, or doing something unnecessary, such as refurbishing the old hut down by the lagoon in such a way that one dared scarcely put a foot inside it. We used it a lot at one time for watching wild life on the water."

Eve remembered, with a quiver, which prompted her to say when otherwise she might not, "You certainly didn't approve when she went to Rhodesia!"

"It wasn't exactly that," Raoul explained curtly. "They had only just returned from America, and there was a lot to do."

"Yet Carol wasn't well?"

"You sound surprised, *ma chère*," he shrugged wryly. "I think Carol made a convenience of her health. Usually she was quite fit."

"And this is why you wanted to keep Michel here when his parents died. So that he might have a stable home?"

"Something like that, *ma chère*," Raoul looked at her contemplatively. "Anyway, we shall see. After we return from our honeymoon his grandparents will come on a long visit, so we will not worry too much about the future right now, *mignonne*."

"A honeymoon...?" Was his voice full of the old tantalising mockery, or did he really mean it? She was never quite sure where she was with him. Her hand clung suddenly to the dark silk of his dressing gown, her face taut with extreme sensitivity as she gave an odd little shudder.

"Need you ask?" He understood the query in her voice and his own was tolerant. "I've been getting everything organised. I find I can't wait until Célèste returns from America to have you completely to myself. There is a small villa I own in the Swiss Alps, which isn't so far away. I know you will adore it."

"Oh, Raoul!" The prospect in front of her seemed so dazzling that she could scarcely accept it without being prone to some doubt. Not for herself—she could never question the strength of her own feelings, but what of his? "How can you be sure," she felt helplessly forced to go on, "how can you be sure I'll settle down any better than Carol?"

"Because I do, my darling." His arm curved hard as it tightened about her. "In fact, merely from watching you since you first came, I can almost guarantee it. But, whether you do or not, it's a risk I must take. Besides, *ma chère*," a glint of dry humour flickered through his eyes, "is it not rather late to be thinking of this now?"

"But—" she began uncertainly, a small devil of perversity driving her.

"No more buts, *petite*." Decisively his lips cut off whatever words she had been about to utter. "Don't you think," he murmured, a slightly roughened edge to his voice, "we've talked enough for one night? Nothing can really matter any more but this, *ma belle enfant*. This will last for ever!" Closely he held her, his mouth lingering on the wide curve of her lips before sliding over the soft silk of her throat, lingering for one threatening moment on the wildly beating pulse before seeking the warm skin of her shoulder, the fragrant appeal of her seductive young body.

"For ever..." There was an unconscious break in her voice as she said it, wholly submissive as she pressed his dark head lovingly to her breast, no thought inside her of denying him any longer. It was a word that would be stamped indelibly on her heart for always. That and this place, this man, with whom she would always be wholly content.

LION IN VENICE

Lion in Venice
Margaret Rome

Jo Domini was known for her impulsive behavior—but telling a man that he must be her bridegroom was certainly bound to get her into trouble.

It wasn't enough that she had insulted Conte Leandro Tempera, aggravated her father and frustrated her sister who wanted to marry. Now she had lashed out in despair at the Italian custom requiring an elder sister to be wed first.

When Leandro accepted her challenge, Jo thought she could provoke him into rejecting her as a bride. But things didn't work out that way. The seemingly calm patient Leandro outwitted her.

CHAPTER ONE

"Jo, if you don't make up your mind to marry soon I swear I'll retreat into a convent, or fade into a decline or... or—"

"Take up acting as a profession? Really, Sara, whosoever it was that stated: 'All the world's a stage' must have had someone very much like yourself in mind!"

Sara's pleading pout hardened into a grimace as she directed a look of dislike towards her elder sister. "Papà always said you ought to have been a boy, but however hard you try you'll never make up to him for the son he never had." She was too lacking in perception, too wrapped up in her own selfish world to be struck by the incongruity of such a statement even when her sister swung slightly on her heel straight into the path of a ray of Venetian sunshine spilling through the window of the *palazzo* perched upon the banks of the Grand Canal. It drew vibrant sparks from hair Titian would have itched to imitate and added extra sparkle to emerald eyes betraying at that moment a gemlike hardness as they rested upon her sister's face. As she stepped forward not even anger could dispel grace of movement from a body which at first sight seemed boyishly slim until her loose silken robe caught and clung to a voluptuous curve of breast, a rounded hip and slender tapering thigh.

"Dear Sara," she mocked, deliberately affecting the very English drawl her sister abominated, "you have achieved your ultimate ambition, have you not? Papà has gone to a great deal of trouble to arrange a marriage between yourself and a personable Italian male. After months of behind-the-scenes negotiations between our respective families, innumerable meetings between yourself and your intended—each, I might stress, with myself as an unwilling chaperone—we have reached the stage of final negotiation when, after a meeting of both families, the contract will be signed and your intended spouse gratified by his success in manoeuvring himself within grasping distance of the Domini millions. Why then is your tongue not dripping with honey and your sharp little claws cushioned with velvet?"

Sara jumped to her feet, a black-haired, dark-eyed bundle of fury. "You make it all sound so sordid! It isn't that way at all, you know very well that Vincente and I were attracted from the first moment of meeting."

Jo nodded agreeably. "An added bonus for him, considering he would have been willing to marry you had you been bow-legged, buck-toothed and peering at him through bi-focal lenses."

Sara's volcanic temper almost reached the point of eruption. Staring down at her from her superior height, Jo registered for the umpteenth time the similarities shared by her younger sister and their Italian father. Both were characteristically dark, volatile and passionately devoted to their beliefs; both were easily swayed by emotion yet conversely were possessed of a hard materialistic streak and the sort of determination that had been the prime factor behind Enrico Domini becoming one of the richest industrialists in England, a country not noted for its generosity towards down-at-heel immigrants.

"How dare you imply that Vincente is attracted only by Papà's wealth!" Sara spat. "I know he loves me as I love him, passionately, devotedly. We live only for the day when we can be married, and it's you, heartless, selfish sister, who keeps us apart!"

"Rubbish," Jo tossed the word across a negligent shoulder as she sauntered back towards the window.

"It is *not* rubbish!" Sara's small foot thumped down upon the carpet. "You know very well that in Papà's family tradition decrees that the elder sister be married first—Papà insists upon it. Gratified though he is by my engagement to Vincente, he won't hear of us setting a date for the wedding until your own engagement has been announced. Oh, he *sympathises*," she uttered a sharp, derisory laugh, at the same time flinging out her arms in a gesture of hopelessness that was entirely Latin, "he bids us have patience. *'Wait just a little while longer, children,'* she mimicked, words rushing like a river in spate across her tongue. *'Venice, the city of Casanova, abounds with attractive men, sooner or later Jo is certain to—'*" She jolted to a halt, just a little too late in applying a brake to her tongue. Appalled by her slip, she waited in tense silence, bracing mentally for the onslaught of a caustic tongue.

"So!" Jo's hiss was more frightening than a shout. "Now it becomes clear why he was so insistent upon my joining you here! I, too, am to be held up for sale in the market places of Venice, dangled as a rich prize beneath the nose of every penniless nobleman in this city of stinking canals who lacks sufficient cash to keep

up his standard of idle living or to maintain the rotting foundations of his crumbling pink *palazzo*!"

"No, Jo," Sara protested, "all Papà wishes is for you to be happy, as happy as Vincente and I, as happy as he and Mammà were..."

"Mammà..." Jo sighed, her taut features softening as memories chased brilliance from her eyes. "I wish she were still alive—she would have championed my aversions to outmoded Italian customs."

Relieved that the storm had been averted, Sara whispered, "You must miss her greatly, you were so much alike. Because of my own rapport with Papà I can understand and sympathise; when Mammà died my loss was great, but yours was far greater." She cocked her head to one side and with birdlike timidity summed up. "You're very English, Jo, no one would believe you have a single drop of Italian blood in your veins. Everything about you is as English as was Mammà—you've inherited her red hair, her fair skin, her precise manner of speaking, her economy and grace of movement, but most of all, I think, her very logical mind. Do you remember how she used to refuse to read us fairy stories when we were children and insisted instead upon reading out suitable articles from the local newspaper? She wanted us, she said, even at a very early age, to be up to date with the affairs of the country, to know about every aspect of English life. I suspect she was afraid we might become swamped by the close-knit Italian community we'd gathered up around us. Her reading used to send me to sleep, but you, Jo, used to drink in every word; I remember how you would both discuss the articles the following day. Mammà would have been pleased, too, about your choice of career; whereas Papà and I were puzzled by your choice, she would have been delighted to welcome a scientist into the family."

Jo eyed her sister's placating face and decided to be kind. "Liar," she grinned, but with such lack of heat Sara was able to relax, "you and Papà were not merely puzzled, you were appalled. Tell the truth," she challenged, "didn't you both decide that I'd chosen to follow an unsuitable, most unfeminine profession?"

"Well..." Sara's glance slid away, "it's perhaps not so unsuitable for an Englishwoman as it would be for an Italian."

"Exactly!" Jo stressed, the warning flicker returning to her eyes. "I would like both of you and Papà to remember that first and foremost I'm English. You may prefer to think of yourself as an Italian and you're quite entitled to do so, providing you don't try to exert pressure upon me to do the same. So oblige me, please, by passing on that message to Papà, tell him in straight, simple terms so that he's convinced once and for all that under no circumstances could I look with favour upon an Italian husband, nor indeed upon any husband at all. At the moment marriage for me is out, there's no room for a man in the future I've planned."

"But, Jo..." Sara's cry was almost a wail, "that means that Vincente and I can never marry!"

"It means nothing of the sort," was Jo's crisp reply. "If Signor Marvese is anything of a man he'll prove it by marrying you with or without the dowry Papà has promised him. Actually, I'm doing you a favour by putting the man to a test, his reaction will help you to honestly assess his worth."

When Sara lapsed into sulky silence Jo returned to

the window to continue her contemplation of the scene outside. The Grand Canal was lined with palaces, the one in which they were at present residing being the most pretentious. They all seemed very big, and more than once she had wondered why the Venetians were so reckless with space when their city was so small. They're show-offs, she decided, show-offs to the world to impress it with their achievements, show-offs to each other, parading in front of friends and enemies the trappings of success. How humiliated they, as a race, must have felt during their slow decline.

Her elegant nose wrinkled with distaste. The Grand Canal seemed to her a cesspit into which fifty-odd smaller canals deposited their rubbish with the rise and fall of the tide. Lines of dark damp brick ran the length of the frontages, evidence that ground floors were flooded during high spring tides. At present the tide was low, exposing slimy bottom steps and the decaying foundations of crumbling palaces.

They had arrived in Venice only a few hours earlier and she had not yet had time to examine the palace in which they were to stay for the duration of their visit. But upon their arrival, while being helped from the private motor boat that had been sent to fetch them, she had heard her father mutter his approval as he stepped on to the *campo* fronting the palace, a paved open area, the presence of which, according to him, denoted that the owner was, or his forebears had been, extremely rich or prominent noblemen, perhaps both.

She turned away from the scene that left her emotionally cold, boredom prompting her to ask, "Who is our host, by the way—I believe he was out when we arrived?"

Sara perked up, obviously this was a subject she was eager to discuss. "Il Conte Leandro Tempera, Vincente's cousin," she beamed, looking for signs that Jo was impressed. "As you know, Vincente's mother was widowed very young. The Conte's father, her elder brother, took both her and Vincente under his wing and when he died his son, Leandro, the present Conte, inherited his responsibilities. Technically he is now the head of the family and as Vincente's home is too small to accommodate us the Conte insisted that we must stay with him."

"How very feudal!" Jo found it impossible to suppress her irritation. "I would have preferred to stay with Nònna Domini, it seems to me ridiculous that we should impose ourselves upon a stranger when we have a grandmother living nearby." When Sara did not reply Jo urged, "Well, don't you agree?" Narrowly she watched her sister nervously pleating the material of her skirt in order to avoid meeting her eyes. Finally, however, when Jo's stare could no longer be suffered, Sara mumbled: "We...Papà and I, decided that Nònna's house wouldn't suit our purpose. We shall be expected to entertain, to return the hospitality extended by Vincente's family, and while in our present circumstances it won't seem odd to utilise the services of an hotel, if we were to stay with Nònna Domini we would naturally be expected to entertain in the family home."

"Naturally," Jo affirmed, her steady gaze fixed hard upon Sara's embarrassed face. "A much more suitable solution, I would have thought."

"Nònna is too old to be bothered," Sara gulped.

"Nonsense, she loves having guests and you know it."

"Her house is too small," Sara continued desperately, "and also it's quite some distance away..."

Jo's honest soul revolted against such blatant prevarication. "You damned little snob! What you really mean is that Nònna Domini's home isn't grand enough, the food which she would cook and offer to her guests with such pride would be too unpretentious for the palates of your high and mighty friends! That *you* should think along such lines is bad enough, but I'm ashamed of Papà—he has always insisted that he's proud of his humble beginnings, yet this conversation would seem to indicate that he's now so pride-ridden he would prefer to forget the mother who toiled ceaselessly to rear six sons on the wages of a Murano glassblower!"

Sara jumped to her feet, the better to defy Jo's anger. "I love Grandmother just as much as you do, and Papà loves her even more, but he's realistic enough to acknowledge that she wouldn't fit into the society within, which we now move. Call us snobbish if you like, but it's you who are a snob—an inverted snob. You've never known poverty, so why claim affinity with those who have? Nònna Domini is comfortably off, Papà has seen to it that she wants for nothing. Yet she refuses to move, even though Papà has offered many times to buy her a more comfortable house in a better neighbourhood. She's stubborn, that one! But if she insists upon clinging to her old way of life she can't object if we, in turn, want to cling to ours. Don't worry that her feelings will be hurt, Papà has gone to her house today to explain the situation and, knowing him as we do, we need have no qualms that he'll do it as tactfully as possible."

Jo swung on her heel, heading for the door separating their adjoining rooms. The expression on her sister's face was disturbing; she was used to her fiery temper and familiarity had rendered her partially immune, but the horrified disgust Jo was displaying was something new and was causing her great unease. Could the course of action she and Papà had decided upon possibly strike others as unacceptably as it was striking Jo?

Jo's accusing voice reached her just as she was about to step out of the room. "The true snob is never satisfied, Sara, there's always another mountain to climb and the higher you go the more people you'll be required to look down upon! Take care you're not left stranded upon your lofty peak, isolated from the warmth of humanity. If you should fall who will be there to catch you?"

"Not you, Jo!" Sara flung a last tempestuous barb, "you'll be bent double from the weight of the chip you carry on your shoulder!"

Left alone with her sizzling thoughts, Jo paced her bedroom, sparing not a glance for the decor which, had she been in a different frame of mind, she would have found delightful. Curtains of priceless lace, delicate cream-coloured webs hanging from ceiling to floor with, here and there, minute, carefully executed darns betraying great age and loving care; matching cover and drapes on a huge four-poster bed; furniture gilded and ornate with legs carved into a semblance of such fragility they looked incapable of bearing weight. Keeping her eyes riveted upon the carpet, she paced, crushing masses of blue bell-shaped flowers beneath her feet, grounding fullblown roses beneath her furious heel.

The insult to her grandmother had cut deep. Jo,

above all, was loyal to her family and her friends. She felt sickened and ashamed of the attitude adopted by Sara and her father, so much so that she felt tempted to pack her bags and leave. But such action would be taken as an affront by Vincente's family, so that course of action was out; angry though she was with her sister she could not deliberately set out to destroy her happiness. Later that evening—she checked her watch—in less than an hour, in fact, the two families were due to dine together at the *palazzo*. Once that hurdle had been vaulted perhaps she would be able to fade into the background, visit Nònna for a few days, then quietly depart for England.

The decision made, she decided in her usual impetuous fashion that her father must be told. Immediately she sped from her room in search of him, running along carpeted corridors, down a wide sweep of stairs, then jerked to a halt in the centre of a huge hall wondering which of the many doors was hiding him from view. He was bound to be back by now, dinner was less than an hour away, so, being punctilious in his habits, she was sure he would have left himself plenty of time to dress for the occasion. He was not in his room, she had checked there first, which meant that he had to be somewhere downstairs.

Her ear caught the murmur of voices. She spun round then like a bloodhound on the scent headed towards the sound, judging that it was coming from behind a heavy wooden door that had been left just a crack ajar. As she hesitated, wondering whether to walk in or to knock, she recognised Vincente's slightly accented voice.

"The elder sister is *una seccatura*—a nuisance—as Sara describes her. Although aware that her father will not allow our wedding to take place until her own engagement has been announced, she flatly refuses to give up her career in favour of marriage."

"So?" a masculline voice filled with an amusement that set Jo's teeth on edge enquired. "And what is this career upon which the *signorina* sets such store?"

"She wishes to become a scientist. Her goal is still some three years away because she is as yet still studying at university. Can you imagine," Vincente's voice rose at the injustice, "Sara and me having to wait three whole years simply to accommodate this obstinate sister?"

"Unnatural," the other voice sympathised. "It occurs to me, however, that there might be a simpler reason why this sister remains unmarried. Could it be possible that she has never yet been approached by any man with matrimony in mind? Personally, I would feel very reluctant to ask a scientist to share my bed; it would require a rare breed of man to make love to a brain machine. Would you not yourself search out a fragrant, willing bundle of femininity if ever the need were upon you?"

"Someone like Francesca, you mean?" Vincente suggested slyly, laughter spilling into his voice.

"Certainly not!" The stern reply implied that Vincente had overstepped the mark. "Francesca's name has no place in such a discussion!"

Without waiting to hear Vincente's stammered apology Jo fled with ears burning, flags of dangerous colour high upon her cheeks. Once back in her room she leant against the door, fighting wild anger jabbing along every nerve, her body so tense it ached.

"Animal!" she hissed denunciation of the unknown male. "Arrogant, supercilious *beast*!" She clenched her fists, wishing it were possible to defend herself physically against his sneers, furious at having been made the butt of jibes he would not tolerate in connection with a woman of his own race. "Francesca, whoever she might be, is welcome to him!"

CHAPTER TWO

HALF AN HOUR LATER Jo, looking outwardly serene, was ready to join the guests assembling downstairs. Sara and her father had both rapped upon her door in passing, urging her to hurry, but as she had a special reason for making a late entrance she had bidden them both to carry on without her. She waited until she was certain that all the guests had arrived before moving towards the door, sustained by an icy calm, having no need to check her appearance in any of the many mirrors she passed on her way downstairs.

Upon reaching the main salon she stood poised in the doorway, waiting to be noticed.

Conversation was rippling from many tongues, bright, curious eyes were resting upon Sara and Vincente who were standing just inside the doorway with their backs turned towards her, flanked either side by Enrico, beaming a proud father's smile, and a taller, slimmer figure with dinner jacket set impeccably upon broad shoulders, dark sleeves baring an exact amount of cuff around brown, sinewy wrists and the back of a head held with such assurance she knew instinctively that she was looking at the owner of the unknown voice.

There was a gasp of surprise, then a second and yet a third before conversation dribbled into silence. Simultaneously four backs turned, seeking the cause of the diversion, and four pairs of eyes lit upon Jo leaning casually against the door jamb wearing ancient jeans rolled up above the knees to show an expanse of multicoloured woollen sock rising from feet encased in grubby sandals; a vivid orange tee-shirt with I AM A BITCH scrawled in black letters across its front, and two hideous green ribbons tied around hair parted from back to front and gathered into two untidy bunches that hung down across each shoulder. Nonchalantly she stared into their outraged faces, then poked the tip of her tongue between lips slashed with purple lipstick, puffed out her cheeks and blew hard until a pink balloon of bubble-gum almost obscured her face.

"Jo, how could you!" Sara's rebuke, blasted on an icy breath, connected with the fragile bubble and it burst, splattering gum all around Jo's mouth. Easily, she scraped it off, wiped her hand across the seat of her jeans, then offered it to the intently watching stranger.

"You must be the Conte. How do you do, I'm Josephine, Sara's sister."

She was disappointed when amusement tugged up the corners of his mouth before an urbane mask was donned. Politely he bowed across her sticky hand before replying in faultless English. "How do you do, *signorina*. I am enchanted to meet you."

"Oh..." When disconcertion clamped her throat she swallowed hard, floundering desperately for words with which to pierce his hateful composure, but was left stranded by a brain that went blank and a tongue that refused to be prised from the roof of her mouth.

The first joust had undoubtedly gone to the Conte!

Her father's anger was her salvation. With a muttered, *"Scusi, signore,"* he grasped Jo tightly by the elbow and marched her out of sight of the scandalised looks being cast by the members of Vincente's family. Her feet barely touched the ground as she was propelled towards a small ante-room where once inside he kicked shut the door before exploding:

"I want an explanation for your discraceful behaviour—and I warn you, Jo, it had better be convincing!" He was very angry! Jo suffered a qualm. With true Venetian intensity Enrico Domini loved his children and had, especially since their mother's death, indulged them disgracefully. Never before had she been the recipient of the ruthless determination that had made him succeed in business where lesser men might have failed. They had always been honest with each other, however, so, though trembling in her shoes, Jo bravely admitted:

"What I did was a gesture of protest against snobbery! When Sara told me about your plan to keep Nònna apart from Vincente's family I felt sick with disgust and terribly ashamed of both of you."

Her father folded his arms across his chest, his expression grim. "So in your usual hot-headed manner you decided to retaliate, without even waiting to discuss the situation. You made a spectacle of yourself by appearing dressed as a ragamuffin before people who set great store upon grace and beauty. In the whole of Venice you will not find a woman or a girl in such a state of utter *déshabille*. That outfit," his glance seared, "might not elevate an eyebrow in the university cities of England, but here women would not be seen dead in trousers—the only slovenly people in the whole of Venice are tourists—yet you disgrace me and your sister by coming down to dinner in an outfit that would make a housemaid shudder! Though you are twenty-three years of age, Jo, and Sara merely eighteen, I sometimes think she is twice as mature as you are."

Jo blanched, unspeakably hurt, not so much by the words which she knew were deserved but by the tone of voice in which they had been delivered. Her father's florid but still handsome face blurred. Quickly she blinked away tears before returning to the attack.

"You had no right to snub Nònna Domini," she choked, "she's worth a hundred of those pampered remnants of an extinct nobility!"

"Do you think me unaware of that fact?" His question rang cold with distaste. "If you had given me the chance I would have explained that your grandmother has made herself quite ill with the worry of having to entertain large numbers of strangers with whom she has nothing in common. She wrote to me while we were still in England, explaining her fears and begging to be excused the duty of playing hostess to Vincente's many relatives. She is old and she is tired; for those very reasons I felt qualms about asking her to take on such an onerous task in the first place, but because it is customary and because I would not for the world have my mother feel slighted I did ask her, Jo."

She stared, appalled, then ran to crumple against his chest almost choking with remorse. "I'm sorry I misjudged you, Papà, I ought to have known better."

Kind arms cradled her until her tears were spent, then prising her shamed face from his shoulder he looked down and sadly shook his head. "What is to be done with you, Jo? Some day I fear your hasty tongue will bring you great grief. You must learn to control your temper, child, to think long and hard before you speak, especially," his voice took on a warning note, "when you apologise to the Conte."

"Apologise to the Conte!" She wrenched out of his arms. "I shall do no such thing!"

"But you will," he insisted thinly, "that is, if you wish to continue studying towards the career you profess to value so much. The British government is good to its students, it provides grants for books, for living accommodation, and education is free, but as its coffers are not entirely bottomless, parents have to help out. You will find it very difficult, if not impossible, to carry on without an allowance. The choice is yours Jo—either apologise to the Conte for your appalling bad manners or face a future full of stringent economies."

She glared, barely able to believe that this hard-eyed, stern-faced man was the same parent who in the past had indulged her every whim. What he had said was true, she could not manage without the allowance he made her. She could wave the banner of independence by telling him to keep his money, but honesty forced her to acknowledge the impossibility of surviving without his financial help within a society where inflation was rampant.

Her reply was rebellious, but her tone was such that he knew the argument had been won. "You wish to teach me a lesson in humility, Papà, is that it?"

"Such a lesson would do you no harm," he admitted, edging nearer a mood of affability, "but mainly I wish the Conte to receive what is his due." He seemed prepared to carry on lecturing at length, but to Jo's relief the sound of the dinner gong penetrated the room. "I must go, the other guests must not be kept waiting. I'll make apologies for your absence, of course, and ask the Conte to spare five minutes of his time once the meal is over. Meanwhile, I suggest you go to your room, clean the mess from your face, and don a dress suitable for your meeting with the Conte." His tone became droll. "An up-to-date version of sackcloth and ashes might be appropriate..."

"Very funny!" Jo fumed when her father had left the room, glaring wildly around at surroundings that seemed suddenly to have adopted an ambience of a penitent's cell. "Apologise to that...that! Oh, *hell*!" She spun on her heel like a furious top, then charged upstairs to her room.

After writhing for an hour with the agonies of defeat she reluctantly admitted herself beaten, scrubbed her face, applied a light film of make-up, arranged her hair into a neat red cap, then, in a wry gesture of deference to her father's wishes, chose a dove-grey dress, its severity softened only by a white collar and childishly prim cuffs. She then sat by the window and waited, her mind a blank, until a maidservant knocked upon the door to inform her that the Conte was waiting for her in his study.

A true Venetian is instantly recognisable by his features, Jo decided as she stepped into the book-lined room and began walking towards a figure seated behind a huge, heavily carved desk. He stood up immediately she entered and motioned her to a chair, waiting until she was comfortable before resuming his own seat.

"Your father tells me you wish to speak to me, *signorina*?" She noted the slightly calculating look in his dark eyes and the enigmatical twist lifting the corners of his mouth. His blade-straight nose was that of a Renaissance prince, she criticised, disliking his air of condescension, mistrusting the guile hidden behind dark, almost oriental features, probably inherited from some long-distant ancestor. She stirred, made uncomfortable by his keen assessment. "You look very different, it is hard to believe that you are the same girl I met earlier this evening—*bellissima*, in fact." This was stated without flourish or flattery, casually flung, as if barely interested. Perversely she felt annoyed.

"My father considers I owe you an apology."

He digested the bald statement, then, smiling slightly, suggested, "Your father may, but obviously you do not?"

She blushed, recognising rebuke, then jumped to her feet. "I'm sorry if I sounded curt, *signore*. Please accept my apologies for any embarrassment I may have caused either you or your guests." She half swung away, but his quiet request detained her.

"Please don't go, *signorina*. Like you, I consider an apology unnecessary—however, there is another matter I would like to discuss." He waved her back to the chair she had vacated. "If you would spare me a few more minutes of your time?"

Surprised, she resumed her seat, but perched on the edge, wary as a sparrow suspecting the motives of a prowling cat.

"Will you smoke?" He proffered a silver cigarette box, withdrawing it when she shook her head. "Not many of my countrywomen indulge in the habit, but I know the emancipated English female is fond of her cigarettes. I believe you are one of those liberated women, a strict upholder of the view that modern woman is entitled to be free to follow her own destiny even if that freedom is detrimental to the happiness of her less liberated sister?"

The gist of his remarks became immediately clear. "Why flirt with words, *signore*? If you think I am being selfish because I choose to ignore my father's old-fashioned decree that I must marry before my sister why don't you come right out and say so? But before you do, let me warn you first that you will be wasting your time. I feel no compunction whatsoever about following my chosen career because, if I were in Sara's shoes, I would go ahead and marry if I were as much in love as she professes to be, with or without my father's permission. The only stumbling block, so far as I am aware, is Vincente's reluctance to go against my father's wishes. That, I interpret not so much as an unwillingness on his part to upset my father's feelings, as a fear that he might become estranged from the Domini fortune."

If she had thought to rouse him to anger she was disappointed. He levelled a long cool look, slowly digesting every facet of her appearance, his eyes sliding downward from her vital red head, tempestuous green eyes, anger-flushed cheeks, then remained lingering thoughtfully upon a passionate mouth set stern to stem further furious words.

"You are very insulting," he told her without heat, his dark eyes morose. "Towards your sister, that is. Sara is so beautiful, so charming, how can you possibly doubt Vincente's love for her?"

"I would doubt any Venetian's capacity to love. You are not a warm people, *signore*. You are a passionless race, excited only by possessions and by the envy of those with less worldly goods—mercenary beyond belief. Shylocks who break hearts without compunction when in search of their pound of flesh. Even traditional serenades, warbled with such touching pathos by your romantic gondoliers, are basically Neapolitan. There are no genuine Venetian love songs because Venetians have never learnt how to love."

A smile flitted across lips that had grown gradually sterner while he listened to her tirade. His voice held no anger when almost lazily he protested, "Come now, *signorina*, are you not forgetting that Casanova, the greatest lover of all times, was a Venetian"

"Indeed not," she retorted. "Casanova was certainly a true Venetian—cold-hearted, licentious and fickle!"

He stood up to tower over her. "It would seem that you have formed a very unfavourable impression of my race during the short time you have been in Venice. Which is how long...?"

She jumped up, the better to combat his encroaching shadow. She felt smothered by his geniality, his refusal to be riled, and irritated by the suspicion that secretly he was laughing at her. "Mere hours," she admitted sharply, "but I have lived a lifetime with your traditions and taboos, have served a long and painful apprenticeship until I now feel qualified to claim myself an expert at seeing through your pretences."

"Some people, Signorina Domini, see only what they wish to see, believe only what they wish to believe. Women are especially prone to this, especially women who are at war with themselves, women who fight to suppress their femininity, who are ashamed of the vulnerabilities of their sex and who, because they are neither physically nor mentally equipped to take up the burdens borne by men, finally turn against the sex they initially tried to ape. *Poverina!* Your father has confessed to me how much he regrets the absence of a son—subconsciously, even during childhood, you must have been trying to fill this void in his life. But by adopting an aggressive attitude you have not supplied him with a son but merely denied him a daughter—one about whose virtues he could rave, one whose sweet disposition would make him the envy of his cronies. As it has turned out, you are simply an embarrassment to him, a bad-tempered wench whose chances of matrimony are depleted each time she exercises her shrewish tongue!"

She stepped back, outraged. This, too, was characteristic of the devious Venetian—the deceptively mild approach used as a matador would use his cloak to conceal the weapon poised to deliver an unexpectedly cruel thrust.

"How dare you!" she gasped, groping for further words of scorn to heap upon his unrepentant head. Her chin lifted so that he was directly in line with twin daggers of danger trained upon his face. "I could marry any man I choose!" she challenged, throwing down the gauntlet. "Any Venetian, that is! There is not a man in this city of merchants that my father could not buy for me. No doubt," she continued in her impetuous fashion, unaware of betraying bewilderment and hurt, "my father is at this very moment offering me up for sale. Indeed, Sara has already let it slip that he brought me to Venice with the specific intention of finding me a husband! He has lectured me on my wilfulness, Sara hardly lets a moment pass without heaping recriminations upon my head and now you, too, have had your say! I ask you, *signore*, would you give up your freedom, revise your way of thinking, enter into marriage with a complete stranger, simply to indulge another person's whim?

She was aggravated by the slow, deliberate attention he gave to the question and was made extremely uncomfortable by the dark stare that seemed to penetrate mental and physical barriers in search of truth.

"I might," he answered slowly, as if still deliberating, "depending on how much regard I felt for the person concerned."

She took his reply as a rebuke, a rebuke which, coupled with all the earlier aggravations of the day, prodded from her a reckless challenge.

"Very well, *signore*, I'll give you the chance to prove your words! You say you're concerned about Sara's and Vincente's happiness; you've condemned as selfish my refusal to be sacrificed upon the altar of matrimony and you've professed that you would not stand in their way if you were in my shoes. I think you're a sanctimonious, lying prig, and for that very reason I feel no fear of putting you to the test...You have my solemn promise that I will marry, *signore*, just as swiftly as the wedding can be arranged."

For once she had managed to surprise him. His eyebrows shot up, his expression a mixture of puzzlement and satisfaction. She held his look, savouring her triumph before slowly spelling out her condition of surrender.

"Providing, *signore*," she stressed with mockery, "*that you agree to be my bridegroom!*"

CHAPTER THREE

HER WEDDING DRESS, they told her, had been hand-stitched over a century ago by nuns of a famous order. The wreath which was to hold in place the matching ivory veil was of pure gold, beaten wafer-thin, then fashioned into finely-veined ivy leaves.

Crossly Jo tried it on, then tossed a derisory glance at her reflection in a mirror. "It makes me look like ruddy Nero!" she muttered, jerking her head so that the wreath slipped, its sharp pointed leaves digging into her forehead. "How could you allow yourself to fall into such a trap, idiot!" she asked fiercely of her mutinous reflection. "Your challenge must have loomed like manna from heaven before the impoverished Conte. What in heaven's name impelled you to call his bluff?"

At the sound of footsteps progressing towards her room she snatched off the wreath and flung it on to the bed. She was standing staring out of the window when Sara bounced in.

"I've just been talking to Leo; he would like to see you as soon as you can spare the time. Naturally, I told him you would come immediately I passed on his message."

"Did you now!" Jo drawled, not bothering to turn her head. "Why, I wonder, did you think I would drop everything and run immediately to answer the Conte's bidding?"

"Because," Sara gave an exasperated shrug, "he is the Conte, I suppose. Though his attitude never demands it, he does command a certain degree of deference from most people."

"Not from me!" Jo's heel ground into the carpet as she swung round to challenge her sister. "The man's nature is as shallow as his purse, and his utterances as meaningless as his title. I've told both you and Father how he tricked me into agreeing to be his wife, and if he insists upon keeping me to my word I'll make life so unbearable for him that before many months have passed he'll be clamouring at the doors of the Vatican begging a special dispensation in order to obtain his freedom!"

Blithely Sara tripped over to the bed and picked up the wreath of golden leaves that was to be Jo's crown of thorns "Serves you right!" she smiled her complacency. "You asked for everything you've got and I for one feel no sympathy for you. Papà warned you many times that your tongue would run you into trouble your feet could not walk you out of, and it's happened just as he predicted."

"I was only trying to prove what a hypocrite the man is!" Jo protested vehemently. "How was I to guess he would drag me in front of all his relatives, giving me no time whatsoever to protest, then announce with great ceremony that I'd promised to be his wife! The gall of the creature!" Her mind shuddered from the memory of the nightmare that had been enacted the previous evening. "He knew I had no real intention of marrying him, yet he gave me no chance to back out of my idiot promise."

"Nor will he ever." Sara's satisfied-cat smile was

very much in evidence. "Actually," she ran a speculative look over her sister's tense body, "I don't think he has any more wish to marry than you have, but he has Vincente's well-being in mind. Leo has always taken his responsibilities seriously; he probably feels that as he's head of the Tempera family it is his duty to resolve the problems of all its members even if as a consequence he has to sacrifice his freedom. Such a man will make an ideal husband, Jo—a better husband than you deserve, in fact."

"But I don't *want* a husband!" Jo lashed back, fuming with impotent anger. "Not even one who's a paragon of virtue, or as rich as Onassis, or as handsome as Omar Sharif! Still less do I want to become the wife of a mercenary Count who's no doubt weighed up very carefully and concluded that his crumbling *palazzo* will benefit from the support of Papà's cheque book!"

"Leo is far too proud—" Sara began hotly, then was left addressing an empty room as Jo raced past, her back held rigid with resentment.

Jo went in search of the Conte and found him in his study. She rushed inside and without preamble began her protest. "Now listen to me, this comedy of errors must be terminated immediately!"

"Comedy of errors?" He rose to his feet, twirling a pen between languid fingers. "Is that a proper way to describe our imminent marriage, *bella*?"

"Don't call me Bella, my name is Jo!"

Her pretended obtuseness did not deceive him. He laughed aloud. "Bella—beautiful. Yes, it is much more appropriate than the masculine-sounding Jo." When he stepped forward she hastily backed away, but was not quick enough to elude the determined hand that fastened upon her shoulder. Held firm, she had to suffer his touch as he entwined a frond of hair wisping her forehead around his lean finger. "May I?" he enquired. Before she realised his intention he had swooped upon a pair of scissors lying on his desk and snipped off the curl, retaining it in the palm of his hand. He released her shoulder to brood down at the red-gold circle lying like a brand of fire against his palm, then he eased from an inner pocket a flat leather case which he handed to her, instructing, "Open it, please."

It sprang apart at her touch, revealing twin lockets nestling side by side upon a bed of white velvet. They looked so incredibly unique she could not suppress a gasp of admiration. Each golden locket was fashioned into the image of a lion—the symbol of the Tempera family whose eldest son was always christened Leonardo, after the king of the jungle. Bushy-maned, with wickedly curving tails, their golden eyes stared jewel-bright, a hard, unblinking stare uncannily like that of the man waiting silently for her reaction. In the centre of each leonine body was a carved glass profile set within four golden claws, one was of a man with classic Roman features, the other a gentler, less severe profile of a girl bearing upon her head a minute replica of the golden wreath each Tempera bride wore on her wedding day.

In silence, Leo lifted from its bed of velvet the locket bearing the girl's profile, pressed a hidden spring, and when it sprang open to reveal a cavity he placed inside Jo's lock of hair. He then snapped it shut and slipped it into his pocket.

"The other one you will retain in your possession," he indicated with a nod the remaining locket. "Anticipating your request for a lock of my hair, I have already obliged. These are traditional betrothal gifts," he carried on urbanely, impervious, it seemed, to her astonished stare. "For many centuries Tempera lovers have exchanged these lockets containing either a portrait or some personal memento. I will provide you with a wedding ring, of course, but in my family the exchanging of these lockets has always been considered more binding than the actual marriage ceremony. You might almost say," he tossed her a smile full of whimsy, "that from this moment on I shall regard you as my bride. Our marriage will not be consummated until after the church ceremony, of course," he thoughtfully reassured her, "but so far as I am concerned you are now the Contessa Josephine Tempera. I hope," he reached out a hand to raise her nerveless fingers to his lips, "that we will share a long and happy association, *bella moglie*."

The endearment broke her trance. She sprang away, putting a yard of carpet between them. "I am not your beautiful spouse, *signore*, not yet! And I promise you that if you insist upon keeping me to my word you'll regret it every day, every hour, every moment of the time we're together. I'm not so gullible as my young sister who fondly believes that her fiancé is captivated by her charms. I suffer under no such illusion! I'm very well aware that the motive behind your own and Vincente's eagerness to marry us is the healthy state of our father's wallet. However," she dared another desperate bluff, "if you are still prepared to suffer the consequences then by all means let us marry. But mark this, *signore*, you will not be treated by me as a husband, there will be no tender exchanges between us and certainly no wild nights of passion. I will accept you only as a *cicisbeo*—knowing how conversant you are with ancient Venetian customs I need not outline what your duties will be." When his lips thinned she experienced a thrill of triumph. Good! At last she had managed to penetrate his insufferable *politesse*, the restrained decorum that was so much a part of the Venetian character. Fired with success, she adopted a more confident, almost cocky manner.

"I was quite surprised, when researching your history, to learn that in eighteenth-century Venice most women were liberated, at least sexually, and were absolutely free to do exactly as they pleased. According to the books I read most of them made the most of it. Each woman, besides having a tolerant husband, had her *cicisbeo*, her recognised companion. After the first year of marriage she was free to choose such a companion with the full consent of her husband, the only provision being that he should be her social equal. I shan't impose upon you duties that are too onerous, *signore*. I shall expect you to attend me constantly, carry any parcels I might gather up while shopping, help me into my gondola, accompany me to the opera and take me to see whatever I might express a wish to see, but I will forgo the pleasure of having you kiss my hand each time we meet." Quite carried away by a sensation of power, she waited with feet astride, her look challenging him to an argumentative duel. If the Conte was determined to enjoy the feel of her father's purse he must also suffer the lash of her whip.

For a long breathless moment while her gaze was held by a cold golden glitter unpleasantly reminiscent of the jewelled lion's stare, she thought her challenge was about to be met. Silence lengthened. The room seemed suddenly to chill. She trembled a little, reminded of the Venetian's devotion, amounting almost to obsession, with the beasts of the jungle. The city was crammed with their stone images, winged lions, aloof lions, fierce lions, lions supporting windows, outstretched on doorsteps, even climbing chimneys and stuck on flowerpots and garden gates. They were carved out of wood, stone, immortalised in oils, and stamped upon leather. Uneasily she recalled a remark she had heard passed about the Venetian character. *"It is understandable that the Venetian should so greatly admire the powerful beast, for bestial too are the men of Venice when the madness of revenge grips them!"*

She jerked away, turning her back upon the silent man who seemed filled with an anger that could rend. She had to escape the ambience of menace filling the room, for the first time her young, courageous spirit was fearful, a fear that quickened her footsteps, that elevated her heart from her breast so that it was trapped, a soaring, panic-stricken prisoner in her throat.

"One moment, please! We have not yet finished our discussion." The command was crisp, decisive, yet held no threat. She halted, then spun slowly on her heel wondering, as her quick eyes noted the half-smile curving his lips and his negligent ease of movement, how she could ever have suspected him of savagery. She experienced an inexplicable pang of disappointment. The lion was but a lamb...

This assumption was responsible for her tone of sharp contempt when she addressed him. "If you're about to say that you've changed your mind about marrying me, *signore*, I shall be only too pleased to listen."

"On the contrary," he replied with such mildness of manner she gritted her teeth, "I consider that we are ideally suited. Besides," he rebuked gently, "have I not just said that so far as I am concerned you already belong to me? No, I merely wish to ascertain that you fully understand the outrageousness of the condition you have just outlined. Are you aware, for instance, that more often than not the eighteenth-century *cicisbeo* was a fop, an unfortunate person who, because he lacked his share of hormones, was more at home in the company of women than of men from whom he received little sympathy and towards whom he felt no affinity? The luckless creature found women tolerant of his shortcomings providing he remained willing to fetch and carry for them, to lend an attentive ear to their troubles, was ever ready to ease a headache by dabbing a cologne-soaked handkerchief on to a pained brow. Husbands were tolerant, as you said. They could afford to be because there was never any danger of their being cuckolded by these creatures. Sex between a woman and her *cicisbeo* was so rare as to be almost non-existent. Even today, the *cicisbeo* has his counterpart in the drawing-rooms of wealthy women all over the world. In France they are named gigolos; I do not know if there is a word for them in your country." His unusual golden eyes glinted with amusement as he challenged, "Tell me truthfully, Jo, do you really believe that I fit into that category?"

Her lips parted to utter a confirmatory insult, but all that escaped was a hissing sigh as she met disquieting eyes, piercing, yet with a hint of pity in their depths that caused her to swallow hard. He did not move a finger, did not utter a word, yet she was very much aware of masculine assurance emanating from his lean body. Vital black hair sprang from his forehead, tutored into neatness by a brush yet hinting that, raked through by fingers, it could erupt into a wilful mass of curls. Thrusting, wide, arrogant nostrils. Eyes—cat-golden. The sensuous, rangy animal stride.

When he growled a half-laugh she had to concede, "No, I must admit that you do not. But in any case," she continued sharply, "it hardly matters, your sexual prowess, or lack of it, does not interest me. All I want to know is whether, in return for the very substantial dowry my father has promised, you intend to accept the conditions I've put forward?"

"But of course," he agreed lightly, "it shall be my pleasure to humour you—at least for the time being."

"For the time being will suit me fine," she spat. "Our alliance will last only as long as it takes to lull Papà into a sense of security and so allow my sister to achieve her objective. I have tried to dissuade her from marrying your cousin, have used every argument I know to prevent her from making what I consider would be the biggest mistake of her life, but she won't listen. She must therefore find her own solution when she eventually discovers—as she most certainly will—that I'm right and she's wrong!"

"It matters a great deal to you that you should be proved right, *poverina*, does it not?"

Condescension, coming as it did from a man whose motives she despised, was galling. "I believe in following my own instincts," Jo retorted. "Once I've made up my mind about a person I'm very seldom proved to be mistaken in my judgment."

"You are a wilful, stubborn creature." His easy smile

had slipped. "However, I do not intend to indulge your appetite for sparring. You are a child still, Jo, and with children one has to have patience—a bitter plant that yields sweet fruit."

"Be as patient as you like," she retorted rudely, "the only fruit you'll pluck will be a lemon!" She stalked out of the room with his laughter ringing in her ears, seething, yet finding time to wonder why the man she so despised, whose actions filled her with contempt, whose mercenary aims she found so distasteful, should have the power to force her to scrabble for cool disdain and be able to arouse her emotion to such white heat that whenever they came into contact she felt a savage urge to inflict pain. She was dismayed by the hatred he aroused in her. If she could keep cool she could cope. Hampered by passion, she was very, very, vulnerable....

CHAPTER FOUR

THE NEXT DAY Jo put the Conte's patience to the test. After breakfast he sought her out and found her staring gloomily out of a window overlooking the Grand Canal. Oblivious of his presence, she was murmuring to herself, "Streets full of water, nothing but streets full of water!" likening the turgid canal to a huge artery from which smaller canals sprang like veins. It was a working day and the waterways teemed with traffic ferrying workmen about their day-to-day duties, refuse barges, parcel-post boats, ambulance boats, milk boats, even a hearse, intermingling with private motor launches, sleek speedboats and, of course, the inevitable gondola. She traced the progress of a *vaporetto*, a green and black painted motorbus lying low in the water with its full complement of passengers. Behind it chugged a cumbersome fruit barge piled high with oranges and great bunches of bananas and in its shadow a solitary man laboriously propelling a skiff full of vegetables he was no doubt hoping to sell in some city market-place.

"Good morning, Jo!" His voice startled her. "Sara tells me you have no pressing appointment until later today, so as I am free myself I decided now would be a good time to take you on a tour of our city." Glancing over her shoulder, he observed with a smile, "Like most visitors, you must be appalled by the congestion and seemingly haphazard progress of our water traffic, but I assure you that you will be quite safe. Accidents, when they do occur, are usually minor. The watermen of Venice are fairly proficient—as they ought to be after fifteen centuries of practice."

"How disappointing." Her answering drawl contained the very essence of boredom. "A squabble between bargemen might have helped to relieve a little of the monotony."

"Do not despair, *vespa*," his mouth tightened with asperity, "I'm sure that with little effort on your part you will find plenty to complain about."

Satisfied that he was needled, she purred, "You may fetch my coat and bag—you can't mistake the ones I want, they're laid out on my bed."

If she had flicked his pride he did not show it. Calmly he walked across the room to press an imperious finger upon a bell. In a matter of seconds a young maidservant tapped lightly upon the door before entering the room.

"You rang, *signore*?"

"Yes, Maria, the *signorina* would like her coat and handbag fetched from her bedroom."

"Si, signore." She bobbed a curtsey and spun round to leave, but was halted in her tracks by Jo's sharp command.

"Don't bother, Maria, the *signore* will do it. Please return to your duties."

"Scusi, signorina... ?" The girl seemed turned to stone, her face a picture of incredulity.

"You heard what I said!" Jo's voice rang with impatience.

Timid though she was the girl hesitated, then swung

pleading eyes upon the Conte, seeking guidance from the tall figure rigid with sudden hauteur. Then, within the blink of an eyelid, hauteur was gone and to the girl's amazement his calm voice instructed, "You may go, Maria, I will fetch the *signorina*'s things myself."

When he followed the girl out of the room Jo's teeth bit deeply into her lip. She ought to have been feeling triumphant—after all, she had successfully demonstrated her authority over the despicable Conte. But it was a Pyrrhic victory—one that left her with a sick feeling in the pit of her stomach and a shamed conviction that, to one girl at least, she represented all that was undesirable in a future *contessa*. However, she could not afford the luxury of qualms at this stage. Already the wedding was being organised—she had less than a month in which to make the Conte change his mind!

When Leo returned he made no reference to her appalling attitude but silently helped her on with her coat before suggesting gravely, "There is a breeze blowing today, if you have a headscarf I suggest you wear it, otherwise your hair will be blown into disarray."

Her fingers closed around a silken square in her pocket, yet perversely she chose to ignore his advice and stalked with chin outthrust outside on to the *campo*.

In common with most *palazzi*, two mooring posts, striped red and white like barbers' poles, had been erected beside the landing stage with, attached to one, a black-lacquered, gold-embossed gondola bearing the twin-lion crest of the Tempera family upon its elegant swan-necked prow. The Conte bypassed this to hand Jo into a sleek, high-powered motorboat, an expensive toy which nevertheless seemed to skulk in the shadow of its aristocratic counterpart. Leo seemed to sense her disappointment when, with a quiet chuckle, he observed:

"Had my companion been Sara, I would not have hesitated to use the gondola, but knowing your preference is for the functional as opposed to the merely decorative I'm sure you approve my choice."

"Quite correct," she agreed coolly, "also my preference for the useful applies not only to objects but also to men."

He was impossible to snub, she fumed as, guiding the craft between a myriad vessels, he kept up a cheerful and informative commentary as they travelled the length of the canal, dodging between heavy barges, slicing through gaps so narrow she many times held her breath until they were safely through, sometimes exchanging good-natured badinage with other navigators while negotiating a jam, other times speeding along a clear stretch of water, foam churning in their wake, the small boat bouncing on top of the waves with a vigour she felt certain was deliberately manufactured. But if he was hoping to hear her complain he was disappointed; she would have drowned without a murmur rather than allow him to think his sneaking, underhanded effort at revenge was having the desired effect.

When, with a flourish that sent the waters of the canal into a frenzy, he drew up at a landing stage she was breathless, flushed and visibly windswept. Her knees shook as he helped her out of the boat on to solid ground, but with an irritable shrug she declined his helping hand and walked unsteadily towards a towering oriental façade that might have been transported straight out of the Arabian Nights.

Glittering gold mosaics executed by Byzantine artists above portals and windows were surrounded by sculptures representing the signs of the zodiac, the Saints and the prophets. Fanciful marble inlays, alabaster statues, gilded weathervanes and petrified palm trees, lilies, grapes, pomegranates, birds and plumes were encrusted on every available bit of space. It was overwhelming—too much of everything, so that the eye became satiated and beauty began to appear grotesque.

"Well?" he murmured in her ear. "What are your first impressions of St. Mark's?" His tone rang with characteristic pride. To the true Venetian there was no city to compare with his, no sculpture so finely executed, no paintings so vivid, no art treasures so costly or beautiful as those gathered into this city of seafarers and merchants who, in past centuries, had plundered the world.

Jo took great pleasure in voicing her opinion. "It looks like the brainchild of some mad oriental warlord. As a whole it's certainly not beautiful, in fact, I consider it's tawdry—like the den of a robber who has stolen what he has been told is rare and costly but which, once it's in his possession, he has neither the taste nor refinement to display to best advantage."

"Come now," his tone was even, "you are judging with a biased eye. Here," he pulled her into a patch of shade, "narrow your eyes against the light and consider again the marble veneers. See how a shower of rain has cast over them a lustrous film, as if the walls were coated with oiled silk."

"I'm sorry," she shrugged out of his grasp, "to me, it still looks ugly."

"We will return again tomorrow." He sounded on

the verge of exasperation. "St. Mark's, indeed all of Venice, can be likened to a neurotic female, one day appearing lovely as a dream and the next wearing a waspish frown." When he took her by the arm and began propelling her away from the object of his pride she sensed with glee that he was annoyed. This being so, she decided to press home her advantage.

"I see no reason," she gasped, having to run to keep up with his stride, "why you Venetians should expect everyone to adopt the same set of values as yourselves. For example, you state that Venice can be as beautiful as a dream, yet one person's dream can be another's nightmare. Of what does a city of Shylocks dream? Of a sun fashioned out of gold? A moon of solid silver? Showers of diamonds, pools of emeralds, mountains filled with precious minerals, earth that yields a hidden treasure trove? Not everyone," she scoffed, "finds pleasure in a miser's horde!"

He stopped suddenly on a narrow bridge spanning an oily eel of canal and spun her round to face him. There was a strange glint in his cat-gold eyes—a warning of a somnolent beast being prodded too far?

"There could be some truth in what you say, little *vespa*," he snorted, "the more I am in your company the more I think my judgment could be faulty."

She grinned, appreciating his choice of adjective. Little wasp! A wasp could aggravate. Its sting, though seldom lethal, could cause great annoyance even to creatures many times its size.

His grip upon her chin was so unexpected she bit her tongue and for a second the pain was so intense she could have cried. "when I first saw you I thought I saw beauty beneath the mask of paint you had daubed over your face. You were a young, immature child, I thought, locked inside the body of a woman, a body of ripe, tantalising curves that would not be disguised even by hideous garments. I felt sympathy for what I imagined was a brave attempt to attack authority, for the resentment of an independent spirit being curbed. Your attitude was defiant, yet I felt it was a tearful defiance, a shell that would crack easily if pressure were applied. I know now that I was wrong on all those counts. You are not a vulnerable, misunderstood child but a bad-tempered, shrewish woman. In fact, the words you wore emblazoned across your shirt that night said it all—you are, indeed, a *bitch*!"

If he had thrown her head-first into the canal Jo could not have been more stupefied. It was a shock, she told herself, that caused a rush of hot tears to spring to her eyes, and fiercely she blinked them away, amazed by her own inconsistency. For hours she had prodded, jabbed and baited him, insult after insult had been heaped upon his head, she had sneered, taunted and reviled. Why then, now that she had managed to upset his damnable equilibrium, did she feel like a sail deprived of wind? Like a cockleshell boat left to the mercy of the elements?

Then temper flared. How dared this impoverished *conte*, this unscrupulous merchant, take exception to anything she said or did?

"Very well, *signore*," she hissed, "now that you've arrived at a true assessment of my worth, can I take it you no longer wish to hold me to my promise? That the marriage will not now take place?"

With one elbow resting on the parapet of the bridge he carelessly but thoroughly scrutinised her. "It most certainly will," he finally decided, "everything will go ahead as planned."

She turned her head away to hide her expression. Disappointment had brought a lump to her throat; she had convinced herself that this man's will would easily crack; he had seemed to bend in which ever direction she desired, yet instead of snapping he rebounded, sometimes painfully, like a steel spring. Much more venom would be needed if she were to rout this beast of prey!

They lunched in a small *ristorante* with an unpretentious frontage consisting of cracked walls, arched windows and hollowed stone steps leading down into a cellar-like room spaced out with very functional tables laid with spotless white linen reaching down to the level of spartan wooden chairs.

Leo seemed well known to the proprietor, who greeted him with outflung arms and a stream of rapid words in a dialect Jo could not understand. When they were seated Leo waved away the menu and order. "*Fegato alla veneziana* and a bottle of Bordolino, if you please, Pietro."

In response to her raised eyebrows he explained. "Calves' liver fried with onions is an experience you must not miss. I think you will enjoy it, but," his tone became dry, "if you do not then I'm sure Pietro could supply you with some English fish and chips."

"I rarely eat fish and chips," she replied coldly, resentful of the implication that she had no palate for good food.

"Excellent, then perhaps we are on the verge of discovering one thing at least about which we will not disagree."

They ate in silence, Leo seemingly preoccupied yet solicitous enough to remember to replenish her glass whenever necessary, and Jo, ravenously appreciative of the food placed before her yet too stiff-necked to put her appreciation into words.

His good humour seemed completely restored by the time they had finished their meal. In an indulgent tone he questioned, "Your father tells me you have visited your grandmother frequently over the years. If that is the case why have you omitted a sightseeing tour of the city before today?"

"We have always stayed with Nònna Domini in Murano. I love it there," she confided, made mellow with wine, "although Papà and Sara often visited Venice I found Murano so fascinating they could never drag me away."

"Your grandfather was a glassblower, I believe?"

"Yes," she retorted sharply, immediately on the defensive.

"An honourable profession," he soothed, sensing that she suspected him of patronage. "Glassmaking has always been based on certain important technical secrets which have been carefully preserved among members of glassmaking families. Close co-operation between the members of a working team is vital to successful glassmaking and as this was most easily assured within a family group, fathers handed down their knowledge only to their sons who in turn instructed their sons. As a matter of fact, during the fifteenth century a law was passed ordering that no one should teach glassmaking to anyone whose father had not known the art."

"There is nothing you can tell me about the industry, *signore*, I have studied the subject thoroughly. Did you know that French glassmakers rated the same privileges as the nobility? Freedom from taxes, for example, and the right to live in manorial style. The aristocrats of Venice, on the other hand, did not become landowners until the sixteenth century and during that period they laid down rules which were designed to protect their class from contamination; strict taboos were enforced to ensure no marriage could take place between members of the nobility and commoners, yet," her chin lifted, green eyes sparkling with pride as they glared at him across the width of the table, "among those whom sons of the noble families could marry without losing their rank were glassmakers' daughters!"

"And quite rightly so." He toyed with a remnant of cheese left on his plate, suppressing a smile before continuing gallantly, "As Venice has declined so, too, has the status of her nobility. As a member of that maligned class, I would like to put on record that I feel proud and honoured to have been chosen as a husband by a glassmaker's granddaughter."

Chosen! Jo could have argued that the blame for that error lay with her impulsive nature, or that it had been a bluff that had rebounded, yet nothing could alter the fact that it had been she who had done the asking.

Humiliation almost choked her, but as she preceded him out of the restaurant she managed to toss across her shoulder the caustic comment,

"Try not to mind too much that your city has become a pawn shop, *signore*. As Napoleon put it: *'Dust and ashes, dead and done with, Venice spent what Venice earned'*. However, she does not sell her heirlooms cheap—be grateful that Papà could afford you!"

CHAPTER FIVE

SIGNORA MARVESE, Vincente's mother, was a fiercely-fond example of Italian matriarch. No woman in the world, in her eyes, was worthy of the great honour of becoming wife to her son. But she was prepared to tolerate Sara, who was dainty, feminine, and satisfyingly *pliable*. Also she possessed one redeeming feature—a rich father.

Jo, on the other hand, she found quite incompatible. The girl was rude, overbearing, shockingly outspoken and showed no deference whatsoever towards Leonardo, her intended husband, nor indeed towards any member of his family. Her prim mouth set as, glancing across the dinner-table, she watched the future Contessa stabbing morosely with her fork a delicious slice of veal that had been beaten thin, coated with breadcrumbs, then delicately browned in butter.

"The dish is not to your liking, *signorina*?" she enquired, her displeasure thinly veiled.

Jo's hand jerked up and the Signora's breath caught as, held by a clear emerald gaze, she had to concede that at times the girl was extraordinarily beautiful.

"What...?" The rudely spoken word caused the Signora to revise her opinion—the girl was impossible, her nephew Leonardo must be out of his mind!

"Forgive my daughter's absorption with her own affairs, *signora*," Jo's father apologised smoothly. "Her mind is no doubt churning with thoughts of clothes and flowers and wedding bells."

When Jo scowled at him he threw a glance that warned: "Behave—or else!" before resuming his smoothing of the Signora's feathers.

"Your wife was English, Signore Domini, was she not?" Vincente's mother enquired. "A cool, distant race, I've always thought, with characteristics completely opposite to your own. You must share with my nephew your formula for successfully managing a wayward temperament. Sara here," she cast her an indulgent glance, "will cause my son no misgivings, I feel sure, but her sister, it seems to me, possesses all the independence of her mother's race. You will have your work cut out, Leo," she wagged a plump, beringed finger in his direction, "to train her into obedient ways."

"I'm not a performing seal!" Jo cast such a withering look the Signora's playful expression immediately froze.

"Nor do I fancy the role of animal trainer, Zia," Leo reproved his aunt. "In common with most Italians you tend to compare English girls unfavourably with those of your own race. You are very misguided. The English have a saying—so well used the truth of it must have been proven over the years—'Do not judge a book by its cover.' Jo's cover," he smiled across at her, "may seem hard and unbending, but I can assure you that I find myself becoming more and more engrossed as I turn each page."

"Yuk!" Jo's utterance of disgust was so loud it brought colour rushing to Sara's cheeks and a steely glint into her father's eyes. "The delusions which mislead men arise from their tendency to believe that to be true which corresponds to their wishes!"

Leo's lips twitched as he saw utter bewilderment clouding his aunt's face, then the frown as she tried to make sense of the ponderous sentence. Even Jo's father was perplexed, uncertain whether or not his tempestuous daughter had once again insulted their host. Kindly, Leo helped them out.

"Jo's argument is sound, but because it deals with a matter upon which she feels strongly she has fallen into the trap of concealing her point behind superfluous words. Reduced to its simplest form, what I'm sure she meant is that men's thought processes tend to run on the following lines:

"All cats are four-legged animals

"Fido is a four-legged animal

"Therefore Fido is a cat.

"In other words, she is telling me that the conclusion I have drawn could just as easily be false."

"Then why didn't she say so in the first place!" Jo's father snapped, made to feel foolish by his daughter's irritating habit of flaunting her intelligence, an annoying trait she quite often employed in order to prove that she was as good as any man. Why, he pondered wearily, looking across at Sara who was happily holding hands with Vincente under the table, could I not have been blessed with *two* gentle, accommodating daughters? What have I done to deserve a virago like Jo who can look so appealing but who is constantly at war with herself as well as with most members of the opposite sex?

Sensitive to his feelings of inadequacy, the Signora

stood up, signalling to the two girls. "Shall we take coffee in the *salotto* and leave these men in peace to sip their port and smoke their cigars?"

To her scandalised amazement, Jo folded her arms across her chest and wriggled back into her chair. "I'm staying here. I like port and I'm not at all averse to a cigar now and again."

"Jo!" Her father's voice thundered through the room. She opened her mouth to argue her right to stay, marshalling all the verbal thrusts that had cut to and fro across the Students' Hall during debates on women's equality, but just as she was about to launch into speech she noticed, out of the corner of her eye, a figure with head bent and shoulders heaving as he tried unsuccessfully to hide the fact that he was convulsed by laughter. Her fury turned on him, the annoyance caused by her father a mere pinprick in comparison to the rage aroused by the man she was being forced to marry.

"Shut up! Don't you dare laugh at me!" Her fists clenched, fingers itching to scratch the length of brown cheeks, as, completely helpless, Leo clutched his sides, swept along on a paroxysm of mirth. "You...you... *conceited, chauvinistic pig*!" She ground her heel into the carpet. "Damn you! I don't know why I even bother to try...!" She swept from the room, head proudly poised, eyes flashing resentment, and ground her teeth when two other masculine voices joined Leo's in a demoralising, humorous chorus.

She had been in her bedroom only a few minutes when Sara, flustered and visibly anxious, followed her inside. Wide-eyed, she watched Jo struggling out of her evening dress, a delicate confection of pale green cotton that had lent to her the charm of a woodland nymph, and gasped a protest when it was flung on to the floor and trampled under Jo's angry feet.

"Jo, what are you doing? You're surely not going to bed already? Signora Marvese has sent me to fetch you; there is something very important she wishes to discuss."

Jo grabbed a denim skirt from out of her wardrobe and began rummaging in a drawer for a matching top. "I don't doubt she has," she gritted, "but I have no intention of sitting with hands primly folded while she lectures me on my faults and outlines the sort of behaviour expected of a future *contessa*. You can go back and tell the old ragbag to get lost—I'm going out!"

"Out?" Sara repeated stupidly, ignoring the insult to her future mother-in-law. "But you can't, not without an escort—it simply isn't done. The Signora will be scandalised, and as for Leo..."

"Oh, for heaven's sake!" Jo turned on her such a look of exasperation Sara shrivelled. "I declare, Sara, the longer you stay in this country the more orientated you become! You're like a snail which for years has been unattached from its shell and now that it's found it has curled into a complacent ball, determined never again to budge! At home in England you and I have gone wherever we wished whenever we wished, sometimes together and sometimes alone. Mere weeks ago the idea of being confined to the house because an escort was not available would have reduced you to hysterical laughter, yet now you're implying that we should embrace attitudes that were rejected by Englishwomen over a century ago. Well, you may be willing to be brainwashed, but I am not! I'm going out now and I'm going alone. If the Signora doesn't like it then she just might, given a bit of luck, persuade her stiff-necked nephew to think twice about holding me to a promise given under duress."

Experiencing a sense of freedom that was amazing considering her modern upbringing, Jo hurried from the *palazzo* and in no time at all was swallowed into a maze of alleyways, archways and winding passages running through dismal back streets, then disgorging with pleasant suddenness into busy spacious squares. Giving no thought as to how she was to find her way back, she followed her nose, tramping along wide, airy quaysides, down ancient lanes, along paved alleyways, then slowed to a saunter when she recognised in the distance the Rialto bridge Leo had pointed out with pride that morning. She crossed its crooked hump and was immediately surrounded by a noisy, picturesque marketplace, then lost all track of time as she enjoyed the banter being exchanged by market traders, examined gilded ornaments, St. Christopher medallions, admired stalls piled high with strings of onions, casually-heaped lettuce, glowing apples, sliced coconut, oranges sliced before her eyes and then offered in succulent portions to tempt her to buy.

With a sticky trail of juice trickling down her chin, she paused before a display of carnations and was hurriedly besieged by an enthusiastic flower-seller with a patter so persuasive she finally staggered away clutching an armful of the cloying, heavily perfumed flowers. The strap of her sandal was chafing her heel, so thankfully she limped towards an outdoor café, collapsed into a chair and deposited her fragrant burden on to a small metal table.

"Caffe, per favore," she begged of the hovering

waiter, then kicked off her sandals preparing to enjoy the sights around her. She was just finishing her coffee when across the rim of her cup she caught a glimpse of bold eyes fastened upon her face before her glance slid away. The obvious admiring Venetian caused her no qualms. Nuisances such as he, she had discovered from past experience, usually shrivelled when at the receiving end of a frozen stare.

To her annoyance her admirer, impelled by boundless conceit, moved his chair closer, leaving mere inches of space between them.

"Buona notte, signorina." A fulsome smile revealed rows of teeth so white and perfect she felt an urge to poke her fist into his mouth, thereby loosening a couple of what he obviously thought were his greatest assets.

"Go away! *Andare via!*" She dismissed him with a wave of her hand.

"Ah, *inglése*!" he beamed, as delighted as if he had found a pot of gold. "I speak English good," he slowly enunciated, baring his tombstone teeth. Impudently he pushed aside her empty cup. "I like English girls very much," he confided. "Let us share a bottle of wine."

"No, thank you," she treated him to a frigid stare. "If you don't mind, I'll just continue to sit here and admire the view—*alone*!"

His toothy smile did not slip. Jo sighed. Regrettably, the reputation of English girls abroad was not good, and though she was irresistibly tempted to defend her counterparts by explaining in very concise terms the difference between liberation and immorality, she did not intend to become drawn into conversation with this pompous nuisance who, given an inch, would take the proverbial yard. So she bit her lip, her stony stare reducing his importance to that of a fly upon the wall. But then, to her great aggravation, he inched forward until their chairs were touching and hissed on a garlic-laden breath, "You like to dance? I know of a place near here..."

"Go and jump in the canal!" Crossly she slipped on her sandals and stood up to leave, turning her back upon the man whose persistence was infuriating. Incredibly, as she bent forward to scoop up her flowers, she felt the fleshy part of her thigh being pinched between two fingers—an old Italian custom which in other circumstances she might have laughed off but which, in this instance, escalated her fiery temper beyond control. Fury added strength to her arm as she swung her heavy handbag at his head. The impact knocked him clean off his chair and as he lay sprawling on the pavement his expression of ludicrous astonishment was so funny she just had to laugh.

The events that followed were like a scene from some farcical foreign film, Jo thought later when given time to reflect. As the amorous Venetian writhed at her feet, howling with pretended pain, an enormously stout woman, gasping and wheezing in her haste, emerged from the interior of the café brandishing a large wooden spoon in Jo's direction. Patrons of the café, obviously very partisan, spilled out in her wake and in seconds she was surrounded by a hostile gesticulating mob whose sympathies, she was left in no doubt, lay with the proprietress and the man on the ground whom she had stooped to comfort. One quick glance was sufficient to confirm Jo's suspicion that he was the stout woman's son, and her heart sank.

Above the screaming tirade of abuse being directed towards her, she heard a whistle blow, then the crowd parted to admit one of the strutting, ridiculously dressed *carabinièri* whose eyes, beneath a cocked hat, gleamed cold as the sword hilt supporting his huge fist. To Jo's disgust he waved her silent and listened carefully to everything the voluble proprietress had to say, then, ignoring her own heated protests that the charges being laid against her were highly inflated, began writing in his notebook.

She lost her cool when his hand descended upon her shoulder and she began to shout, feeling prickings of genuine fear. "The woman is mad! I had no intention of murdering her son—I was merely defending myself. In fact, if in England he had attempted the same impertinent action I could have quite easily had him arrested and charged with indecent assault. Look, I can prove what he did!" Forgetful of Italian modesty, she hitched up her skirt to search for the beginnings of a bruise she felt certain had appeared on her thigh. Gasps of horror from the watching women and jeers from the men recalled her sanity as, feeling shame out of all proportion to her crime, she hastily covered up the pulsating bruise.

"You will come with me *signorina*." The policeman's voice echoed with distaste. "I am charging you with violence and with offending public morality. Do not try to argue," he placed a hand as big as a palm leaf upon her shoulder and began pushing her before him. "You English girls are a nuisance, you tempt our sons, unsettle our daughters and outrage our parents with your immoral ways. If I had my way you would all be banned from our shores, but as it is," he shrugged regretfully, "I am only authorised to lock you away."

It could not be happening! she thought frantically, not really *happening*. She must actually be experiencing a nightmare, one so realistic she could feel the waves of the Grand Canal rocking the speeding police boat and actually feel the sword, buckled around the waist of the musical comedy figure sitting next to her, digging into her leg. The breeze seemed real enough as it rushed through her hair, as did the stars twinkling in a midnight blue sky, also lights strung out along the canal, their reflection decorating the water with an endless jewelled fringe.

The stern-faced man seated behind a desk in the police station was too down-to-earth to be other than human. He committed to writing all the lies that had been told about Jo, then, without even lifting his head, waved her out of sight. Roughly she was escorted along a dank passageway, down a flight of stone steps, then pushed inside a dimly-lit room that would have fitted inside one of the cupboards housed within the *palazzo*.

The cold, comfortless cell, the hard mattress, the leaden pillow, were all very real. She slumped down upon the bunk and leant sideways so that her burning forehead was in contact with bars of cold steel and thought, not of her enraged father, her scandalised sister and outraged future in-laws, but of the calm, unflappable Conte, desperately wishing that—just this once—he was by her side.

"Oh, Jo girl, you've done it this time!" she squeezed the whisper past the lump in her throat. "There'll be hell to pay!"

CHAPTER SIX

AT FIVE O'CLOCK the following morning Jo was given a bowl of water, a coarse grey square of towelling and an offensively-smelling sliver of soap. Shuddering her disgust, she dabbed water over her face and bathed eyes that felt gritty with lack of sleep. After patting her face dry, she combed her hair through with shaking fingers, wishing she had thought to retrieve her comb from the handbag the police had taken into their custody the previous evening.

The wash refreshed her. She sat on the edge of the bunk feeling hungry but at the same time nauseated, which was just as well, because when breakfast arrived she took one look at the metal bowl containing some unrecognisable brown mess and pushed it aside. For ages, it seemed, she sat watching the sun moving gradually from the lip of a window situated high, just beneath the level of the ceiling, until it disappeared from sight leaving the cell once more dank and grim. She shivered, dejection washing over her. The grim-faced policemen had refused to listen when she had begged to be allowed to contact her father. Back at the *palazzo* they were bound to be worrying—after all, to go out alone for a short while was one thing, but to stay out all night was quite another.

Her mind raced, filling in the time by preparing the

long and complicated explanation that was bound to be demanded of her. She had no idea of the time, but a further meal had been offered and rejected before she heard the rattling of keys, urgent footsteps, and a resonant voice, strange in tone as it snapped an order to some unfortunate offender, yet hearteningly familiar.

She jumped to her feet and stumbled forward, so that the sight that confronted Leo as he approached the cell was that of a small, frightened figure caged behind bars, with eyes that seemed enormous staring out of a pinched, ashen face.

"Dannazióne!" He allowed himself the luxury of one expletive as he waited, savagely controlled, until the guard's fumbling fingers had turned the massive key, then as the cell door was flung open he opened his arms to receive her.

To Jo, at the moment, it seemed the most natural thing in the world to fly through the cell door and bury her head deep into his shoulder. She heaved a great shudder of relief and Leo's arms tightened into a protective circle, his lips brushing her brow as he murmured tender, soothing phrases. He comforted her until she had stopped trembling, then, keeping her pressed to his side, he guided her along the passageway, up the stairs and into the glaring brightness of the police station's main office.

There seemed to be a great deal of commotion, many hurrying footsteps, many voices raised in voluble argument, but Jo kept her face pressed into Leo's shoulder, ashamed of weak tears that had welled into her eyes.

An authoritative voice, tinged with bluster, began protesting, "*Signore*, how were we to know? The girl was wandering the streets alone, late at night. She caused a commotion in a local café and we were sent for—what were we to think? We had no alternative but to arrest her!"

It was typical of Leo that he did not raise his voice. Leo—the lion who never roared, the beast without a bite.

"Enough!" he silenced them coldly. "I will return later."

Even Jo sensed the anger contained within the few quietly bitten words and was moved to feel a stirring of sympathy for the men who fell into an uncomfortable silence broken only by the shuffling of feet and a gruff, embarrassed cough.

As he handed her into the speedboat and ascertained that she was comfortable before taking over the controls she chanced a glance at his profile. His lips were a stern, straight line, compressed as if to stem words he could not trust himself to speak. His face, taut as a mask, had a hint of greyness beneath its tan and his eyes, lashed thick and black, looked haggard devoid of their golden gleam, dulled with searching through a long and worrying night.

Once back at the *palazzo* he again took command. As soon as she stepped into the main hall her father, Sara, Vincente and his mother descended upon her, firing rapid questions, barely waiting for her stumbling answers before asking yet another.

"Jo, what on earth happened?"

"Jo, where have you been?"

"Where, may I ask, did you spend the night, *signorina*?"

"Why didn't you send a message, Sara was frantic with worry!"

In response to the bell Leo had pressed a maid-servant appeared.

"Maria, take the *signorina* up to her room, see that she has a hot bath, something light to eat and is left undisturbed for the rest of the day."

"But, Leo!" Sara protested, "we must know—"

"Your sister is in no state to answer questions just now. This evening, if she feels inclined, she can satisfy your curiosity, but until then I insist she is left in peace to recover from her experience. Go now with Maria," he instructed Jo. Then more kindly, "If you feel well enough you may join us for dinner this evening."

For once it was a great relief to do as she was told. Her head was aching, eyelids would not be willed to stay open over heavy eyes. She felt unclean, and stepped eagerly into the bath Maria had prepared, then afterwards, warm, dry, and smelling sweetly of talc, she climbed into the huge four-poster and was asleep before Maria had tucked the bedcovers around her.

Hours later she stirred, opened her eyes, then, with a long, luxurious yawn, rolled over on to her back.

"Ah, at last you have come back to us, *nipotina*!"

"Nònna Domini!" Jo turned dazed eyes upon the figure seated in a chair drawn close to the bedside. "Whatever are you doing here?"

"I was brought here early this morning by your very charming *fidanzato*!"

"My betrothed...? Oh, you mean the Conte!"

"Naturally," the old lady spoke severely, "is he not the one you have chosen to wed?"

"Well...er..." Jo struggled upright, then, deciding the subject needed more thought, she dodged the issue. "But I don't understand, Nònna, why he found it necessary to bring you here."

Her grandmother was small, slender, with a sweet expression and a mouth that could adopt very determined lines when occasionally she felt inclined to be stubborn. "When he told me that you were missing I asked if I might return here with him. In the early hours he came to my house. Seemingly, all during the night he had explored every avenue in search of you and I was his last resort. His disappointment was great when I told him I had not seen you, but even then, at a time of great personal anxiety, he was courteous enough to apologise for disturbing my sleep and for being the bearer of such worrying news. He begged me to return to my bed, but when I insisted I would not rest until I knew you were safe he brought me back to the *palazzo* so that I would be near at hand when finally he discovered your whereabouts—which I had no doubt he would do," she chuckled, at ease now that her favourite granddaughter was safe. "You have chosen as a husband a very determined man, *nipóte*, one who would have upturned every stone in Venice had his search been much longer prolonged."

Jo stared, the image of Leo in such a frantic state was not an easy one to visualise. "I think you may have misjudged him a little, Nònna. The Conte never allows himself to become agitated, he is at all times cool, unflappable—even remote."

Her grandmother turned upon her a gimlet stare. "Just how long have you known the Conte?"

Jo swallowed hard and began plucking at the bedsheet with nervous fingers. Here was her chance to gain an ally. She was very fond of her grandmother and she knew the fondness was returned. Perhaps, with the aid of her wisdom, they would be able to find some way out of her predicament. "I've known him only a few days," she began in a rush. "The engagement came about through a silly wager, but nevertheless the Conte insists upon holding me to my promise because he needs the marriage dowry Papà is providing."

Her grandmother seemed not one whit disturbed. With a shrug of her thin shoulders she observed mildly, "If such is the case, then you are indeed fortunate. Consider how you would have felt if the man with whom the wager had been made were not the young and handsome Conte Tempera but an old, ugly specimen of manhood, the sight of whom would make a young woman cringe. But then I think I do you an injustice, *nipóte*," she chuckled at some private joke. "It has been said that you favour your mother, but in one respect at least you are very like your father. It would be very hard, I might even say impossible, to force either of you into a situation that was not to your liking. You profess to dislike the Conte, are suspicious of his motives and say you are angry about his insistence that the marriage must take place. Think deeply, child, be as honest with yourself as you are with others. Are you not secretly gratified by the fact that you have managed, albeit with seeming unwillingness, to capture the man you wanted?"

"Nonna!" Jo bounced out of bed and glowered down at her grandmother. "By implication, you're reducing me to a level of silly flibbertygibbets like Sara whose sole ambition in life is to find a husband! Very much to the contrary, I'm anxious to continue with my

career, the only men needed in my life are those whose brains I can pick. I'm not averse to male companionship, indeed, I enjoy it in the right place and at the right time, but marriage has no part in my plans. So you see how ridiculous is your implication that I deliberately engineered the situation that's causing me so much unhappiness!"

Nònna Domini stood up, looking unimpressed. "Poor Jo," she sighed, "if only I could hold up a mirror to your soul! I feel so sorry for the young girls of today who live in a world which does its best, night and day, to change the nature of woman, to strip her of her femininity, to convince her that wedlock is a padlock, to argue against our sex's most natural instinct—that of bearing children. You must fight against such insidious propaganda, Jo, if you are ever to discover your true self. Otherwise you will starve—not from lack of bread but from lack of love."

Her grandmother, Jo decided, once she had been left alone to dress, was old and pitifully out of touch with modern-day life. She shrugged slim shoulders into a strapless black dress, low-cut at the front and plunging deeply at the back, held in position by sheer will power and the genius of a cutter who had measured, cut, snipped and tucked the material in order to obtain the maximum adhesion using the minimum of support—a dress which demanded the utmost sangfroid of its wearer and culled gasps of admiration, willing and unwilling, from wondering observers. Each time she had worn it she had asked herself: will it stay put. It always had. The hypnotic effect of smooth, unblemished shoulders and milk-white curve of breast, half hidden, half displayed by a flimsy film of net, was sensational.

Tonight she felt she needed the boost the dress would give her. Anxiety about her welfare had had time to wane; if the going should get tough she would need all the armour the outfit would provide.

She was putting finishing touches to her hair when Sara entered the room. As Jo turned from the mirror Sara's frown was very much in evidence. "Oh, no, Jo, you're not in an 'I dare anything' mood again!"

"I don't know what you mean." Calmly Jo swung round to the mirror, allowing Sara the full benefit of a back bared to well below the waist with, outstanding against one shoulder blade, a black, circular mole, perfectly placed. "A devil's kiss," her mother had once laughingly proclaimed it, much to Jo's delight and Sara's trepidation.

"Something gets into you whenever you wear that dress," she frowned, "you take such delight in shocking people." Her rather censorious tone changed to a plea. "Please, Jo, try to behave tonight. Papà is already very angry with you, Signora Marvese and Vincente have both been shocked and bewildered by your actions, whereas Leo..."

"Yes...?" Jo swung round to challenge her sister. "Tell me about Leo, is he, too, shocked, angry and ashamed? I must admit he didn't seem to be when he delivered me from jail this morning, but then he's too much of a gentleman to show his displeasure to a lady in distress. Tell me what you think, Sara. Did last night's escapade do the trick, has Signora Marvese finally managed to persuade the Conte that as a Tempera bride I leave much to be desired? Come, tell me what harsh words were bandied about during my absence."

Jo was expecting a spirited reply from her usually

voluble sister, but to her surprise Sara did not react as expected. She stood in dejected silence, her bottom lip quivering, then in a gesture of utter hopelessness crumpled, a tight ball of misery, on to Jo's bed and began to sob. Jo started towards her, sensing that this time Sara was not acting, that her tears were tears of real despair. "Sara, what's wrong?" She shook her by the shoulder. "Were you so worried about me? I'm sorry I caused you all so much concern. I didn't mean—"

Sara's head jerked up, an expression of unmistakable dislike on her tear-streaked face. "*You* are sorry!" she choked. "You're not half so sorry as I—sorry that my happiness is in the hands of a person such as you, sorry that you have the power to destroy my life, sorry that instead of a sister with my well-being at heart I have one who's selfish, stubborn, concerned about fulfilling her own desires even if she wrecks my life in the process!"

Jo sank down beside her. She was used to such recriminations, but this time Sara was not railing against what might happen but what already had happened. "Tell me about it," she demanded crisply, knowing soothing words and denials would be useless.

Sara gulped, then rolled on her back, staring at the canopy above the bed as if on its lace-patterned surface she could see projected an image of the scene that had occurred the night before. "When you ran out of the *palazzo* last night Signora Marvese went in search of Leo demanding that he should follow you and fetch you back. To everyone's surprise he seemed unperturbed, merely shrugging and making some oblique remark about a kitten pent up becoming a tiger which we did not understand but which seemed to satisfy Papà, because he, too, made no further objection. For an hour or so we played cards. Your name was never mentioned, yet your absence hung over the room like a cloud. Then finally, when it was midnight and you'd still not returned, the signora could contain her anger no longer and began to rant and rave, demanding of Leo that he should call off the wedding, saying you were not fit to be his bride and that your actions would bring disgrace upon his name. By that time I could tell that Leo, too, was worried, but he made no reply, just brushed her aside as he strode out of the *palazzo* to begin his search. This incensed the Signora so greatly she turned on Papà. It was terrible, Jo!" She sat upright, gulped back a quivering sob and with eyes mirroring the extent of her misery continued reliving the nightmare.

"Her remarks became outrageous, too outrageous for Papa to endure. It was when she accused you of being morally lax that he lost his temper and they began to row in earnest. Vincente and I tried to intervene, but we were shouted down. After many bitter exchanges, the Signora incensed Papà almost to the point of apoplexy by declaring that the late Conte, Leo's father, would turn in his grave at the idea of his son marrying someone as unworthy as yourself. "If one of my daughters is not fit to be accepted by the Tempera family, *signora*," he exploded, "then neither is the other! That being the case, the marriage between Sara and your son will not now take place—I here and now formally withdraw my permission!"

"Oh, glory...!" Jo's breathed explanation was drowned by a further outburst of sobbing from Sara.

Both of them knew how impossible it could be to change their father's mind once he had come to a decision. The future for Sara seemed bleak.

Jo left her sobbing on the bed and began pacing the room. Something drastic would have to be done. Although she held no brief for Vincente, whom she considered to be a weak and vacillating character completely under his mother's thumb, to Sara he represented all she wanted from life. Sara, too, possessed her share of Domini single-mindedness. She had set her heart upon becoming Vincente's wife and was liable, if thwarted, to become a creature of unbearable moods and depressions.

"And it will be all your fault," Jo told herself gloomily, searching her mind for a solution.

There was only one—time and time again her mind shied away from it, but finally it had to be faced. She would have to go through with her marriage to the Conte, it was the only way her father's ruffled feathers could be smoothed. Signora Marvese could not influence Leo as she did her son, so her dissenting voice would quickly be silenced.

Jo's fists clenched as she fought the influence of an inner voice crying out against the forfeiture of freedom, against the coercion of being forced to marry when marriage was the last thing she had intended, against the wrench of being deprived of a career whose challenge she would have enjoyed, especially when she would have become one of a small female minority within a male-dominated sphere. But she owed a duty to her sister—she would have to fulfil that duty and leave the rest to the gods. If the Conte was still interested in obtaining a bargain bride then let the sale be finalised!

She sought him out, anxious to test his reaction to the decision that had been made, her pale, subdued face quaintly at odds with her flamboyant outfit. He was pouring out pre-dinner drinks and when she stepped inside the *salotto* he looked up and saw her image reflected in the mirror directly facing him. Their eyes collided through glass and for a second she felt startled by the golden, alert gleam that traced her reflection, lingering longer than was polite upon smooth, curving shoulders outstanding stark as alabaster against a density of filmy black bodice. She tensed, expecting censure, but he turned to face her wearing his usual expression of urbanity to observe.

"You are not wearing your locket. It would look well with that dress."

"I don't agree." She stepped farther into the room, projecting bravado, yet feeling an annoying quirking at the knees. "You Venetians have an unfortunate tendency to paint the lily. We English, on the other hand, consider simplicity has more impact."

"Beauty needs no adornment, eh?" without consulting her wishes, he handed her a glass of pale golden sherry. "In this instance I will not argue with that." As Jo accepted the proffered glass she blushed, made to feel naked as his slow, interested glance slid along a slope of shoulder, down a curvaceous breast, then plunged to linger among tantalising shadows cast by net enthralling, mysterious as midnight.

"I've come to apologise." Fiercely she suppressed the tremor in her voice as, casually turning aside, she exposed the devil's kiss startling against a white expanse of shoulder, to his interested gaze.

"This time, *cara*, I consider an apology is justified. Last night I suffered some very anxious hours."

She swung round, puzzled by a voice that had sounded strangulated, then decided she had been mistaken as she searched a face impassively unreadable.

"Yes," she jerked, struggling with a surge of depression. "Sara has just been telling me about the row and I want to do all I can to patch things up between Signora Marvese and my father. But before I do so, you must let me tell you the true details concerning last night's fiasco. The police wouldn't listen to anything I tried to say, but I'm sure you will give me a fair hearing." She drew in a deep breath and without giving herself the time to wonder why it was so important that he should believe her, launched into her explanation.

Leo heard her out in silence, one arm draped casually across the shelf of a fireplace sculpted from black marble, the other occupied with a goblet of fine crystal, twirling the stem within sensitive brown fingers as, with dark head bowed, he paid rapt attention to its swirling contents. Giving him no time to interrupt, Jo spoke in a tumbled rush, watching for any change of expression, however slight, upon the regal profile etched with cameo clarity against a background of black stone.

His lips quirked once when, her voice raised in indignation, she recounted the flesh-pinching episode, but he let it pass without comment, continuing his mood of sombre contemplation until, her explanation finished, she began with disjointed phrases to outline her remedy for undoing the harm her actions had caused.

"It seems I now have no alternative but to marry

you—my first duty must be towards Sara. Your aunt, I'm sure, must already be regretting her thoughtless remarks, but Papà will not be easily mollified. So if I can somehow convince him that I really *do* want to marry you then I'm sure he'll raise no objection. Our marriage will remove every obstacle threatening Sara's happiness.

Leo jerked upright, spearing her with a look of glacial displeasure, "Forgive my obtuseness, but I had formed the impression that you had already promised to become my wife. Arrangements for our wedding have been in process for some days, yet you speak as if only this minute you have reached a final decision?"

Jo cast him an uneasy glance, suspicious of a calm that seemed cast like oil over turbulent emotions. With a nervous shrug she crossed over to the window before attempting an explanation. "I know I promised to marry you," she gulped, "but I somehow never really expected to have to carry out that promise. To me, the situation has always seemed unreal, as unreal as Venice itself, a ruined city full of relics, a museum wherein antiquated customs have to be brushed aside like the cobwebs one keeps brushing from one's face and from out of one's hair. A city peopled with beings living in the mediaeval past, women who revel in servitude and men with attitudes to match. Can you blame me," she appealed desperately, "after living the sort of life I've lived, for thinking I'd stepped into some kind of fairy tale, an Alice in Wonderland dream inhabited by unbelievable creatures that would disappear the moment I woke up?"

He moved with lithe, cat-like tread, demolishing the width of the room in the time it took her to draw breath. She would not have believed his grip could be so cruel, fingers that dug into the soft flesh of her shoulders, flexing hard, gouging a depth of unbearable pain. He was very angry, she realised, as he released his grip upon her shoulder to enclose her slender neck within one hand, at the same time fastening the other upon her waist to jerk her forward against his chest. Her terrified eyes caught his expression as his head lowered, the glitter of eyes flashing cold fury, nostrils flaring wide, a savagely resentful mouth intent upon punishment.

He kissed her only once, a kiss of long duration that began chilling as steel against steel, then gradually, as metal melts, developing a relaxing warmth that rose to bearable heat, then progressed into scorching flame that erupted ultimately into a frightening flare of passion. No devil's kiss could have inflicted a more searing impression than his. She felt marked for life, not unobtrusively like the mole crushed beneath his hand, but blatantly, so that the whole world would look at her and know that she was his.

He released her so suddenly she sagged against him, her red head, dejected as a broken match, supported by his comfortless shoulder. As if from miles away his voice resounded, suave, composed, echoing none of the passion they had shared.

"Nothing becomes real until it is experienced, *bambina*. I regret having had to waken a dreamer, but I could not allow you to enter into marriage with a man you look upon as a shadow. I'm human, *tesora mia*, as are you; together we will find love in marriage."

"Love!" Jo choked out the hateful word. "Love could never usurp the loathing I feel for you!"

He shrugged. "Love, hate, they are both qualities of passion. At least you have said goodbye for ever to your limbo of illusion. Perhaps now, having been shaken from your cradle of indifference, you will really begin to feel.

Jo's blood ran cold as she stared into the face of a stranger. A lion without a roar, she had labelled him, a beast without bite. The menace of the jungle was all around him—how could she have failed to see, how could she have forgotten that of all God's creatures there is but one that cannot be made the slave of the lash—the cat, the family with the lion at its head.

CHAPTER SEVEN

THEIR WEDDING DAY dawned bright and golden. As Jo stepped outside the *palazzo* on her father's arm everything seemed to be glittering, as if artists had mingled sparkling wine into their paints or fairies had waved their wands over buildings, dusting them with diamonds.

The Conte's crested gondola was bobbing at its mooring post and as she stepped inside a steadying hand was offered by one of the menservants dressed for his role of gondolier in a splendid pink uniform. He looked slightly self-conscious, Jo thought, as carefully he arranged her veil over velvet cushions. Signora Marvese had demanded a ceremony worthy of the house of Tempera. In the old days, she had insisted, Venetian brides had been celebrated throughout Europe for the magnificence of their clothes and the grandeur of their weddings. So the city's leading coiffeur had dressed Jo's hair, had shampooed, snipped and brushed until it resembled a length of red-gold silk. The front was combed severely back to accommodate the wreath of golden leaves worn by Tempera brides and the rest, entwined with golden thread, had been fashioned into a scroll that rested low on the nape of her neck. Her shoulders were bare and her dress, borrowed from legions of previous brides, had a full skirt, a nipped-in waist, and was fashioned out of priceless silk damask woven with golden threads.

A crowd of sightseers had gathered outside the *palazzo* hoping for a sight of the bride. As Jo waited for her father to join her a breeze lifted her veil, exposing white, set features, a firmly disciplined mouth, and eyes mirroring a depth of uncertainty. Oohs and aahs of satisfaction came from the watching women—it was as it should be; the Conte's young English bride, though reputedly headstrong, was nevertheless conscious of the honour about to be bestowed upon her.

With a fluttering of pink satin ribbons the gondola set off towards the church with, following in its wake, a trail of motorboats transporting the wedding guests. The church was not far from the *palazzo* but, although all traffic on the canal gave way to the gondola with much blaring of horns and goodnatured badinage, the journey, to Jo, seemed interminable. She schooled herself to return friendly waves and to smile her appreciation of good wishes being yelled by spectators lining the canal, but her heart grew heavier by the minute until, when finally the gondola drew up in front of the church and a priest, at once beaming and benevolent, advanced to greet her, she felt her body was encasing a leaden weight.

Leo, looking indescribably distinguished in a morning suit, was waiting inside the church, the interior of which, as she walked down the aisle towards him, was merely a blurred impression of wooden-beamed ceiling, tall arcades, painted cherubs, and a scent that seemed the very essence of mediaeval Venice, a mixture of flowers and Oriental spices that caught in her throat, causing her to choke on her responses.

Surprisingly, she had become too numbed over the past weeks to argue her dislike of the vow to obey. Her own lethargy surprised her. She felt she had been sapped of the will to fight, as if the combined pressures of Leo, Vincente, the Signora, Sara and her father had bludgeoned her spirit, reducing the scratching kitten to a bleating lamb.

When the Conte slipped a heavy gold ring upon her finger she gasped and involuntarily jerked her hand away. But Leo was prepared for such reaction and grasped her firmly by the wrist while the ring was slid into place. Then it was all over. She and the Conte were man and wife—choirboys were singing of it: an organ was joyously pealing a hymn in praise of it; guests were laughing and chatting of it, and the priest, beaming and rotund, seemed enormously proud of the part he had played in sentencing her to a lifetime of bondage.

Leo lowered his head and before she could dodge out of the way brushed her cold lips with his own.

"Che duri per sempre, cara," he murmured, holding her still.

May it last for ever!

"Not if I can help it!" she hissed in a most unbride-like tone. His eyebrows shot up, then with a small smile of reproof that set her teeth on edge he led her up the aisle, out of the church, and towards the beribboned bridal gondola with, on its high-necked prow, the crest of lions with cold, glittering stare.

Back at the *palazzo* a feast had been prepared, a culinary triumph masterminded by Signora Marvese, who was in her element when sufficient money could be spared to imitate the grandeur of yester-year. It was a buffet luncheon, hot and cold meals served to the guests' individual choice. White-fringed, pink-curled hams, succulent barons of beef still hot from the oven and basking in their own sizzling juices, tender chickens with crisp brown skins that crackled at a bite, huge prawns, blood-red salmon, grilled bacon rashers wrapped artistically around slices of tender liver. There were innumerable side dishes, iced-sponge cakes oozing cream, crystal bowls containing a wide selection of desserts, the inevitable *lasagne* and *misto mare*, a fried pot-pourri of unbelievably delicious seafood.

"Shall I fetch you something to nibble, Jo?" Sara zoomed upon the bridal pair as they waited at the entrance of the main *salotto* to welcome stragglers. "You must be starving," she urged, full of concern now that she could look upon her sister as an asset rather than an obstacle. "You wouldn't eat breakfast and also, if my memory serves me correctly, you refused supper last night. I'll get you a devil on horseback," she coaxed in response to Jo's wave of dissent, "that's one delicacy I've never known you to refuse."

"Yes, please do that, Sara," Leo accepted on Jo's behalf, "we shall have to remain here a few minutes longer, so by all means supply Jo with her devil on horseback."

"Don't bother," Jo refused coldly. "I've had my fill of devils for one day." As she scowled at Leo, her meaning unmistakable, Sara protested:

"How can you imply that Leo is a devil—he's too much of a gentleman!"

"According to Shelley," Jo fixed her with a stony stare, "sometimes the devil *is* a gentleman!"

Sara's shoulders lifted in despair. Casting Leo a sympathetic glance, she appealed of him: "How will you tame her temper, Leo? She's already driven Papà and myself almost to despair, what remedy will you employ that we have not?"

"A soothing tongue, perhaps." Leo's grave answer held a hint of rebuke that made Sara feel decidedly uncomfortable. The Conte could be gently cutting when he wished. For a surprised second she felt almost sorry for Jo, who had stated emphatically on more than one occasion that this descendant of the Lions of Venice was no more ferocious than a toothless tomcat. He, on the other hand, seemed very intuitive of Jo's needs—for the understanding he seemed to think her family ought to have supplied. She shrugged, deciding their characters were too complex for her simple mind, then twirled on her heel to go in search of Vincente, her pleasant, undemanding fiancé who would bring no upheaval into her placid life. How glad she was that he differed so much in nature from his cousin—the man whose imperturbability made her shiver, a man, she sensed with rare insight, who would not enjoy victory without a fight.

When the last of the guests had been greeted, leaving them free to mingle, Leo raised Jo's hand to his lips, brushing her cold fingers with a kiss.

"You have behaved very well today, *cara*. Indeed, for the past weeks you have seemed almost docile." His smile was wry as he enquired whimsically, "Is it possible that you have at last come to terms with the idea of having me as a husband? It would be nice," his golden eyes flicked across her set features as if in search of encouragement, "if our honeymoon could begin in harmony rather than in discord."

All of her pent-up frustration was contained in the

scornful look she threw his way. "If you think that then I must be a better actress than I thought. However, if my behaviour has pleased you then it must have also met with Papà 's approval, which was my sole aim But now that we're married and Papà can't go back on his promise to allow Sara and Vincente's wedding to take place I shall revert to normal by adding one more vow to those I've already pledged today—you have my word, *signore*, that from this day onwards you will bitterly regret having taken me for a wife!"

The unshockable Conte shrugged off the threat and politely offered her his arm. "Our guests are waiting. For the next couple of hours do please continue acting out your role of radiant bride."

It was hard, yet Jo somehow managed to do as he had asked, mixing freely with the guests, laughing, chatting, her manners impeccable as she was introduced to members of the family she had never previously met. Carefully she noted each introduction, expecting to be confronted by Francesca, the girl whose name had teased her mind since she had heard it mentioned by Vincente in a teasing, flippant manner that had aroused Leo's anger. But the introduction never came.

She pretended it was a game, that each of Leo's relatives was an adversary who had to be charmed, and managed with such success to fool them that by the time the reception was in full swing Leo was being inundated with congratulations from envious friends.

"What an angel you have brought into the Tempera fold, Leo!" one infatuated uncle exclaimed, bemused by the beauty, wit and charm of his new niece.

"An angel with a temper, nevertheless, Uncle Nuccio," Leo countered with a smile, sliding a fond arm around Jo's waist.

"I have always preferred temper to meekness," his uncle approved. "The latter I regard as a dishonest vice and the former as an honest virtue."

"How nice of you to champion me, Uncle," Jo cooed, stroking a seemingly possessive hand along Leo's arm to administer a vicious secret nip. It must have felt agonising, but he did not flinch. Rather white around the lips, he covered her punishing fingers with his hand, exerting crushing pressure until she released her grip, all the while continuing an urbane conversation with his uncle.

Her sparkle lasted until the last ritual was being performed, the act of the bride and groom distributing to their guests dainty lace pouches with draw-string ribbons, decorated with minute posies of flowers, each containing a handful of sugared almonds and a small card printed with the names of the bride and groom, the place and date of their wedding. It took time, because a few pretty phrases had to be exchanged with each beaming recipient so that, by the time the last favour had been handed out, Jo felt she was dragging a heavy cloak of weariness around with her, and wondered how much longer she could maintain her artificial air of gaiety.

When she stumbled Leo's arm shot out to steady her, his keen glance noting the droop of her mouth and faint shadows beneath her eyes. He looked around for Sara, caught her eye, then indicated with a wave that she should join them. She came immediately, giving an understanding nod when Leo instructed:

"Our duty is done, we can leave now without giving

offence. Most of the guests will remain for hours yet, but I've no doubt that you and your father will cope with the help of Vincente and my aunt." His last words were phrased as a question and when Sara nodded assent he smiled approval, then suggested, "Perhaps you will accompany Jo upstairs and help to get ready for our journey? I suspect she is feeling very tired."

For once Jo did not argue with his judgment. She *was* feeling tired, and depressed, and apprehensive all at the same time. Blood rushed with fevered, panicky haste through her veins at the thought of being isolated, completely marooned from society, except for the man she had just married. They were to spend their honeymoon in a villa set upon the edge of the lagoon that was used by the Tempera family during the hot summer months. She had been aghast when Leo had suggested it, but her protest, owing to her father's presence, had been mild; her acceptance of the plan all part of the deal to keep Enrico Domini's volatile temper sweet.

In a quiet, subdued mood, she allowed Sara to help her out of the costly wedding finery and into a dress of blue and white checked gingham in which she had the appearance of a troubled infant. Sara was blind to the nuances of expression chasing across her sister's face; she was preoccupied with the wedding dress, fingering the material with admiration and envy.

"How I wish I could wear this dress for my wedding!" she yearned over the rich damask, "but even if it were allowed I couldn't get into it," she decided petulantly, "the waist is far too narrow."

"You could always forsake pastries for a while," Jo replied absently.

"I could, couldn't I?" Sara brightened. "Do you suppose if I did—" she hesitated, then sighed, "no, I haven't enough willpower to shed the required number of inches in the time allowed. Vincente is most eager to set a date for our wedding—if he had his way it would take place tomorrow."

"If only it could," Jo breathed inaudibly, "I would get my release that very day! How much easier it would be to bear the bondage of marriage if I knew it was to last for only one day!"

Guests crowded on to the *campo* to wave the happy couple goodbye. It was early evening and as Leo nosed the motorboat down the canal Jo huddled in her seat, beset by cold shivers even though sunshine was dancing upon the water, the canal a long silver ribbon with, foaming in their wake, scintillating diamond spray.

Soon they were out in the lagoon, speeding across its width towards the Lido, a vast, glittering beach resort full of hotels, shops, nightclubs, and even a casino. It seemed a strange choice of abode for a man who cherished his solitude, who seemed to incorporate within himself all the qualities of Venice, her supreme conceit, her patronising pride, her high and mighty façade.

But he sped the length of crowded beaches crammed with sun umbrellas, ice cream vans, shrieking children and barking dogs with a haste indicative of distaste and did not slow down until they had reached a quiet stretch of shore enmeshed in weeds and creepers and littered with tree trunks and many-coloured sea-shells. Here, signs of habitation were few, so it came as no surprise when he sidled the boat into a narrow creek so thickly fringed with weeds and long grass they might have been explorers pushing a way through an uncharted river in some dark, unknown continent.

Without comment, he helped Jo out of the boat, then, retaining her hand in his, he hauled her up a narrow path, through a tangle of wistaria and bougainvillea until they emerged into a lawned garden with, set in its middle, a white creeper-covered villa, skilfully placed to gain the maximum ventilation in the heat of summer. The impressive structure was topped by overlapping double roofs, upcurving like sails ready to take the breeze, supported by tall slim pillars that gave to the house an appearance of being delicately balanced, poised between air and sea.

They approached up steps following the rise of the land and entered a cool, black-tiled hall.

"The staircase connects two entrances to the house," Leo explained, "one from the front and the other, the one we have just used, from the back. It virtually divides the house into two," he smiled, seeming to guess that Jo was nervously wondering how many bedrooms it contained. "Your room is the one under the larger of the roofs," he supplied. "The one beneath the smaller roof is mine."

Relief untied her tongue. "The wide-spreading roofs are very distinctive," she stammered, "like huge wings hovering protectively over a nest."

He laughed at her description but seemed pleased. "They were not designed purely for decoration but were logically shaped to collect rainwater for the cistern and to cast welcome shadows during high summer. As there are no internal walls the air circulates. As you can see, the masonry of the walls has been left untouched, again to give added coolness. Heating has not been installed as it was built essentially as a summer house, but water is heated by geyser and fuel for cooking is supplied by gas cylinders. Come, I'll show you to your bedroom and once there I suggest you rest for an hour or two. You look tired, *cara*. It would please me if you were rested enough to enjoy the dinner I have planned especially to celebrate our first night together."

The bedroom into which he led her was a continuation of the spartan simplicity favoured throughout the villa, holding a modern divan, a couple of chairs and a length of wall consisting entirely of wardrobes with, in its centre, an aperture out of which had been fashioned a dressing-table with mirror, and a glass shelf to accommodate bottles and jars. Underneath was a set of built-in drawers in which to store lingerie.

Leo leant against the door jamb, hands thrust deeply into the pockets of his slacks, and smiled a whimsical smile as he watched her walk across to the window. Patiently he waited for her reaction to the view, then, when she did not speak, he prompted:

"Well, what do you think?"

An indrawn breath was her only reply. Standing splendid in isolation, the villa afforded panoramic views of vivid blue sea and cloudless sky. Below was the green slope leading down to the shell-strewn, wave-kissed, lonely shore that was to be exclusively theirs. It was an ideal love nest, an invincible eyrie, a paradise for lovers—especially for lovers on honeymoon who had need of a beautiful setting, freedom from human distraction, and time to explore the minds of partners who, in spite of having knowledge of each other, might discover their companions possessed of strange, complex facets of nature never previously guessed at.

Leo frowned when he saw her shiver. His voice, terse and clipped, seemed to indicate that there was an edge to his patience.

"I'll leave you to relax. Perhaps later, when you are rested, you will feel more inclined to voice your appreciation—or lack of it!"

When the door slammed behind him she began mechanically to unbutton her dress. He had sounded upset. Disappointed that she had uttered no word of praise for the villa in the sun whose delights he had expected her to appreciate? She was far too tired to appreciate anything and was especially resistant to voicing any admiration lest her husband should take it as a sign of softening or even of encouragement.

She dragged weary feet across the room and sank down upon the bed. In one respect she agreed with him. She must sleep if she were to prepare her tired spirit, her weary body and numbed mind for the frightening days—and nights—that loomed ahead.

CHAPTER EIGHT

"ARE YOU AWAKE, *cara*?"

Jo struggled through half-sleep, dreaming that a huge bird of prey with wings outstretched was hovering over her bed. She stared blankly at the shadowy form, fighting rising panic, and her fear did not subside when Leo's face swam into focus, his dark head thrown into sharp relief by a halo of sun, a huge ball of fire slipping slowly past the window.

"You sleep like a child." His tone was indulgent, almost paternal, but the eyes sliding across the pale creamy slope of shoulder were not. Made suddenly conscious that she was wearing nothing but a flimsy slip, she blushed, a slow embarrassed tide of pink rising in her cheeks. "Also you blush like a child," he teased, "a contrary child who is at one and the same time liberated and prim."

"I am not prim!" she denied indignantly, jerking upright in order to prove him wrong. She was hard put to it to appear nonchalant when appraised by bold, appreciative eyes. She slid slim legs from the bed and stood up, searching for some protection, however flimsy, for her scantily clad body.

With a grin he reached for a pale peach negligée lying across the foot of the bed. "Is this what you are looking for?" He quirked a black eyebrow. "I don't see the necessity, it is still quite warm."

It was warm, in fact the room felt unbearably hot, yet Jo snatched it from his outstretched hand as if suffering the chills of winter.

"How did it get here, in any case?" she demanded crossly, belting the negligée tightly around her waist. "And what, now that I have time to think of it, are you doing in my room? You might have had the decency to knock!"

With a feline ease of movement she found disconcerting, he relaxed upon her bed and raked a cool, possessive glance over her fumbling attempts to fasten tiny buttons at her neck. "Let me help." His speed of movement was startling, within the space of a gasp he had abandoned his relaxed pose and sprung to her side with effortless, leonine ease. She backed away, confused by his quick change of attitude from lazy docility to stalking predator all in the space of a few short hours. Her hackles rose. It was the piper who was supposed to play while his benefactor chose the tune! She, not he, should be the one in control.

It was not easy to sound authoritative while brown fingers were fumbling at her throat, wrestling with tiny buttons. "Will you please go now, and don't enter my room again without permission!"

He feigned an expression so pained she was infuriated. "If I am to be forbidden access to your room how am I to carry out my duties? If you wish the services of a *cicisbeo* you must learn to tolerate my presence while I run your bath and help to brush your hair. See," with a controlled violence that jarred her nerves he slid aside the wardrobe door, revealing a rack of neatly hung dresses, "already I have unpacked for you! Next I shall run your bath and while you are soaking I'll put the finishing touches to the dinner I prepared while you were asleep. Come now, little *vespa*," brown fingers abandoned the buttons in order to cup her infuriated face, "you must admit that I am keeping to my part of the bargain. To ban me from your bedroom would indicate a reluctance on your part to continue on such a basis—I might even be encouraged to think that the ministrations of a husband would be more to your liking!"

He was enjoying a joke at her expense, Jo fumed, not one whit fooled by a subservience made false by a ring of mockery. He was calling her bluff, daring her to opt for one of two equally unacceptable roles—she could choose to have his shadow constantly dogging her footsteps or agree to accept him as a husband, with all the privileges and intimacies such a status implied. She did not hesitate.

"Very well," she stared cool contempt, "by all means carry on with your duties. I'd like my bath in five minutes, please."

If he was disappointed he did not show it by so much as a flicker of an eyelid. Indeed, her decision seemed to please him, judging from the smile flickering around his mouth and the satisfied tone of his answer.

"So be it, *mia bella contessa*!" He lifted her clenched fist to his lips and brushed it with a kiss.

"Stop that!" She snatched away her hand, then was furious with herself for betraying tension.

When he departed, grinning, in the direction of the bathroom, she sagged down on to the bed feeling drained and completely deflated. He was playing with her emotions as a cat plays with a mouse—a well-fed cat, uncertain whether or not he could manage a further tender morsel. And she *was* tender, very tender, very young, very green. Yet she would never allow him to guess the qualms she was experiencing, the water in her veins, the jelly in her knees, the choking lump that rose to her throat, all warnings of his dangerous presence.

She dragged herself upright and was glad she had when a few seconds later he again entered the room.

"I shall lay out your black dress—what there is of it," he twinkled. "Wear it, please, I find it very fetching."

She gritted her teeth. The black dress had been consigned to limbo, she had instructed Maria not to include it in her luggage as she never intended to wear it again. Someone must have countermanded that order—the someone whose golden eyes were alight with devilment as they challenged her across the width of the room. To refuse to meet his challenge would be an admission of defeat.

"Shall do." Her indifference was well acted. "But as there will be just the two of us for dinner it hardly seems to matter which dress I wear."

Nevertheless she took great pains with her appearance, in spite of the profound contempt she felt for the man with whom she was about to dine. Instinct warned her that she would find need of every weapon in her armoury if she were to successfully combat whatever tricks the baffling Conte had up his sleeve. In common with most Italian men he was fond of playing cards. Often Jo had watched and marvelled at his daring while playing bridge, bidding boldly on hands of little strength, bluffing his competitors into losing their confidence, taking his time to plan out his campaign, counting the tricks that were certain to be his, the top trumps, the aces, then cleverly manoeuvring so that tricks were gained that ought never to have been his. His consummate skill was measured by the value he extracted from cards of small significance. Only now was she beginning to realise how cleverly he incorporated the same technique into everyday life; the thrust and parry, the skilled judgment, were arts he had cultivated to a nicety. She would need to keep a sharp lookout for recognised moves and be ready to block each one with the appropriate counter-move.

She went downstairs looking coolly beautiful, but with every nerve vibrant, ready to alert the senses at the first hint of danger. Leo met her in the hall and escorted her into the dining-room. Alarm bells jangled in her mind when she was confronted by an atmosphere reminiscent of a sultan's harem. He guided her towards a beautifully appointed table set with silver cutlery engraved with the Temperea crest—the twin-headed lions with a cold glance that seemed to follow her everywhere. Dark blue candles, displayed with satanic sophistication in sconces of silver, flickered with devilish glee across diamond cut crystal goblets, their beauty reflected upon the surface of a table satined with the patina of age. A glorious centrepiece of freshly gathered roses spilled virginal white against cool green foliage—a pungent, forceful reminder of her bridal bouquet. Dim, seductive lighting, romantic background music barely audible to the ear, and a suave, watchful companion, his dark profile strikingly outlined against the whiteness of his dinner jacket, all combined to make an attack upon her senses, resulting in a frantic, panicky warning being transmitted to her brain: *Watch out!*

A deep breath helped steady stampeding nerves into a steady trot, so that his keen eyes gleaned no information from her face as she accepted with languid ease the champagne he poured into her glass. She sipped appreciatively, then dispelled the intimacy surrounding them by observing:

"Isn't it rather dark in here? I like to see what I'm eating—could we please have more light?"

His eyes narrowed, weighing up, she judged, whether the request had been made out of nervousness or necessity. She rejoiced inwardly when, with a small shrug of annoyance, he complied with her wishes by pressing the switch of a small table lamp tucked away in a far corner of the room.

He left her in peace while they enjoyed their meal, which was simple but expertly cooked—prawn cocktail enlivened by a tangy sauce, tender steak accompanied by a crisp salad and a dessert of Kirsch-flavoured raspberries smothered in cream. Jo drank recklessly, then, realising that this was pleasing him, covered the top of her glass with her hand when he made to top it up.

"No more for me, thank you."

"Don't you like champagne?" he queried, raising one eyebrow in the devilish quirk she had begun to dread.

"Yes, of course, but I've had sufficient, thank you."

"Nonsense," he overruled, removing her hand from the glass in order to pour a stream of golden bubbles into the crystal goblet. Rashly, she lifted it to her lips and drained it dry, savouring its effervescence, only to feel nonplussed when he filled up her glass once again. "I felt sure this wine would be an appropriate choice," he grinned. "Champagne has an equal number of followers in heaven and in hell."

"And to which of those places do you consider I belong?" She tilted her chin, exposing a slender curve of throat he seemed to find captivating. Slowly his eyes caressed a creamy slope of shoulder, then plunged to continue the exploration he had begun the first time she had worn the dress.

"Who knows precisely where angels dwell?" he murmured, his eyes upon the deeply plunging cleavage between her breasts.

To her annoyance her emotions erupted into utter confusion, forcing her to fight to suppress a burning tide of colour rising into pale cheeks. Agitated by his deliberately intimate mood, she reached for her glass, hoping the sudden movement would distract his attention, but her fingers missed the bowl, connected with the stem, and sent the glass crashing on to the table. A stream of golden liquid ran swiftly across the shiny surface and over its edge, straight into Leo's lap.

"Damnation!" Instinctively he jumped to his feet to avoid the worst of the spill. Jo grabbed a napkin and ran to help, babbling her apologies while she dabbed surplus liquid from his jacket.

"How clumsy of me! I'm terribly sorry, that was unforgivably careless..."

A hand clamped down upon each of her shoulders and drew her upright until her troubled eyes were staring into a face no longer mocking, eyes kindling golden flame, a mouth set almost grim.

"Jo! *Io ti amo!*" he groaned, pulling her forward until her head was resting against his heart. Before she could pull away his arms tightened around her waist, she felt the heat of his hands flat against the cool bareness of her back as he bent his head in search of her lips. It was a powerfully virile kiss that drew unwilling response from the very tips of her toes, then proceeded to rage rampant through her helpless body. She was nothing if not human, as susceptible as the next girl to a scene set for seduction—the magic of candlelight, the heady scent of roses, romantic music that aroused yearnings so new to her they were unrecognisable, intoxicating wine that had weakened her defences and left her vulnerable to the advances of her savagely-attractive husband.

Afloat on a cloud of champagne, she stretched on tiptoe to slide her arms around his neck and fired his passion to melting point by returning kiss for kiss, answering need with still more urgent need, heightening the hunger within him with abandoned caresses.

She did not protest when he swept her from her feet to carry her upstairs to her room. Gently, almost reverently, he laid her upon the bed, murmuring hoarse endearments while he unzipped her dress, then, with one quick flick of the wrist, consigned it to a far corner of the room.

The expertise with which this action was carried out reached like a shock of ice water upon Jo's seduced senses.

"No!" She began to struggle and turned on her side in an attempt to wriggle out of his arms. It was then that she felt the fiery imprint of his lips upon her shoulder as, drawn irresistibly to the devil-dark mole, he murmured:

"How I have longed to do that, *cara*! How does it feel to be branded by the devil?"

"Utterly degrading!" she spat, managing, with the advantage of surprise, to escape his loosened grasp. With her back turned towards him she shivered her way into a negligée, uttering condemnation in a spate of angry words. "Some of the blame must be mine, I don't understand why I allowed it to happen...How simple you must think me, a naive idiot, one whose head is easily turned by flattery, by a stage set for seduction! You played your hand brilliantly, *signore*, masterminded all the tricks, discovered I was vulnerable, then exploited my poor head for wine for all you were worth! But mercifully I recovered my senses in time to trump your tricks!" She swung round, searching for his outline in the darkened room, and found him gazing out of the window into a dark velvet sky. He was silent, tense, uncannily still.

"Please remember in future," she stormed at his unresponsive back, "that I am the one who holds all the aces. Papà paid you to marry me and I'm never going to allow you to forget it!"

He strode towards her, his face strained and very weary. She backed away, but was cornered when she came up against solid wall. When Leo reached out to touch her she flinched away and his mouth tightened. However, his grip upon her shoulder was kind.

"Don't say any more just now, Jo, not while you are in a temper. I can understand your feeling shocked, puzzled, a little ashamed, perhaps, but you have no reason to be, child, for are not our passions ourselves? A moment ago you demonstraed that you can be a passionate, generous lover—if ever you allow yourself to be. All you need is more time, while I, on my part, should have shown more patience. Sleep on it, Jo."

She was afraid she was going to cry, sobs were crowding her throat causing an aching pain which, however much she swallowed, would not be eased. Then anger came to her aid, although what she had intended to be a lighthearted laugh developed into a grating in her throat.

"Really, *signore*, you speak as if you were addressing a child! I'm no stranger to passion, nor am I easily shocked. You are so pitifully old-fashioned in outlook," she forced a stiff smile. "Few girls of my age remain virgins in these enlightened days!"

Lightly, his thumbs moved over her shoulders. "Why are you trembling? Are you cold?" he surprised her by asking.

"No," she jerked.

"Are you afraid of me?" he continued calmly.

"Of course not!"

"Then why are you trembling?"

She pulled out of his grasp, ran across the room and flung the door open wide. "If I am trembling, *signore*, it's certainly not with fear. What would you say," her chin tilted defiantly as he crossed towards her, "if I were to tell you that, had you succeeded in seducing me, you would not have been the first man to do so?"

He paused a foot away, subjecting her to a steady stare. "If that is a hypothetical question then an answer would be superfluous—but if it is based upon fact..."

"Yes," she goaded, "what then?"

He reached out to encircle her throat within gentle fingers before menacing in a mildly pleasant manner: "I should quite probably strangle you."

CHAPTER NINE

Jo WAS stretched out on a lounger at the edge of the swimming pool watching Leo cleaving through aquamarine water, his strokes clean and powerful. He had already swum the length of the pool about two dozen times, yet his movements were relaxed and tireless. It seemed quite likely he would continue swimming for ages yet. They had been at the villa for three days and not once during that time had he referred to the incident that had occurred on the first traumatic night. He had reverted to treating her with paternal indulgence, respecting her wish to be alone, making not the slightest demur when, each morning after breakfast, she had disappeared down the path leading to the shore to continue her exploration of the many small coves, to search for unusual sea-shells or just sit for hours dabbling her feet in the lukewarm sea.

But after three days, her explorations exhausted, solitude had begun to pall, so this morning she had surprised him by lingering over breakfast until curiosity had prompted him to ask:

"You seem to be at a loose end, have you nothing planned for today?"

"Er...not really. I may go down to the beach later."

"Why not join me for a dip in the pool, then after lunch we could go for an outing?"

She dithered. The casually extended invitation had held not the slightest hint of urgency, her acceptance or refusal, it seemed, was a matter of complete indifference to him. Consequently, her acceptance was equally casual.

"I might as well, I suppose..."

Since the day after arrival at the villa a maid had come each day from a nearby village. She did not live in, but arrived in time to cook breakfast and left each evening after dinner. She appeared at Jo's side bearing a tray holding a large jug of freshly-made lemonade and a plateful of almond biscuits.

"Thank you, Dina," Jo smiled at her pleasure as she heaved into a sitting position. "Leave the tray on the table, will you, I'll pour out when the *signore* joins me."

Dina returned her smile and bobbed a curtsey, but as she walked away her simple features wore a perplexed frown. The *signore*'s young wife was so beautiful, yet how, she wondered, did the English manage to keep their island populated? For three whole nights the *signore* and his bride had occupied separate bedrooms and for three whole days the *signora* had wandered off on her own, leaving her new husband alone in the villa. Her own husband had refused to believe her when she had told him of their sleeping arrangements. "No, no," he had pooh-poohed, "the Conte is too virile a man to adopt the life of a celibate, especially not on his honeymoon. The strain of it would be too much for him—after all, is it not widely known that such a situation can affect a man's brain?" Still, Dina's frown lightened, at least today they had not gone their separate ways, so perhaps tonight...!

Leo heaved out of the water and stood teetering on the edge of the pool, flexing his muscles while hot sun dried rivulets of water from skin tanned brown as a nut. Jo averted her eyes from his whipcord body, wondering how she could ever have been misguided enough to liken him to a toothless tomcat. Granted, this lion had no roar, but she knew to her cost that he had teeth, teeth that had bitten gently into her skin to inflict the pain of ecstasy. A flood of colour accompanied the memory and she reached for the jug of lemonade, hoping her blush would go unnoticed. But nothing she did seemed to escape his keen glance.

"You look hot." He dropped down on to the lounger next to hers. "Perhaps you should seek more shade," he frowned, "your pale skin is not yet acclimatised to our heat." His solicitude grated upon nerves sparked into expectant life by vibrant kisses and a wildly arousing touch; in three whole days they had not quietened down, her pulses still jerked at his approach, her spine tingled if he so much as brushed her arm with his sleeve, and her wayward heartbeats became annoyingly erratic when occasionally her eyes collided with his golden, enigmatic gaze. She despised her weakness. Irritation was evident in her voice when she enquired:

"How much longer must we remain here?"

His face appeared to darken as cloud drifted across the sun. "You are bored with the villa already?" he asked lightly. "Perhaps the fault is mine for neglecting your entertainment. I am a devotee of solitude, but I'm apt to forget that others do not share my preference. As we shall be remaining here for a further two weeks I must remedy the error."

"Another two weeks!" Jo gasped, her eyes wide with

dismay. "Do we have to? Why can't we return to Venice before then?"

"Because the *palazzo* is in the process of having its foundations strengthened, an exercise which entails the building of a watertight caisson around the building so that concrete may be injected into the foundations."

Her lips compressed. "You've wasted no time in making use of my dowry! Were you afraid Papà might change his mind?"

"Not at all," he assured her smoothly, shrugging aside the insult. "It is simply that such work can be carried out only at certain times of the year and this happens to be one of those times."

"It's probably a case of good money being wasted," she scoffed, impelled for some reason to upset his damnable composure. "According to experts, Venice is slowly sinking into the lagoon."

Gravely he nodded. "There are many places in the city where columns and doorways, once at ground level, are now well below it. Often, when paving stones are removed, the remains of another street built in the Middle Ages when the lagoon was lower are found about a yard below. All over the city one may find evidence of rising water—balconies and windows that have had to be heightened, stone animals with paws awash by the tide, and many damp, rotting brick walls. The sinking process could be arrested, but only at phenomenal expense. At present, we Venetians are more concerned with keeping our city afloat than with rescuing her from drowning."

It was silly to feel resentful of a city, yet obviously the subject of Venice and her wellbeing was constantly in the forefront of his mind, to the exclusion of all others. Venice, Bride of the Sea, was Leo's true and only bride and he would do anything, make any sacrifice, to ensure the safety of even one small part of it.

She jumped to her feet and stood, rounded and lovely in a curve-hugging bathing suit golden as the sun, and told him abruptly, "I've had enough of sunbathing, I'm going inside." Puzzled by her obvious ill humour, Leo nodded agreement, then watched, frowning, as she flounced out of sight.

Moodily, Jo stared around her bedroom wondering why she was feeling so unsettled, so nervy, so unlike her usual confident self. She crossed the room to stare gloomily out of the window, trying to decide what to do. The prospect of going down to the beach loomed uninviting; she had already explored its possibilities to the utmost, and so too, the gardens and the house. So the day yawned dull and depressing. Then she recalled Leo's suggestion that they might go on an outing and her spirits lifted. The suggestion had been casually put—he might even have forgotten—nevertheless she had better be prepared just in case he should come in search of her.

She showered, then spent a few minutes deciding what to wear. He had not indicated in which direction they might go, but hoping he might suggest a visit to the Lido she plumped eventually for a cotton sundress, green to match her eyes, with a short matching jacket in case there should be a breeze. Comfortable white sandals and a pouch bag that could be carried over her wrist were all the accessories needed to complete an outfit that was chic, gay and functional.

She sat down to wait, silently urging Leo to come and fetch her, so that when eventually he did rap upon the door she flew to open it, then waited with suppressed excitement for him to speak.

Slightly taken aback by her swift appearance, he hesitated, then smiled, well pleased. "Good girl! As you are ready, we can set off immediately."

"Where are we going?" Eagerly she fell into step. "And how are we going to get there?"

"By car, of course," he answered her last question first. "Didn't I mention that the villa is not far from the main road and that we keep a car garaged here permanently?"

"A car!" she said eagerly. "In that case, we could go as far as—"

"The Lido?" he quizzed, his lips curling upwards.

"How did you guess I wanted to go there?" she faltered.

"Dear Jo," he teased, "you have the look of an infant anticipating a day at the seaside. If you were not so fashionably dressed I might be tempted to supply you with a bucket and spade!"

The run down to the beach resort was both interesting and invigorating. Leo's powerful, long-nosed sports car purred along, eating up miles of empty road and Jo, who lately had begun to wonder how the impoverished Conte could afford the luxury of a summer villa, was prompted to wonder further about the ownership of such a ruinously expensive car. Following this trend of thought, she blurted impulsively:

"Leo, why don't you get a job?"

Ever so slightly he swerved off course. "I thought I had one," he answered mildly.

"You are deliberately misunderstanding me," she retorted. "I know you consider yourself to be fully employed looking after your family's interests, but when I speak of a job I mean a job that *pays*!"

"Don't all jobs pay in one way or another?" He slanted her an amused look. She fell into puzzled silence. Leo, though reputedly impoverished, nevertheless maintained a high standard of living—a villa, a car, a private gondola, priceless heirlooms housed within the *palazzo*, numerous servants employed to do his bidding, all were proof that he did not go short of cash from somewhere. Yet obviously he had no intention of discussing his financial position. Improvements to the *palazzo* were being paid for by her dowry, but how, she pondered, was he managing to pay for the rest?

But it was not a day to favour moody conjecture. The car was purring the length of a road running alongside an expanse of sea, glass-smooth, sparkling with a brilliance that hurt the eyes as it was caught by the glare of the midday sun. Through gaps in the foliage Jo caught glimpses of beaches crowded with sun-lovers, promenades lined with restaurants protected by gay striped awnings and the towering façades of hotels, brazenly modern, impudently defying the mediaeval majesty of Venice dimly outlined across the water.

He parked the car near the sea-front. "The day is yours," he told her, indulgent as a father prepared to reward an obedient child, "do what you will with it."

"Let's just stroll," she begged, captivated by glimpses of streets lined with wistaria and bougainvillea, wishing they could be here at night to see the effect of fairy lights hung in loops and cascades, twinkling with gaudy brilliance against the dark sky. She inhaled a deep breath of shrimp-flavoured, salt-tanged air, her feet pitter-pattering rapidly as she tried to keep up with Leo's rangy stride. He seemed deep in thought as he strode, head down, hands plunged deeply into his pockets, sparing not a glance for the exciting modernity of their surroundings.

"Would you mind slowing down a little?" she gasped, trailing a pace behind him. He stopped so abruptly she cannoned into him and would have stumbled but for his quick grasp upon her elbow.

"How thoughtless of me," he frowned, very much put out by his unintentional discourtesy. "I didn't realise—" He broke off, spotting a vacant table in a nearby pavement café. "Sit here while I order some refreshments—you look hot. Fool that I am for rushing you through this midday heat!" As sun rays fell upon her hair, firing its dark red beauty into glowing life, he shot suddenly, "Why aren't you wearing a hat?"

"I didn't think a hat would be necessary," she confessed. "It felt so cool up in the hills."

"Let me move your chair closer under the sun umbrella," he instructed. After she had complied he ordered, "Now sit there and don't move until I get back."

By the time he returned Jo had been served lemonade and was savouring its coolness through a straw. When his shadow fell across the table she looked up and saw that he was laughing. A trifle shamefacedly she apologised, "I ought to have waited for you, but I was parched." Like a satisfied kitten she sat back and licked a small pink tongue around her lips. "I asked the waiter to bring you a drink too," she indicated a second glass, "you'll enjoy it."

"No, thank you." His glance flickered with obvious distaste over the glass of violently-green liquid. "Here!" He tossed what looked like a bundle of straw into her lap.

"That was the least conscpicuous object I could find, I hope it fits."

It was a sun-hat fashioned out of plaited straw, high-crowned, its wide brim left abruptly unfinished so that when Jo tried it on a fringe of straw fell across her face, reminding him of an urchin Huckleberry Finn.

"How do I look" she giggled.

He raised his eyes in despair. "At one with your surroundings." His look disparaged everything within his vicinity. The fastidious Conte in his impeccable suit, silken shirt and flowing tie was distinctly out of tune.

With her usual impetuosity, she leant towards him and proffered: "I've often thought you would benefit by occasionally adopting a less staid attitude in public."

"Staid...?" His nostrils flared.

"Oh, well, dignified, if you prefer—they're one and the same thing really. You don't like it here, do you?"

"I have never professed affinity with sticky buns, gaudy shops, poisonous drinks," he cast a further disgusted look at the offending lemonade, "howling children bulging up to the ears with ice cream, and their yelling parents supposedly out for a day's enjoyment yet exasperated to the point of murder by their ill-behaved offspring. However," he sighed, "for your sake I will try to put up with them, just this once."

"Why not try to enjoy it, just this once?" she retorted impudently. "Just for today, couldn't you try to forget that you are Il Conte Tempera and pretend to be a young man of no particular standing intent upon seeking fun. We could pretend we've just met," she sparkled, carried away on a tide of rash impetuosity, "two strangers thrown together by accident, with a whole day at their disposal to get to know one another.

But you would have to cast off your starched image or it wouldn't work!" she declared with engaging candour. "To get rid of your jacket and tie might be a good way to start."

For a few perilous moments she thought she was about to be slated for her impudence. Expressions of pride warring with temptation crossed his face and as he hesitated something about her animated expression helped him to reach a decision. Showing a hint of self-consciousness she would never have associated with the haughty Conte, he drew off his tie, slipped it into his pocket, then shrugged broad shoulders out of his jacket.

"Satisfied?" he quizzed.

Tapping the tip of her nose with a thoughtful finger, Jo frowned. "There's something still not quite right," she puzzled. Then her face brightened. "Try rolling up your sleeves."

"Rolling up my...?"

"Sleeves," she insisted firmly.

With great reluctance he removed silver-crested links from immaculate cuffs and proceeded to roll very expensive blue silk over his forearms. When he had reached past his elbows, she leant across and rather shyly undid the three top buttons of his shirt. The improvement was startling. Bare brown throat rising from out of a winged collar, a tangle of black hairs exposed upon a broad chest, muscles rippling under silk, all combined to make him look relaxed and very much younger. The transformation was complete when he grinned, his white, even teeth outstanding against a tanned skin.

"I feel like a soldier deprived of his uniform, uncertain who I am, and unsure how I am expected to behave. Decently dressed I felt civilised, whereas now...!" He shrugged, leaving the rest to her imagination.

Jo almost choked on the last of her lemonade. What had she done? Fervently, she wished she could learn to think before she spoke. The courteous Conte she could handle—she was not so sure about this rakish image conjured up at her own foolhardy request!

CHAPTER TEN

As they sauntered along the promenade, Leo took Jo's hand and she did not object. With sun dancing a lively jig upon the water, sky blue as a madonna's cloak, and the sights and sounds of merriment all around them, it was surprisingly easy to forget that the man whose fingers were curled around her own was Il Conte Leonardo Tempera and not one of her casual, undemanding student friends.

Leo seemed to have cast off dignity with his coat, his eyes behind smoky glasses smiling as he looked down at her, not with paternal indulgence, but showing the spontaneous grin an attracted man might bestow upon an attractive girl. Her spirits rose light as her footsteps as she tripped alongside him, pointing out the grace of a seagull outlined in flight against a backcloth of cloudless sky, pausing to worry over a crying infant who seemed to have become detached from his parents, then murmuring her relief when, just as she was urging Leo to intervene, a worried father approached to scoop the distressed child into his arms.

"You have a caring heart, Jo. The welfare of others, even those who are unknown to you, means a great deal, does it not? This is a very unusual trait to be found in a girl such as yourself brought up in what most people would consider the lap of luxury. Who instilled within you such concern? Not your father. In common with most men of his standing he seems too wrapped up in business affairs to spare much time for introspective thought, while Sara," he hesitated, wishing to be kind, "has always seemed to me a little self-centered."

They were leaning their elbows upon a low wall, looking down upon an anthill of humanity spread across the sands. There was none of the usual distaste reflected in his expression as he watched the antics of families fighting for their pleasure, jealously guarding their conquered strips of territory from encroaching invaders. It was a completely new world to him, Jo realised. An insight into the difficulties experienced by the common herd, the struggle for breathing space never encountered by the man to whom the huge, empty palace of Tempera was home and who, up until now, had considered solitude and space were rights granted to every man. The realisation caused her a pang of pity—the very last emotion she would normally have associated with the imperious Conte.

"My mother took great pains to impress upon me the need for compassion towards others less fortunate than ourselves," she explained haltingly. If that sounds patronising it isn't meant to be," she rushed on, "my mother was of a nature so loving and giving she would have reacted the same even if we'd been living in poverty. Money, possessions, status, were of secondary importance to her. I remember asking once, with all the anxiety of childhood: 'Mammà, what will become of Papà if ever he should lose his money?" Her answer chased from my mind every childish fear. 'Riches have wings, my darling,' she replied, 'sometimes they fly away. But children are poor men's riches, so long as he has the love of his children he will never know poverty.' "

She lapsed into silence and Leo's grip upon her fingers tightened. "How old were you when she died?" he asked.

"Twelve," she sighed. "The worst possible age." Then, unwilling to linger on a subject still tender, she questioned, "And what about you? I've never heard you speak of your mother. Do you, too, find such memories painful?"

She was startled by his careless shrug. "I have no memories," he surprised her. "My mother died when I was born."

"Oh...I'm sorry."

He smiled, teeth flashing white against nut-brown skin. "Tender heart," he teased. "Why should you be sorry? What is that saying you English have: What one has never had one cannot miss?"

"But that simply isn't true!" she objected, touched to the heart by a picture she had conjured of a baby nursed in strange arms; the cuts and bumps of an exploring toddler left unhealed by a mother's kiss; the worries of a schoolboy having no one in which to confide; the stresses of adolescence and the struggle into maturity—all situations in which a mother's understanding were priceless. "Perhaps your father tried twice as hard, as mine did, to make up for your loss?"

He shook his head, allowing more loneliness than he knew to colour his tone as slowly he explained, "I saw very little of my father, he spent most of his time abroad, leaving me in the charge of nurses, and tutors—and my aunt, of course. According to her, my father resented me, could never forgive me for taking my mother's life in exchange for my own. If he had stayed in Venice, if we had been given the opportunity to get to know one another, perhaps I could have replaced her in some small way, but it was not to be."

"Your aunt told you *that*!" Jo choked, horrified by the insensitive treatment meted out to a motherless boy. No wonder the lonely child had grown into an even more solitary man. Guilt had been heaped upon his shoulders. Time and tradition had graced him with a veneer of self-confidence, yet with such a history he must surely carry inside of him a feeling of guilt, a conviction even, that he had no right to happiness. Compassion brimmed over. Impulsive as ever, she advised him fiercely:

"I don't know how you can bear to continue living in a house full of such unhappy memories! Why don't you close it up, forget that it ever existed or, if that isn't possible, make up for your lonely childhood by filling the *palazzo* with children so that their happy laughter, their stampeding footsteps, will chase out all your childhood ghosts!"

He threw his head back and laughed so loudly everyone in their vicinity smiled and looked ready to join in. Startled, Jo looked up, then caught her breath. Etched against a background of blue sky his profile rejected dark, attractive appeal. Muscles rippled in his throat and as he continued to laugh his chest heaved, dislodging from a tangle of dark hairs a silver medallion that swung crazily on a fine silver chain.

"Oh, darling Jo!" he grinned, bending down to peer into her indignant face. "I would like that! I really would..."

Suddenly, as they stared into each other's eyes,

everything seemed to hush, waves lapped silently upon the shore, children's screams faded to a whisper, their parents' shouts mere echoes of what they had previously been. Even the birds' raucous cries seemed muted, the chimes of an ice cream vendor advertising his wares deadened by a thudding noise, a heavy pounding filling Jo's ears. When he removed his sunglasses, then disposed of hers, she found she was staring into eyes no longer alight with laughter but intensely dark, mirroring fathomless feeling.

"A home full of happy children," he spelled out slowly. "If only it were possible, Jo. It could be," he insisted softly, "if you could only bring yourself to accept me as a husband."

At that moment she recognised the pounding in her ears as the beating of her heart. She bit her lip, hovering between mistrust of his silvered tongue and an urgent will to believe. He sounded at that moment as if he were prepared to forsake even Venice, his bride of the sea, if in exchange he could have his very mundane wish. She shook off his spell. What he was experiencing was mere whimsical longing, a momentary urge that would pass, leaving embarrassment in its wake if she were fool enough to take him seriously. Sincerity was as much a stranger as was laughter to the inhabitants of the Palazzo Tempera.

So she broke from his compelling glance, uttered a shaky laugh, and completely shattered the spell by declaring brightly, "I'm hungry, aren't you? Let's find something to eat."

Leo's only physical reaction was a slight tightening of his grip before he set her free, then, in a tone so matter-of-fact she blinked, he agreed with her suggestion.

"Very well, we'll try one of the hotels along the front."

"Oh, but..." She dug in her heels, resisting the pressure he was exerting upon her elbow as he attempted to guide her away from the promenade.

"But what?" he quizzed, replacing her sunglasses as she frowned against the glare.

"Couldn't we have a picnic?"

His doubtful look confirmed her suspicion that he had never known the childish pleasure of an alfresco meal, with a salt-tanged breeze adding flavour and lack of ceremony bestowing piquant freshness to plain fare.

"If that is really what you want," he conceded reluctantly.

"Oh, it is, it is!" She tugged his arm in her eagerness. "There are shops down the side streets where we can buy bread and cheese—and pickles, if you like pickles?"

"I do." He sounded surprised by his own admission.

"And a poke of shrimps would be nice," she cajoled, sensing his weakening, "and some fruit to finish off."

Not only did they find all that they required, they also bought swimwear and two large bath-towels before making their way back to the beach. But after ten minutes of stepping over browning bodies in a fruitless search for space, Leo rebelled.

"Let's go back to the car—I know of a private beach nearby where we can relax and be undisturbed. The owner, a friend of mine, is away at present, but if he were here I know that permission to trespass would be gladly given."

Jo relented with a nod. He had behaved beautifully considering his dislike of crowds and his abhorrence of modern-day noise. The least she could do was to fall in with this one solitary suggestion when, during the whole of their time here, he had set out expressly to please her.

The cove was a mere ten minutes' drive away, but they might have stepped into another world when they parked the car and began descending a sloping path leading down to a crescent of fine sand bearing not one human imprint upon its smooth surface. They stacked their basket of goodies beneath cool foliage, then went behind rocks to discard clothing that had begun to feel cumbersome in the heat.

Jo emerged feeling slightly selfconscious in a one-piece bathing suit patterned with garish, fullblown roses, its mixture of colours having been the least offensive she could find among garments piled high upon the counter of a one-roomed shop. Doubtfully, she looked down. At the time it had seemed an unnecessary extravagance to seek out a more expensive suit—after all, her drawers at the villa held at least a dozen swimsuits and this cheap one had been purchased for only one unforeseen swim. Yet, with one huge rose enclosing her waist within the grip of hideous lime green petals, she began having second thoughts.

Her feet felt weighted as slowly she began walking down to the beach, dreading the sight of Leo's eyebrows elevating and his lips quirking as he tried to contain amusement. But when she looked up and saw him sidling from behind a rock it was she who had to laugh at the tall, usually elegant figure wearing an expression of utter disgust as he peered down at shorts made up of striped material in violently clashing colours offensive to the eye. His expression was just too much. Laughter began as a choked gurgle deep within her throat, then spluttered past compressed lips to emerge as an hilarious shout that might have disturbed the slumberers on the Lido beaches.

He was not amused. Showing a glint in his eye that boded ill for Jo, he stepped forward and accused, "I ought to have known better than to allow you to shop for me! You chose this diabolical garment deliberately, did you not?"

"I'm afraid so," she spluttered, holding her sides as a fresh spasm of laughter rendered her helpless. "Mine," she gasped, indicating her own costume, "was the best of a bad bunch, so I searched out something equally hideous for you in case you should be tempted to make comparisons!"

Instinct warned her to run even before he made his first step towards retaliation. She flew down the beach with a speed that kept her within inches of his outstretched hands and plunged into the water to dive swiftly as a minnow determined to outwit a shark. But gradually his dark shadow overtook her and she was enmeshed by hands that gripped her waist, then showed no mercy as they administered a ducking that left her breathless. Desperately she clutched rock-hard shoulders and pleaded in small breathless gasps:

"Please, Leo, no more! I'm sorry, truly I am," she half laughed, half choked, "so no more ducking, *please*!"

"You *are* a bitch." Never had the words been spoken with such a tender intonation.

She went very still within the circle of arms that tightened fractionally before surrendering her to the emotionless embrace of the sea. Minutes later all she could see of him was his dark head bobbing above the waves as he directed all his energies and frustrations towards a battle with the waves.

She was dry and stretched out on her towel by the time he returned. He dropped down on to the towel she had draped upon the sand a careful yard away, then, catching her peeping through lowered lashes, he requested politely, "I'm hungry, do you mind if we eat now?"

Experiencing a mixture of relief and disappointment, she scrambled to her feet and ran to fetch the basket, avoiding his eyes as she shared out the bread and cheese, shrimps and fruit while he uncorked a bottle of wine. Two plastic cups were utilised as goblets for wine that flowed like soothing nectar down parched throats. Handsful of crusty bread were torn from a long, cigar-shaped loaf, delectable hunks of cheese delivered a sharp bite upon the tongue, delicious shrimps were denuded of their armour, then slowly savoured before teeth sank into peaches so luscious the juice overflowed on to their chins. Surreptitiously, Jo wiped hers away with sand-encrusted fingers, then, replete and contented, they both rolled on their backs to laze, enclosed within an atmosphere of silent companionship, a feeling of togetherness too ethereal, as yet, to be named. They slept like weary children with arms outstretched, their fingertips almost, but not quite, bridging the yard of dividing sand.

After ten blissful minute's Jo wakened from her nap. Cautiously she moved, bewildered by a trapped sensation, then went very still when Leo stirred in his sleep and tightened his grip around her wrist. She chanced a quick look, wondering if he were feigning sleep, and was disarmed by a small smile of contentment hovering around his relaxed mouth. He looked so defenceless in sleep; it was easy to discover traces of the boy he had once been in thick lashes lying in dark crescents upon high cheekbones. How often those lashes must have swept down to hide tears he had been taught were unseemly in a future Conte. How often his mouth must have quivered with hurt inflicted by his insensitive aunt. And how often his lean frame must have tensed to suppress an urge to run to the father who had rejected him, seeking comfort and a little of the love he had been denied.

Her heart lurched. Leo seemed destined never to enjoy a loving relationship. Even his wife, she recalled bitterly, had been chosen with finance rather than emotion in mind.

She stared down at him, allowing herself the momentary weakness of wondering what it would be like to be loved by such a man. She knew his touch could arouse her to barely endurable heights of passion, the scarring imprint of his kisses would remain on her lips for ever. She shivered, remembering how her body had responded to caresses so expert they had repelled and she had to force her mind to accept the fact that although Leo had made it plain he would not be averse to claiming his rights as a husband, his main objective in marrying her had been the price she carried on her head.

She quivered a sigh, trying to lash up scorn, to arm herself with the hatred she assuredly felt for this man. But the venom seemed to have been drawn from her sting, in place of an armour of hatred she had been left clutching a veil of vulnerability so lacking protection it could be pierced by the quirk of an eyebrow or a casually flung smile.

She was jerked back to reality by a fixed stare. Embarrassed colour flooded her cheeks. It was stupid to feel panic-stricken, wondering how long he had been awake—there was no possible way he could have read her thoughts!

His words, however, seemed to disprove this theory. Slowly, concentrating his interest upon her heightened colour, he mused aloud, "Today, in some subtle way, you seem different. Your attitude is gentler, less reserved. Your words are spontaneous expressions of happiness instead of barbs directed by a suspicious mind. You are always beautiful, Jo, but today your face has acquired a special glow." Though his words were slow his movement was swift as he rolled on his side to throw an arm around her, pinning her to the sand. Mesmerised, her brave resolutions evaporating swift as droplets beneath the sun, she quivered beneath his shadow, straining to cull the will to resist from a weak, traitorous body.

"Today has been wonderful, has it not, *amore mia*?" The magnetism he was projecting was overpowering. Panic clutched at her throat and squeezed it tight. She felt nerveless and weak as an infant utterly dependent upon the whims of its minder. Finding words impossible, she pleaded with her eyes, mutely appealing to him to be kind. She was at that moment blissfully prepared to be taken, to be loved, to be mastered...!

For long breathless seconds they stared into each other's eyes, conscious of an aura of inevitability, a strong, vital attraction that drew them closer yet at the same time bade them pause to savour for a while joyful anticipation. As his head descended her lashes lowered, shy in case the trail of heat blazing through her body might be reflected in her eyes. His shadow blotted out the sun and she was glad to use darkness as a cloak during the long-drawn-out, almost unendurable seconds of waiting.

Her mouth was quivering, anticipating his kiss, when he uttered a sharp, savage curse and flung away. With his shadow removed the sun blazed down. Jo flinched from its scourge and rolled on her side, fighting an urge to cry as an agony of humiliation ran sword-sharp through her body.

"Come, it is time for us to go." His touch was impersonal as he helped her to her feet, but she turned her face away, conscious that she was not yet sufficiently in control to hide the ravages of rejection.

She hated the steadiness of his voice, the cool impersonality that contrasted so violently with her own emotions, when casually he suggested, "Let us return to the villa now. I see no reason why such a pleasant day should not be prolonged, so I have decided that tonight we will return and visit the casino. Would you like that...?"

There it was again—the damnable paternal intonation she so resented! Bolstered by temper, she rounded on him. "As a special treat for an unworldly infant?" she taunted sarcastically, "or as an apology for insincerity?" She wanted to hurt him, enjoyed the white pinched look around his mouth, the sombre darkness of his eyes. "By all means let us enjoy what the Lido has to offer." She tried to make her voice sound eager, as if the prospect he had presented filled her with delight rather than the dread she was actually feeling. If today had been a pattern for days to come she knew she would not stay the pace. Like a jaded Casanova, he had experimented with her emotions, then, showing a humiliating lack of enthusiasm, had decided that she did not measure up to the ghost from his past: Francesca. His rejection was even harder to bear than his persistence had been. But all of life was a lesson and if nothing else this episode had taught her one important lesson—never again to believe him capable of sincerity!

As she followed him towards the car she could not help but wonder why, with a carpet of warm sand beneath her feet, a ceiling of blue sky, and the hot breath of summer on her back, she should be feeling as if it were three o'clock on the morning of a cold, dank, miserable winter's day.

CHAPTER ELEVEN

DINA WAS DISPLEASED with her employer. All during dinner he had picked morosely at his food, sparing barely a glance for his young wife sitting opposite. She had nurtured great hopes that today would bring about a change of attitude between the two and when after lunch they had set off on their outing in such high spirits she had felt certain that the cloud had lifted and that at last the honeymoon was about to begin.

At a nod from the *signore* she whipped a plate from beneath his nose and enquired stiffly, "Shall I serve dessert now, *signore*?"

"I beg your pardon...? Oh, none for me, thank you, Dina." Then, as if suddenly reminded that he was not alone, he added, "What about you, Jo, are you ready to sample yet another of Dina's delicious concoctions?"

Dina bridled, not one whit mollified as she glanced at the Contessa's pale, unhappy face. She was wearing a dream of a dress, a floating chiffon affair coloured cool leaf green, and from the transparent cape hugging unblemished shoulders her neck rose slender as a stem, her burnished hair, bathed by the rays from an overhead lamp, fiery as her courageous spirit. But her green eyes were sad and the usually tempestuous mouth had quivered noticeably several times during the silent meal. In the space of a few days the Contessa had entered from childhood into womanhood, from a tight bud into a blossom just waiting to be plucked. But the Conte seemed not to have noticed. Was he blind? Or was it that he simply did not want to see?

"Sorry," Jo smiled her apologies to the anxiously hovering maid. "I'm sure the sweet you have prepared is excellent, Dina, but I couldn't eat another bite."

Even the fact that his wife's healthy young appetite had deserted her did not seem to disturb him. With a lack of concern that made Dina fume, he rose to his feet and suggested politely, "Then as we are both satisfied, we might as well go."

"Satisfied!" Dina murmured under her breath as she stood in the open doorway watching the Conte helping his wife into the car. "The satisfied do not love, they nod off with boredom!" Her brow wrinkled. And yet boredom had no place in a relationship such as theirs. The tension between them could almost be felt, it was as if they were both foolishly skimming over an ocean whose depths were about to be ravaged by subterranean upheaval!

Earlier in the day Jo had wished she could see the coloured lights strewn across the dark evening sky. But the sight, spectacular though it was, gave her spirits no lift. Since their return to the villa she had fallen into a state of numbed hurt, a quiet, introspective mood Sara would have termed a sulk but which was actually a cloak to protect nerves too raw to bear the pain of probing. Many times she had shied from searching for answers to the questions hammering against the doorway of her mind. Questions such as: Why am I feeling so hurt? Why should the fact that he finds me unattractive matter so much? What possible difference can it make when, at the earliest opportunity, I shall be leaving him?

Once, Jo recalled a childhood memory, she had fought with a cousin who had picked up one of her favourite toys. The girl's mother, much to her own mother's indignation, had remarked coldly: "Jo, I'm afraid, is a little spoiled, covetous of that which is denied her."

Had her aunt's assessment been correct? When Leo had tried to put their relationship on a more intimate footing she had spurned him. Was she now coveting the toy she could not have, did she want his attention only because she, in turn, had been spurned?

When Leo drove straight past the casino she turned her head, watching the huge palace of fun receding into the distance. "It is a little early yet," he replied to her unspoken question. "Although the gaming rooms are open the atmosphere will be not quite right. There is a night club not far from here that puts on a passably good cabaret, we will spend an hour or two there, and then make our way to the casino later. Agreed...?"

He spared her a quick second to turn his attention from the road in order to smile down at her. Her heart jolted, then began beating at a furious rate. "Very well," she stammered, "anything you decide is fine by me." She then subsided into silence, waging inward war against emotions completely out of control.

Enrico Domini liked his daughters to move in sophisticated circles, consequently Jo was no stranger to affluence. Yet the nightclub into which Leo led her was unlike any she had previously visited, seeming more of an exclusive club, a rich oasis secreted within a strip of bawdy desert and reserved exclusively for the privileged few. While a doorman spirited away the car they were welcomed inside by a beaming manager who immediately summoned a waiter to escort them to a table made intimate by a screen of palm leaves, yet situated conveniently near to the circular dance floor. Lighting was discreet, sufficient glow to enable faces to be recognised if one should wish to recognise, yet dim enough to make deliberate oversight excusable. Thick carpets muffled the footsteps of waiters rushing to pander to the appetites of late diners and Jo's seat, when she sank into it, hugged her within an embrace so comfortable she felt immediately relaxed.

"Champagne...?" Leo suggested as the wine waiter hovered.

"Lovely," she accepted, leaning back in her seat and wriggling her toes, prepared to enjoy the music the small band of musicians was about to play.

The sound that eventually issued was completely attuned to their surroundings, discreetly intimate with a throbbing, romantic beat.

"Would you like to dance?" Leo's offer came as a sweet surprise and was eagerly accepted.

"Yes, please, I'd love to!"

As she slipped into his arms her grandmother's advice came, unsolicited, into her mind. *"Be as honest with yourself as you are with others, Jo!"* It was hard to admit even to herself that all she wanted was to feel his arms around her, to be able to slide her hands across his broad shoulders, to rest her head against his heart and drink in the hard, warm strength of him. At first he remained aloof from her attractions, but as the dance progressed and the floor became crowded he was forced to tighten his protective arm and gradually she felt muscles knotted tensely beneath her outspread fingers beginning to relax as he was wooed by the pleasure of sweet music, an enjoyable atmosphere, and the encouragingly approachable attitude of the girl in his arms.

"Precocious minx..." His breath tickled her ear. "Why have you suddenly decided to flaunt your femininity, to parade your very considerable charms before a susceptible husband? I warn you, Jo, that you are acting unwisely. Unless—" He broke off, leaving a question hanging in the air.

Her heart began to spin. More than anything in the world she wanted to test his reaction to the tremendous, amazing, even frightening secret she was only now daring to recognise. All day knowledge had been banging on the door of her mind demanding admission, but she had refused it entry. Now, feeling a great sense of relief, she faced the truth behind messages that had been transmitted for days by a pounding heart, racing pulses, vibrant nerves and an agonised yearning which had been nameless. She knew now that its name was love. A glorious, exciting, ecstatic feeling, so strong it had overridden pride and doubt and even the humiliation she had experienced that afternoon.

"Well, Jo?" His lips descended lightly against a pulse throbbing madly at her temple. Riotous emotions erupted and she began to tremble. Within the swaying crowd of dancers their seclusion was such that she was able to press flushed cheeks against his chest and to stammer:

"Leo, something tremendous has happened. I must tell you...you must know..."

His perception was such he sensed immediately that

some momentous decision had been reached. He pulled her closer and urged, "I must know what, *cara? Tell me!*"

At that precise moment the music reached its finale with a long-drawn-out crescendo of sound that penetrated their absorption, jogging them into the realisation that they were the last couple remaining upon the dance floor. Reluctantly they drew apart, but he kept tight hold of her hand as he led her back to the table where a green foiled bottle was plunged up to its neck in a bucket of crushed ice. Not once, as they waited until a waiter had decorked the bottle, did his eyes leave her face—a face made even lovelier by a soft glow lighting her eyes, the tremulous lift of her mouth, the rise and fall of colour in her cheeks.

After interminable seconds the waiter finally departed, leaving them alone with two glasses of wine sparkling between them, golden, effervescent, with minute bubbles rising from the depths to explode on to the surface—a wine reserved especially for toasts, for well-wishing, for glorious, exciting occasions. The glint in Leo's eyes told her that he had almost reached the end of his patience. She drew in a deep breath.

"Leo, I—"

"Leo! Tesoro mio! I could hardly believe my eyes when I saw you leaving the dance floor! Is it really you?" The voice, shrill, feminine and extremely penetrating, sliced stiletto-sharp between them, demanding a response Leo seemed loath to provide. With a muttered imprecation audible only to Jo, he rose to his feet to extend a polite greeting towards the unwelcome intruder.

"*Buona sera*, Francesca, I hope you are well?"

"*Benissima, caro,* but you could have found that out sooner had you taken the trouble to call. Where on earth have you been these past weeks?"

So this was Francesca!

Jo's senses were alerted by the proprietorial tone in which the question had been voiced. It had not been a light enquiry, more a demand for explanation of absence.

Blandly ignoring what amounted almost to rudeness, Leo nodded to Francesca's escort before replying with polished smoothness.

"Perhaps an introduction will serve as an explanation. Jo," he smiled down at her bewildered face, "I would like to introduce two very old friends of mine—Signorina Francesca Pellegrino and her brother, Mario."

Francesca barely acknowleded Jo, but her brother looked intensely interested, his dark eyes admiring from a distance. His mouth dropped agape, however, when Leo continued, "Francesca, Mario allow me to present the Contessa Josephine Tempera—my wife."

Francesca was extremely attractive, Jo thought, a dark-eyed, black-haired Latin beauty with a full passionate mouth and carefully controlled hour-glass figure. She projected the arrogance of one who took admiration for granted and the poise that only breeding can bestow. She must also be very wealthy, Jo concluded, eyeing a dress that was the product of one of the leading fashion houses, and diamonds flashing at throat, ears and wrists that looked fabulously expensive, if a little ostentatious for an occasion such as this. But Francesca had need of all the poise she could muster in order to weather the blow Leo had dealt. For one stunned moment her eyes flashed over Jo with such resentment in their depths that she shivered, then her blazing eyes settled upon Leo's face, searching his bland expression for signs of humour.

"You are a great joker, Leo," she husked. "It *is* a joke, is it not...?"

Mario, sufficiently like his sister to have been her twin, shuffled his feet and gave an embarrassed cough. "May we all sit down?" he suggested awkwardly. "We seem to be attracting a great deal of attention."

Jo glanced around and saw that he was right. Every eye was upon them. Leo and Francesca were obviously well known to the club's clientele and the drama of the moment was such that even the discreet Italians had forgotten themselves far enough to gape. During the few moments it took for waiters to fetch extra chairs, Francesca was able to rein in her emotions to the extent of composing her features—but not her eyes. Jo felt their stab upon her face and body as slowly she was examined, assessed, then dismissed as a nonentity.

Francesca's very first sentence was evidence that she intended mischief. Fixing a hard, angry stare upon Leo, she grated, "As you have made no denial I must assume that you were speaking the truth. But why all the secrecy, *caro*? Did we not agree, during our long and happy association, that there was to be no commitment on either side? Surely," her voice softened to a silky meaningful purr, "such old friends as we were entitled to an invitation to your wedding? Or were you perhaps afraid that I might have made a fuss, might have tried to persuade you to change your mind? Knowing how persuasive I can be, Leo, were you afraid that I might do just that...?"

Jo's heart descended like a stone. In just a few succinct sentences Francesca had painted a portrait of unmistakable intimacy. She had not been naive enough to imagine Leo a complete celibate, no attractive man could reach his age without having had at least one serious affair. But he might have had the decency to rid himself of surplus female entanglements before taking a wife!

Mario's appalled gasp was partially drowned by the sound of music as the band resumed playing, but Leo's concise reply was not. With a nonchalance Jo found incredible, he leant across to pat Francesca's hand while in a half reproving, half bantering tone, he chided,

"Come now, Francesca, enough of the dramatics! Mario and I are well aware of your penchant for making a great deal of fuss about nothing, but my young wife is not. See how you have shocked her." His tone was dry as he flicked a glance across Jo's ashen face. "Child that she is, she has placed the worst possible meaning upon your innuendoes. As for the wedding invitation, you would certainly have received one had you not been visiting Paris at the time the ceremony took place."

Francesca shrugged off his explanation, seemingly satisfied, now that barbs had been shot, to smile apologies all round, then settle back in her chair with feline grace. "I will forgive you this time, Leo, *caro*," she purred, "but I shall expect prior warning of any future happenings."

"Such as a marital rift!" Jo muttered beneath her breath, struggling to retrieve remnants of shattered dignity. What a guilible idiot she had been! She ought to feel grateful to Francesca for preventing her from committing the ultimate act of idiocy. Knowing the motive behind Leo's insistence that they should marry, having, as early as this afternoon, been presented with proof of his lingering devotion to Francesca, had she actually been ready to admit to Leo that she had *fallen in love with him*?

Her gratitude towards Mario knew no bounds when politely he asked if she would care to dance. "Yes, please," she accepted with alacrity, and swept from the table with chin held high in defiance of Leo's enquiring stare.

Mario was an excellent dancer and though, in her upset state, Jo stumbled once or twice, his expert guidance covered up her mistakes until she was composed enough to concentrate all her mind upon following his lead. She was relieved that, at first, he did not attempt to make conversation but gave her time to adjust, so that when he did finally speak she was able to give him her complete attention.

"My sister and I have been friendly with Leo since childhood. Our two families have always been close, our fathers and grandfathers were business partners, consequently our families visited each other regularly. Which is why Francesca and I are apt to look upon the Palazzo Tempera as a second home—and everything and everyone in it as being of special interest to us."

"Please don't attempt to vindicate Leo," she requested gently, "there is really no need."

"There isn't?" He looked surprised.

She shook her head. "None whatsoever," she confirmed hardly, deciding she owed Leo no loyalty "Our marriage was an act of convenience on both sides. It's a long story and I won't bore you with it, but rest assured, *signore*, your sister's innuendoes caused me no grief. Indeed, I found her remarks less than interesting."

He expelled a soundless whistle. There was something wrong somewhere, he sensed, but as yet he could not guess exactly what it was. But Leo's wife was certainly a product of her race; it would be interesting to discover if she were ice all through or merely frozen on the surface.

As the band swung into a foot-tapping Spanish number he decided to gauge his companion's depth of fun. Whisking her into the centre of the floor, he began stomping out the rhythm with his feet while at the same time twirling, spinning and weaving Jo at arm's length in the manner of a matador brandishing his cloak. Surprise was her first reaction, then elation took over as she entered into the spirit of the dance with all the fervour her supple young body could demonstrate. Excitement rose to fever pitch as she lost herself in the dance, aware yet uncaring that the rest of the dancers had formed a watching circle around the perimeter of the dance floor and were clapping wild encouragement to the spectacular couple, extracting every ounce of enjoyment from their performance. The band repeated the tune once, twice, three times more before, their energies spent, Jo and Mario gasped a laughing protest, whereupon the band responded by sliding into a slow, seductive tune.

As Jo made to leave the floor Mario detained her with a grasp upon her elbow. Pulling her back into his arms, he dared wickedly, "You have implied that Leo's feelings are a matter of complete indifference to you, but I think he has asked to be punished a little and knowing how possessive an animal he can be, I think I know just the way to do it! Let's flirt a little," he dared her. "Leo will be furious, but we might find it enjoyable."

Temptation was strong and she was as weak as Eve. "All right, let's!" she agreed recklessly, thereby proving to Mario that she had lied. If she did not care about her husband's opinion she would hardly go out of her way to vex him, he reasoned. She was trying to fool even herself by professing indifference, yet the very lie was proof of Leo's superiority. Mario suppressed a secret smile, he felt no great affection for his sister, but he valued Leo's friendship highly—a friendship he was about to put at risk!

Momentarily shrugging off his misgivings, he pulled her closer and as she snuggled up to him, entering into the spirit of the game, he rested his cheek upon her bright head, reminding himself firmly, as her perfume drifted beneath his nostrils, that the beautiful girl in his arms was the property of his tight-lipped friend whose chilling eyes were following their every movement as they swayed together in time to the music.

It was Jo's idea that Mario and Francesca should accompany them to the casino. Francesca was delighted.

"How kind of you to invite us! Naturally we would love to come."

Mario's reply was less effusive but equally sincere. Their flirtation was coming along nicely—with the help of the champagne he was pressing upon Jo at every opportunity. The one disappointing factor was Leo's change of attitude; instead of the jealousy Mario had earlier noticed he had, after an initial coldness, reverted to sitting back and being entertained by Francesca, who was an expert handler of men. Jo had been quick to sense his lack of interest, hence her increasing bravado. She knew she was behaving badly, flirting openly, drinking too much champagne, but so long as her desperate unhappiness remained hidden she did not care.

During one rare moment when she and Leo were left alone he reached for her hand. Carefully examining each perfect fingernail, he observed mildly, "You are running dangerously close to making a spectacle of yourself, *cara.* I can understand your preference for Mario's company, he is a very entertaining young man, but do you have to make your pleasure quite so obvious?"

She turned upon him a look of wide-eyed innocence. "Surely I'm doing you a favour by keeping him occupied? You obviously have much to discuss with his sister."

"On the contrary," he objected sharply, "we are merely chatting, covering old ground."

"But that's even better, isn't it?" she countered sweetly, choking back her hurt. "How fortunate you are to have a friend who knows you so well that conversation is superfluous—so much can be expressed in long intimate silences!"

CHAPTER TWELVE

THE CASINO was brash, exciting and so crowded it was easy for Jo and Mario to become deliberately lost. He supplied her with a pile of chips, then proceeded from table to table, explaining the intricacies of each particular game. She had no need to pretend absorption, gambling was new to her, a thrilling fascination that grew as fast as the pile of chips on the table in front of her.

"Beginner's luck!" Mario termed it, as time and time again her chosen number was called and winning chips pushed her way. Intoxicated with success, she was reluctant to leave, but finally yielded to Mario's persuasions when, with a quick glance at his watch, he reminded her, "It is two o'clock, Jo, I think we'd better start looking for the others, don't you?"

"Perhaps you're right," she sighed. "Will you cash these chips for me while I fetch my wrap? I'll meet you in the foyer in about five minutes."

Mario was a long time returning. A little lost without his support, Jo wandered into the foyer feeling conspicuous without an escort. Noticing a screen of palms, she made towards it hoping to hide from the curious eyes of people grouped around the foyer chatting idly as they prepared to leave. The hum of voices was all around her, yet as she sought the protection of huge, outspread leaves one voice reached her above the rest, its pitch penetrating even thought its tone was subdued. Realising that Francesca and Leo were seated behind the spread of greenery, she jerked away, but her feet remained rooted to the spot as, holding her breath, she waited for Leo's answer to the question she had just heard Francesca put to him.

"Why did you marry her, Leo? She is not of our nationality, not of our culture—indeed, everything about her is directly opposite to the sort of woman with whom you are accustomed to associating."

"Perhaps that is why." His light tone gave nothing away.

"Oh, come, Leo, don't be evasive," Francesca's voice dropped to a husky whisper. "Am I not entitled to know? For years you have skirted around the subject of marriage and have avoided—with admirable gallantry, I must admit—the wiles of women eager to become the next Contessa. And there have been many, elegant, soiphisticated and very worldly, yet along comes this simple English girl who, so far as I can see, has nothing more to commend her than moderate good looks and a somewhat naive manner, yet you immediately marry her!"

For the life of her, Jo could not have moved away.

"You are a woman of the world, Francesca," she heard Leo drawl. "I married Jo for one very obvious reason, surely I have no need to spell out to *you* what that reason is?"

Jo could have screamed her impatience during the long suspended silence that followed. She had begun to suspect that they had moved away and was about to dare a peep around the leaves when a voice so dejected it was barely recognisable as Francesca's replied, "How

I envy you, *mio caro*, and how I wish I could be lucky enough to share the same good fortune! Soon I, too, shall have to marry. Mario and I are an extravagant pair. And why not," she sounded irritable, "when we were brought up from birth to believe that money was plentiful? From childhood to adolescence we lived the sort of life expected of the children of a family of high position. It was not until our father died that we learned that there was very little money left and that the only way we could continue with the life-style to which we had become accustomed was to capitalise on our assets, such as they are."

She gave a hard laugh. "They are not many. Good looks, an ability to wear clothes well, knowing the right people, moving in the right circles are talents that qualify us for one thing only—a wealthy marriage. A few weeks ago while we were visiting Paris, Mario almost managed to save us from bankruptcy. The daughter of a German industrialist who was staying at our hotel became infatuated with him. All seemed to be going well until one morning we came down to breakfast and discovered that she and her father had left suddenly the night before, leaving no forwarding address nor even a note of goodbye. So now," she sighed, "it is up to me. These diamonds are all that is left of the family fortune. We shall sell them and take a cruise on the proceeds, hoping that one last wild gamble will result in my winning a wealthy husband. Wish me luck, Leo," she pleaded in a husky whisper, "wish me the same sort of luck you have had yourself."

So sickened she felt sure she was about to vomit, Jo stumbled her way back to the powder room and, finding it empty, leant her back against the door, quivering with shocked disgust. Venetians were noted for their mercenary outlook, yet Shylock himself could be compared favourably with Leo and his friends!

Wish me the same sort of luck you have had yourself! Francesca's meaning was plain. She, too, would settle for any gullible fool with sufficient money to satisfy her craving for material possessions!

It seemed a long time before she was able to compose herself sufficiently to make her way back to the foyer, but as Mario was still not in sight it must only have been minutes. He appeared at her side just as she was considering taking flight, hailing a taxi that would transport her miles outside of Leo's vicinity. She felt she could not bear to look, much less speak to him. That he had married her for money was bad enough, but that he should discuss the situation openly with Francesca, preening himself on his good fortune, was treachery beyond belief—even for him!

Mario put her dazed look down to tiredness and was concerned. "I'm sorry, Jo, to have kept you waiting so long, there was a queue and those damned cashiers could not have been slower! Let me help you with your wrap; the others can't be far away. Oh, there they are..." Mario signalled to them and they began making their way across the foyer. Jo hated Leo's spurious concern when he chided:

"Heavens, child, you look exhausted! The sooner you are in bed the better."

Mechanically, not knowing what she said or how she said it, Jo made her goodbyes, nodding agreement with Mario's insistence that they must meet again soon and watching with frozen indifference while Francesca stood on tiptoe to kiss Leo's cheek and whisper a final word in his ear. As she sat in the car on the homeward journey, mute and deaf to his remarks, she felt his anxious glances and when he drew up outside of the villa she jumped out of the car and ran inside, paying no heed to his anxious: "Jo, is something wrong...?" when she sped blindly past him.

He followed her upstairs, as she suspected he would, but received no reply when after trying the locked door he called out, "Jo, let me in! I insist upon knowing whatever it is that has upset you."

Standing rigid by the window, she covered her ears and blanked her mind by concentrating all her attention upon a huge yellow moon coasting languidly across fathomless sky. She would not cry, she promised herself, gulping back a sob, then closed her eyes when the moon began wavering through a mist of tears.

"Jo!" Leo's voice had become dangerously calm. "I mean to come in—must I break down the door?"

"No!" She spun from the window. "Leave me alone, can't you? Please, just leave me in peace..."

Her broken plea seemed to have the desired effect. Footsteps moved away from the door, then there was silence. But relief was momentary. Seconds later there came a crash as his shoulder connected with a wooden panel, the flimsy lock gave way under pressure, and the door burst open. Lean, purposeful, he stepped across the threshold, pausing long enough to draw in a deep, steadying breath before condemning without anger:

"That ought not to have been necessary. Now, tell me why you are acting like a sulky child."

Tears dried on her cheeks as she swung to face him, her slim body defiant, her expression contemptuous. "I *was* a child—a simple innocent—but this evening I grew up! And as for my sulking—have I not the right to feel resentful, especially after overhearing your very enlightening conversation with Francesca?" Poker-stiff, she turned her back on him. "I had become reconciled to being married for money, but obviously for you the outcome has not been satisfaction enough. Why couldn't you preen in secret instead of boasting to others about your stroke of good fortune?"

His hand descended heavily upon her shoulder. "I haven't the faintest notion of what you are talking about." His pretended bewilderment was infuriating. "Exactly what is it that you are implying? So far as I can recollect there was nothing said between Francesca and myself that should cause you the least concern." His brow wrinkled, giving an impression that he was striving to remember. "Francesca was feeling upset, melancholy. These past few years for her have not been easy, she has had many worries—"

"The main one being how quickly she can emulate your example by finding herself a wealthy partner!" Jo spat.

His brow cleared. "Ah, now I am beginning to understand! Francesca opened the conversation by asking why I married you and you, having been allowed to labour under certain misapprehensions, have obviously drawn the wrong conclusion from my reply. There is something which you ought to have been told sooner, Jo, information which, because of what some might term a form of conceit on my part, I deliberately withheld. But now I think the time is right to tell you—"

"More lies? No, thank you, I've heard enough!"

Her abruptness caused him to frown. He hesitated, searching her face for a hint of softening, but after thoroughly examining a defiantly tilted chin, stubborn mouth, and stormy eyes flashing green-diamond dislike, disappointment darkened his face. His lips tightened into a grim line. She knew she was being handled with kid gloves when he reached for her hand and urged quietly:

"Let us sit down and talk reasonably, Jo."

Hating his ability to make her feel childish, she snatched her hand away. "We have nothing to talk about!" She spun on her heel and flounced across to the window, hoping her rigid back would serve as a sign of dismissal. But the iron-willed Conte was not easily intimidated. She sensed he was mere inches away when he joined her at the window, sharing the intimacy of a darkened bedroom lit only by moonlight casting a silver veil over vibrant hair, downcast lashes and cheeks pale as the ghost she resembled as she trembled in the moonlight.

He was close enough to touch her, yet he resisted the temptation and addressed her in a calm, controlled voice. "How are we ever to reach an understanding if we do not talk? It is wrong that so much should be left unsaid between us. Occasionally, I have hoped that we were moving towards deeper understanding—mere hours ago we were happily exploring each other's minds, enjoying each other's company, testing each other's humour and finding it sound. Can you deny, Jo, that there have been moments today when you were able to forget that on our wedding day you vowed to hate me, the man you insisted you were being forced to marry?"

Ignoring the softly phrased questions, the reminders that turned her knees to water, she seized upon the one remark that revived her anger. "Are you daring to imply that I was *not* forced to marry you? Like my grandmother, have you foolishly concluded that deep within me are yearnings I'm too gauche to recognise?" A laugh grated past her lips. "If that is so, then how little you know me! Let me remind you that up until our marriage I was well on my way to becoming a scientist and that for years now I've mixed with the opposite sex in an atmosphere where frank discussion of every subject—including and especially sex—is accepted as normal, just as the liberty of women is normal and their right to have an equal say. I'm very jealous of that right, so believe me, if I were in love with you I wouldn't hesitate to say so!"

Leo thrust his hands deep into his pockets as if resisting an urge to shake her free of female arrogance. Yet his tone retained its even tenor when he vexed by her pointing out:

"Your argument would be sound were you not confusing boys with men. My own experience of English students has taught me that during their years of study they are slow to mature, full of youthful bravado yet still firmly under the family wing. Your Welfare State makes this possible by cosseting them from childhood, throwing them lifelines of grants, scholarships, and monetary aid in order that their progress through the shallows of life is made painless. Consequently, they become lazy, reluctant to strike out unaided. These boys you mistook for men no doubt treated you with sexless camaraderie. To them you were an equal—a good mate, I think you would term it—demanding no more of you than you were willing to give. They denied you your womanhood, Jo! Such a situation could never occur in my country where a boy is thrown in at the deep end of life, emerging as a man filled with the urge to master, to protect, and above all to love the woman he has chosen to be his wife." Suddenly he closed the gap between them until he was close enough to breathe into her ear, "Don't be afraid of the lion, *cara*, he has far more to offer than the playful puppy..."

Mesmerised by his persuasive argument, Jo caught a sharp breath and for one unthinking moment was almost bewitched into leaning back against the shoulder looming temptingly close. Then Francesca's image flashed before her eyes, throwing a dash of sanity on to her fevered senses.

"You do well to liken yourself to a beast of the jungle," she charged bitterly, wanting to move away but fastened by invisible chains to his side. All the applicable characteristics are yours—cunning, stealth, and a complete lack of compassion for those less ruthless than yourself."

He recoiled from her vehemence yet kept anger from his voice when softly he reminded her, "You did not think so this afternoon, nor again this evening when your mouth trembled as you whispered of a secret you wished me to share. What was it that you were so eager to tell me, Jo? Had you, at last, begun to recognise...love?"

She twirled round to face him, cat-green eyes spitting fury. "Your imagination is excelled only by your conceit, *signore*! I must admire and respect if I am to love!" Her throat closed around the word and to her utter dismay she felt tears spurting beneath her lids. Quickly she turned her head, but he had caught their glint in the moonlight. His hand snapped upwards, imprisoning her chin between forceful fingers.

Steadily, almost sadly, he noted her distress and a flash of what could have been regret was reflected in his eyes. Painfully Jo bore his scrutiny, throat too tight to admit speech, her spirit cowed by a weight of unhappiness. She braced, expecting to have to suffer more of the tolerance she detested, but this time when he spoke his voice held a sharp edge.

"If it is any satisfaction to you, I will admit that today you have tormented me almost beyond endurance. Endlessly, I kept having to remind myself that you needed more time, that you must not be rushed. Nevertheless, there is a limit to my patience, Jo, and it is all but reached. You are young, you are innocent, but you are also my wife and I do not intend to wait for ever. I have tried—*Dio, I have tried*!"

He released her chin to run fingers through his hair, an unprecedented action for the immaculate Conte. "I have tried to be reasonable, to make allowances for your youth and for your volatile temperament." He bent towards her with such suddenness she was startled, alarmed by the hint of danger contained within a rock hard jaw outthrust in anger. Then to her relief temper dropped from him like a cloak as, sounding almost weary, he continued, "More than anything in the world, little *vespa* I wanted you to come to me of your own free will, to admit to feelings you have as yet refused to acknowledge, to be warm and soft and loving as I know you can be, as I have longed for you to be. Perhaps it is foolish of me to hold on to the key that could unlock your mind of suspicion, but I wish it to be used only as a last resort. Victory will be all the sweeter if you bring me love that is strong enough to overcome doubt. I could take you now, my wife. Here, alone in this house, I could take you by force, with only the seabirds to hear your protests and the pounding waves to drown your screams."

She recoiled from the threat, putting yards of space between them, her eyes wide with revulsion.

"Don't worry," his tone was dry. "I am not quite the beast you think me. I will wait a little longer, be a little more patient, and with luck the kitten might decide to purr instead of scratch."

Nervously she edged away, sensing an extra quality in his manner, an assurance that had not been present before, a relaxed frame, a secret smile playing around his lips that seemed to indicate a certainty that sooner or later victory would be his. She stood with head bowed, a green-clad wraith bathed in moonlight that drew him like a magnet.

"Jo..." A shudder ran through her when he reached out to clasp her lightly by the shoulder, "why must you always fight me? I am tired of this war between us. Life could be so wonderful if only you would lay down your arms, not in defeat, but in sweet surrender."

His magnetism was such that she did not rebel when his arm slid around her waist, drawing her close. She felt she was drowning in eyes dark with emotion yet kindling with a lick of hungry flame. *"Ti adoro,"* he murmured hoarsely. "Come to me, *amore mio*, please...!"

She hesitated within the circle of his arms, a tender trap held loosely so as not to frighten, offering the choice of swaying forward or jerking away. Almost she succumbed to the bait, urged on by pounding heartbeats, by a body yearning for his touch, by a quivering mouth hungry for his kisses. He was devilish clever, a hunter with a silken snare, a lion who preferred to coax rather than to pounce.

It took overwhelming willpower to break away. Trembling, tearful, her emotions a wildly knotted tangle, she stumbled until the width of the room lay between them.

"Sorry, I can't oblige," she choked. "I have no intention of playing second fiddle to Francesca."

He went very still. "If I had wanted Francesca would I have married you?"

Her forced laughter grated shrilly through the room. "Of course you would, so long as both she and you remain dedicated to living beyond your means! You are both misers, *signore*, and a miser's avarice entombs all other passions!"

CHAPTER THIRTEEN

WEARY OF RIDING an emotional seesaw—one minute high with hope, the next plummeting into dejection—Jo avoided taking breakfast with Leo the next morning. Yet he sought her out, stalking easily down the path leading to the beach where he found her sorting idly through the pile of unusual seashells she had spent the previous hour collecting.

For once he did not comment upon her childish pursuits but suggested in a voice grave but nevertheless firm, "We promised to call upon your grandmother, remember? I think today would be as good a time as any to pay her a visit."

She started to her feet with an alacrity that was far from complimentary to her husband of just a few days. "I should like that very much," she agreed. "I'll go and change." His thoughtful eyes followed her jean-clad figure all the way, as she sped along the path leading up to the villa.

She had spent a restless night tossing and turning, wondering how she was to endure three more weeks of torment. Like a puppeteer Leo jerked the strings of her emotions first one way and the other until she felt confused and uncertain of both her own feelings and his. One remark in particular had caused her to fret. He had implied that he was possessed of knowledge which, if confided, would cause her to revise her opinion of him. After much fruitless speculation her tired brain had rebelled and she had dismissed the remark as being yet another fabrication, an exercise in confusion evolved by a devious mind.

She dressed carefully for her visit, wanting Nònna Domini's approval, knowing that to arrive wearing trousers would be to instantly arouse her displeasure. So she chose to wear the Quaker-grey dress in which she had appeared before Leo as a penitent and was pleased with the look of demureness conjured up by a white cowl collar and spotless cuffs. To enhance this image further she brushed her hair until it glowed like silk, a banner of red, bright as courage, curling past slim, squared shoulders.

Leo made no remark about her appearance when he helped her into the boat, but as she settled into her seat she shifted uneasily, wondering if his enigmatic smile showed insight into her wish to curry favour with the grandmother whose sympathies had always seemed to err upon the side of the charming Conte.

Murano was a large island with an atmosphere very different from the rest of the Venetian communities. An island of waterborne peasants, Jo had always considered it, with its tenement blocks, lines of washing and clutter of small glass factories, grubby buildings built of red brick, with tall blackened chimneys and a wooden landing stage in front of each one. "It is a pity," Leo read her mind, "that this once beautiful island should have been left to fall into such a state of disrepair. At one time Murano was considered the playground of Venice, covered with a wealth of vines and fruit trees, where aristocrats of the day kept luxurious apartments. But that was before the island was turned into a glass foundry. So many fires had erupted in Venice that all furnaces within the city were compulsorily removed to Murano, which then became the principal glass producer of Europe."

"Is there any truth in the belief that Venetian tumblers will break into fragments if the merest drop of poison is poured into them?" she asked, a trifle shy of her lithe husband, casually dressed in light slacks and a shirt, black as his windtossed hair, with top buttons left undone baring a strong tanned throat. Sunlight glistened upon the medallion strung around his neck on a silver chain, and as he responded to her question with a grin of amusement her heart lurched, bedevilled once again by audacious charm.

"That romantic theory has many times been disproved," he teased, amused by her obvious disappointment, "yet knowing how tenaciously you cling to your illusions I've no doubt you'll continue believing it to be fact."

"Can you blame me," she countered bitterly, "if I find illusion pleasanter than reality?"

He was still frowning when he pulled the boat in at the landing stage in front of her grandmother's house, one of a dismal terrace, its bricks grimed with the smoke from nearby factories.

"The *signora* is out visiting a friend!" called out a neighbour leaning inquisitively from an upstairs window. "Oh, it is you, Signorina Domini!" she recognised Jo. "Your grandmother will be back shortly, I'm certain, she is seldom absent from her home for more than an hour. Unfortunately she left a mere ten minutes ago—would you care to come inside my house and wait?"

"Thank you, no," Jo declined hastily, "you're very kind, but I should like to visit the factory while I'm here. Perhaps when my grandmother returns, you would be good enough to tell her that we've arrived?"

"Si, signorina, that I will do."

Almost apologetically Jo turned to Leo, whose frown had not lifted during the interchange. "Do you mind if we visit the Renucci factory?" she enquired meekly, suspecting that a visit to a glass factory would be regarded by him as less than a novelty.

"No," he surprised her, falling into step as she began to walk, "it is many years since I last visited a foundry; it is time my memories of the art were revived."

Jo had never found her grandmother's neighbours very forthcoming, but she had excused their surliness with the reminder that years of poverty and hard work could not help but result in resentment. Yet surprisingly, Leo was welcomed warmly when they entered the factory; every man present seemed intent upon shaking his hand, many calls of welcome, warm as the heat blasting from the furnaces, echoed down the long room. The owner himself appeared to greet them and to guide them around his establishment with voluble compliments and an immense amount of pride.

Jo felt piqued. For many years her grandfather had worked as *padrone di fornace* in this very factory. Diligently he had guarded the secret of the constitution of each batch, had planned the work programmes for each day, decided what items should be made and how many, had been responsible for keeping the tough craftsmen in order and when necessary had rolled up his sleeves and worked alongside them. But even this fact had not seemed to entitle her to more than a courteous nod from older workers who remembered him. Her appearance had been *tolerated*, never welcomed as it had been today.

Sensing her aggrievement, Leo explained as he introduced her to the owner, "Signor Renucci's products were greatly favoured by the house of Tempera. Much of the glass housed within the *palazzo* was made here, exquisite, greatly admired pieces whose value has increased enormously over the years." He turned his attention to the proprietor. "I should like to make my wife a present, Signore Renucci, a piece of crystal of a design and purity equal to those which we treasure as heirlooms today. But first, with your permission, we will wander through the workshops before making a choice from your treasure-house."

"It shall be my pleasure to serve you myself," the delighted owner bowed over Jo's hand. "Until this moment I was well pleased with the contents of my showroom, but I fear the Contessa's beauty will outshine everything displayed upon my shelves."

Heat from the furnace was not wholly responsible for colour rioting in Jo's cheeks as she walked by Leo's side, enduring his arm around her shoulders while he guided her through the stages of manufacture, imparting information gained through studying the industry in depth instead of merely skimming the surface as she had herself. In spite of her embarrassment she was deeply interested, paying rapt attention to his expert commentary. They lingered before a master glassblower hard at work beside his furnace, looking proud and self-assured, with two young apprentices handing him tools as he flourished a long pipe in his hand. Like a magician performing before an audience, he raised the pipe to his lips and puffed out his cheeks until a small bubble of glass appeared at the other end. Slanting a glance at Jo, he gave a twist of the wrist, a further delicate puff, then waved in front of her nose an as yet unidentifiable form. Swiftly he twiddled the pipe between his fingers, sliced with an iron rod, added a dollop of molten glass, then for a swift second plunged the rod into the heart of glowing embers. Then with a theatrical flourish he withdrew it to sever a glacial umbilical cord with a snap of iron shears. Triumphantly he placed the finished article at Jo's feet, gesturing sweating apprentices to clean up his implements in preparation for his next performance.

The swiftly-fashioned offering was simple but exquisite—a delicate, shapely bell, its ringed handle the circumference of a finger with, set alongside, a dainty crystal tear which later would be suspended from a fine chain and inserted within the bell to act as a clapper.

"To remind you of your wedding day, Contessa," the burly glassblower bowed proudly. "After polishing, it will be suitably boxed and presented, together with our very good wishes to yourself and the Conte, that you may enjoy a happy and fruitful marriage."

She somehow stammered her thanks, then, with Leo grinning widely by her side, set off towards the showroom where Signor Renucci was waiting.

Leo took an interminable time deciding which of the many examples of enamelled and engraved, clear and opaque, fluted and plain, ornate and simple pieces of glass would make the most suitable present for his bride. Finally he settled for a fragile crystal goblet engraved with a frieze depicting a maned predator, unmistakably a lion, bounding in pursuit of a smaller, terrified shape which Jo sensed had appealed to his humour as being that of a timorous kitten cowering behind a flourish of foliage.

"Piteous eyes that stab the heart," he glinted down at her, indicating his choice to the hovering proprietor. "See how cleverly the artist has portrayed the small animal's anticipation of suffering?" Ignoring the proprietor's interest, he reached out his hand and with one taut finger levered up her chin until he was probing green, uncertain depths. "To anticipate," he warned softly, "is to endure more than is necessary, *cara*."

Her grandmother was waiting on the doorstep when they arrived back at the house. She welcomed them with a kiss, then ushered them inside, casting a questioning glance over Jo's pale face but making no comment until they were seated in the comfortable, spotlessly clean living-room. Not until coffee had been poured and a plateful of small biscuits passed around did her grandmother settle back in her chair to chide Leo lightly, "I had expected to see my granddaughter blooming, *signore*, instead of which she is sad and pale as a chaste little nun."

Colour flared in Jo's cheeks. Her grandmother was impossible to deceive; her eyes grew shrewder, her tongue more cutting with age.

Leo, however, refused to be embarrassed. Casting a negligent eye over Jo, a picture of confusion in her grey dress with Quaker-prim collar and cuffs, he observed lightly, "You must know that Jo is a creature of contrasting moods, one day outrageous, the next demure. Today she has opted to be the subdued young penitent—why, I am not quite sure, but I do not complain. It is not every man who can awaken each day to a new and different wife. I must confess I find the experience both challenging and intriguing."

Nònna Domini looked pleased. "Good," she leant forward to pat his hand. "Jo takes more understanding than most, needs firmer discipline than most, but I can see that she is in sympathetic hands. Now," she sat upright and beamed at them both, "I have some good news for you! Sara and Vincente have set a date for their wedding. It is to take place next week. Your father, Jo, demurred at first, he wanted them to wait at least until you and Leo had returned from your honeymoon, but after pressure was brought to bear, he was finally persuaded that a one-day interruption would not be too upsetting for you both. He stipulated, however, that you were not to be told until the very last minute. A message was to have been sent the day before the wedding summoning you both to attend.

"Happily, your arrival here today has made that unnecessary. All arrangements have been made, invitations sent out, and preparations for the wedding feast are well under way. It is exciting, is it not?" she appealed, bird-bright, "having two weddings in the family within the space of a month? I suspect, Jo, that your father is feeling relieved as well as pleased—the responsibility of controlling two wayward daughters was becoming a great strain. You too, *signore*," she addressed Leo, "must be pleased that your cousin's future has been decided. Sisters married to cousins is a very tidy arrangement, I think. So beneficial that the outcome might almost have been planned."

Beneficial! The benefit was all on one side, Jo fumed.

Both Leo and Vincente had been up for sale and her father had considered them a good investment!

So moody and withdrawn did she become that when the time came for them to leave her grandmother drew her to one side, showing obvious impatience. "I don't know what to make of you today, Jo! Your manner has been most ungracious, especially towards the attentive and very charming Conte. I am beginning to suspect that you have been spoiled, child. Can't you show a little more gratitude towards your husband?

Gratitude for what? Jo fumed inwardly, at the same time managing somehow to smile. Gratitude that her father had been rich enough to meet the Conte's price?

When Leo swung the boat in a wide arc, starting upon the return journey to the wild and lonely shore, she felt she was a prisoner being deported into exile. Steeped in depression, she sat silent, her demure expression hiding a mind in turmoil as she explored every avenue of thought directed towards a solution to a situation that was becoming more unbearable by the minute. Her grandmother's news had practically effected her release. With the arrangement for Sara's wedding so well advanced her father's hands were virtually tied, for to cancel the wedding at such a late stage would be to inflict cruel unhappiness upon Sara and humiliation upon the Tempera pride. Therefore, she reasoned, escape was now possible. The only problem remaining was how!

When Leo attempted to help her along the path leading to the villa she jerked away, loathing his touch. That her revulsion had been communicated was obvious by his tone when he halted her progress through the shrubbery with the clipped, icy observation:

"I am fast reaching the conclusion that my handling of you has been all wrong. Patience, I thought, was all that was needed. I told myself that once removed from her father's indulgence the child would develop quickly into a woman. But as the days have passed and you have grown progressively more wilful, more prone to moods, I have been finding it very difficult to control an impulse to turn you across my knee and administer a good spanking!"

With unusual roughness he pulled her towards him, eyes glittering coldly as they travelled her defiant face, daring her to rebel. "Well, which do you prefer—slaps or kisses?" It sounded like an ultimatum! "This situation has remained tolerable because only we two were aware that it existed. But very shortly our seclusion is to end and we will be once more surrounded by family and inquisitive friends. I utterly refuse," he clamped, tightening his grip upon her arm, "to be the recipient of any further remarks similar to those voiced by your very observant grandmother."

His black head swooped until his lips were a fraction from hers. "The old lady was correct," he murmured, softly threatening, "you do have the look of a chaste, untouched nun. It will be my enjoyable duty to remedy that. By the time we leave this island I promise you, *cara*, that everyone who wonders shall have his curiosity satisfied. One glance at your expressive face will be sufficient to confirm that you have experienced the sweet tempestuous passion that is the reward of every dutiful young bride!"

"You should be so lucky!" Panic caused her to revert to the vernacular favoured student friends whose attitude towards authority had always been brusque.

She jerked away and began running towards the villa, not stopping until she had gained the safety of her bedroom where she leant her back against a door rendered useless as a barricade because of a shattered lock. But he did not follow her. For almost half an hour she waited, tense body pressed hard against the door, before gradually she was able to relax.

"Well, Jo," she muttered to herself as she paced the room, "it's now or never—those were not idle threats, he meant every word. Which follows that you must leave here tonight at the very latest!" She paced and pondered until she was weary, latching eagerly on to one escape plan after another, then discarding each as hopeless. If she were to try to escape by car the sound of the engine would bring him running, even if she were fortunate enough to find out where he kept the keys. To walk to the Lido and then catch a waterbus to Venice was out of the question; she would be missed and followed long before she had reached the town. She thought of asking Dina to help, then dismissed this as placing an unfair burden upon the conscience of the girl who, though sympathetic, would nevertheless feel she must remain loyal to her employer.

Then with a flash of inspiration she remembered the haste with which Leo had followed her from the landing stage. Was it possible, had his anger been consuming enough to have caused him to forget to remove the ignition key from the motorboat? The more she thought the more convinced she became that he had. Unfortunately it was too dangerous to check; the sight of her slipping down to the landing stage might serve as a reminder, and she dared not risk that. She would have to act very carefully; her attitude during dinner must be sufficiently disarming to make him think escape was the last thing on her mind, then, once the meal was over and darkness could provide cover, she must think up an excuse to leave him for a while. If her acting were convincing enough, and his suspicions lulled, she should be halfway across the lagoon before he began wondering about the length of her absence.

She took great pains with her appearance. The dress she wore for dinner had to be flattering enough to disarm him, yet must not hamper her progress when she ran down to the beach. Her final choice was a widely-flaring evening skirt, chestnut brown with matching sequined jacket, but with tight, full-length sleeves that would protect her arms from the evening breeze. Swiftness would be the essence of her escape. There would not be time even to grab a wrap, so bearing this in mind she slid a long chiffon scarf through the bracelet on her wrist. Its protection would be flimsy, but at least it would turn a little of the chill from her exposed neckline. She felt proud and rather clever as she twirled before a mirror, then began pacing, nervous as an actress awaiting her cue.

The ordeal began immediately Leo pushed open the door and strode into her bedroom. He was handsome enough to play the part of any woman's hero, she admitted grudgingly, avoiding eyes that raked approval over her body, bold, unrepentant eyes showing a glint of... *anticipation*?

Inwardly shivering, she forced herself to smile and move towards him. Looking pleased, he admitted dryly, "I half-expected to find you sulking—either that or dressed in the most objectionable manner in the hope of cooling my ardour. But, as usual, you have surprised me by appearing quite enchanting. Can it be that once again I have misjudged you? Have you suddenly become mature and wise enough to accept without a fight that which you sense is inevitable?"

She cringed against the need for diplomacy. Curbing a feline urge to scratch and spit, she schooled herself to purr, "To argue against the inevitable is a waste of time. Rather than rail against a storm I put on a raincoat."

His golden eyes glowed. Halting her progress towards the door, he clasped both her hands in his and turned her round to face him. Softly, with a pleased smile playing around his lips, he asked, "Is this your way of admitting surrender, Jo?"

"Perhaps," she choked through a throat agonisingly tight, wishing for one reckless moment that the lie were truth. "Give me a little more time, Leo," she stammered, then hoodwinked him completely when with a small breathless laugh, she admitted, "You'll probably think me foolish, but I'm...I'm feeling rather shy."

She had never felt more ashamed when, with protective tenderness, he tucked her hand into the crook of his elbow and began escorting her downstairs.

CHAPTER FOURTEEN

As DINNER progressed Jo was astonished at the extent of Leo's blindness to the trap she had prepared, at his eagerness to swallow her bait. They ate by candlelight, speaking little as each course progressed, Jo because she was too busy trying not to cry and Leo because he had no wish to rush the victory she had hinted was imminent, content to bide his time until the meal was over and Dina had gone home, leaving them to their solitude.

But once or twice their fingers touched, the small contact causing her simultaneous pangs of fear and delight. She sensed his eyes upon her downbent head but would not look up. She must be performing well, she congratulated herself, or he would not be sitting opposite looking benign as a well fed jungle cat, his golden eyes slumbrous, yet ready at his partner's whim to join her in play. Nervously she laid down her fork. To stroke a lion took nerve enough—from where would she find courage to inflict a wound?

When the meal was finished Dina served coffee, then cleared away. Not long afterwards she popped her head around the door to beam, "With your permission, *signore, signora,* I will go now. Unless there is anything else you wish...?"

"Nothing, thank you." Leo's obvious desire to be

left alone with his lovely wife delighted Dina. *"Buona notte,"* he dismissed her firmly, "we'll see you tomorrow."

Dina's exit signalled the end of the prologue—now it was time to continue with the play!

"Shall we move into the *salotto* where it is more comfortable?" he suggested. Jo implied agreement by rising to her feet, then she hesitated, eyes widening as if at some sudden reminder. "Oh, how careless of me! All during dinner some small doubt has been nagging at the back of my mind, and now I've realized why! Just before you came into my room I lit a cigarette and for the life of me I can't remember stubbing it out. Wold you excuse me while I slip upstairs and check?"

"Don't bother, I'll go..." Leo offered, but she had almost reached the door.

"No," she insisted, "I won't be more than a few minutes."

Hastily she closed the door behind her, then ran hell for leather to the back entrance, through the garden, then along the path, blessing her foresight in choosing to wear serviceable sandals instead of the spike-heeled, fragile bundle of straps she usually favoured. Without sparing time to even glance across her shoulder she sped onwards, her brown-clad figure almost invisible in the darkness. When at last she reached the boat she tumbled into it, groping feverishly in the darkness for the feel of the vital key without which the engine would not start. For five minutes she groped, sobbing with her anxiety, unwilling to accept that no key had been left for her to find, then she slumped against a seat shivering with the cold of despair.

"Hypocrite, thy name is woman—Josephine Tempera, to be precise!" The bitter accusation scythed through the darkness. "I congratulate you, *bella*, for acting out your lie with astonishing sincerity!"

His words pierced her shell of despair, sending heat racing through her veins as fiery temper erupted. Jumping from the boat, she quivered in front of him.

"You dare to call me a hypocrite! *You*, who did not hesitate to marry me while carrying on an affair with Francesca—*you*, who spoke of wanting a loving wife, a mother for your children, when, as everyone in Venice is aware, what you really wanted was a share of my father's wealth!"

Golden eyes glittered in the darkness, chilling, intent, menacing as those of a jungle cat who has been prodded and aggravated beyond endurance. Sensing within him a violence never before encountered, Jo began backing away, but had taken no more than a step when the predator pounced. Ferocious fingers clawed into her shoulders as he jerked her forward and proceeded to shake her violently until her teeth chattered and her head felt as if it were about to snap from her body, at the same time clipping words through tightly compressed lips. "Wild, wilful shrew! This time you have tried me too far, I am determined you shall be tamed!"

Fear came to her aid, fear of the ferocious stranger who had taken the place of the even-tempered, hard-to-rile Conte who had brushed aside her insults and smiled indulgence of her childish whims. With all the spirit of a firebrand kitten she tried to wriggle out of his clutches and when her efforts met with no success resorted to the ultimate feline defence of raking vicious fingernails down the length of his cheek.

"Diavolo!" Instinctively he lifted his hand to the scratches and the second her shoulder was released Jo wrenched away and fled into the darkness.

Thorns stabbed through her long skirt, impeding her progress as she stumbled through undergrowth, over rocks and boulders, then finally on to a firm stretch of sand. Gulping in a couple of sharp, painful breaths, she picked up her tattered skirts and ran blindly, neither knowing nor caring where her flight would end, anxious only to put as much distance as possible between herself and the man whose footsteps she could hear pounding in her wake. Terror fluttered inside of her like the wings of a frantic bird when she stumbled and fell, losing precious minutes in the race. Her terrified senses assured her that Leo was quickly making ground; even as she scrambled to her feet she imagined she could feel the heat of his breath searing the nape of her neck.

She screamed aloud when an impact behind the knees sent her sprawling face downward upon the sand. Rough hands rolled her on to her back and for seconds, too winded to speak, she had to be content with glaring indignant defiance into his unrepentant face.

"Beast!" She choked on a mouthful of sand. "You took an unfair advantage—rugby tackles belong on a rugby field!"

"Just as honeyed responses belong on the lips of a woman who intends to honour her promises," he countered tersely, pressing the weight of his body on her legs and grasping each of her wrists so that she was effectively pinned to the ground. "Now, you will listen to what I have to say!"

She shuddered from the breathed threat but was too

tightly held to offer physical resistance. "Talk all night, if you like," she retorted bitterly, "I shall simply refuse to believe a word you say."

Exercising the utmost control, he ignored her taunt and proceeded in tight, clipped tones. "First of all, let us dispose of the least important matter—namely Francesca. She and I have been friends since childhood, that perhaps has made her feel she is entitled to show a proprietorial interest in my doings, I don't know—all I do know is that there has never been the slightest romantic attachment between us."

Inside of her, frantic wings ceased flapping and went very still. "Knowing what a minx she can be, I should have thought to warn you of her liking for drama and of her unfortunate tendency towards making innuendoes that are completely devoid of truth, but to be honest, these past few weeks Francesca has been the very last person on my mind. However, now that she has accepted our marriage as fact, you will probably discover that she can be a very good friend, loyal, partisan to a fault, and genuinely delighted—in her ignorance—that we have found happiness together. Her request, 'Wish me the same sort of luck you have had yourself', was influenced by thoughts of love and not, as you suspected, by thoughts of money."

When Jo uttered a derogatory "Huh!" he winced, but continued bleakly, "Now that small item has been disposed of I can deal with the matter that has caused you most concern—namely that of finance. I had hoped to explain in more favourable circumstances, had even been foolish enough to hope," his lips twisted wryly, "that after getting to know me better you would have no doubts left to erase. But as you are still so obviously bigoted against me, so unresponsive to reason, I think the time has come to tell you that far from being a pauper, I could match, lira for lira, the total amount of your father's wealth."

Sand-encrusted lashes flew up over green eyes brilliant with disbelief. "You must consider me every kind of a fool if you expect me to believe that!" she spat contemptuously.

His patrician features hardened; obviously the Conte was not accustomed to being accused of lying. "Proof can be supplied if and whenever it should be needed," he replied, flaring nostrils indicating his distaste of the whole subject.

"My father would have mentioned—" she began.

"Your father was requested by me to avoid the subject," he cut in. "For reasons already stated, I did not wish you to know. However, I will free him of his promise so that when you ask him—or anyone else you might care to question—he will tell you that far from being the dilettante you think me I have for many years worked upon the restoration of my city's ancient buildings. During the course of such work I have acquired not only a reputation as an expert but also an embarrassing amount of the commodity upon which you set such great store: money. I did not seek such wealth, my main consideration was the preservation of irreplaceable buildings for the benefit of future generations. Towards such an end I would gladly have worked for nothing."

Jo closed her ears against the sincerity in his voice, reluctant to believe that she could have so badly misjudged him, *refusing* to believe it. Suffering his piercing look, she relaxed, twisted her lips into the semblance of a smile and enquired, sweetly mocking, "Do you have any more fairy tales to tell me? If not, I should like to be released so that I can return to the villa."

For what seemed a very long time Leo stared down at her, golden eyes dark with anger. A huge moon sailed from behind cloud, bathing in its silver glow the girl outstretched upon the sand in the attitude of an offering awaiting sacrifice. The sight seemed to incense him, the glitter she feared appearing once more to terrorise her as slowly his black head lowered towards lips whose tilt of bravado was denied by a quiver of dismay.

"But I have not finished with you yet, *amore mio*." She blanched from the softly growled threat. "Did you not hear me promise that before we left the island the shrew would be tamed?" When he kissed her it was as if her bones melted into the sand, leaving behind a weak, helpless body completely at the mercy of hands that blazed a trail of fire along a smooth line of shoulder, a curve of breast, a slender hollowed waist, then lingered against a length of thigh. He laughed softly against her lips, revelling in his dominance, satisfied that he held her spellbound.

That small laugh of triumph was his undoing, the whip that flogged awake her pride and drove a stab of cunning through her numbed mind.

"Leo...!" Instilling melting tenderness into her voice, she snuggled against him. "Darling, what a fool I've been..." He drew a pleased breath, then when his imprisoning arms relaxed into a loving embrace she whispered messages of remorse into his ear, at the same time furtively stretching a hand behind his back, groping for a weapon of defence among the sand. She almost gasped her relief when her fingers closed around a large stone. Giving herself no time to think, she grabbed it and thrust it with all her might against the back of his downbent head. The thud as it connected was sickening. Panic-stricken, she clawed her way from under him when he slumped senseless, then again she fled, this time in the direction of the villa.

Great gasping sobs escaped her as she forced herself not to look back, not to think about the unconscious body laid out defenceless on the beach. She had to reach the car before he came round; this was her last chance of escape from a now desperate situation and she dared not allow it to slip through her fingers.

Tears were streaming down her cheeks when she stumbled into the villa, then raced upstairs to Leo's bedroom where she hoped to find the car keys. She was shaking so much she could barely turn the doorknob, but after a deep breath to steady her nerves she thrust open the door and ran inside. The room was bare, monastic even, but as she ran across to the dressing-table his presence was so strong it felt almost physical.

A faint tang of aftershave was emanating from behind a half-open door leading into the bathroom, the aroma of a recently-smoked cheroot teased her nostrils, a bathrobe flung across the bed brought vividly to mind the inert body stretched out on the sand, and as her shaking fingers searched through the articles on top of the dressing-table they brushed against a gold cufflink, upturning it so that her eye was caught by the baleful glare of a monogrammed lion. Swiftly she jerked her hand away and ran across to a wardrobe, sliding open the door in search of the jacket Leo had worn when last he had garaged the car. It seemed an unforgivable intrusion to rummage through the pockets of immaculate suits, but she forced herself to do it, searching feverishly, conscious that at any moment he might appear in the doorway bitter, angry, and thirsting for revenge.

When at last her fingers closed around a bunch of keys her relief was so enormous she sagged against the wall until she had mustered sufficient strength to resume her flight. She blessed her good luck when, after negotiating the stairs and hall without incident, she ran outside to the garage. Clouds had dispersed and a full moon was throwing sufficient light to make the unlocking of the garage doors easy. Seconds later Jo was nosing the powerful sports car out of the garage, her shaking body crouched over a wheel held in tense fingers. She had managed to outwit the athletic Conte who in the past had outrun, outwalked and outswum her at every opportunity!

Then almost without volition her foot stamped hard upon the brake pedal. Why was Leo not in hot pursuit? It was against his nature to admit defeat, so what possible reason could there be behind his non-appearance?

The nose of the car was jutting out into the roadway leading to the Lido, a mere half hour's drive away, yet she switched off the engine, pulled on the handbrake and stared wide-eyed through the windscreen as a dreadful thought struck her. Could the blow she had struck have killed him? Was he lying on the beach felled by a mortal blow from a stone directed by her own reckless hand?

"Oh, no...!" she moaned, covering her face with shaking hands. "Please, God, no...!"

She could not afterwards recall her journey back to the beach, but stamped indelibly upon her mind was the sight of Leo's prostrate body lying immobile on the sand where she had left him. Incoherent prayers were interspersed with agonised gasps as she stumbled down the path and ran to drop on to her knees beside him.

"Leo! Leo, my darling," she sobbed, "please speak to me—don't die, I couldn't bear it if you should die!" She had no idea what she said or promised during the five long minutes while she rolled him on his back, brushed sand from his hair and forehead and began stroking his cheeks with frantic fingers. "Leo," she choked. "My darling, I love you so much!"

Dredging her memory for hints on first aid, she slipped her hand inside his jacket to search for a heartbeat and felt a steady, comforting throb beneath her palm. Immeasurably relieved, she strove for further reminders and recalling instructions on how to administer the kiss of life she propper herself up with one hand on either side of his head and lowered her mouth towards his.

The moment their lips touched he came alive—vitally, excitingly alive—with arms that crushed her close and warm, passionate lips that murmured hoarse, adoring condemnation as he rolled her back against the sand and proceeded to punish her in the most wonderful way possible for all the heartache, frustration and pain she had inflicted during the past traumatic weeks.

Surprised, breathless, and utterly confused, Jo nevertheless realised that she had been tricked. Yet the delight of knowing him to be alive overruled every other thought in those first few startling seconds. The agony of mind she had endured when she had thought him dead, the idea of living her life without his teasing, his tormenting and above all his tenderness had almost caused her own heart to stop beating. Those moments had convinced her that her career, her freedom, even the heartache of being married for reasons other than love did not matter, all she wanted was the feel of his arms around her, his kisses upon her lips, and to hear the meltingly tender expressions of love which at that very moment were being whispered into her ear.

"Io ti amo, mia cara! Oh, *tesoro mio,"* he groaned, burying his lips in her bright hair, "I had almost given up hope. Tell me again what you told me when you thought I could not hear," he pleaded urgently. "Look at me with your honest eyes and let me see the truth reflected there when you speak."

Jo did not pretend. Sliding her arms across his broad shoulders, feeling muscles flex beneath her touch, she admitted in a small, broken whisper, "Leo, my own darling, I adore you so much I couldn't bear the thought of living without you..."

Never had the reward for surrender been so sweet. Gathering her into his arms as if she were infinitely precious, infinitely fragile, he sought her lips, drawing the heart from her body with a kiss achingly tender, a kiss that pledged a lifetime of devotion and set a seal upon her heart, marking her for ever with the stamp of the possessive Temperas.

There were no stars in the sky brighter than her eyes when, suppressing the tide of passion rising within him, he pulled her to her feet, concerned as ever for her wellbeing. "Come, *cara*, let us return to the villa."

"But why...?" She stretched out her arms as if to embrace all about her, enchanted by the beauty of the night, by the silver moon with its huge benevolent smile that seemed to be lingering on its pathway through the heavens to enjoy the sight of their happiness, by the soft murmur of waves upon the shore sighing a song of envy, by the warm bed of sand that had enclosed them within its warm embrace.

"Because," he shook her gently, a tolerant smile playing around his mouth, "though you may perhaps not have noticed, my darling, the breeze is growing colder. And besides that," he drew her close to nuzzle into the warm hollow of her throat, "in years to come when we are recalling our wedding night, I do not wish you to be able to rebuke me for having spent it on a cold, comfortless beach."

He felt the quiver that ran through her and tightened his arm, holding her very still. "Are you afraid of me, Jo?" he asked quietly.

To his relief she nestled closer to his heart and assured him with a contented sigh, "Never of you, Leo."

He hugged her so that she felt cosseted as a child wrapped in a cloak of love and rocked her slightly as he promised, "I shall be gentle, Jo. Trust me...?"

"Always." She reached up to stroke his cheek as if he and not she were in need of reassurance. "Always and completely, my darling."

They savoured the short journey back to the villa, strolling along the path they knew would lead them to paradise, yet lingering every now and then to kiss, to caress and to talk, dispersing every last doubt. Gazing across the sea to where the lights of Venice were glittering in the darkness, Jo spoke in a wondering murmur. "Had I not turned back because I was worried about you I would be in Venice now. You tricked me by pretending to be unconscious," she reproved him. "I suffered agonies thinking you might be dead."

"Good," he teased, squeezing hard where his hand rested on the curve of her waist, "you deserve to share a little of the suffering I have endured on your account." He then amended his severity with a kiss before continuing in a more serious vein, "After you hit me I was stunned for a few seconds, and when I had shaken off my daze my first impulse was to follow you, intending first of all to dump you in the sea and then alleviate my anger by administering a thorough spanking."

"You wouldn't have...!" She rounded on him indignantly.

"I assure you, my darling, that I would," he replied, controlling quirking lips with difficulty. "However, upon reflection, I decided that if you were able to leave me—as you thought, unconscious—then obviously there was no chance of your ever loving me and the dream I had cherished from our first moment of meeting would have to be discarded, I would have to accept, finally and irrevocably, that you were not the girl for me."

Halfway towards the villa he stopped to cup her small, serious face between his palms. "Thank God you did come back, Jo! As I lay there on the beach listening to the revving of the car that was taking you away from me I descended into hell and believed I would never surface. Then you came running, sobbing your fears for my life, and it suddenly seemed that agony had served to intensify joy."

After a kiss to ascertain that she was real and not a mirage, Jo betrayed her uncertainty by latching on to one particular remark. "You said," she swallowed hard, "the dream you had cherished from our first moment of meeting...?"

"You sound as if you find that hard to believe," he reproved her gently.

"How can I believe it," she continued, desperately wanting to be convinced, "when I first appeared before you dressed in the most hideous garments I could find, with a mask of paint covering my face that wouldn't have disgraced a clown."

"That made no difference," he assured her with such sincerity her heart soared. "I must admit that when you appeared, defiant and outrageous, in front of my easily shocked relatives, my first impulse was to laugh. Then I saw behind the façade, recognised courage, and realised that beneath the mask of paint the little clown was crying."

"Oh, Leo," she crumpled against him, "how tolerant you are—and how well you know me."

"You are part of me, my heart," he told her simply, "with you I hear one word and understand two. My only regret is that we have wasted so much time." He stooped to lift her into his arms as the outline of the villa loomed before them. "I am greedy for you, little wife. If life were as permanent as the shadows cast by mountains I would not worry, but as it can be compared with the shadow of a fish skimming through water every precious moment must be savoured."

Impatiently, he kicked open the door of the villa and carried her over the threshold. For a time there was movement and laughter inside, then one by one lights were extinguished and only a broadly smiling moon was permitted to share the secrets of the silent villa.